A Cottage in the Country

BY THE SAME AUTHOR

Living Dangerously
The Rose Revived
Wild Designs
Stately Pursuits
Life Skills
Thyme Out
Artistic Licence
Highland Fling
Paradise Fields
Restoring Grace
Flora's Lot
Practically Perfect
Going Dutch
Wedding Season
Love Letters
A Perfect Proposal
Sumer of Love
Recipe for Love
A French Affair
The Perfect Match
A Vintage Wedding
A Summer at Sea
A Secret Garden
A Country Escape
A Rose Petal Summer
A Springtime Affair
A Wedding in the Country
A Wedding in Provence
One Enchanted Evening
Island in the Sun
From London with Love

Katie Fforde

A Cottage in the Country

BLOOMSBURY PUBLISHING
LONDON · OXFORD · NEW YORK · NEW DELHI · SYDNEY

BLOOMSBURY PUBLISHING
Bloomsbury Publishing Plc
50 Bedford Square, London, WC1B 3DP, UK
Bloomsbury Publishing Ireland Limited,
29 Earlsfort Terrace, Dublin 2, D02 AY28, Ireland

BLOOMSBURY, BLOOMSBURY PUBLISHING and the Diana logo
are trademarks of Bloomsbury Publishing Plc

First published in Great Britain 2026

Copyright © Katie Fforde, 2026

Katie Fforde is identified as the author of this work in accordance
with the Copyright, Designs and Patents Act 1988

This is a work of fiction. Names and characters are the product of the author's
imagination and any resemblance to actual persons, living or dead,
is entirely coincidental

All rights reserved. No part of this publication may be: i) reproduced or transmitted
in any form, electronic or mechanical, including photocopying, recording or by
means of any information storage or retrieval system without prior permission
in writing from the publishers; or ii) used or reproduced in any way for the
training, development or operation of artificial intelligence (AI) technologies,
including generative AI technologies. The rights holders expressly reserve this
publication from the text and data mining exception as per Article 4(3) of the
Digital Single Market Directive (EU) 2019/790

A catalogue record for this book is available from the British Library

ISBN: HB: 978-1-5266-9078-4; TPB: 978-1-5266-9068-5; EBOOK: 978-1-5266-9066-1

2 4 6 8 10 9 7 5 3 1

Typeset by Six Red Marbles India
Printed and bound in Great Britain by Clays Ltd, Elcograf S.p.A

To find out more about our authors and books visit www.bloomsbury.com
and sign up for our newsletters
For product-safety-related questions contact productsafety@bloomsbury.com

To Desmond Fforde, 6th of January, 1947–21st September, 2025. With love, for 53 years, and always.

Chapter One

Late May

'I'm fairly sure you're going to love this one, Fiona,' said Hattie as she and her clients surveyed the property they had just parked in front of. 'I certainly do. Not so sure about you, Lance, although the bones are all there.'

Hattie, whose job – passion even – was finding houses for people, led the way round the house to the back. Behind them was a garden with borders full of delphiniums, cosmos, peonies and larkspur. Beyond that were trees with rambling roses climbing up them. A summer house was covered in wisteria which provided wafts of perfume on the breeze. Late May was Hattie's favourite time of year for gardens, and this one was sure to melt even the coldest heart.

Now, she turned a big iron key. 'We're using the back door, which as you know is the country way. And the front door is a bit stiff.' In fact, it was completely seized up through lack of use but she didn't feel the need to share that particular piece of information.

Before she opened the door, which led straight into the kitchen, she paused. 'The current owner is an artist, and isn't what you'd describe as a minimalist.' Lance would describe all the pretty things inside as clutter, but Hattie knew Fiona would love the look as much as she did herself.

She didn't say any more, she just gestured for them to head in before her and let her clients take in the huge space. This was the third property she had shown them and was the one that matched their requirements the best. And although there was approximately a ten-year age gap between them, Hattie and Fiona had become friends over the last few months, meeting for coffee and a trip around the shops on a couple of occasions. She wanted Fiona to have the house of her dreams. This could be it.

But only the range cooker (minus the stained orange Le Creuset casserole on top) and the double Belfast sinks could be crossed off Lance's extensive kitchen wish list straight away. As yet, there was no vast granite island, no handleless built-in cupboards, and the floor, although made out of the required golden stone flags, was uneven, shiny with age, and there was no heating underneath.

Instead of the island, there was a large refectory table, scarred with use, surrounded by mismatched kitchen chairs. Instead of the fitted cabinetry, there was an ancient dresser, a huge chest of drawers and a few cupboards for storage. (Hattie would refer to at least one of them as an armoire, should she need to describe it.) The rest was open shelves, full of jugs and mugs, jars full of wooden spoons, ladles, whisks and any other conceivable kitchen utensil. Brightly painted plates, vintage biscuit tins and other kitchenalia covered every inch of the shelving. And where there were no shelves, there were paintings, wooden spice racks and printers' trays filled with tiny knick-knacks, a name in lights, and a few awards for prize-winning cakes. Hattie knew Lance would struggle with this aesthetic even though none of it would remain if they bought the house, but she also knew by now that he wouldn't be led so she simply had to hope he was prepared to look beyond it.

Extra to Lance's list were a couple of deep window-sills, currently covered in basil, parsley and chilli plants in hand-thrown pots. Another row of windows looked out on to the flower-filled garden.

A beam provided space to hang a collection of wicker baskets, jugs, drinking vessels, corn measures and loving cups. On an antique side table stood an old stone jar filled with dried flowers, hydrangeas, honesty and grasses. (Hattie knew that Lance would hate this.) An ancient sofa nestled near the range cooker and a grandfather clock stood proudly behind. A few rag rugs were scattered in front of the sofa and the range.

'I think you'll agree,' Hattie said after a few moments' silence, when the ticking of the clock became suddenly deafening, 'it's the classic country kitchen.'

Fiona sighed deeply. 'It's perfect!' A few moments later, when her fiancé hadn't responded, she added, 'Don't you think so, darling? Is it third house lucky?'

Lance never showed what he was thinking. Hattie was very good at reading body language – she'd had to learn over years of house viewings – but she still couldn't work out if he was discerning or contrary. He never seemed quite satisfied with anything he saw.

He laughed indulgently. 'It's very dated, don't you think? All those wonky cupboards, nowhere proper to keep anything? Where would we put the big fridge we'll need? And the dishwasher isn't even integrated.'

'If I can direct you here,' said Hattie, opening a door to a room that once would have been a larder. 'You'll see this is where the current owner keeps the American fridge, the KitchenAid, ice-cream maker and coffee machine. So you have options, and plenty of room for any other equipment you may need.'

Hattie could, of course, suggest a firm who could build them a beautiful fitted kitchen, or just put a door on the dishwasher, but she wanted to gauge how they really felt about the place first.

'Let's have a look at the sitting room. It's a good size.' She laughed gently. 'Again, it's a matter of using your imagination. I don't think the current decor will be to your taste.'

As Lance had already rejected a house because he didn't like the sofas, Hattie felt this warning was necessary. And to be fair, in the past she'd had to struggle to get past some very large leather suites herself.

The room was of generous proportions with a colossal inglenook fireplace at one end. In it stood a large wood burner. Opposite this was a huge sofa covered in kilims and bright rugs. At right angles to this was another sofa, not matching, but equally bright. The dark wooden floorboards were covered in Turkish rugs. There were comfortable-looking chairs dotted about, placed next to tables with lamps and piles of books. The whitewashed walls were hung with abstract paintings. It was all very personal, but, Hattie felt, a reasonable buyer should be able to see beyond the artwork.

Lance didn't say anything except: 'I suppose we could put the TV on that wall.'

Fiona didn't comment. Hattie got the impression that she liked it, but didn't want to say.

'I like this big hallway,' she said, looking round as they left the sitting room. 'It's an extra room. I like the table and chairs being here.'

'Is there a formal dining room?' asked Lance, apparently not sharing his fiancée's enthusiasm. He gave a small smile. 'It is on the list.'

'There is a room that could certainly be used as such,' said Hattie, opening a door, 'but it's nicely set up as a snug at the moment. It's where they keep the television. The present owner uses the hall at Christmas.'

'I can just see the Christmas tree in corner,' said Fiona. 'And fairy lights all down the stairs.'

'So, it's short of reception rooms?' asked Lance as he went into the snug. He was obviously not so invested in Christmas.

'It's a lovely cosy sitting room,' said Fiona, following him, sounding a little deflated.

Lance didn't seem impressed. 'Do you think we could see the bedrooms on our own, Hattie?' he asked. 'It might be easier?'

Hattie smiled in agreement, secretly relieved. Glad of a few moments to herself, she went to sit in an armchair by a window embrasure in the hall. There was a mirror next to it, angled to bring in sunlight as well as a view of the garden. She was relaxed about her clients going upstairs, knowing there were four generous doubles, two bathrooms and a walk-in wardrobe up there. Surely even the particular Lance would be pleased? She turned her attention to the garden borders.

Quite suddenly, Hattie was no longer looking at an early summer garden, but at a hotel bedroom. In the bed was Lance, but the woman was dark-haired and very thin; she looked nothing like Fiona. And she was wearing nothing but scarlet stockings and a suspender belt.

Hattie shook her head to clear the vision. It didn't happen often but she sometimes found herself seeing things. Possibly things that hadn't yet happened, but she knew they would happen eventually and she found herself unable to ignore them. She'd had these visions all her life and quickly learnt not to mention them to her family; they struggled with her enough as it was.

She took some deep breaths and glanced in the mirror; she saw that her freckles were standing out against her suddenly pale face, and her eyes looked greener than ever. She didn't want to look as if she'd just seen a ghost, although in a way she had. Now she ran her fingers through her hair, her dark curls being forgiving of such treatment.

She then went to the kitchen for a drink of water. She could hear Lance and Fiona coming down the stairs.

'The upstairs is a vast improvement on down here,' said Lance. 'We'd like to see the garden now. On our own.'

A flash of anger stabbed her. Not only was Lance a man who was about to, or already had, cheated on the lovely Fiona, but he was rude and unappreciative too.

'What a good idea,' she said. 'Late May is the very best time for gardens.'

Fiona gave her a quick, shy smile, and followed her fiancé out of the house, leaving Hattie wondering what on earth she could do with this new information about Lance. Her visions were anything but a gift at times like these.

Chapter Two

It seemed that a summer house covered in white wisteria, beds full of roses, and love-in-a-mist spilling over the lawn didn't impress Lance. Although there was space for one, and money in the budget, there was no swimming pool. The drive needed repairing and the paddock (Hattie couldn't remember why they needed a paddock) was too small.

She took a breath and gave it one more shot.

'One of the many joys of this house,' she said, 'and yes, I am trying to sell it to you, is that the village is only a short distance away and it's lovely. It has the usual general store – run by volunteers—'

Lance groaned.

'And a few delightful shops selling other things. My friend Rose – I'm sure I've mentioned her before?' Fiona nodded. 'She has her shop that sells lovely things, soft furnishings, scarves, vintage finds from France. And there's a wine shop that is also an amazing delicatessen, as well as a proper little haberdashery and fabric shop.' She paused. 'The pub is excellent too.'

'I'm sure you'll be telling us the village hall has tai chi, Pilates and Hatha yoga classes,' said Lance. 'As well as an active WI. I'm not interested.'

Hattie forced a smile. She loved the village because, apart from anything else, her favourite house in the world wasn't far away.

'Or maybe you don't think this is the one? I may have a couple of other houses we could consider but I need to do a bit more research first.'

'This one is close, but no cigar,' said Lance with a smile that made Hattie feel patronised and murderous at the same time.

She took a breath and returned his smile with one of her own. 'Don't forget you will need to compromise. No one ever gets everything on their wish list for a house: it's like finding a partner.'

Then she wished she hadn't made that analogy. Poor Fiona had no idea quite how much she was compromising with Lance.

'I don't expect to have to lower my standards, Hattie,' Lance said.

'Well, just have a think about it,' said Hattie briskly. 'I'm afraid I have to leave now. There are a couple of dogs at home who need to be fed.'

It seemed to take ages to usher them out of the house.

Once in her car, she forced herself to stop and think for a moment. She couldn't in good conscience ignore her vision of Lance. He was cheating on his fiancée before they'd even got to the altar. He didn't deserve Fiona, with her dimples and her messy bun. And he certainly didn't deserve that lovely house! Fiona had told her at their first meeting, held at her mother's house, that her parents had given them a very generous deposit. So if they married, when the inevitable divorce came along Lance would get half of it. This was so unfair. No, she'd have to find a way to help Fiona see what was going on.

Hattie might even be able to find her a lovely home to buy for herself in the wake of it all.

It was all very well having visions, she reflected, but it would be more useful if they offered solutions. Instead they just gave her dilemmas which, in this case, seemed impossible to solve. Although they did sometimes show her a glimpse of a happy couple and when she had those she knew she needed to help pair the two up. It had led her to being known as a bit of a matchmaker. It didn't work on her own account, of course. Nothing so useful!

She did a couple of shoulder rolls and looked at herself in the mirror. She still looked a bit pale, her freckles prominent. She looked very different from the other women in her family, who were blonde and angular. Apparently she took after her wild Irish great-grandmother, who had eyes 'as green as gooseberries' and was hardly ever mentioned – and was missing from most of the ancient family photographs.

As she started the car, she wondered why she was worried about her appearance when it was only Luke who was likely to see her. He was due to pick up his dogs soon and although he had a key to her house and could help himself to them, she always preferred to do a proper handover.

Frank and Fearless were Springer spaniels that he'd had from puppyhood. They were so good and beautiful with their white and brown coats and dark brown eyes to match. She would miss them.

'Were they all right?'

Luke didn't bother to say hello. He was leaning in the door frame wearing his working clothes, which were dusty and hung off his tall frame but somehow suited him. His work boots always made him look like he meant business, Hattie thought. Looking at him you could somehow tell he was the best builder around. He'd spent the last few days working in Cornwall, which was out of his normal territory: he was involved in a huge restoration project on the coast and kept having to disappear for days or weeks at a time. Hattie missed his easy-going presence in her life when he was away – but right now she was indignant about even the faintest suggestion that Frank and Fearless might have been anything but perfect. Usually he took the dogs with him, but he was staying somewhere unsuitable this time and so Hattie had offered to have them; it was always a pleasure.

'When are they ever anything but good? Will you have a cuppa?'

'Please.' He put his hand in his pocket and produced a packet of biscuits. 'I bought you these. Cornish Fairings. A local speciality.'

'You didn't need to do that!' she said, taking them. 'Let's go and sit in the sunshine.'

It wasn't long before the two of them were looking over the fields and hills. 'I'm going to miss this view,' Hattie said. 'So many houses are on the wrong side of the hill and you don't get the vistas.'

'How much longer will you be here?'

'Another three months. I must start looking for somewhere.'

'Somewhere more permanent? It's ridiculous, a property hunter without a home of her own.'

'That's what my parents always say. And my sister.'

'I know you struggle with them, but your family are right about this. Moving from house-sitting job to house-sitting job every few months must be very unsettling.'

Luke was a good friend, and she knew he was talking sense because everyone – including the postman – said the same thing. But it had to be the right home. And although she'd saved as hard as she could, she didn't have a huge deposit and had recently spent a lot of it on a new car: a tough four-wheel drive that could cope with any road conditions, and if necessary pull a client's car out of trouble. She'd since regretted not just leasing a car, but she'd been offered such a good deal she hadn't been able to resist.

'I quite like the variety. I promise I'll never live anywhere who won't let Frank and Fearless come when they need to.'

'You know it's not—'

'I know,' she interrupted. Luke wasn't one for chatting and Hattie felt it was a kindness to spare him sometimes.

Luke got up. 'I'd better be going.'

Frank and Fearless heard the words and were at his side in an instant. Hattie and Luke walked round to the front and, as always, Hattie looked on in admiration as Frank and Fearless leapt into the car the moment it was open, and waited, panting, for their master to join them.

'They're so good,' said Hattie, not for the first time.

'And they know they're not allowed on the sofa in my house,' said Luke.

'I like having something to cuddle.'

There was a moment's silence between them before Hattie went back to her doorstep. It was a very full silence, one she didn't know how to handle.

She decided to ignore it, waved goodbye and went back inside to have supper. Her sister called just as Hattie's omelette was ready to put on the plate. She tucked her phone under her ear and slid it out of the pan anyway. She didn't want it to burn.

'I've got something I need to ask you,' said Leonie.

As her sister never wasted time with pleasantries, Hattie wasn't offended. Leonie probably wanted to know if Hattie thought the value of her house had gone up since she last asked. But being her elder, she still thought of Hattie as the baby sister, who couldn't quite be trusted and needed to be guided. It was a role that had been enhanced when Hattie was little, and had failed to realise not everyone saw things that weren't in the room, and that it was best not to mention it if you did. She soon learnt never to talk about her visions to her family. She didn't really understand them herself. Her pragmatic relations wouldn't have a chance. Telling them would just make them worry.

'Ask away, I'm here.'

'I might need to come down and ask you.'

'From London? I'm sure you don't need to do that!' Hattie was horrified at the idea. She was tired and had a lot to do; just the thought of a visit from her sister would take what remained of her emotional energy.

'All right, I'll just ask you.' Leonie obviously didn't want to drive down to see her any more than Hattie wanted to see her. 'Can you take Xander for a couple of months?'

Hattie put her fork down. 'What do you mean, take him?'

'There's a college near you that's perfect for him.' She took a deep breath before she continued; Hattie could almost see her reading from a list she'd put together before picking up the phone. 'He hasn't been happy at school. This place has a reputation for helping kids recover from difficult phases ahead of big exams. He's got a place, it's mid-term, which is not ideal, but he'll have GCSEs next year so I don't want to miss the chance to get him in there.'

Hattie's sister had been a single mother for a long time but she'd never asked Hattie for help before.

When Hattie, dumbfounded, said nothing in reply, Leonie continued. 'I've got to work abroad for a few months – it's a temporary thing in Switzerland and they've made it very clear they'll find a way to fire me if I don't go. You know I can't lose this job, not with Xander to look after.'

Hattie opened her mouth to respond but her sister still wasn't finished. 'You're his aunt. You have to have him. Please.'

Hattie didn't quite know where to start. 'But surely he can't just attend a college on a temporary basis?'

'Of course not. If it goes well I'm considering moving out of town. My house would sell for a fortune. I thought he could try it for the second half of the summer term. And if it works out, he can stay on in September.'

'Won't it be hard for him, joining halfway through the term?'

'He'll be fine! I'm sure.'

Hattie could see that having come up with the idea of sending her son to her sister's, Leonie wasn't going to give up on it, no matter what Hattie thought.

'What about his father? Couldn't Xander go to college there?'

'He lives in Scotland, Hattie, as you well know!'

'But, Lennie, I hardly know Xander.'

'And whose fault is that? You hardly ever come to Mummy and Daddy's Sunday lunches!'

This was true: Hattie did avoid the lunches that Leonie drove down from London to attend. They were full of ritual built around overcooked meat and a forensic examination of Hattie's life and how it could be so much better.

'You know I often work at weekends.' This was partly true; she did work on Saturdays sometimes.

'Well, never mind that now. Is it OK if I bring him next week, on my way to Mum and Dad's? It's a trek to go via you but I have to say goodbye to them before I disappear to Switzerland.'

Hattie took a few calming breaths. 'Xander is the most precious person in the whole world to you. Why would you leave him with a sister who has absolutely no experience with children? And even less with fifteen-year-olds.'

'I have no choice. I'll be there tomorrow week around two. And he only eats pasta with ketchup. You have to give him a daily vitamin pill.' And Leonie hung up.

Hattie looked in the fridge and eyed the bottle of white wine. She drank very little these days (something her parents considered faddish – a bottle of wine between them every night kept them going). But sometimes…

She had reached for the bottle when her phone rang again. It was her best friend, Rose. 'Are you up for a barbie? Sam's cooking and we've got some lovely steak.'

An evening with Rose and Sam would be relaxing and fun and she needed that after the day she'd had. She heard herself saying, 'Do you want me to bring anything?' She would put the forgotten omelette into a stir fry the following day.

She was at her friend's house forty-five minutes later. It would have been sooner had it not been for yet another telephone call – this time from her mother, who had evidently spoken to Leonie.

Although Rose had said she didn't need to bring anything, Hattie had cut a bunch of herbs: parsley, thyme, mint and some coriander.

'Oh, thank you!' said Rose, burying her face into the bouquet. 'They smell amazing and Sam will be delighted.'

'They're only out of the garden.'

'But you make them grow,' said her friend. 'Wherever you live, there are always amazing herbs. You must be part witch. Now, come round. There's a sun lounger with your name on it.

'Wine?' asked Rose as they walked through the house, a haven of bright colours, mismatched patterns, rugs, cushions and eclectic paintings that always lifted Hattie's heart. 'Or some sparkling water I've put cucumber and lemon into to make it seem special?'

'Water, please. That sounds delicious.'

'Only you could get excited about water,' said Rose. 'Now sit down and relax. I'll bring it out to you.'

Sam was turning steaks on the barbecue but when he saw Hattie he put down his tongs and came over to give her a warm and brotherly hug.

'How are you, Hats?' he said.

'Fine, thanks.' Hattie smiled fondly at him. He was the only person who called her Hats and she allowed it because he was married to her best friend. And although he was completely unaware, he and Rose represented her most successful match to date.

Rose knew this because she was one of the very few who knew about Hattie's visions. Hattie had had to explain in order to get her friend to go to a very random fund-raising event that had nothing to do with either of them. Rose had been sceptical but went along to please Hattie and so met her future husband. Rose had been convinced ever after.

Rose put a misted glass into Hattie's hands. 'Now, tell us why you sounded so stressed.'

'Did I sound stressed?' She took a bracing sip of flavoured bubbles. 'It's my sister—'

'What's she said now?' asked Rose, who had a glass of red wine by her side.

'It's not what she's said, it's what she's done!'

Rose and Sam were aghast at the outrageousness of Hattie's sister's request. Sam had handed out crunchy baguettes filled with sliced steak and fried onions before Hattie got to the follow-up phone call from her mother.

'She said, "Harriet! It's vital that you do this for your sister. I know you don't seem to care about it, but family is the most important thing! Your nephew needs you. You must step up." She really said all that. I wouldn't have minded so much if I hadn't already told Leonie that I'd do it.' She sighed and took a bite of her sandwich. It was delicious, the steak perfectly cooked, the onions complementing it, and just a smear of homemade salsa. 'My family prepare long speeches and then insist on delivering them even if they're not necessary. It's very annoying.'

'Are you sure you don't need a glass of wine? You could stay the night,' said Rose. 'I know you have excessively strict rules about drinking and driving.'

Hattie shook her head. 'I feel better for getting it off my chest. And it's Xander I feel sorry for. Stuck with an aunt he barely knows in a strange place, going to a new college.' She paused. 'Xander has been struggling with school, so this is a new opportunity and I want it to go well for him.'

Rose took a moment before responding. 'I can see why Leonie might want Xander to give this a go. And also why she has to go to Switzerland to safeguard her job.' She took a sip of wine. 'It's a compliment in a way. Your sister is devoted to her son; she'd never do anything she didn't think was right for him.'

Hattie nodded. 'I hadn't looked at it quite like that before. It *is* a compliment.'

Later, in the kitchen, while Hattie and Rose were clearing up, Rose said, 'So are you going to tell me why you look washed out? It's not your sister, is it? Have you had a – you know – vision?'

Hattie exhaled and nodded.

Rose looked firm. 'You have to tell me!'

Hattie was actually quite glad to talk about it. Rose might have some ideas on how the situation could be helped.

'It was horrible. We were in a really gorgeous house that would have been perfect for them if Lance wasn't so unbelievably rigid that he can't ever see beyond the decor. They'd gone upstairs to look at the bedrooms on their own and suddenly I was looking at him in bed with another woman.'

'Gross!'

'I know! And his fiancée is so sweet. She's pretty and cheerful and kind. And this snake has – well, another snake on the side! How am I going to let Fiona know without telling her? I really like her; I can't let her marry that man.'

'God no! But what can you do?' Rose put the kettle on while she spoke. She knew some sort of hot beverage was required.

A few minutes later, Hattie was sipping mint tea made with the mint she'd brought with her. 'Fiona – that's the woman – is staying with her parents until the wedding which is only a few weeks away. I could make an excuse to go and see her.' She took another sip. 'I could offer to take her to another house?'

'A house just for Fiona? Do you know of anything suitable?'

'I do. And it would be perfect for Fiona but no good for them as a couple. He wants a sweeping drive, which it hasn't got. Apart from that, it's a great house.'

'So?'

'I could try and get a good conversation going about Lance being in London a lot and see what I can do. Fiona might realise this isn't the house for the two of them, and with luck, she might realise that Lance isn't the man for her, either.'

'It's a shame your special powers aren't more manageable,' said Rose. 'Why can't you find someone lovely for Luke, for example?'

'I've tried! But I never have visions for him and he never likes any of the women I find for him in the normal way. And no, he's not gay.'

Rose pursed her lips. 'Do you want more tea? Chocolate?'

Hattie got up. 'No, thank you. I should be off. I've got a busy day tomorrow. But thank you for tonight, I needed it.'

Chapter Three

The following week, Hattie sent Fiona a message asking if she could ring her. It was before 9 a.m. but Xander was due to arrive in the early afternoon, so she didn't have much time. She was sure Fiona would be awake and as she was constantly glued to her phone, she would answer.

'Can I take you to a really lovely house?' said Hattie when Fiona called back. 'Early this morning is the only time we can do it. I really want you to see it before anyone else has a chance. It's going on the market on Monday.'

Fiona sighed, obviously tempted. 'I'd better not. I have so much to do for the wedding. And Lance is in London.'

Hattie was prepared for this. 'It's just a little preview. No point in dragging Lance to something he'll hate. Shall I pop round anyway? I'm over that way and can call in.'

Fiona sighed. 'Oh, all right then.'

Hattie decided this was not a hard 'no' and after they had disconnected she got in the car, hoping her lies wouldn't catch her out.

When she arrived, Fiona's mother opened the door to her. 'I'd be delighted if you could take Fiona out for an hour or so,' she said rapidly. 'She's so stressed about the wedding and she can't stress if she can't look at the spreadsheet or worry about Lance liking the colour of the bridesmaids' dresses.'

Then Fiona appeared in pyjamas covered in pink elephants. 'Mum! Invite Hattie in! Oh, you haven't met, have you? Mum, this is Hattie, house hunter extraordinaire, and this is my mother, Sheila.'

Hattie and Sheila exchanged smiles. 'Fiona talks about you a lot.'

'We did have a very bonding early meeting involving a shared piece of chocolate gateau,' said Hattie. 'It was so delicious, but Lance was very disapproving of us for putting so much refined sugar into our bodies.'

Sheila laughed. 'That sounds like Lance! There's coffee in the kitchen: come through,' she said, leading the way.

'I haven't got much time...' Hattie said to Sheila's back.

When they reached the kitchen, Sheila turned to her daughter. 'Darling, why don't you pop some clothes on? It would be good for you to get out of the house and if you could pick up some milk while you're out, it would save me a trip to the shops.'

When Fiona had gone upstairs, Sheila said, 'I'm quite worried about her. She consults Lance on absolutely everything, and what sort of a man is interested in bridesmaids' dresses?'

Hattie nodded, aware this question didn't require an answer. 'Is he in London a lot?'

Sheila was pouring coffee; she nodded. 'Of course. It's where his work is and Fiona gave up a job she loved there. But why do they want to live down here? Why not a nice little flat in Shoreditch?'

'It is lovely down here. And it's where you are.' Hattie smiled. Sheila wasn't very like her own mother and she could imagine Fiona wanting to live near her. 'I feel we've got to know each other over the viewings and she's quite a home bird really, isn't she? She's going to have such fun decorating a house, putting her stamp on it.'

Sheila pursed her lips. 'As long as she doesn't feel obliged to consult Lance on every detail. And I'm sure she'll find a nice little part-time job – part-time so she can "be a proper wife" to Lance, as he put it. But I don't think Fi should want to live near her parents when she's first married. I'm worried, I can tell you.' She paused. 'I've got no one else to discuss it with. Fiona's father just thinks I'm fussing.'

Hattie was worried too but didn't know what to say. She put a comforting hand on Sheila's instead. It was reassuring to think she would have an ally if she managed to separate Fiona from the horrible Lance. She took a sip of the too-strong coffee Sheila had given her. 'I'm afraid I haven't got long...'

Sheila left the room so she could shout up the stairs. 'Hurry, darling! You don't need make-up on.'

Fiona appeared a couple of minutes later looking like a twelve-year-old, pretty but unadorned.

'Thank you for being so quick,' said Hattie, abandoning her coffee. 'We can nip along and see the house and then get the milk.'

As they left the house, Hattie spotted a mobile phone on the hall table, but she didn't mention it. If it was Fiona's, it sounded as if it would be good for her to be away from it.

Unfortunately, Fiona remembered her phone when they were hardly out of the drive. She wanted to turn back but Hattie accelerated instead of turning round. 'We'll call Lance from my phone when we get to the house. We can send a picture if you like the place.'

Fiona sighed and sat back in her seat. 'I need to ask him what he thinks about the bridesmaids' dresses.'

Hattie said, 'My mother would say that bridesmaids' dresses were a pink job and not for men to worry about.' This wasn't quite true but she wanted to make Fiona laugh.

It did. 'My mother has said the same, but Lance wants to know every detail about the wedding. He's very meticulous about everything, even what I wear. When I first met him he sort of examined me and said I should wear sapphires because they'd complement my eyes. So romantic!'

'Mm,' said Hattie, non-committal.

'I always ask his advice before I buy anything now. I love that he's so interested. He likes to know all about my clothes and my make-up. He's changed my style quite a bit.'

'And you don't *mind* him changing your style?' Hattie tried not to show how horrifying she found this thought.

'Of course not! I love him! I want to be perfect for him.'

'I'm sure you're perfect just as you are!'

'No. He'd like me better if I was thinner and more sophisticated. I've been on a diet. I'm hoping my dress will have to be taken in when I next go for a fitting.' She paused. 'Once a month, he weighs me.'

Hattie's mouth went dry. The affair was one thing, but was this lovely young woman a victim of coercive control? If it wasn't that, it was something very similar.

'I think you've got a wonderful figure.' She paused, unsure what to say next. She was saved by their turning coming into view.

'The house is just up here.'

As Hattie negotiated the narrow lane to the house she wondered if she should confide in Fiona's mother and leave it up to her to separate her daughter from Lance. What would she do if she was only Fiona's friend and not her house hunter? Hattie very rarely mentioned her visions but without doing that, and risking sounding completely bonkers, what could she say?

'How many bridesmaids are you having?' Hattie asked. 'I'm sure you've told me.'

'Just little cousins and things, so six.'

'No adult ones?'

'No. Lance isn't that keen on my friends. We can be quite silly when we get together.'

Hattie forced a laugh. 'I bet you had a hilarious hen do. Did you go abroad?'

'I decided against having a big affair. Mummy asked a group of my oldest girlfriends round and we had cake and Prosecco at her house. It was fun.'

Hattie tried to ignore the little sigh that followed this, exclaiming instead, 'We're here! Now, I know it's not exactly what you asked for but it's good to challenge yourselves sometimes.' She got out of the car.

'Like the "mystery house" on *Escape to the Country*?' asked Fiona, following Hattie to the front door. 'That's always the best one, isn't it? Oh, can we take a picture of the front and send it to Lance?'

'Let's do that later. There might be a better opportunity for a good picture. We'll get you in it too.'

Fiona laughed merrily. 'As if! I've got no make-up on!'

Hattie bit her tongue on the question of whether Fiona got up before Lance so she could put on subtle make-up and then get back into bed. She had a horrible feeling the answer would be yes.

'We'll go in the back door,' said Hattie. 'In through the kitchen. You might need to use your imagination as this kitchen hasn't had anything done to it. But the Belfast sink is original and the range still works, although it might be tricky to cook on.'

Fiona didn't speak. Hattie watched as the young woman took in the tall mantelpiece over the range where the current owner had displayed a pair of Staffordshire dogs. Next to the dogs was a spill jar, flat-backed, depicting a shepherdess and a rather squashed lamb. A jam jar with marigolds in it took up the rest of the space.

There was one deep windowsill behind the sink, with a collection of dusty succulents, several empty stoneware storage jars, and old pots that once contained marmalade, potted meat or Stilton cheese. There was a cupboard, old but attractive, and a small dresser, full of decorative plates and the detritus of life stuck into jugs and mugs that hung from hooks and filled the shelves in front of the plates.

As well as the period charm and quaintness, there was a good cooker to supplement the range, and a dishwasher.

'I love this,' said Fiona with a sigh. 'It's got all the things I like. But Lance would say it's too small and cluttered.'

'The sitting room is a bit bigger, but I'm afraid there's no separate dining room, which I know Lance wanted.'

'It's lovely!' said Fiona on seeing the sitting room. 'It's a good size, and there's the dining table so we could still entertain formally.'

Hattie could see how much Fiona loved the house. 'Why don't you pop upstairs. There are four bedrooms. Not enormous, but big enough. Two bathrooms...'

'What I love about this house,' said Fiona a little later, 'is that it's full of charm and all the things I love but has the mod cons we all need. I think it's so clever that they've fitted the washing machine and dryer upstairs. It's where you take your clothes off, after all. Why do we carry them downstairs and then up again when they're clean?'

They had explored the cottage garden, which was slightly on the steep side but offered amazing views, when Hattie said, 'Which bit shall we take a photo of for Lance? I think these views would be great. If you put in bifold doors you'd have this view from your sitting room and your kitchen.'

Fiona shook her head. 'I don't think Lance would like this house. It's too small for him. He likes a bit of grandeur and he has his heart set on a sweeping drive.' Fiona laughed although Hattie sensed she didn't really feel it was funny.

'It's going for quite a lot less than your top budget. There'd be change to spend on alterations.'

Fiona shook her head. 'I don't think this house should be altered. It's perfect as it is.'

There was a lot Hattie would have liked to add to that statement but she realised she'd have to tread carefully with Fiona if she were going to help her see Lance for what he really was.

★ ★ ★

Hattie's phone rang as she drove back home. It was her sister.

'Hattie? Can you talk?' Leonie demanded.

'I'm driving. Can it wait?'

'Are you on hands-free?'

'Of course,' said Hattie, wondering why her sister always made her feel tired.

'I can't bring Xander to you after all. You'll have to pick him up.'

'Have to, Lenny? Surely, I don't have to do anything.' It was unlike her to challenge her sister but since she'd learnt all those awful things about Lance that morning she felt less ready to be compliant.

'Oh, you know what I mean! I'll put him on the train. I hope he'll be all right. He's only fifteen…'

'And so will be fine on the train on his own. Far younger children travel on trains on their own.'

Leonie ignored this. 'But you'll collect him from the station?'

Hattie heard anxiety in her sister's voice, which she knew was her way of feeling love. 'Of course, otherwise he'll never find his way to my house. What time?'

Chapter Four

To her annoyance, Hattie was a few minutes late to pick up her nephew at the station. She'd been held up by a solicitor who was being a bit slow doing the conveyancing for a client and Hattie had called on him in person to remonstrate rather than send an email. It had been effective but, having been just a little bit firm with him, she had felt obliged to look at a lot of pictures of his newborn baby and hear how very, very tired he was. It had been one of those days, she thought, sweeping into the station car park.

'Xander!'

She hugged him and felt him stiffen. Her sister wasn't much of a hugger. She probably greeted her son with a pat on the back. To his credit, Xander managed a small smile in response.

'I'm really thrilled you've come to stay for a while, but I feel it's only fair that I tell you just how inexperienced I am in dealing with people under twenty. To be honest, I'm better with people around thirty-five. But I mean well. And you've got to promise to tell me if I'm being really annoying.' Hattie looked at him and decided not to ask how he was feeling about his first day at college just yet. 'The car is this way.'

Despite her feelings about her sister bouncing her into this situation, seeing Xander standing by his rucksack outside the station had wrenched at her heart rather. She was determined to make his stay with her as good as it possibly could be.

They stowed his rucksack in the boot and got in.

'Although Lennie – your mum – told me you only ate pasta, I went shopping anyway. I thought it would look so unwelcoming if you arrived at my house and there was a packet of penne on the table next to the vitamins I have to give you.'

Another grunt. Hattie realised she was more experienced interpreting the sounds that Luke's dogs made than those her sister's son did.

'You never know, you may find you have a liking for kimchi you previously didn't know about. I mean, I think it's fairly disgusting but apparently it's very good for gut health.'

She looked across to check for cars at the crossing and snatched a quick glance at Xander. Was there a slight lift to the corner of his mouth or had she imagined it?

'In theory, it's ten minutes' walk from my house to the station, but it's at least twenty going back. The hills, you know. You'll get used to them.'

When they arrived Hattie opened the back door to the house she'd been living in for the past six months and she knew instantly that something was wrong. There was a dripping sound. She knew what it was. It had happened soon after she'd moved in. Luke had told her then she should tell the owner and ask him to have it fixed.

'Go on through to the sitting room. Put the telly on if you want. I'll just see what I can do about this leak.'

She'd have to call Luke, but felt just a little bit guilty for putting upon him even before she'd done it – and a tiny bit *more* guilty because she hadn't mentioned the problem to her landlord.

But she paid very little rent for the house, which belonged to a property developer. Hattie was keeping it maintained (after a fashion) and lived-in until it sold. But negotiations had begun and so she'd been given three months' notice.

It was a nice property. It had three good bedrooms, a cosy sitting room with a wood burner and a kitchen she had made her own. It was one of her better house-sitting spots, she thought, going upstairs with a bucket to catch the drips.

Coming down again, she saw that Xander had opened the double doors on to the garden and was standing on the terrace. She was glad: she so wanted him to feel at home here.

Luke, to Hattie's huge relief, answered. She usually got his answerphone message. As the builder preferred by people with old houses and people who had pretensions, he was always in demand.

'Hey, Hattie, what do you need?' he said.

'Why do you assume I need something?'

'Well, don't you?'

Hattie sighed. 'Yes, of course. I'm afraid I do. The tank in the attic is leaking again and I've got my nephew Xander staying for a while.' She wasn't sure why this made the leak seem more important, but it did.

'I'll be over.'

'I'll give you supper.'

She loved cooking for Luke. He was appreciative but discerning. He was a good cook himself, but he had the patience to follow a recipe all the way to the end which was something that Hattie never managed. Her cooking style was like the rest of her, haphazard and unorthodox but successful. She could always make a delicious meal out of whatever was available. Her parents and sister found this gift really annoying and Hattie suspected her wild great-granny had shared it.

After hanging up, Hattie explained the situation to Xander, who had come in and seated himself down at the kitchen table. She gave him a Diet Coke (forbidden fruit).

'So I must feed him. He mostly lives on food you buy at petrol stations and it's not healthy.' She opened the door of the fridge, which was now full of what she thought of as Xander food, although it was possible that Xander wouldn't eat any of it. 'I think I'll do special fried rice. It's his favourite.'

'Is Luke your boyfriend?' said Xander.

Hearing this question from her nephew's lips took Hattie aback, but not so much that she couldn't explain. 'No. Luke is a very dear friend. People often ask me if he's my boyfriend because they don't believe men and women can be friends with each other without anything else doing on.'

She put two onions on her chopping board. 'It's a special friendship. I could never risk anything bad happening to it.'

'What do you mean?'

Hattie wondered if it was the fact that Xander hardly spoke that made him so direct. 'If anything romantic started and it went wrong it could spoil the friendship irrevocably. I couldn't risk that.'

Xander nodded. Hattie wondered if he'd used up his daily ration of words.

She'd thought about it, of course she had. When they first met, she'd been struck by how handsome and kind he was – she'd have been mad not to have considered it. But they'd both been with other people and by the time they weren't, she and Luke had slipped into an easy friendship.

A little while later, Frank and Fearless bounded in through the double doors and bounced on to the sofa to make a big fuss of Xander.

'Horrible dogs,' said Luke, following them.

'Dogs off!' commanded Hattie, aware she didn't know if Xander was dog friendly or not.

The dogs immediately jumped off the sofa, but Xander said, 'No, leave them.'

Hattie saw them get back on to the sofa and settle with their heads on Xander's lap. He smiled slightly and seemed to relax. And Hattie let out a breath too. Maybe it would be all right.

While Luke was up in the attic, putting some wonder product on the leaking water tank, she carried on cooking. Soon there were large bowls on place settings and she got out a bottle of wine and glasses from habit and then realised no one would be drinking it.

'Would you like another Diet Coke?' she asked Xander. 'I know you're only supposed to have one a day, but it is your first night.'

'Water is fine.'

Luke came down and looked at Hattie sternly.

'That should last a little while, but you must speak to your landlord.'

'I will mention it, but I can't make demands. I'm lucky to be here.'

'You're protecting his investment. You'd be doing him a favour.'

'OK then. If you put it like that.' She smiled. Luke grunted. He knew as well as she did that while she'd mean to report to Aiden, her landlord, she'd probably forget because of all the other small but time-consuming things she had to do as part of her work. Luke was one of the few people who realised what hard work being a property finder was. Most people thought she was a combination of Kirstie and Phil but only did what Kirstie and Phil did on television, showing nothing of the tireless research and many, many hours that had to be put in first.

When Hattie served out the fried rice she put some in all the bowls without consulting Xander. She knew he probably thought she'd forgotten about his 'pasta only' diet but in fact she thought he might like something different if no one was making a big deal of it.

And so it proved. There wasn't much conversation as everyone seemed hungry. Hattie offered seconds and Xander and Luke both had some.

'What about cheese?' said Hattie when everyone had finished. 'I'd have made a pudding if I'd known you were coming, Luke.'

'Hattie is the only person I know who still makes proper Bird's Custard,' Luke said to Xander. 'She's a wonderful cook. You've struck lucky living with her.'

Hattie laughed. 'Xander isn't here for my cooking – thank goodness – but because he can walk into town to college from here.'

'It's quite far. Mum used to drive me to school.'

'I'll drive you if I can. Or pick you up, but it's better if you're independent. You might like to hang out with your friends after college.'

'I haven't got any friends,' said Xander.

'Frank and Fearless seem to like you,' said Luke, indicating the dogs who had their heads on Xander's knees, one each side.

'I've never been around dogs before. Mum doesn't like them. She says they're messy.'

'They are,' said Luke. 'If I didn't have them my house would be immaculate.'

'If you overlook all the dust and grime you bring back home with you every day,' said Hattie.

'I'm a builder. That's what happens.'

'What sort of things do you build?' asked Xander.

'I restore old houses mostly,' said Luke. 'I'm what's known as a heritage builder because I use all the old techniques.'

'He's a posh builder, Xander,' said Hattie. 'It means he has brie and cranberry in his sandwiches instead of cheese and pickle.'

Luke laughed. 'True. Maybe I should add that nugget to my website. It might encourage a better class of client.'

'You've got more work than you can handle as it is,' said Hattie.

'Also true.' Luke got up. 'Anyway, I must be off. So no cheese for me now, but thank you very much for supper.'

'It was a pleasure and I always love seeing my best boys.' She caressed both dogs behind their ears.

'I think I might be jealous,' Luke muttered. But before Hattie could read anything into this he had whistled and the two dogs were following him out to the car.

'Are you *sure* Luke isn't your boyfriend?' asked Xander a couple of minutes later.

'No!' Hattie couldn't emphasise this enough. 'He's my friend! Can you pass me those bowls?'

'Does that really mean he can't be your boyfriend, ever?'

'I'm afraid so.' She finished stacking the bowls in the dishwasher. 'Glasses?'

'I still don't understand why.' Xander's expression was all innocence.

They went on clearing away the things in silence. 'The thing is,' said Hattie when it was all done. 'Friends are so special, especially as an adult. It's just not worth the risk.'

Chapter Five

When Xander had forty-five minutes to get to college, Hattie braved his room, armed with tea and toast. 'Xander!' she said to the shape lying in the bed. 'I'll take you to college but you have to be ready to leave in fifteen minutes. After that and you'll have to walk. Here's your breakfast.'

Her sister hadn't warned her Xander might not get up and although she knew she shouldn't, Hattie felt responsible for him getting to college for his first day. It was like looking after Frank and Fearless, she realised. To begin with, they had been just creatures to feed and clean up after, but very soon they had become creatures she cared about.

To her surprise and admiration, Xander was in the kitchen bang on time. His hair was wet and he'd brought down his plate and mug. 'Thank you so much for breakfast, Aunt Hattie,' he said. 'Shall we go?'

'Not so much of the aunt,' said Hattie, to disguise the fact she was impressed and a little touched by her nephew. 'But well done getting ready so quickly.'

'I just slept through my phone alarm,' he said. 'Mum usually comes and shouts at me a few times and, eventually, I get up. She never brings me tea or anything.'

'I'm not sure I could do shouting first thing in the morning,' said Hattie, 'but I'm making tea and toast anyway.'

'Sweet.'

'You are, Xander, darling!' said Hattie and was rewarded with a smile which was almost concealed behind his teeth.

Having delivered her nephew to his place of education, Hattie looked at her phone and realised, if she was quick, she could call in on an old friend before meeting Nick, one of her most challenging clients, to show him yet another property he was unlikely to want to buy. She never gave up on a client, but if she was ever going to, Nick could be the one. For now, she headed out of town and up into the hills. She loved her old friend dearly but she had to admit, the fact that Mary lived in Hattie's dream home added to the joy of visiting her.

Her friend Mary was sitting in her chair next to the window looking into the garden. At nearly ninety, she wasn't very fit and did a lot of sitting. But there was a range of bird feeders, all well filled, beneath the branches of a field maple for her to look at as she sat, and she was always cheerful when Hattie came to visit.

'Hattie, darling! How lovely to see you!'

Hattie kissed Mary's crumpled cheek, which felt and smelt like rose petals. 'And you! As always, I'm on the run, but had time to pop in. Can I make you anything? Toast and honey?'

Mary had carers who made her breakfast but Hattie knew she wasn't always hungry when they came and sometimes fancied a snack a bit later instead.

'I'm fine,' said Mary, 'but I'd have a cup of tea if you want one for yourself.'

Hattie went to the kitchen and switched on the kettle. This was probably her favourite room in the house. It wasn't huge but it had room for a table and six chairs, windows with wide sills where white-painted flower pots full of scarlet geraniums added cheer. There was a long wooden work surface under which a bright curtain hid deep shelves. There was a fridge, a four-burner cooker and double Belfast sinks. On the wall next to the sinks was a plate rack. Simple, but with everything one could need. She made the tea quickly and settled herself next to her friend. 'How have you been?'

'You saw me last week, darling. Nothing much has changed.'

Hattie laughed. 'I wondered if your great-nephew had done anything about that patch of damp in the kitchen. It's getting worse. I could easily get Luke to come and sort it out for you.'

'I know. And as I also know how busy Luke is, I am very grateful for your offer, but Clive says he has it in hand.'

Hattie sipped her tea so she didn't accidentally express her feelings about Clive. He was supposed to look after his great-aunt but Hattie didn't think he did it very well. In his turn, he resented Hattie for being close to Mary. Once she had left him a note suggesting a bit of repair work on a gutter and he had taken deep offence. As Clive held the purse strings, if Luke did do any remedial work, he wouldn't get paid. Hattie would try to pay him, but Luke wouldn't permit it. So it was all a bit awkward.

'I do think you have the best view in the Cotswolds,' said Hattie, 'and I speak as one who has quite a good view of my own.'

'Except it's not your own, is it, darling? How much longer are you there for?'

'A few months.' Hattie was deliberately vague. She didn't want Mary to worry about her, something she was prone to doing.

'You know I'd leave you this house if I could,' Mary went on. 'I'd love to give you some security.'

'You can't leave it outside the family, Mary, you know that.'

'True,' said Mary, 'but I've realised there's nothing to stop me leaving you a small legacy which would help you buy something, even if not this cottage.'

'You don't need to leave me anything,' said Hattie, putting down her cup and getting up. 'You've given me years of friendship and I hope you'll give me many more.'

'Not too many, darling. I'm getting on.'

Something in the way she said this made Hattie anxious. 'But you feel OK? Nothing wrong really?'

'Nothing specific. I just feel tired.'

'Being nearly ninety will do that to you,' said Hattie. 'Now I've got to go. My next client is most exacting.'

'Is that Nick?'

'Yes, it is! I am so indiscreet, I shouldn't have told you his name. Maybe "exacting" is unfair – he's... discerning.'

'Don't worry about that. Being "discerning" is not a bad thing. Besides, I'm not going to tell anyone. I have no one to tell!' Mary laughed, but it brought home to Hattie how few people Mary saw these days.

'Are you sure you don't fancy a nice care home?' Hattie asked. 'With company and more social life?'

'I do actually, but Clive says they're far too expensive.'

'But—' She didn't want to state the obvious by saying if she sold her house it could fund a care home, certainly for a good few years.

'Clive says it's cheaper to get someone to pop in a couple of times a day.'

'Yes, but there would be book clubs and handicrafts. You'd enjoy that.'

'Well, I would, but I can't go spending Clive's inheritance, can I?' Mary laughed to indicate she was joking, but Hattie knew she wasn't.

Hattie nodded. 'OK, well, we'll revisit this conversation. I must go. Can't keep my client waiting! I'll be back to see you soon.'

As Hattie started her car she realised she would be a bit late but didn't regret calling in on Mary. Currently her friend needed company more than she needed carers and more than Nick needed to view this house.

Hattie's client Nick had found the property successfully and was wandering round the outside speculatively.

After a brief 'Hello,' he said, 'It's a bit big,' as Hattie appeared.

'It's in budget and is a great investment. Let's get inside.'

Hattie stayed in the kitchen, which was primitive and smelt slightly of drains. Nick had definitely stated 'no work' on the form he had filled in for Hattie, but she was sure if the rest of the house was right, Nick would accept this compromise. If he had any sense, of course. Hattie never assumed people would be sensible when it came to buying houses. It was not only the biggest amount of money anyone was likely to spend, it was also the one which needed commitment from both head and heart. Nick hadn't shown much in the way of heart so far, so Hattie was hoping the investment angle would win him over on this one.

She could hear Nick's footsteps overhead and knew he was in the bathroom. It was in the right place, but otherwise she feared he would find everything was wrong with it. He obviously didn't linger in there for long.

She was just thinking what she would do to the kitchen if it was hers when she had another vision. It was of Nick. He was in the kitchen of the house, although it now had a big island in it. He was raising a glass to someone Hattie couldn't see. The expression in his eyes was of pure love. On the island was a straw basket with a scarf spilling out of it and there was a pair of sunglasses. When it faded, Hattie helped herself to some water and went to sit down in the old armchair next to the range. Why was she seeing this? Was she really expected to help her most discriminating client find love? She closed her eyes.

'Having a power nap?' said Nick, jolting her from her thoughts.

'I'm just testing out the fixtures and fittings. What do you think?' she added.

He shrugged. 'If you overlook that it's absolutely not what I asked for, and it needs completely gutting, it's a good house.'

Hattie lit up, she had not expected that. 'So, what do you want to do? Shall I sort a second viewing with a builder?'

Nick nodded. 'Why not?' He smiled slightly and Hattie had a glimpse of how attractive he could be.

Although exhausted from her latest vision, Hattie was pleased as she locked up the house. It did have a lot of potential and if Nick found the person he was obviously going to fall in love with, they could be very happy here.

Chapter Six

It was Sunday. Luke had offered to entertain Xander so Hattie could get on with her paperwork. Hattie was very pleased how easily Xander had fitted into her life – as she had fitted into his. He hadn't actually gone to or from college under his own steam yet, but he was eating pretty normally and while they didn't have long chats, their shared silences were friendly. He had gone so far as to mention a couple of friends he hung out with and he seemed happy to go into college.

She had just finished her work and was wondering about going and joining Xander and Luke when Fiona's name came up on her phone. As anxiety about Fiona was a constant she answered it immediately.

'So sorry to bother you on a Sunday!' said Fiona, sounding bright if apologetic. 'But I've made the mistake of telling Mummy how brilliant you are and now she wants to ask for your help with something. She needs a local friend. Only if you want to, of course, and aren't too busy.'

'I'm not too busy at all,' she said. 'Is it house related? I hope she's not planning to move out of that lovely place.'

'Oh, not at all! Can we tempt you over with lunch?'

★ ★ ★

As Hattie drove, she considered how annoyed she'd be if any of her friends who worked for themselves used up their precious free time helping out a client's mother. But Fiona wasn't just any client; she really felt they had become friends and she liked Sheila, Fiona's mother. Her job couldn't always be neatly packed into office hours.

Sheila smiled when she opened the door. 'My husband and Lance are playing golf – some special match; they won't be back until much later so it's just us girls.'

Hattie smiled, glad Rose wasn't there to object to being called a girl.

'Come on through to the kitchen. I'll make you a sandwich.'

'Mummy's sandwiches are famous – at least in the family,' said Fiona. 'Would you like a glass of fizz?'

'I won't, thank you very much, but the sandwich will be very welcome.'

'Are you sure?' said Sheila. 'Now we've opened the bottle, we'll have to finish it or my husband will find out and be grumpy.'

'I'm sure you'll manage to drink it all without me.' Hattie smiled again. Rose wouldn't be happy about Sheila's last statement either, and nor was she. If two grown women wanted to drink champagne and could afford it, it was nothing to do with anyone else.

In between questions about bread, toasted or untoasted, mayonnaise, mustard and other vital queries, Fiona started to explain what Sheila's problem was until – after a tall sandwich had materialised on a plate in front of Hattie – Sheila felt able to explain herself.

'The thing is, we haven't lived here long, only a couple of years, and I haven't been accepted into the local community properly. I mean, everyone's been really friendly, but they don't ask me to things.' Sheila took a sip of her champagne. 'I thought things were going better but then we made the blunder about the flowers for Fi's wedding.'

'Oh?' Hattie dabbed at the corner of her mouth with her napkin.

'Yes,' said Fiona. 'Lance wanted us to use this London florist – it's where all the smart couples are going for their flowers. Their website is stunning.'

Obviously less impressed by the stunning website than her daughter had been, Sheila went on: 'And when the flower guild, from the church, found out, they were all dreadfully offended that we weren't going to ask them to do the flowers. The woman in charge told me off. Apparently, almost all the flowers are provided by the members of the guild so it earns the church some money which it badly needs. The Lady chapel needs restoring.'

'Do you need the name of a good builder? I can certainly provide that. My friend Luke—'

'If only it were that simple,' said Sheila. 'Of course I offered to make a donation but they refused. Newcomers can't buy their way in. They have to make a real contribution, not just throw their money around. Rachel – I don't really feel happy calling her that but she did say I should – was very frank.'

'So... how can I help?'

Sheila took a breath. 'I need you to provide people for a quiz.'

'How do you mean?' Hattie was mystified.

Sheila exhaled sharply. 'I promised Rachel – she's the leader of the flower guild and every other organisation in the village – that I'd come up with at least two teams for her quiz night, which is a really good money spinner, apparently. It seems that might be enough to absolve me.'

'Two teams?' asked Hattie. 'How many in a team?'

'Six,' said Fiona. 'Daddy's not very keen but he's said he'll come. Lance likes quizzes, but otherwise it's only Mummy and me. We don't really know anyone else around here. And besides, I'm not much good at general knowledge. Lance thinks some of my answers are hilarious!' She laughed as if she agreed with him. Hattie wasn't convinced.

She took a breath. 'OK, let me think. You need twelve people in total?'

'Yes, and we've only got four,' said Fiona.

'I'm sure we could find a couple more people though,' said Sheila. 'I wonder if Mrs Witcombe likes quizzes?'

'Mummy, you know Daddy would go mad if you asked our cleaning lady to be on our quiz team. He'd say it was overstepping boundaries.'

'Well,' said Hattie, 'I can almost definitely promise you five people. Xander, my nephew, may only be a teenager, but he'll be good on popular culture and technology. Not sure if he likes quizzes but he's obliging, on the whole.'

'Lance is brilliant on technology but he thinks all modern music is rubbish, so help with that would be handy,' said Fiona.

'Haven't you any old friends who'd come over?' asked Hattie. 'It would be fun.'

'There're my old chums the Craigs. Camille and I were at school together and he's American. They've come over from Vermont for the wedding and they're making a trip of it,' said Sheila. 'I didn't think a village quiz would be their thing, but I can ask. If they don't fancy it I could ask another couple. We've got plenty of room to put people up. One of the reasons we bought this big house was so we could have friends to stay.'

'What about you, Fiona?' asked Hattie. 'Is there anyone you could invite? Someone who might be good at celebrities?'

'Lance doesn't like my friends.' Fiona sounded bleak.

'He can't hate all of them!' said Sheila. 'But he can't object to anyone I want to invite. What about the Jenkinses? They could bring Sophie? She's very sensible, and the three of them would fill up the two teams.'

'I suppose. Lance hasn't met Sophie, so maybe that would be fine.'

Sheila pursed her lips. 'Much as I love him, I don't think I can allow Lance to have a say in who I invite to my house.'

Fiona blushed and then took another sip of champagne. Hattie had the feeling this was a discussion that had been had before. It must be so hard for Fiona, she thought, trying to keep both her difficult fiancé and her mother happy. She got to her feet. 'I must go and rescue Xander and Luke from each other. I promise I'll try to fill a team for the quiz. When is it, exactly?'

'Friday,' said Sheila

'This Friday? That's horribly short notice.'

Sheila nodded. 'And horribly near the wedding.'

'Oh? Remind me when that is? I know you've told me.' Hattie smiled at Fiona.

'The twenty-second of June. The happiest day of my life.'

'Oh, don't say that,' said Hattie. 'It implies that life is all downhill from there!' As soon as the words were out of her mouth, she regretted them. Hattie couldn't imagine that Fiona's married life would be a bed of roses but she hadn't found a way to help Fiona see what Lance was like: he might not even have had his affair yet. 'That's pretty!' she said quickly, to hide her feelings. She pointed to a woven shopping basket with leather handles hanging on a hook in the hall. 'Is it French?'

'Yes. It's Mummy's but I do borrow it quite often,' said Fiona. 'It's very useful. You can just fling everything in.' She laughed. 'Lance says I use it like a dustbin, and fill it with rubbish.'

At the same time as Hattie was thinking what she'd like to fill Lance with she realised when she'd last seen a basket just like it: in the vision she'd had of Nick. It wasn't enough on its own to identify Fiona, or more frighteningly her mother, but it was enough to make her add Nick's name to her list of potential quiz attendees. 'Right, well, as I say, I'm going to make up a table for Friday. Get us a good range of experts.'

'That would be really kind,' said Sheila, as if Hattie had promised her half a litre of blood. 'Here are some leaflets with all the details on them. There'll be supper and a bar. Food will be free – I'm bringing chocolate roulades for pudding – but drinks won't be. Or maybe there's one free drink? I can't remember. But I'm not letting anyone pay for their tickets,' she added firmly, just as Hattie had opened her mouth to ask how much it would be. 'This is our mess. You're doing us a favour as it is.'

Hattie took the leaflets and gave Fiona and her mother a quick hug goodbye.

★ ★ ★

Hattie thought about the basket, and how she might invite Nick to the quiz without seeming like she was asking him out herself. But it had to be done. If he and Fiona appeared to hit it off, she could assume it was the right basket; if not, it obviously wasn't. But she wasn't quite happy about this. She wanted to know for sure. It wasn't going to be easy for either of them to show interest in each other with Lance there.

She parked the car and walked up through the grounds of the pub – Luke had texted to say where he and Xander had gone – to where she could see them sitting at the top of the garden, where the view was best. It was a beautiful summer afternoon and Hattie never stopped being grateful for living in such a beautiful area.

'Hi, guys!' she said, aware of a sudden rush of happiness at seeing them. The dogs, Frank and Fearless, who'd been settled quietly under the bench, got up and made a huge fuss of her. 'Can I get you drinks? Not you,' she said to Fearless, who was particularly affectionate.

Luke unhooked his long legs from the bench and got to his feet. 'I'll get them. What are you having? And do you want anything to eat? We've already had lunch, but they'll stop serving food soon.'

'Lime soda, please, but nothing to eat.'

Luke nodded, and after a quick command to his dogs to stay, set off towards the pub.

'So, how was it?' Hattie was a little anxious; she'd left Xander with Luke when they didn't really know each other. Luke had offered, and to her surprise and relief, Xander had accepted the offer of spending Sunday morning with him.

Xander nodded. 'Cool.' He didn't elaborate, but as far as she could tell, he wasn't unhappy.

'You haven't spent all morning at the pub?'

Xander shook his head. 'No. We went to an old house Luke is working on. But I found out he used to be into electronic music, like I am. He's still got quite a lot of kit. He said I can use it any time.'

'That's good.' Hattie wasn't sure she knew about Luke's musical interests and certainly didn't know about Xander's. 'So you had a nice time?'

Xander nodded.

Luke came back with drinks and packets of crisps. Seeing him walking up the hill with the tray, Hattie noticed how easily he moved, his faded linen shirt loose on his body, his equally faded jeans flattering his long legs. She reached for her bag, so he wouldn't notice she'd been looking at him.

'So, how do you feel about quizzes?' Hattie asked when everyone had had time to sip their drinks.

Luke nodded. 'I like them. No good at sport or popular culture though.'

Xander shrugged. 'Never watched one.'

'I'm talking about a real-life quiz, not one on television. And I really hope you'll come. Sheila, Fiona's mother — she's my client — Fiona is, I mean — needs people for a quiz team.'

'When is it?' asked Luke.

'This Friday,' she said. 'Very short notice.' She pulled out a couple of leaflets. 'You'll be my guests, of course, and there's a supper which sounds pretty good.'

Luke looked at the leaflet. 'I'll come if I can but I'm back down in Cornwall next week. I might not be able to get back in time.'

'Oh, don't rush back for it!' Hattie felt suddenly guilty. 'It doesn't matter if you can't come.'

'I can't come either,' said Xander.

Hattie shook her head. 'You're an essential part of the team, Xander, you don't get a choice.' She paused. 'I'm going to ask Rose and Sam if they can come. You'll like them,' she said to Xander.

'I'll certainly try and make it, Hattie,' said Luke.

He didn't often use her name and suddenly it felt meaningful. 'Thanks!' she said, hoping she didn't sound breathless.

It was easy to convince Rose and Sam to come to the quiz; they loved a night out.

'I'm hoping it won't go on too long,' said Hattie.

'It probably will,' said Rose. 'If they're raising funds there'll be raffles and all sorts. You can have a power nap before we go.'

'I'm nearly thirty-five, not nearly ninety!' said Hattie. 'Anyway, I'm needed. Bye, bye.'

Hattie could find no genuine reason to get in touch with Nick; she'd already organised a builder to come and see the house with him but the appointment wasn't for ten days or so. In the end she decided to just invite him. She tapped on his number. 'Nick! How are you doing?' she said when he answered, surprisingly quickly.

'Thank you for your interest, Hattie,' he said lightly. 'I'm fine. Now why are you ringing me? I do hope the builder hasn't pulled out of our meeting. Although it's got everything wrong with it, I'm really excited about that house.'

'That's good to hear, but no, nothing to do with that. I'm hoping you can do me a favour…'

'What's that?' He sounded curious.

'Could you come to a quiz this Friday? Do you like quizzes? You strike me as someone who'd be good at them.'

This made him laugh. 'Really? Or are you desperate?'

'Both. It's local. There's food and one free drink, and a very desperate woman who needs to fill two teams. That's not me, by the way. I'm only desperate by association.'

'Well, you're in luck. I do like quizzes. My knowledge of flags and the Periodic Table is outstanding.'

'Oh, Nick, that's amazing! I can't do flags and my knowledge of the Periodic Table is only what I've learnt from *Pointless*.'

'I'm rarely at home in time to watch that.'

Hattie swallowed. 'And would you like to bring anyone? A partner?'

Too late she remembered she officially knew he didn't have a partner; she really just wanted to know if he had any sort of girlfriend.

'No, just me. I'm currently single, as you should know.'

'I know you're only looking for a property for you, but you could have a red-hot lover who you don't happen to want to live with,' Hattie blurted out, sticking up for herself.

'Could I indeed?' He sounded quizzical.

'It happens.' Hattie laughed, and as she disconnected she realised she was getting to like him.

Chapter Seven

'Are you sure I have to come?' asked Xander, when they were waiting for Nick to pick them up to go to the quiz (he'd insisted). 'Mum often leaves me in the house on my own. I'm always fine.'

'You're not coming for your sake, but for the team. A young person is always a huge asset, so my friend Rose tells me. Besides, you might have a good time.'

'I wish Luke was coming.'

'Why's that?' Hattie felt the same but didn't really know why. She didn't think he was a natural quizzer.

'I like him. He's cool.'

'You know there's a film called *Cool Hand Luke*?'

'Is it good?'

'I've never seen it. I'm no good at film or pop music.'

'Pop music!' said Xander disgustedly. 'Who listens to that?'

Luckily Nick drove up before Hattie could expose herself to even more ridicule.

They were early, which meant they could still find space in a car park which was rapidly filling up.

'There are obviously lots of people coming,' said Nick. 'Your friend will be pleased.'

'I just hope she managed to get enough people. I've only rounded up five and she wanted two teams of six.'

'It's not your job to provide people for her teams,' said Nick, possibly realising that Hattie felt responsible. 'You're only doing it out of kindness.'

'Of course. Let's go in.'

Sheila's name was on a couple of tables, so Hattie claimed one of them. 'I wonder if she's got a sixth person for us?' she said, knowing she was going to wangle it to be Fiona if she possibly could.

'Glass of wine?' asked Nick. 'You may as well. And, Xander, what about you? Coke OK?'

As Xander nodded, Hattie replied, 'One glass then. Red, please.'

'I hope it's drinkable,' said Nick, and set off to the bar, which was a table covered with a cloth and various bottles of wine. Fiona had told her that Lance had donated six bottles. He had an excellent palate, apparently. With luck, she'd get a glass of the wine he had chosen.

Nick came back with the drinks. 'I gathered from the women running the bar that Mrs Anstruther-Jones, who's in charge, will fill up any teams with fewer than six members with random people who aren't already on a team. Which is a bit like Russian roulette – they may be brilliant or they may not be.'

'It will be more fun to have people we know,' said Hattie, determined not to miss an opportunity for Nick and Fiona to meet.

'Though maybe someone who's a cricket expert could be useful.'

'Maybe,' said Hattie.

Rose and Sam arrived shortly after and Hattie made the introductions. She was pleased and relieved to see that Nick, who had seemed fairly grumpy when she first knew him, was being pleasant. He was brisk, yes, but not without charm.

Xander managed to make 'hello' noises and Rose and Sam kindly didn't press him for more. Hattie could tell Rose was sizing Nick up. She was always trying to get Hattie paired up – she reckoned she owed her, and she wasn't far wrong.

Everyone sat down to sip their drinks and nibble on the snacks, while looking at their watches.

'I want to nab one of Sheila's party,' said Hattie. 'But where are they? It's nearly time to start.'

At that moment the door of the hall opened and a group of people came in, Sheila leading the pack. Hattie ran over.

'Hi!' she said enthusiastically. 'Can I bag Fiona for our team? Luke couldn't come unfortunately, so we're one short.'

'Fiona's not really known for her general knowledge, is she?' said Lance, giving his fiancée a squeeze. 'So you're welcome to her.'

'Do you mind, Fiona? We'd be so grateful. That leaves you one short, I see, but Mrs Very Long Name will assign you someone at random.'

Lance laughed. 'You'd probably do better with one of them than with my lovely Fifi here.'

Hattie hooked her arm through Fiona's and was about lead her to her team when her eye was caught. 'Oh!' she said to Sheila's friend. 'What a pretty scarf!'

The woman put her hand up to touch it. 'Isn't it? Sheila lent it to me. I suddenly remembered how cold village halls can be, even in summer, so Sheila produced this. I really like it.'

So did Hattie, but for different reasons. 'It goes well with your top. Now come along, Fiona,' she said, leading the way to her table.

'I'm quite glad not to be with Lance and Daddy, they're so confident they're going to win and won't let me give any answers anyway,' said Fiona when the introductions had been made.

'Oh, that's a shame for them,' said Nick with a smile. 'Because *we're* going to win.'

'Well said!' Rose patted his arm encouragingly. 'I'm afraid I can get awfully competitive, although as there are such huge gaps in my knowledge, I'm very willing to let other people give answers.'

'Can I get you a drink?' Nick asked Fiona.

'Don't worry. We're just about to start,' she replied, obviously not wanting to be a nuisance.

'There's plenty of time,' said Nick calmly. 'What would you like?'

'I don't suppose they've got any Prosecco?' she said.

'I think they have. What would you like otherwise?' Nick said.

'Something not too – you know – alcoholic.'

'He's very nice,' she said, when Nick had gone.

'Yes, he is,' said Rose, trying to catch Hattie's eye.

Mrs Anstruther-Jones scraped her chair back and the hall quietened. She announced that because in past years there'd been the implication that teams marking each other's papers was not perhaps a method to be entirely trusted, the papers would now be marked by the committee. 'The raffle will be drawn while the marking is being done so it won't be a late night. A list of prizes is on the back of the leaflets.'

'Ooh, a week away in a Paris apartment,' said Rose, reading the list. 'That would be amazing. Have we bought raffle tickets?' Sam knew his cue and dutifully approached the bar for tickets.

At last the quiz began. The first question was asked, and heads drew together.

Although Hattie could be a keen quizzer, tonight she was intent on studying Nick and Fiona for signs of chemistry. He was very courteous to her, that was certain, but he was being very polite generally. It was hard to know.

'We seem to be doing quite well,' said Rose. 'Xander, your knowledge of computer games is encyclopaedic.'

'That's not what my mum would call it,' he said, but was apparently pleased with the compliment in a quiet way.

Once Fiona realised that her answers were given the same weight as everyone else's, she started to make more suggestions. But only Nick said much during the round on flags. It was the last one before the interval.

Lance came over. 'How are you doing? We're pretty well spot on apart from that last round,' he said. 'Even the ladies made a contribution when we had to recognise celebrities. Who says reading *Hello!* is a waste of time!' He laughed in the way of a man who definitely thought reading *Hello!* was a waste of time.

'Fiona was good on the birds round, wasn't she?' said Rose.

'Oh, yes. Sheila was good on those too,' Lance acknowledged. 'And I suppose you had the computer games round licked,' he said to Xander.

'Yes,' he said.

'He was also good on the film round,' said Rose. 'He was the only one among us who knew anything about Francis Ford Coppola. I just about knew he'd directed *The Godfather*—'

'Oh,' said Lance, still patronising, 'that was a tough one, wasn't it? No shame for not getting that. We did, of course.'

'*The Conversation*,' said Xander. 'So did we.'

'Oh,' said Lance again, deflated. 'Does anyone need a drink? What have you got there, Fiona? Prosecco? I didn't know they had that.'

'It was under the counter,' said Nick. 'Very nice red, Lance. I gather we have you to thank.'

The conversation then went on to wine and most of the group tuned out.

'I don't know if I want Lance's team to win or not,' said Fiona, obviously forgetting that, officially, it was her mother's team. 'He'll be so... grumpy if they don't.'

Hattie and Rose found themselves exchanging glances. 'Well, there's not much we can do about the results,' said Rose.

'And people need to learn how to be good sports,' said Sam. 'I think we're doing rather well. More raffle tickets. How much are they again?'

Everyone was very generous in their buying of raffle tickets. 'Mummy's offering to take someone to the opera in that stately home,' said Fiona.

'What a very generous prize!' said Nick.

'Do you think so? Lance said that no one wanted to go to the opera in a muddy field, even if there was a picnic. Luckily Mum wasn't in earshot when he said it!' Fiona laughed.

Hattie realised that she quite often laughed when she was telling stories about Lance, as if they were actually funny, and didn't reveal him to be utterly vile. She wondered if, deep down, Fiona knew what her fiancé was like.

The second half of the quiz began. Xander, who'd lost all his shyness by now, was very active in some quite rarified questions.

'Mummy said people travel for miles to come to this quiz because the prizes are good and the questions are hard. Apparently pub teams like the challenge.'

'So Lance will be up against some stiff competition,' said Rose.

'And so will we!' said Hattie.

As far as she could tell, her team was doing very well. Her knowledge of history and literature had been used up and now it was mostly Nick, Xander and Sam who were coming up with the answers in the geography round. Fiona's knowledge of the Kardashians had proven pretty useful too.

'They'll wish they had you on their team,' said Hattie. 'Lance has been sending longing looks in this direction.'

'That may be because he's missing you,' said Rose.

Fiona laughed. 'Maybe! I think the wedding is making him very stressed.'

'It's because he's paying too much attention to detail,' said Hattie.

The last question was answered, papers were gathered in. Both of Sheila's teams stood up and went to visit each other.

'That was so difficult!' said Sheila. 'No wonder Rachel finds it hard to get people. Although I was able to get the Dartford warbler question. We needed you, sweetie, for the popular culture although Camille was very good.'

Sheila's old friend, Camille, still wearing the scarf that Hattie had seen in her vision of Nick, brushed away the praise. 'It was Lance. He knew everything! You're marrying a very clever young man, Fiona.'

'I know,' said Fiona proudly. 'I'm so lucky he chose a goofball like me.'

'Being good at quizzes isn't very high up on the list of reasons to pick a husband,' said Rose.

'Although intelligence is,' said Hattie. She agreed with Rose wholeheartedly but didn't want to antagonise Lance.

Xander suddenly yawned. He could have been bored by the conversation going on around him or he could have been tired. Hattie looked at Nick, catching his eye.

'Do you need to go?' he said. 'I'm busy first thing too. If you're ready, I'll take you.'

'But you won't know who won!' said Fiona.

'You can text me,' said Hattie.

'You might have won a raffle prize,' said Sheila.

'You can tell me about that too,' said Hattie.

She suddenly felt uncomfortable and she couldn't tell if there was an atmosphere or if she was just tired and bored, but either way, she wanted to leave.

'I think we did really well!' she said, when she and Xander were settled in Nick's car and on the way home. 'You really are good at quizzes, both of you. Although we may not have beaten Lance's team.'

'I should bloody well hope we have,' said Nick. 'I don't think he knows as much as he thinks he does.'

'Fiona was good too,' said Xander, to Hattie's surprise. 'It was a good quiz.'

'She was,' Nick agreed. He paused. 'So – er – I gather Fiona is spoken for?'

'Yes, she's engaged to Lance,' said Hattie.

'Shame,' muttered Nick, to Hattie's huge satisfaction.

To gloss over the slightly awkward silence, Hattie went on, 'I'm so glad you enjoyed yourself, Xander. I know I dragged you along against your will but you were really useful.'

'Yes,' agreed Nick. 'You must have really pissed off Lance with that film question.'

He said this in a way that made Hattie feel there was a very good reason for Nick's obvious aversion to a man he'd only just met. But with the wedding only a week away, was it too late to get Fiona and Nick together?

Hattie had a text from Fiona, sent at past midnight. 'We won! Lance is not happy. It's my fault. I shouldn't have played for your team.'

Hattie resolved to do all she could to help Fiona see sense in the next week.

Chapter Eight

The following morning, Hattie received a brisk phone call from Rachel Anstruther-Smith. 'You've won a raffle prize. The week in Paris. Congratulations! But your table did buy a lot of tickets.' She paused for breath. 'Now I gather you're a property hunter? I wonder if I could just ask you a couple things – nothing official – just general advice…'

Hattie made herself comfortable. In this instance, 'general' meant 'free'.

No sooner than she had disconnected than there was a WhatsApp from Luke. *Fancy lunch at mine today?*

What's the occasion? she typed back.

I have a new BBQ. Given to me by a client.

What time? Shall I bring salad?

Bring dressing. 12 pm.

Hattie found herself excited to be seeing Luke; she'd been missing him. They usually had a barbecue nearly once a week, but with him being away so much, this summer she felt she'd missed out. She went to Xander's bedroom. She knocked on the door. 'Are you up for a barbie at Luke's today? You don't have to come, but we'd love it if you did,' she added.

'OK. What time?' Xander was peering out at her from under the duvet.

'In an hour?'

He nodded and turned over.

Hattie took a bit more time, applying subtle make-up. If he's going to trouble to cook for us, it's only polite to dress up a bit, she told herself. She pulled on a much loved dress that was easy to wear but always made her feel good. Then she found herself adding some scent Luke had once said he liked.

She'd found a few books to take to her old friend Mary, who lived quite near Luke, and had picked a couple of quick posies – flowers for Mary, herbs for Luke – when Xander appeared in the kitchen. There was an aura of dampness about him which implied he'd had a shower. Hattie smiled her approval. 'Do you want something to eat? Barbecues can take a while sometimes.'

Xander nodded. 'Toast?'

Hattie knew she should have told Xander to make his own toast but she was in a good mood this morning.

'So did you enjoy the quiz?' she said as they drove along.

'Yeah. It's nice to win.'

'Don't you often win things, Xander? You seemed to know a lot.'

'Yes, but not the things my mum thinks are important.'

'You mean the computer games and things?'

He nodded. 'And film. She thinks films are a waste of time.'

'Film studies are perfectly respectable.'

'I know. But I don't want to do film studies.'

Hattie experienced a moment of sympathy for her sister.

'So what do you want to do? Any ambitions or thoughts about how you're going to earn your living?'

'No,' said Xander.

Hattie sighed. 'Fair enough. I was thirty before I knew what I wanted to do when I grow up. And when I do, I may well change my mind.' She glanced across at him, hoping for an acknowledgement of this admittedly feeble joke. Nothing.

But when Luke came out from behind his house to welcome them, preceded by Frank and Fearless, as enthusiastic as always, Xander brightened up. He exchanged manly nods with Luke and then Hattie went in for a hug, still holding the bunch of herbs she had brought for him.

Luke was good at hugging. It was firm, long enough and friendly. Hattie had a whiff of soap and shampoo and Luke before she was released. Just for a second they regarded each other and then he said, 'I like that dress.'

'I wear it a lot,' she said. 'You probably like what's familiar.' She looked away sharply, to cover the sudden flutter in her heart.

'I've always liked it,' he said. 'Now, what are you going to have to drink?'

'Actually, Luke, would you mind if I just popped across to see Mary first? I've got some books and flowers for her. Unless everything is sizzling hot and ready to serve.' She smiled. She could see burgers and steaks in a cool box by the newly lit barbecue. 'Xander? Will you be OK?'

Xander nodded. 'Is that all right, Luke?'

He smiled.

As Hattie walked back to her car it was with the impression that Luke and Xander would be very happy in each other's company. She smiled too.

Mary was pleased to see her. She accepted the flowers and held them while Hattie found a vase.

'It's so kind of you to bring me books,' said Mary. 'The mobile library used to come but I don't think it does any more and when you haven't got much else to do, you get through the reading material very quickly.'

They both sat and Hattie asked, 'Maybe I could take you to the actual library? If we arranged it?'

'That would be lovely, but I know how busy you are. I usually like the books you bring anyway.'

Hattie trawled charity shops when she had time, looking for suitable reading matter. She knew Mary enjoyed a good range of books, from romantic fiction to quite gritty crime and psychological thrillers, but she was sometimes annoyed she didn't get a chance to choose what she read herself.

'I could take you to the library, or a bookshop, anytime,' she said.

'To be honest, I don't have much energy for visiting shops these days. I can manage with what you bring me.'

'Maybe you should think more about moving into a home? A nice one would have a library, or bring you books.'

Mary nodded. 'I know, but as we said before, sadly they are dreadfully expensive!'

Hattie paused, trying not to say what she felt. She failed. 'If you sold this house – which would go in a flash even in the state it's in – you could live for quite a long time in a very upmarket home.'

'What do you mean "the state it's in"?' Mary was offended.

'I'm sorry – I didn't mean to be rude. I mean the fact that there are a few damp patches here and there, the kitchen needs rationalising – there's that little larder in the kitchen which takes up space where the fridge should be. I love larders, I really do, but you could put a bigger one at the end of the room. It could be very stylish.' She paused. 'I probably shouldn't read interior design magazines.'

'No, do go on. Tell me what you think needs fixing.' Mary smiled, reassuring Hattie that she was no longer offended.

'There are a few window panes with cracks in them which makes the house look a bit uncared-for. And I like the roses going all the way to the roof, but maybe they could be tied back, so they don't grab you as you go past? And magnolia paint – so last century!'

Mary laughed.

'You should tell Clive that he'd get far more money for it if it was in better repair. How old is the boiler?'

'Not as old as I am,' said Mary, 'so it should be OK for another couple of years. It probably needs servicing though.'

'But the views are sensational! A little careful tree felling would make them visible in summer, not just when the leaves are off the trees. And the rooms have lovely proportions. There are beams, but not too many or too low. Two good fireplaces and nice pale stone flags that help keep the rooms light. And if the damp patches could be treated and repainted, it would look so much better. I'd snap it up!' Hattie laughed, to hide her disappointment about the fact she could never have this cottage, which was her dream home. Hattie knew she was flogging a dead horse but couldn't help herself. Clive's selfishness when it came to his great-aunt never failed to enrage her.

'That's very useful. Thank you. Now, would you like a drink of some kind? Sherry? Tea?'

'Actually, I shouldn't stay as I've left Xander with Luke. He's doing a barbecue. But I could certainly get you something. What do you fancy?'

Twenty minutes later, Hattie had made Mary a sandwich, a pot of peppermint tea with fresh mint from the garden, and had done an online shop for her, using her own credit card as she always did. Although Mary had carers, they couldn't buy her groceries beyond the occasional bottle of milk.

'You will let me know how much it comes to, won't you, dear?' said Mary, who was already looking brighter. 'I can ask Clive to get the cash out for me.'

He'd love that, thought Hattie. *He* should be doing Mary's online shopping, not her. The trouble was he was a bit of a Luddite himself. 'Well, thirty pounds should cover it,' she said, although she knew exactly how much it would be and thirty pounds wouldn't cover it.

'Are you sure? I've got that much in my bag. Hand it over to me, there's a good girl.'

As Hattie walked back to the car, she wondered why she had lied about the cost of the shopping; it was because she knew Clive would harangue Mary if he thought she'd spent too much and she really didn't want that. A ninety-year-old woman deserved the good biscuits.

★ ★ ★

Luke and Xander were chatting enthusiastically when Hattie rejoined them. As neither of them were exactly verbose, she wondered what they'd been talking about.

'Xander's been telling me about the quiz,' said Luke. 'It sounds as if it was good.'

'Winning always helps,' Hattie said, and was about to tell Luke about the trip to Paris as well, but she held back. She hadn't quite decided what to do with that prize yet. Her immediate instinct had been to give it to Rose and Sam but someone else might need it more. It was open-ended so there was no hurry. Only very briefly had she considered going herself, but she had no one to go with.

'The other team were pissed off that they didn't have me on the team,' said Xander. 'They needed someone for computer games and music.'

'Don't let my sister hear you using words like "pissed",' said Hattie mildly. 'She'd tell me I'm bringing you up all wrong.'

'It's not your job to bring me up,' said Xander.

'Not the point. She'd say I was a bad influence and, to be fair, she's probably right.'

'Time to eat,' said Luke, getting to his feet. 'What would you like, Hattie? A burger, some steak? A bit of everything?'

They stayed far longer than Hattie had intended but it had been such an enjoyable afternoon, sitting in the sun, eating, chatting and watching her nephew come out of his shell. He had such an attractive smile: he would be a heartbreaker, one way or another, fairly soon. Eventually though, she heaved herself out of her deck chair.

'Luke, we must go. We've outstayed our welcome by several hours, I'm sure, but it's been so lovely,' she said.

She saw a glimmer in her old friend's eyes she couldn't interpret. 'It's been a pleasure, Hattie.'

And as they hugged goodbye she wondered if Luke had held on to her just a fraction of a second longer than usual. On her part she had found it harder than usual to let him go.

The following evening, Hattie was sorting out washing when her phone went. It was Sheila. What could she want at this hour?

'Hattie? I'm so sorry to disturb you but Fiona's distraught. I don't know who else to turn to. She talks about you all the time so I hope you don't mind me ringing.' There followed a series of muffled sounds where Hattie could just make out a general sense of chaos amid some choice phrases: 'the wedding', 'Lance', 'called off'. 'I don't know what to do or who to turn to.'

Hattie sighed. 'Do you need me to come over?'

Sheila sighed deeply in her turn. 'Could you? I would be so grateful. I don't know how to deal with this. And Malcolm is worse than useless.'

'I'll be right there.' Poor Fiona, Hattie thought, though whatever had happened to call the wedding off had probably done everyone a favour, not least Hattie who now wouldn't have to find a way to separate the pair. The least she could do was go over to offer some comfort to her friend.

But what about Xander? Would it be OK to leave him alone in the house at night? He'd say yes if she asked him, of course he would. Maybe she'd picked up some of her sister's anxiety, she thought as she found Luke's number.

'Hey,' he said.

'I'm sorry to disturb you at this time of night—'

'It's only nine o'clock,' he said.

His voice was so comforting. She took a breath.

'I've got to go out. There's a drama with Sheila – you know? The mother of the bride, who organised the quiz?'

'I don't need a full CV – how can I help?'

'While I'm sure Xander would be absolutely fine here on his own—'

'Drop him off as you swing by. Pack some things and I'll take him to college in the morning.'

All her tension melted away. 'Oh, Luke! You are so kind! I lo— I'm loath to think how I'd manage without you. We don't have any near neighbours he could call on if there was a problem.'

'More than happy to have him,' said Luke.

As she knocked on the door of Xander's bedroom she realised how close she'd been to telling Luke she loved him. She did love him, of course, but as a friend. And words like 'love' shouldn't be used casually, she decided.

Xander was delighted when Hattie told him what was happening and didn't object to packing some things. Hattie allowed herself a couple of seconds to wonder how her sister would respond if she heard her son had gone to spend the night with a man she didn't know at a moment's notice. Not well, was her conclusion as she started the car.

★ ★ ★

Sheila almost dragged her into the house the moment she rang the bell.

'Come in, do! I don't know what's going to happen. Fiona is beside herself.'

As Hattie followed Sheila into the kitchen, she wondered where Sheila's friends the Craigs were. Perhaps they'd gone touring before the wedding.

Fiona was standing at the kitchen table in her dressing gown, tear-stained and looking desolate. Her father was sitting at the end of the table, a large glass of something by his hand. Sheila took hold of her daughter and gently led her to a chair.

'You'll feel better if you have something to eat,' she said.

'Food isn't always the answer, Sheila!' said her husband.

'What's going on?' asked Hattie, sitting next to Fiona, hoping the name of her father would come back to her shortly.

'Lance wants to call off the wedding,' said Fiona.

'Do we know why?' asked Hattie, secretly thinking again that this was very good news.

Fiona nodded. 'He doesn't think I'm committed enough to him. I've let him down.'

Hattie took a breath. 'How have you done that?'

'I didn't lose weight before the wedding. He thinks I don't care if I'm a fat bride although of course I know perfectly well he doesn't want one of those. I did try hard, I really did, but it wasn't enough!' Fiona's voice broke.

'She hasn't eaten a thing today. I've only just found out about it,' said Sheila quickly.

'Oh God,' said Hattie. 'Why did he think you hadn't lost weight?' she asked Fiona.

'He came to the latest dress fitting,' said Sheila. 'The dress fitted perfectly; Fifi looked a dream, didn't she, Malcolm?'

'I can imagine,' said Hattie. Her mind was whirling, wondering why they didn't have a wedding planner to sort out this mess — she was a property hunter, for goodness' sake! What on earth were they expecting from her? Had she been a wedding planner, she realised, she would not have let the bridegroom near any dress fittings.

'I don't see what all the fuss is about,' said Malcolm. 'Eat less between now and the wedding: you're bound to lose a bit of weight.'

Hattie and Sheila looked at the man sitting at the end of the table, glass in hand. 'She doesn't need to lose weight,' said Hattie.

'How do you know?' Malcolm said belligerently. The whisky in his glass was probably not the first.

'By looking at her,' said Hattie, fully aware that it wasn't her place to say these things. 'She's got a lovely figure.'

'Lance doesn't think so,' said Malcolm. 'She's more Shetland pony than racehorse, that's for sure.'

Fiona visibly slumped in her seat.

Hattie took a breath and bit back the retort she wanted to make. She turned to Sheila. 'I couldn't trouble you for a cup of tea?' She could see the kettle on the Aga, spluttering slightly. While whisky obviously wasn't a good idea, a cup of tea would help.

'Of course!' Sheila got to her feet, her chair making a dragging sound on the quarry-tiled floor.

'I'm sorry, Hattie,' said Fiona. 'I don't really know why Mum rang you, but you are good at organising things.'

'What do you want me to organise?' Hattie asked quietly.

'I want you to get Lance back for me.' Fiona's eyes filled with tears again. 'Tell him I'll do anything – go on a juice diet, have those injections – but please, get him back for me!' Fiona sniffed and then took a soggy tissue from her pocket and wiped her nose.

Sheila placed a mug of tea by Hattie and she took a heartening sip.

'Are we a hundred per cent sure Lance doesn't want the wedding to go ahead?' she asked. As she was fairly sure he stood to gain a lot by marrying Fiona, she was surprised he was calling it off.

'He does want to marry me!' Fiona wailed. 'But only if I'm thinner. I can be thinner! I have a whole week.'

'Plenty of time to lose any extra poundage,' said Malcolm.

'Except there isn't any extra!' snapped Sheila.

'So, you want me to go and talk to him?' said Hattie, wishing that Sheila would say 'Yes, and give him hell' but aware that she wouldn't.

'Yes, please,' said Sheila. 'I wouldn't trust myself and Malcolm has had far too much to drink.'

'I'm absolutely fine!' said Malcolm.

'I'm perfectly happy to go,' said Hattie. It wasn't true, but she didn't want Malcolm on the narrow lanes of the Cotswolds. 'Is he nearby?'

'He's at a holiday cottage,' said Fiona. 'I'll send a link to your phone.'

Chapter Nine

Hattie found the house without difficulty but sat outside in the car for a few minutes. Although she felt Lance deserved to be flung into the seventh circle of hell for what he was doing to Fiona, she was a bit scared. It was after ten at night, far too late for social calls, and he would almost certainly shout. If it weren't for her visions she would never have got so involved with this couple. Reprimanding misbehaving bridegrooms was not part of her job as a property hunter. Nor even as a new friend. She hadn't even been invited to this wedding. She took a deep breath and got out of the car.

When Lance opened the door, he did not look distraught and disappointed, he looked annoyed. 'What are you doing here?'

'I imagine you know,' said Hattie. 'Can I come in?' As she asked, she went through into the house.

'Did Sheila send you?' he asked.

Hattie found her way to the sitting room. The hallway was too narrow for her to say what she needed to. 'The whole family sent me. They want to know if you mean it when you say you want to call off the wedding. Actually, that's not true: it's me who wants to know that.

The family, Fiona in particular, wants you not to call it off. She's distraught.'

'So she should be,' said Lance. 'Silly thing should have done what I asked and got herself in shape for the wedding.'

He was so cold about it, thought Hattie. He really doesn't care. He just wants everyone to jump through hoops for him. Although she didn't want him to know, she felt she had to tell him what Fiona had said. 'Fiona will go on any diet invented – including complete starvation – to help her lose weight for the wedding.'

He seemed pleased. 'Good. She's paying attention to my wishes at last.'

'From what I've seen, Fiona has done absolutely everything you've asked and more. There's nothing she wouldn't sacrifice to make you happy.'

'Good!'

Hattie couldn't help herself. 'And you have taken everything from her. Her friends, her hen night, the joy of keeping the wedding dress a surprise. You've been a bully from start to finish! And it's my opinion that Fiona is well shot of you.'

He laughed. 'I don't think she agrees with you.'

Hattie exhaled. She knew he was right, and she'd undertaken to get Lance back for Fiona. She also knew now that he had every intention of marrying Fiona and had just wanted to torture her before the wedding.

'So you'll be there? At the church? On Saturday?'

'And you'll stop interfering in what is absolutely nothing whatever to do with you?'

Hattie stood her ground but didn't speak.

'I'm firing you as our property hunter,' he went on. 'I never want to see you again, and if I do – well – you won't like it!'

'I'm sure I won't,' said Hattie and walked out of the house.

She called Sheila when she was back in the car. She didn't really want to go all the way to the house if she could avoid it. She had a lot to think about and needed space.

'It's going to be all right,' she said when Sheila answered. 'Lance will be there. Although I should say I think it would be better if the wedding was called off.'

'I just want what Fifi wants,' said Sheila. She sounded exhausted.

'Well, there we are.'

'Hattie, thank you. I don't know how we'd have managed without you – hang on, Fiona wants a word…'

'Hattie?' said Fiona, sounding painfully young and vulnerable. 'Will you be my bridesmaid? I don't mean walk down the aisle or anything – but come here on the morning, help me get ready? I'd love to have a friend on the day. I can't put it all on Mum, all the doing up buttons and things…'

'Of course,' Hattie heard herself say. She liked Fiona a lot and she found in this moment that she pitied her too, isolated from the world by her own partner. 'What time would you like me?'

'After breakfast? About half past nine?'

'I'll be there.'

When Hattie disconnected she wondered what on earth she was getting herself into. She had to assume this meant she was wanted at the wedding though what Lance would say to that she wasn't sure. And, of course, she had absolutely nothing to wear. She'd get in touch with Rose in the morning, she resolved.

Hattie drove home. Before she felt able to relax, however, she had to make hot chocolate. She found the bottle of whisky in the back of the cupboard and added a slug. It was going to take something powerful to get her brain to turn off, she realised.

Chapter Ten

When she picked up Xander from college the next day, he was in good spirits.

'Hi!' she said. 'Did you have a good time with Luke?'

'Yup. He's cool.' He paused. 'Mum rang me.'

'Oh, good! How's she getting on?'

'Fine. She likes Switzerland, I think.'

'Great,' said Hattie cheerily, wondering what Xander's caveat was. She could hear there was one.

'I didn't tell her I was at Luke's. I thought it might make her kick off.'

'Oh.'

'You know what she's like,' went on Xander.

'I do, but Luke's a very respectable person. You didn't need to hide the fact that you were staying with him.'

'Without you there? Does she know Luke?'

Hattie said, 'They've met, but she doesn't know him well.'

'So she could make a big fuss about it.'

Hattie considered telling Xander that he shouldn't refer to his mother as 'she' but decided against it.

She called Rose later in the day when she'd got through quite a lot of jobs, which included looking at a house that might suit Nick if his second viewing with the builder didn't go well. She'd soon realised it wasn't right for him but might be right for someone else.

'Hattie!' said Rose. 'How's things?'

Hattie explained her need for a wedding outfit, knowing Rose would relish finding her the perfect thing, even if she only had her own wardrobe to choose from. 'My clothes are either really old or work-related. Smart trousers and country jackets.'

'That'll be huge fun,' said Rose. 'I'll get Sam to pick you up so we can have wine. When would you like to come? For supper, obviously.'

'Thanks! That's really kind.' She'd leave something cold ready for Xander – wedding conversation wouldn't be his thing. Of course she'd immediately wondered if Xander would like to go to Luke's again, but with a pang she remembered he'd gone away.

Hattie disconnected a little later, very grateful for her good friends. She had caught some of Rose's enthusiasm for a wedding that was doomed before the first chord on the organ had been heard.

She stood in Rose and Sam's bedroom examining herself in the mirror, although her mind wasn't really on the job. 'The thing is, Rose, I can't let the wedding go ahead.'

'Because the groom is a coercive control freak who bullies his bride before they're even married?'

'That's about it.'

Rose exhaled and sat down on the bed on several cotton skirts that would now need ironing. 'But how are you going to do it? Will you stand up at the "if anyone knows any just cause" bit?'

'I really don't want to. I want to avoid drama as much as I can.'

'But what else can you do? Could you take Fiona aside and say, "Your fiancé is vile and is already cheating on you"? She would say, "How do you know?" and you'd have to tell her about your visions.'

'I don't know! What do you think of this dress? With luck no one will see it because there won't be a wedding.'

'That, I'll have you know, is a very expensive dress! OK, I got it off Vinted, but it's practically designer. You should be proud to be seen in it.'

'I would be very proud to be seen in it under any other circumstances.'

'It does look lovely on you. In fact, I'd better give it to you as it's not so great on me.' Rose took a breath. 'You're a sort of bridesmaid so you'll go to the house early?'

'There are little bridesmaids, I think.'

'Not relevant. You'll have to help Fiona get dressed.'

'That's the plan, yes,' said Hattie.

'And her mum – Sheila? Is she on your side about all this?'

'I think I could get her on side. But her father isn't. He is obviously a bit like Lance. Which may be why Sheila is so worried.'

'So if you and Sheila talk to Fiona, wouldn't that have an effect?' Rose started hanging up the discarded dress-choices.

Hattie bit her lip. 'What do you think? She's madly in love with this man who has her exactly where he wants her. Your newest friend and your mother say he's a wrong 'un and you should call off the wedding of your dreams? Can you see that working?'

'No.'

'I've done hardly anything except think about what to do and I haven't come up with any answers.'

'Didn't you tell me you'd had a vision about Nick and Fiona?'

'Yes, but I'm not a hundred per cent sure the woman in the vision is Fiona. I mean, the basket and the scarf I saw were in her house, but I might not be right.'

'Nick did seem to like Fiona at the quiz.'

'Yes, but he didn't hit on her or anything,' said Hattie.

'And that's a good thing! He knew she was with someone else!' Rose was adamant.

'So, what you're saying – or rather what you're about to say – is that I have to tell Nick about all this and see what he can do?'

'Erm, I was a little bit behind you in coming to this conclusion, but I do agree. And if that fails and you can't get through to her, the wedding will have to go ahead and you'll have to be supportive through the divorce. You know lots of solicitors.'

'Who mostly deal in conveyancing,' said Hattie.

'Let's have another glass of wine and then you can ring Nick,' said Rose. 'Let's go downstairs. And take the dress.'

Hattie was glad of the second glass of wine and of Rose hanging over her so she couldn't back out. Hattie made dozens of phone calls every day, they held no fear for her, but this one was different.

'Nick? It's Hattie.'

'I know that. It told me before I answered.'

'Listen, I've got a very strange favour to ask you. Could we meet at the Coach and Horses for coffee, so I can ask you?' Hattie knew this pub would be deserted at coffee time and she'd be able to speak freely.

'I assume this is nothing to do with buying the house? I'm seeing the builder this week. Why don't you just ask me now?' asked Nick.

'It's complicated. I need to see you face to face.' Or did she? Was she just putting off the awful moment when she'd have to burden Nick with all this?

Nick was silent for a few moments. 'OK. I could manage that. Eleven o'clock?'

'Well, he's agreed to meet me,' she told Rose and Sam when she hung up, although they must have gathered that.

'Well done, Hats,' said Sam.

Hattie nodded. 'And could you take me home now?'

The goodbyes took a little while. Hattie had so much to thank Rose and Sam for.

Chapter Eleven

Although she was early, Nick was waiting for her in the pub, a cup of coffee in front of him. Hattie was relieved. It would be so easy to find an excuse to duck out of this, but now he'd seen her she couldn't run away.

'Hey, Nick, thank you so much for agreeing to meet me.'

'You sounded rather desperate on the phone. Not like you. Coffee?'

He made appropriate signals to the woman polishing glasses behind the bar.

'So, what is it?'

Hattie swallowed, wishing he'd let her have a few sips of coffee first.

'Nick, I really need your help.'

'To rob a bank, obviously, going by the expression on your face.'

She managed a smile. 'To be honest, it's almost as bad and possibly twice as hard.'

He leant forward, his attention fully engaged.

'Do you remember at the quiz, the nice girl on our table—'

'Fiona. Yes.'

'Well, you might also remember that she's getting married, to Lance. Who's not so nice.'

'I remember.' He pursed his lips but didn't comment further.

'I want to stop the wedding. Now, before you say anything, let me give you my reasons.'

He nodded. Hattie took a breath and then her coffee arrived, interrupting her momentum.

'You were saying?' said Nick when Hattie's coffee was served.

'Actually, I want *you* to stop the wedding. I've thought for ages about how I could do it, and I can't think of a way.'

'Why do you think the wedding should be stopped?'

'Firstly and most importantly because Lance is horrible to Fiona. He bullies her. Secondly, I think he stands to make money out of marrying her, divorcing her and taking half of whatever house they buy. Finally, I know for a fact that he's unfaithful to her.'

Nick looked very stern. But crucially, he didn't ask her how she knew that Lance was cheating.

'Have you thought about stopping the wedding in the traditional way?'

'Yes, but I really don't want to do it. It would be so upsetting—'

'Stopping the wedding however you do it is going to be upsetting. Have you talked to Fiona about it?'

'She won't hear a word against Lance. She says his behaviour is a sign of how much he loves her. The other day he said he wanted to call the wedding off because she hadn't lost enough weight.'

'She doesn't need to lose weight!'

'I know. He's a monster.'

'That's a polite word for him.'

Nick's quiet anger was very reassuring. Hattie relaxed a little. 'I think we're right. We must stop the wedding happening if we can. We may not be able to do it, of course. It won't be easy. But we'll have tried. And if the wedding goes ahead, we'll just have to be supportive and hope it ends gently.'

'We want to avoid that if at all possible.'

'I'm so grateful to be able to share this with you. I've been so worried,' said Hattie, suddenly feeling deeply fond of the man who until recently was just her most discriminating client.

'Of course, I can't promise anything. When is the wedding? And do you know who'll be driving her and her father – presumably – to the church?'

'I can find out,' said Hattie.

They discussed details of the wedding. Hattie told him everything she knew and said she could ask for more details on some pretext, if that would be useful. Nick wrote everything down. Then he put away his Moleskin notebook and said, 'I'm not sure why you've asked me to help but I find myself compelled to try, for Fiona's sake. She's a lovely woman. She doesn't deserve to be shackled to a man like Lance.'

And Hattie left the pub feeling lighter than she had in days.

Chapter Twelve

Suddenly it was Saturday morning, the day of the wedding. Xander had assured Hattie several times that he'd be fine on his own, and as she finally left the house in her borrowed clothes (including a hatinator which had made Xander snort with laughter when she put her head around his bedroom door to say goodbye), she realised she had turned into Xander's mother: over-anxious. Though quite what could happen to him while he was lying in bed she wasn't sure.

But when she arrived at Fiona's house, any thoughts about her nephew faded. Sheila opened the door to her. 'Thank goodness you're here, Hattie. Come in.'

Fiona was in what was obviously her parents' bedroom. Her hair was in heated rollers and a make-up artist was applying concealer under her eyes. She looked as if she'd been crying.

'Hello, everyone!' said Hattie, not sure of her role, but deciding to think of herself as a cross between a bridesmaid and a wedding planner. She felt glad she hadn't actually had to plan anything, although keeping people's spirits up looked as if it was going to be a tough challenge. 'Are we all excited? Fiona? You must be longing to get into your dress!'

Too late, Hattie spotted Sheila shaking her head, indicating that Hattie shouldn't have mentioned the wedding dress.

'Not really,' said Fiona. 'I haven't eaten all week but I still weigh the same as I did last week.'

'But you'll look amazing in it!' said Hattie.

'You looked really lovely in it at your last fitting,' said Sheila.

'It's really hard to lose weight if you haven't much to lose,' said the make-up artist. 'I'm Pippa, by the way.' She extended a hand to Hattie.

'I don't know what Lance is going to say,' said Fiona. 'He could call off the wedding again.'

'He's not going to see you coming up the aisle on your father's arm and think: She's too fat, I won't do it,' said Hattie, hoping some straight talking would help.

'He might,' said Fiona, barely audible.

'Well, if he does,' said Sheila bracingly, 'we'll have the party anyway. It'll be fun!'

There was a silence when everyone in the room, even Pippa, seemed to give the impression that they felt a party without a wedding would be more fun than with one.

'Glass of Prosecco, anyone?' said Sheila.

'Actually, I'd love a cup of tea!' said Hattie. 'I feel I should keep my wits about me.'

'Why?' asked Fiona. 'Have a glass of Prosecco if you want one!'

'I'm a sort of bridesmaid,' said Hattie. 'I might need to sew up your skirt, or send out for fish and chips. Anything!' She laughed in a lighthearted way that didn't convince anyone.

'I think some Prosecco would be a good idea,' said Pippa. 'I'm nearly finished here – I'll have to touch up later anyway. We can have a glass and then I'll do Fiona's hair. After that we can put on the dress and see just how beautiful you are!'

Sheila found a bottle and some glasses and then handed the bottle to Hattie to open. 'Sorry,' said Sheila. 'I've never been able to open bottles of fizzy wine.'

Hattie poured the wine, longing for a cup of tea even more now. Then there was a knock on the door.

'Photographer?' said a smiling woman. 'A couple of candid shots?' Her smile froze slightly as she looked around.

'You'll have a glass of fizz with us?' said Pippa. 'I think a few bubbles would make us all feel – weddingy!' She smiled.

Pippa was doing her best to keep everyone cheerful. The photographer took some shots of Fiona with her heated rollers although it was obvious – to Hattie, at least – that she was not looking the radiant bride everyone expected her to be.

Sheila disappeared to make Hattie's tea and Pippa passed around glasses. Hattie didn't think that Prosecco was going to help Fiona but it probably wouldn't hurt either. She might need a little Dutch courage if she was to be persuaded to call off the wedding herself. Hattie checked her watch: not long until Nick's plan could swing into action; she hoped they'd got it right. Everything seemed to be taking so long! And the little bridesmaids hadn't arrived with their mothers yet.

'All right,' said the photographer. 'Mum's back! Hair and make-up look amazing – time for the dress!'

She clicked away as the dress was removed from its cover and Fiona slipped off her dressing gown.

'Let's have a shot of the bride's mum doing up those lovely pearl buttons on the back.'

Sheila did her best but after a couple of moments she gave up. 'I'm sorry. I've got a bit of arthritis in my thumb. Hattie, you do the buttons up for me. Pretend to be me.'

Hattie obliged, and kept her face out of shot as the buttons were done up.

'What about a shot with the bride and her dad? That can be very sweet. Proud father and beautiful bride…' suggested Pippa.

Sheila shook her head. 'Not now. I'm afraid Malcolm has got "father of the bride" nerves so he's busy pacing downstairs.'

'What's he worrying about, Mum?' said Fiona, now buttoned into her dress, her arms covered in delicate lace.

'He says he doesn't want you to be late, but it's not really about that. I happen to know he's been thinking about your wedding since the day you were born,' said Sheila. 'He may have stressed himself out a little.'

Fiona was clearly taken aback. 'I don't want to be late either,' she said eventually. 'Lance specifically said he didn't want to be waiting like a lemon for me to turn up.'

Hattie looked away. She was certain she wasn't the only woman in the room wondering how a bridegroom could talk like that to his bride.

Malcolm insisted on his daughter having a good swig of brandy from his hip flask before they got into the wedding car, to 'settle her nerves'. He seemed to have quite a long pull himself before he apparently felt his own nerves were settled. 'That'll put hairs on our chests!' he said as he helped Fiona in. Fiona managed a weak smile and Sheila arranged her train.

'We'll be right behind you, darling,' said Sheila and then the door was closed.

'Do you mind giving me a lift to the church?' Sheila said to Hattie, having disappeared into the house for a few minutes. 'I lent my car to Camille and Malcolm's obviously got the keys to his car in his pocket. He doesn't really like me driving it so taking them with him is a habit.'

'No problem,' said Hattie. 'Let's hope they give us time to get to the church before they do.'

Sheila nodded. 'I'd like to make sure her dress is hanging right before she goes into the church.'

'And that the bridesmaids all have their headdresses the same way up. There was a moment there with the mums all arguing about it. And the bride should definitely arrive last,' said Hattie firmly.

'That'll be difficult with Malcolm in charge,' said Sheila. 'He hates being a second late and is very nervous. I happen to know that brandy isn't the first drink he's had this morning.'

'Is there any reason why he's so nervous, do you think? He's happy about the wedding?' While she really didn't want to mention it, she wanted to give Sheila an opportunity to talk about her feelings if she wanted to.

'Of course he is. He thinks Lance is amazing. "The son he never had" and all that. I think he just doesn't like being part of something where he isn't in control.'

Hattie nodded, but couldn't find much to say in response. She sent up a silent prayer for Nick's plan to work; it was clearly Fiona's only hope now.

★ ★ ★

'It looks like we've beaten the bride to it!' said Hattie, finding space for her car a little way away from the church gate.

'That's good! We can recover from the morning and then sort Fiona out when she arrives.' Sheila paused. 'I suppose I ought to say hello to Lance first.'

'Do you and Lance get on OK?' asked Hattie, although she had seen them together a couple of times.

'He's not my favourite person, to be honest, but he's apparently the love of Fifi's life. He may soften up as the years go by. Malcolm is quite like him. I've learnt to manage him. Fiona will have to do the same with Lance.' And with that she took off towards the church.

The space looked beautiful, thought Hattie as they entered. Lance's choice of florist might have caused a lot of local ill feeling but she had to admit they'd done a wonderful job.

The pews were full and Lance and his best man were in their places, Lance looking around impatiently. Most grooms would be nervous, thought Hattie, but not Lance.

It was odd to be at a wedding where you knew hardly anyone, she thought, searching the seats for someone she recognised. She spotted Camille and her husband. They could give Sheila a lift to the reception venue if Hattie got the call she was hoping for.

Hattie followed Sheila back out to the church porch where she was anxiously awaiting her daughter. 'Where can they be?' she said, when she saw Hattie.

'The wedding isn't due to start for another five minutes, and although no one wanted Fiona to be late, she might decide to go round the block, have a few minutes to get herself focused.'

'I wish her luck with that, if it's her plan,' said Sheila. 'If Malcolm has anything to do with it, she'll be here and marched down the aisle before the cat can lick her ear.' She paused. 'Sorry, that's something my father used to say. I can't help thinking about him just now. He was never keen on Malcolm but I insisted on marrying him.'

'Do you regret it?' asked Hattie tentatively.

Sheila didn't reply for a few seconds. 'He gave me Fiona and she's worth everything. I couldn't love her more.'

The vicar approached, a friendly woman of about Hattie's age. 'Sheila? Do you want to take your seat?' She looked at Hattie, obviously wondering who she was.

'This is Hattie,' said Sheila. 'She's my – my best woman.'

'Very good idea to have one. The bride's mother can feel quite lonely on the day. She's usually been such an important part of all the planning and organising and, come the wedding, she's often expected to sit by herself and do nothing.'

'I'm going to sign the register,' said Sheila. 'I insisted on that.' She paused. 'My husband's very old fashioned. He doesn't really think women should sign forms.'

The vicar laughed. 'He probably doesn't approve of me either!' she said.

'Probably not,' said Sheila.

Time seemed to pass incredibly slowly. Lance stormed up the aisle to wait for his bride by the door. He probably wanted to give her a blast of disapproval before he forsook all others as long as they both should live. The irony of it hit Hattie – they weren't even married and he'd probably already broken this vow. She decided if

Nick couldn't stop the wedding, she would stand up at the appropriate moment. She'd have to.

It was twenty minutes past the appointed time when Hattie's phone went. She left the church to answer it. It was Nick.

'I've done it. I got rid of Fiona's father and we're taking time to talk things through. But she wants to talk to her mum. She didn't have her phone on her – no pockets in a wedding dress.'

'I'll get her.'

While Sheila and Fiona were talking, Hattie wondered what on earth Nick had done. Had he hijacked the wedding car? And how had he got rid of Malcolm? He must have shown an impressive amount of initiative, she realised, hugely relieved that she didn't have to interrupt the wedding herself. Far better that it had never started, she felt. She wandered a little way away and looked at her watch – it was half an hour after the wedding was supposed to have got going.

Sheila came running up and handed Hattie her phone. 'It's all off. Fiona's not coming. She... she couldn't go through with it. I... I...' She stopped and took a deep breath, making a visible effort to pull herself together. 'And Malcolm's back at the house; he needs me to pick him up. He confessed to drinking a bit in the car. Can you possibly give me a lift? I can't bear to go through all the explanations so I can ask Camille for mine back.'

Hattie nodded. 'Let's go.'

A few seconds after they'd set off, leaving Lance none the wiser, pacing outside the church, Sheila said, 'It's all the most godawful mess and Malcolm is going to be fit to be tied but I'm really glad this has happened.'

Hattie nodded.

'I think we should still have the party, don't you? We'll have to pay the caterers anyway so we might as well.'

Sheila was thinking aloud, she didn't need Hattie to reply.

'I blame myself entirely for all this going as far as it has. I knew Lance was a bully. My marriage has been very tricky and I've managed, but I don't want that for my only child.'

'Fiona could go to my house,' said Hattie, before Sheila could blame herself any more. 'Lance doesn't have my address. Nick could take her there until we think of a plan.' She paused. 'Presumably she packed for a honeymoon? Could you get me her case? I could take it home so she could get out of her wedding dress.'

Sheila nodded. 'Good idea!'

'But I don't want Malcolm to see me, to know I'm in any way involved, or he might tell Lance.' Hattie didn't want to deal with an angry Lance again if she could possibly help it.

'How will I get it to you, then?'

They were nearly at the house. Neither woman spoke, both frantically thinking.

'I'll have to take Malcolm's car,' said Sheila. 'I'll have to give him coffee in case he's more drunk than just over the limit. I'll also have to tell him that the wedding is off and he has to tell all the guests.' She paused. 'I'll say I need to use the bathroom, go upstairs and throw Fifi's case out of the window. Malcolm will be in the sitting room, in the front of the house, so you could collect it. I'll keep him occupied.'

'OK,' said Hattie. 'That seems like a plan.'

Sheila hadn't warned Hattie that she'd have to climb through a hedge to reach the case that was on the lawn but she plunged in and got through, hoping she wouldn't catch Rose's dress on anything. She couldn't think of a better way of getting out of the garden, so she climbed back through it, clutching the case to her.

Hattie couldn't help laughing as she saw a stately Rolls-Royce climbing the hill to her house, just in front of her. As it was a single-track road and there were a couple of cars coming towards her, she pulled into a passing place to watch the Rolls turn into her entrance and park. She saw Nick get out and bang on the front door and Xander open it with some confusion. Then the car door opened and Fiona emerged in her wedding dress. She had taken off her veil and abandoned her bouquet. Hattie breathed a sigh of relief.

Chapter Thirteen

'Hi, everyone!' said Hattie, calling from the car as she retrieved Fiona's case from the boot. 'Fiona! I've got your case here, if you want to get out of your dress.'

Xander regarded his aunt, clearly relieved that he didn't have to play host. 'Hattie! You look like you've been pulled through a hedge backwards.'

'Hardly surprising,' said Hattie, 'although, to be fair, I went through it forwards. Do please go in!'

Nick took the case from Hattie and led the way. Fiona, who was looking pale and tear-stained, followed when Hattie took her arm. 'Let's get you upstairs and into some more normal clothes,' said Hattie.

'I haven't got any normal clothes,' said Fiona. 'Lance doesn't like normal clothes.'

They were all in the kitchen, which wasn't large. 'Xander? See if Nick wants a beer or something. Fiona, you come with me.'

She managed to get Fiona up the stairs and into her bedroom. She put the case on the bed and opened it. 'What do you want to wear?'

Fiona thought for a moment. 'Jeans and a T-shirt. Like I used to wear before I met Lance.'

Hattie rifled gently through the case. There was a pair of silk capri pants but they were hardly jeans. 'Do you mind wearing something of mine?'

'I'd prefer it. Lance chose all those clothes.' She looked at Hattie gratefully.

Hattie laid out a selection of items from her own wardrobe. 'Will you come down when you're ready? Or do you need a hand with the buttons?'

'I need a hand.' A few seconds later, when Hattie had lifted away the confection of lace and silk, Fiona said, 'I thought I loved that dress but I never felt comfortable in it.'

'You looked utterly beautiful in it. But then, you are.' Hattie smiled. 'Shall I pop back and get you when you're dressed?'

'I'll come down.'

Hattie didn't leave the room immediately. 'Do you – did you – feel safe with Nick?' Hattie was aware that she had been taking a huge risk asking Nick to help. She hardly knew him. If it hadn't been for her vision he would never have come into her mind to help Fiona.

Fiona nodded. 'He's so kind, isn't he? I remember meeting him when we did the quiz and thought he was really nice. I didn't know he was a limo driver and what a coincidence that he works for the company we booked for the cars.'

Hattie bit her lip. She wasn't absolutely sure what Nick did for a living, but she was fairly sure limos didn't come into it.

Downstairs, Hattie sent Xander and Nick out on a fake errand for milk. She suddenly had the feeling that Fiona would need some space.

When Fiona came into the kitchen, Hattie was glad she had asked the others to go shopping. Fiona looked hollowed out in a pair of jeans that hung off her and a T-shirt washed to the palest pink and no bra. Hattie realised she had probably been wearing something complicated and constricting under the wedding dress.

'Are you hungry?' Hattie asked.

'Toast,' said Fiona. 'Have you got bread? I haven't had toast and Marmite for months.'

Hattie cut bread and put it in the toaster. 'Would you mind telling me what happened? Not if you don't want to, obviously. Tea?'

Fiona nodded. She sat down at the table and put butter on the crust of bread that was there. 'It was a miracle really. I was so unhappy but I couldn't see a way out.'

'Oh, love, that's awful,' said Hattie.

'So we set off in the car – Dad had a hip flask he sipped from a few times and offered to me. I didn't have any. I thought I'd be sick. I felt ill enough as it was. Then, when we'd gone a little way, Dad said, "This is the wrong way, you fool!" Nick said – I hadn't noticed it was Nick, I was too wound up with everything. Nick said he'd heard that a load of sheep were loose on the usual way and we had to take a detour.'

'Golly,' said Hattie, impressed by Nick's ingenuity.

'And then Nick took a call on his phone, through his ear, you know, and said Dad was wanted urgently back at the house. He said that someone had rung and it was urgent.' Fiona paused while Hattie buttered the toast that had now popped up. 'Dad went ballistic and said we'd be late for the wedding. Nick said he'd drop Dad off and make sure I got to the wedding on time. I knew

Dad was nervous about walking me down the aisle, so he didn't say anything.'

Hattie cut more bread. She got the impression that Fiona was enjoying telling her story.

'Nick dropped him off and then we sped away, really fast. But we hadn't gone far before he pulled into a lay-by and asked me if I'd like to think about whether I wanted to get married or not.' Fiona paused, apparently losing focus a bit.

'What did you say?' Hattie prompted, desperate to know the story.

'I realised I hadn't thought about it. Not ever, I don't think. Lance proposed, gave me this enormous diamond.' She waggled her finger. Hattie wasn't an expert but she guessed it to be about two carats. 'And suddenly, that was that. We were getting married, buying a house, moving to the country.'

Hattie took out the second lot of toast and started buttering. 'Are you happy with Marmite or do you want something sweet?' she asked.

'Marmite every time. You have no idea how absolutely delicious this is. I haven't eaten a carb since I met Lance, I don't think. Or since he decided he wanted to marry me but only if I was slim.'

'You are slim.'

'But not thin! Not thin enough to give him status,' said Fiona. 'Apparently. I let him down by being podgy.'

Hattie took a breath to protest but let it out again. She wanted to know the rest of the story. 'So you decided you didn't want to get married?'

'Actually, I started to cry. Nick came and sat next to me in the back of the car and handed me tissues and water. Eventually he said, "I'll take that as a no, then." Fiona smiled at the memory. 'Even though I was crying so hard I had to laugh. And I knew I didn't want to marry Lance and the wedding had to be called off.' She gave a shuddering sigh. 'I told him I didn't want to marry Lance, but I thought I still had to. Nick told me the wedding didn't have to happen.' She bit into her toast. 'Then he rang you and I spoke to Mum.' She yawned. 'Would you mind if I lay on the sofa for a bit?'

Two minutes later, Fiona was fast asleep.

'She must have been exhausted,' said Hattie as she and Nick surveyed the sleeping Fiona, now covered with a blanket.

'Poor darling,' said Nick softly. 'What I'd do to that man if I had the chance.'

'What did you say happened to Xander?' Hattie asked, wanting to change the subject.

'Oh – we met a guy called Luke? In the shop? They were obviously old friends. Xander asked if he could spend the day with Luke. Luke said yes and invited Xander to make music at his house. Luke said he'd drop him home tomorrow but to text if you're worried. That's OK, isn't it?'

'You seem to have gone to a lot of trouble to do the right thing. But Luke is very nice. And it's fine. Now, how much do I owe you for the milk, and what can I make you to eat?'

'Nothing and nothing,' said Nick. 'I'll make myself a sandwich. Then I suppose I'd better get that Rolls-Royce back to its rightful owner.'

'You must tell me how on earth you managed to persuade people you were a limo driver?'

Nick smiled. 'A lot of ingenuity and a bit of bribery did it.'

Hattie watched as Nick wielded ham, tomatoes, mayonnaise and butter.

'I'm just a bit worried about Fiona,' said Nick over his shoulder. 'Where can she go? Lance is bound to come looking for her.'

'Actually, I've got an idea about that. Hang on a minute.'

Hattie went to her bedroom and found the raffle prize and ran back downstairs with it. 'I won this at the raffle they had at the quiz. It's a week in someone's flat in Paris. She could go there for a week at least to think, although I don't much like the thought of her being alone.'

Nick looked thoughtful. When he spoke, it was hesitantly. 'Do you think Fiona would like – might consider going to Paris with me?'

Hattie lit up at the idea. It was much too soon for anything romantic, of course, but hoping as she did that Nick and Fiona might be right for each other, if she'd read her vision correctly, this was too exciting to not encourage. 'You'll have to ask her.'

'Or you could ask her? I don't want her to feel pressured in any way. I mean – you know me, but she doesn't. It's probably a mad idea even to think of it.'

'I'll ask her.'

Nick handed her a sandwich with so much filling she'd have to eat it in small stages. 'Here.'

'Thank you.'

'But, Hattie, isn't there anyone you'd like to go to Paris with?'

Just for a second she pictured herself and Luke sitting at a café table in Paris. It wasn't a vision, it was just a momentary dream. She shook her head and cleared her throat to bring herself back to sanity. 'Not really. Besides, I've got Xander staying.'

After she'd watched Nick drive the Rolls down the hill, Hattie cleared up the lunch and sat on the armchair next to the sleeping Fiona. Then she got up and changed the sheets on Xander's bed for something to occupy her time and stop her thinking about Luke. It was crazy, she'd seen him only a week ago. How could she be missing him?

Fiona came to at about six o'clock.

'How are you feeling?' asked Hattie.

'A bit weird. Is the wedding really off?'

Hattie nodded. 'Would you like to stay here tonight? My nephew is spending the night with my friend Luke, so it's just us.'

'That sounds nice. Would you mind if I called my mum? I haven't got my phone.'

Hattie handed over her phone. 'I'll make us some supper to give you some privacy.' She paused. 'Would frying pan pizza be OK? I was going to make that for my nephew.'

'That sounds perfect. Anything with carbs is fine by me!'

'Go and talk to your mum. I'll be in the kitchen.'

While Hattie cooked she could hear Fiona and her mother were having a long conversation but of course couldn't hear what they were saying.

The pizza was under the grill browning before Fiona came back.

'Lance hasn't taken it well,' she said. 'Mum said he was spitting tacks, whatever that means.'

'It means he's angry.'

Fiona sat down at the table. 'He would be. He's been made to look a fool. Although Mum said everyone seemed to enjoy the party. Daddy's spitting tacks too. He thought Lance would be good for me.'

Hattie smothered a snort at that idea. 'Glass of wine?'

'Yes, please. I haven't been drinking either. I've just been having bone broth and green smoothies.'

They ate in silence for a few minutes; then Fiona said, 'The trouble is, I don't know where to go. I want to go home but can't as I need to keep right out of Lance's way. And Daddy's.'

'Well, I was talking to Nick about this earlier. I won a week in Paris as a raffle prize at the quiz. Would you like to go there?'

'On my own?' Fiona didn't look keen.

'Actually, Nick offered to take you. Of course it would be just as friends, but he felt a bit odd about asking you himself.'

'He was incredibly kind to me,' said Fiona. 'So calm and gentle. So unlike Lance!'

'Nick… cares about you.'

'He doesn't know me!'

Hattie laughed. 'True! But would you feel safe with him if you went to Paris together?'

'Oh, yes. Absolutely. In a way I never felt with Lance. I felt he owned me but didn't really like me.'

Hattie was silent, keeping back her opinions on Lance. There was no need to pile in now that the wedding was off.

'Have a think about Paris,' she said instead. 'Nick will come back in the morning and you can make a plan if you want to.'

Fiona nodded; she didn't seem against the idea at all.

'More pizza? Or shall I find the box of chocolates I've had in the freezer for a while?' Hattie offered.

'Chocolates! I didn't know you could freeze them!'

'You definitely can.'

Fiona had gone to bed and Hattie was just clearing up when her phone went.

It was Sheila. 'Hattie? Can you hear me? I'm in the coat cupboard.'

'I can hear you.' She didn't bother to ask why Sheila was in the coat cupboard – there would presumably be a good reason.

'Lance has worked out that the wedding being called off was something to do with you. I let the cat out of the bag. I'm *so* sorry. He's furious.'

'Oh, dear.'

'I'm ringing to warn you. I know you haven't got your home address on your website or anything but he's determined to find you.'

'Is he likely to come tonight?'

'He shouldn't drive as he's been drinking but I don't think that would stop him.'

'OK.'

'You'll be all right?'

'I'll be fine. I'm safe here, I'm sure. And I'll keep Fiona safe too. She's probably asleep by now.'

'Good. The poor girl must be worn out by all this.'

'Yes! It's been lovely to see her eat and relax.'

'Thank you so much for all your help, Hattie. You've saved our daughter.' There was a wry laugh. 'Although my husband might take longer to be grateful.'

Hattie laughed too. 'That's OK. I don't need his gratitude.'

'I'm grateful enough for both of us, I'm sure.'

'I was very happy to be able to help.'

It was only after she disconnected the call that she suddenly began to feel nervous. The cottage was far from any neighbours and Hattie had never minded this before. But the thought of Lance tracking her down, coming to her door to threaten her and Fiona, made her heartbeat increase.

She picked up the phone again. 'Luke?' she said when her call was answered. 'Could I possibly borrow Frank and Fearless?'

Chapter Fourteen

'What do you want them for?'

She hesitated for just a second too long, aware she should have got her story straight before she'd called.

'I'm coming over,' said Luke, and he hung up.

Hattie still hadn't worked out what to say before she heard Luke's truck pull up and the sounds of people getting out. The dogs arrived first, quickly followed by Xander.

'What's up, Hattie?' he asked.

'It's complicated. Come in. But don't go to your room, it's got Fiona in it.'

'Oh!' said Xander. 'I leave the house for an evening and you rent my room out to someone else!'

Hattie smiled, grateful to him for lightening the mood. Then Luke came in. He looked… not cross exactly, she thought, but resolute.

'So?' he said.

'Well, come in properly,' she said grumpily. 'I'll make some tea.'

Her mouth had gone dry and she was desperate for a cup, but even more, she wanted a bit longer to think what to say.

She brought through a tray of mugs and a plate of biscuits. Xander would appreciate them even if no one else would.

'So?' said Luke, looking at her over his mug.

He had a way of talking that was quiet but very firm, she realised. She wasn't sure she'd seen this side to him before. Right now it was wonderfully reassuring.

'It's a bit complicated, and sorry for dragging you out,' Hattie said. 'I could have managed with Frank and Fearless, I'm sure.'

'Really, Hattie,' said Luke. 'Surely you know me better than to expect me to just lend you my dogs without a proper explanation.'

Hattie sipped her tea. 'OK. The thing is, I've got a girl – young woman – staying with me—'

'So quick to replace me,' said Xander, shaking his head.

'And her – well – the man she left at the altar earlier today might find out where she is. And if he does, he'll quite probably come here and he'll be very angry.'

'OK,' said Luke, crossing one long leg over the other, 'so your plan, if this man arrived at your door, angry, looking for his bride and finding you in his way, would be to set Frank and Fearless on to him?'

'I don't think Luke thinks much of your plan, Auntie Hattie,' said Xander.

'Don't call me that! Of course I'd hope it wouldn't come to that. Fiona's mother wouldn't tell him where she was, and she doesn't know where I live anyway. The chances of him rocking up here are tiny.'

While everything she'd said was true, Hattie wasn't convinced.

'Really tiny,' said Luke. 'I'm going to stay here until we know they are non-existent.'

Relief washed over Hattie but then she started to protest. 'You can't sit up all night, Luke.'

'I can if I want to,' he said. 'Now why don't you get to bed?'

'Fiona's in Xander's room,' said Hattie. 'But this is a sofa bed: you could go there, Xan. Luke, you take my room. I'll slip in next to Fiona. It's a double bed.'

Hattie didn't actually intend to share a bed with Fiona but she knew Luke wouldn't take her bed if she didn't pretend she was going to.

Luke shook his head. 'Let's make up the sofa bed for Xander, but I'm staying down here. You go to your room, Hattie, and try to get some sleep.'

Something about the way he said it told Hattie there was no point in arguing.

Hattie's room was very comfortable. She had put an armchair by the window with a Welsh wool rug over the back. She had designed it as a reading nook and now she sat there, the rug over her knees, and found her book on her phone. She had no intention of going to sleep.

She wasn't sure if she'd dreamt the sound of a car, or if there really had been one, but she was downstairs in a flash. Luke was standing by the front door and the two dogs stood beside him, all as still as statues.

Luke put his finger to his lips. Hattie nodded.

The car must have been parked a little way away from the house and the driver must have been quiet on purpose. Hattie could hardly discern any sound, although one of the dogs whimpered.

'What time is it?' Hattie breathed.

'About one,' Luke replied.

And then suddenly there was a banging on the door so loud Hattie's heart pounded. She heard a door opening upstairs and Fiona came running down.

'I'll deal with this,' said Luke quietly. 'Fiona, make sure you stay out of sight.'

The banging came again. 'Who is it?' said Luke.

'I've come for my wife!' Lance shouted. 'I know she's in there!'

'You must have the wrong house, mate.'

'I don't think so!' bellowed Lance. 'Let me in so I can look.'

'You must be joking,' said Luke calmly. 'I'm not letting a nutter who bangs on my door at this time of night into my house.' One of the dogs let out a well-timed bark at this.

There was a pause. 'Who are you?' asked Lance.

'None of your business, mate, but I'm just a man who you've woken up for some mad reason. Now I suggest you go home and sleep it off, before I call the police or set my dogs on to you.'

'But this is her house!' said Lance.

'Whose house?'

'The madwoman, the property hunter – what's her name?'

'I don't know what her name is, or what your name is, but I'm going to be calling the police if you're not off my doorstep by the count of ten. And I'm letting the dogs out then too.'

'Tell me who you are!' demanded Lance.

Luke unlocked the front door and let the dogs out.

Frank and Fearless were, Hattie knew, the most gentle dogs ever but they were very well trained. Luke's arm waved them forward and they surged towards Lance, who didn't wait. He ran back to the car as fast as he could, the dogs keeping him company.

Luke whistled them back as Lance got in the car and reversed it back down the lane.

Hattie managed to get the kettle on before her knees gave way. Fiona joined her at the table. 'Who is he?' she whispered, pointing to Luke, who was relocking the front door.

'Luke. He's my friend.'

'He's a hero!' she said.

Luke came in. 'Hi,' he said, 'you must be Fiona. I'm Luke.'

'You were amazing!' said Fiona. 'Thank you so much for fighting off Lance.'

Luke gave her a half-smile, which made him very attractive, Hattie thought. 'It was Frank and Fearless,' he said.

Fiona leant down to pet the dogs, who seemed unaware that they'd played a starring role in a drama. 'They were very brave,' said Fiona. 'Lance has always frightened me, I think.'

'Well, he won't be back tonight, I don't think,' said Luke.

Hattie had a moment of panic thinking that Luke might go home now.

'You're not going, are you?' said Fiona, to Hattie's relief.

'No. We'll stay until I feel it's safe for me to leave,' said Luke.

'What's going on?' asked Xander, who came into the kitchen rubbing his eyes. 'I heard a lot of shouting.'

'It's a long story,' said Hattie. 'Now, who wants a hot drink? Or shall we just go to bed?' A terrific yawn overtook her.

'You go to bed, Hattie,' Luke said, walking around the kitchen counter. 'I'll make drinks for anyone who wants one. What about you, Fiona?'

'I'll go back to bed in a minute. I feel too shocked to sleep just yet. And I have been in bed for hours.'

'That's because you probably haven't slept for days – or even weeks,' said Hattie.

Fiona nodded. 'I've been so nervous about the wedding. Now it's as if the elastic has snapped. But I'm still on edge.'

'Hardly surprising,' said Luke, 'if you were planning to marry that—' He hesitated.

'You can say it,' said Fiona. 'Or I will. He was – is a bastard.'

Hattie nodded. 'But he's out of your life now.'

'I just hope he's out of your life too,' said Fiona.

'He is,' said Luke. 'I'll see to it. Now go to bed, Hattie. You're dropping. Fiona, I'm going to make you a special Horlicks.'

'What's special about it?' asked Xander.

'It's got brandy in it,' said Hattie. 'And you can't have any.'

'Bed,' said Luke firmly.

Happy to be ordered about in this instance, Hattie went upstairs.

Within moments she was in her night clothes and under her duvet. She plumped up the pillow and closed her eyes.

Hattie was awoken by the smell of frying bacon. She pulled on some clothes and went downstairs.

Luke was cooking bacon and Fiona was making toast. The kettle was on.

'Morning!' said Fiona. 'I was going to bring you up some tea. Bacon sandwich? On toast or bread?'

'Toast please, but tea first.'

Fiona was a different woman, Hattie thought, watching her bustling about, cheerful and practical.

'Good for you finding the bacon. I've had it in the freezer a while.'

'I knew you'd have some somewhere,' said Luke with a casual smile. 'For emergencies.'

'It's not exactly an emergency,' said Fiona. 'But I was starving hungry.'

Hattie smiled, happy to see Fiona so relaxed and obviously enjoying herself.

'How do you like your tea?' Fiona asked. 'And your phone's been pinging. Shall I bring it to you?'

Hattie nodded. Someone, Luke probably, had put it on charge for her. There were a lot of missed calls. 'Nick's rung me,' she said. 'I'll call back.'

'Hattie?' said Nick. 'Is everything all right? I've been worried.'

'Everything's fine,' said Hattie. 'Would you like to come for breakfast?'

'Yes please. What can I bring?'

'Eggs? We've got bacon. Anything else you might want to eat. I do have plenty of bread.'

'Is Nick coming?' asked Fiona, handing Hattie a plate with a bacon sandwich on it.

Hattie was pleased to see how keen Fiona seemed. 'Yes. He'll want to talk to you about going to Paris.'

'Paris?' said Luke. 'Sounds nice.'

Just for a second Hattie remembered her daydream of being in Paris with Luke. And for another second, she felt inexplicably hollow.

'It'll be well out of Lance's way,' said Hattie. 'Which is the point.'

Nick appeared with a full shopping bag. 'Where did you find that's open?' asked Hattie. 'It's not ten o'clock yet.'

'There's a little shop near me that opens early on a Sunday morning,' said Nick. Then he caught sight of Luke, turning bacon in a pan.

'This is Luke,' said Hattie.

'We met in the shop yesterday—' said Nick.

'Luke saved us last night,' Fiona interrupted. 'He was an absolute hero.'

'Why did you need saving?' Nick was horrified.

'Lance found us,' said Fiona, and told Nick the story.

'It's hard to believe these lovely animals can be threatening,' he said a few minutes later, caressing Frank and Fearless's silky ears.

'They can't really,' said Luke. 'But a pair of dogs running at you can fake it pretty well.'

'If I'd thought for a moment that bastard would be able to track you down here, I would never have left you,' Nick said.

'You had to get the limo back,' said Hattie. 'And it never occurred to me he'd find out where I lived either.'

'Now, you've got a trip to Paris to plan and I've got things to do. I'm going to push off now,' Luke announced.

Fiona ran and put her arms round him. 'Thank you so much!' she said.

Seeing Luke return the hug so easily gave Hattie another funny feeling. When Fiona had released him, and Luke had left the kitchen, she followed him to the hall. 'I must thank you too,' she said, and regarded him, wishing she could wrap her arms round him and have his arms round her. But the moment was gone, she realised. She couldn't hug him now without it looking odd.

She said goodbye and went back into the kitchen, feeling momentarily bereft.

'We need to get Fiona's phone,' Nick was saying.

'And different clothes,' said Fiona. 'If we're getting the phone anyway, I can ask Mum to pack some things for me if she can.' She shuddered. 'I hope she'll be all right.'

'She will be,' said Hattie. 'Her friends are there if anyone gets nasty.'

'And if she can't pack you a case, we can buy you clothes in Paris,' said Nick.

'If you won't be ashamed of me, I'd rather have my old clothes. Lance went through my wardrobe saying what I could keep. There wasn't that much. I was supposed to get rid of the old stuff but I didn't. It's in a bag in the loft.'

'We'll get you your clothes,' said Nick. Hattie could see it dawning on him just how much Lance had interfered in her life.

'You should ring Sheila,' said Hattie, handing Fiona the phone.

Then Xander emerged, slightly surprised to see that Luke had turned into Nick, but not unduly bothered. 'Although we were making a really good tune,' he said. 'It's so great that Luke is into it too.'

'I'm afraid I don't know anything about electronic music,' said Hattie. 'Why didn't your mother tell me it was one of your interests?'

'She doesn't know. She wouldn't get it. It's OK though. I manage.'

'I think you should tell her.'

Fiona came back into the room. 'Mum says she'll meet you in the church. She said it was the one place she felt sure Lance would never set foot in again. Daddy too. She's going to encourage everyone to go to the pub for lunch and then slip into the pews.'

'Do we know what time?' asked Nick. 'We need to book our Eurostar tickets. Although I think it might be a good idea to stay in London and go early tomorrow morning. I want to get you away from here as soon as I can.' He frowned suddenly. 'Hattie? Can you make an offer on the house for me – the figure we discussed after I saw the builder? I don't want to lose it.'

Hattie nodded. 'Of course!'

'I would like to get away too,' said Fiona. 'Although nothing really happened, I found last night frightening.'

'Me too,' said Hattie. As she thought about it the fear and anxiety came back to her. The nearly silent approach, the hectic banging on the door, the subsequent confrontation. Luke was such a rock. The thought of trying to deal with Lance on her own made her heart race. 'So, what time should I go and get your phone from Sheila?'

'She'll let us know.'

Hattie suddenly wanted her house to herself. She was tired and had been through a stressful time. As a single person she was accustomed to a certain amount of solitude.

'I'm just going to pop into the garden and pick some herbs,' she said. 'For peppermint tea and things.' She found kitchen scissors and a plastic jug to put the herbs in and went out of the back door.

She took her time wandering round the little garden, going through a calming routine. She checked the apples – too early to pick but a good crop. She rubbed a leaf of a salvia to smell its sweet spicyness, and then, using the scissors, cut off several dead rose heads. It was only when she felt a bit more herself that she actually picked anything. But her jug was full by the time she went back in. She would put them in a pretty vase for the kitchen table.

'Your phone rang and I saw it was Mum so I answered it,' said Fiona.

Hattie laughed. 'And what did Sheila say?'

'If you set off now, she'll be at the church.'

'OK, I'll find my keys.'

'And I called Luke,' said Xander. 'He said I can go over and finish making the tune we started yesterday.'

'Oh.' Her first reaction was to ask if that was really OK with Luke, but then she realised he was more than capable of saying no.

'So can you drop me off on your way?' Xander went on.

'Of course. Are you ready?'

'Yup.'

'Thank you so much, Hattie,' said Fiona. 'I don't know what I'd have done without you and Nick.'

'You don't have to think about it,' said Hattie. 'Come on, Xan.'

Hattie let Xander out of the car at Luke's but didn't call in herself. She wanted to get the phone and Fiona's clothes as soon as she could. Then Fiona and Nick, lovely as they were, would leave so she could have some space.

The church was full of the expensive wedding flowers Lance had demanded but it was very still. Sheila was sitting at the front, a case on the pew next to her. Hattie walked up the aisle.

'It's all so beautiful,' said Sheila. 'To think it was for something that was so ugly.'

'Not any more,' said Hattie. 'Fiona escaped before it was too late.' She sat down next to Sheila.

'I still don't know how you managed it,' Sheila said.

'Nick was the one who managed it.'

'I wish I knew more about him. I don't want Fifi rushing into the arms of someone else on the rebound.'

'I don't think she is rushing, and Nick is a good man.'

'That's something. I remember him from the quiz. He seemed nice.'

Hattie hesitated for a moment and then said, 'What about you, Sheila? Will you be all right?'

'With Malcolm? I'm going to give him a bit of time. He never bullied me as badly as Lance bullied my little girl.' She gave a rueful laugh. 'I'd better give you her phone and her clothes so she can run off to Paris with a gorgeous new man. It sounds so romantic, doesn't it?'

'It certainly does.' Hattie laughed.

'I'm so grateful to you,' said Sheila. 'If ever there's anything I can do for you, let me know.'

'I will,' said Hattie, thinking it was unlikely. 'But I was so happy to help. Fiona is a sweetheart and the thought of her with that brute was heartbreaking.'

Chapter Fifteen

The moment Hattie had waved off Fiona and Nick she went into the back garden and sat in her favourite seat, turned her face to the sun and closed her eyes. It was bliss. The sun was warm but not too warm and the silence broken only by birdsong was instantly calming. She planned to stay there until she was so hungry she had to move, which might be quite a long way off.

She thought about Sheila and how awful it must have been for her, watching her beloved only child being ensnared by a coercive bully. She thought about Lance, how angry he had been to have Fiona taken from him although he had never intended to be a proper, faithful husband to her. She thought about Nick, her discerning client who was now a patient suitor, almost like a knight of old.

Then, inevitably, her brain turned to work. Working for herself meant she never quite switched off and the wedding had been a distraction. She stayed in the sun for a few more blissful minutes and then went inside to check her emails. Try as she might, she was never as good at sitting still as she wanted to be.

There was one from a potential new client who had a detailed and very specific wish list. A grand period property. A flat plot but with far-reaching views. A cobbled stable yard, a wildlife pond that definitely had frogs in it, a small orchard to include Bramley apple trees, five acres of level pasture and good stabling. The budget was about half of what would be required to find this unrealistic dream.

Rather than answer the email, Hattie decided to visit Mary, which meant visiting her own unrealistic dream home in the form of a cottage on a hill which had the views her potential client wanted. She picked flowers first, and retrieved some cheese scones from the freezer.

Hattie felt her old friend was a little frailer than usual and wondered if she was eating properly. She heated the scones and buttered them, wishing she'd brought more of them as Mary would insist Hattie ate them too.

'Shall we sit in the garden?' Hattie suggested. 'It's so lovely! I'm thinking of taking on a new client who wants exactly what you have with regard to views and an orchard.'

'Well, I may not need this house for much longer,' said Mary cheerfully. 'You could sell her this!'

Hattie shook her head. 'Sadly your stabling would be inadequate, and you lack a cobbled stable yard.'

Mary laughed, as she was supposed to. 'I might as well hang on here a bit longer then.'

When Hattie had made the tea and brought everything out to the table and chairs that were perfectly placed to make the most of the views, she asked, 'Is Clive not willing to let you move yet?'

Mary shook her head. 'It's not that I'm unhappy here, by any means. I love this cottage, but it is a little large for me and needs more upkeep than I'm able to give it.' She raised a hand. 'But of course I'll ask you if I think I need a builder. Clive is determined to get "top dollar" for it and probably wants to use his own man to do any necessary work.' Hattie could hear him saying this. 'And it goes without saying, he doesn't want me to move until the market is absolutely right.'

'The market is pretty good for properties like this, Mary. It's a perfect spot. Near a village but rural, a good-sized plot but not unmanageable. It would be snapped up.' She didn't add 'by me' because she knew it would be beyond her means.

Mary regarded her. 'I think we both know why Clive doesn't want to sell really. He doesn't want the value of this house going towards me being in a care home.'

'It's your house and your money, Mary! Would you like me to help you sell it? And with finding the care home?'

Mary shook her head. 'It's very kind of you, darling, but Clive owns half of this. I can't sell it without his agreement.'

Hattie gasped. 'Did I know that?'

'I always try and forget it myself,' said Mary. 'I may not have told you.' She seemed a little embarrassed. 'To be honest he talked me into it years ago, which means I'm stuck. I keep hoping to persuade him to sell, but...' She shrugged. 'You do make wonderful scones, dear.'

Hattie laughed as best she could but she was furious – and depressed – at the thought of her old friend being in the power of a man like Clive.

Hattie stayed with Mary a bit longer than she had intended and the sun was fading as she headed for home. As she turned into the lane she saw a car parked a little way away. She stopped and reversed to where she could turn; she was almost sure it was Lance.

She headed for Luke's, all thoughts of solitude abandoned. He would take her in. Now she thought about it she realised she had been mad to think Lance would forget about her. She had been a vital player in his public humiliation and he wouldn't forgive her.

Chapter Sixteen

'Hattie! Hey!' said Luke. 'I was going to bring Xander over later. Oh – what's the matter?'

Hattie had thought she was looking her usual cheerful self but Luke saw instantly that something wasn't right.

Hattie greeted the dogs to give herself time to think how to phrase it. 'I'm fairly sure I saw Lance's car parked near my house. I'd gone to visit Mary—'

'Come in,' he said. 'You'll want to stay the night. Have a glass of wine.'

Luke's tall, reassuring presence soothed Hattie more than the wine did. Luke put a bowl of her favourite crisps by her chair too.

'Where's Xander?' she asked.

'In the cabin. I've still got quite a lot of equipment from when I was into making music and he's finding out how to use it. Something I never really did properly.' He paused, obviously thinking. 'He can sleep on the sofa bed in there. You can have the spare room.'

'I didn't know you had a spare room. I thought you had a room where you kept table drills and other equipment.'

He smiled. 'It is rather full of other things at the moment, but there's a bed in there too. I'm a bit low on bedding.' He paused. 'I'm going to go over to your house to check out the situation. I'll pick up some things for you.'

'If you got my duvet and pillows – Xander's too – that would make things easier for you here. I'll help him sort things out if that's all right.'

Hattie hadn't often been in the wooden cabin in Luke's garden. In theory it was his office but she knew it had got filled up with other things. But there was a sofa bed and a telly and an electric kettle. Xander would be happy in there.

He nodded. 'Good idea. And when I know what's going on and have everything you need, I'll get fish and chips on the way back.'

Hattie was usually resistant to being looked after. Looking after people was what *she* did. But she found herself very comforted by Luke's casual but firm command of the situation. She stopped feeling foolish for running away from a car that might not have been Lance's. Luke made her feel it was the sensible thing to do.

Xander took her sudden appearance in his stride and didn't mind being told they were staying the night, but when he was asked about his fish and chip order he wanted to go with Luke. 'I never know what I want until I'm in the shop.'

'I've got an errand to run first though,' said Luke. He glanced at Hattie, obviously wondering if he should go on.

'Luke's going to check there's no one hanging about at home. But the person who might have been there may well have gone. If he has, you can help Luke find stuff we need for here.'

Luke nodded. 'And if there's any chance Lance is still hanging around, Xander can stay in the car. But will you be all right here?' he asked Hattie. 'I'll leave Frank and Fearless.'

'I'll be absolutely fine,' said Hattie, knowing it to be true. The fact that Lance couldn't find her was very reassuring.

'So, a small cod, salt but no vinegar on your chips?'

She nodded. Luke knew her very well. It was a very comforting thought. Comforting and also another feeling she wasn't ready to acknowledge.

Hattie used the time to clear up, her way of thanking Luke for his hospitality. The house was obviously lived in by a man who didn't spend much time there. In theory, he was doing the place up: it was a project. But being a builder, he got very little time to attend to his own house. There wasn't a lot of clutter but there were a few books, plans for buildings, the usual electronics and a lot of dog hair. She tidied the surfaces without disrupting anything, ran the hoover round and then found a cloth and wiped the building dust that must have come in on Luke's clothes. Then she put plates in the oven to warm for the fish and chips. An insistence on warm plates was one of the idiosyncrasies she and Luke shared.

As she moved around the house, she wondered if Luke's house would ever be finished when he spent so much time on other people's. It wasn't quite her sort of house, she realised. There was nothing wrong with it, but it lacked the charm and character that, say, Mary's cottage had. Although she knew it would suit many people, if Luke ever got round to completing the work on it.

Hattie set up the sofa bed in the cabin for Xander, and investigated the spare room for herself. She moved a ladder, a saw horse, a couple of buckets and the bags of tools to one corner. Then she saw that it was pleasant enough and had a good bed in it.

She realised at that moment that she would likely need to leave her house before her tenancy was finished. She wasn't sure how she could stay there knowing Lance could show up at any moment.

By the time Luke and Xander got back she had resolved to email her current landlord, Aiden, and give him the rough details. With luck he would have another property she could move into — and fairly soon. If it was just her, it would have been easy. She could stay with Rose and Sam, or another couple of friends who'd be happy to put her up for a few days, but she had Xander to think about. If she had to, she'd find an Airbnb for them to live in, but it was an expensive option she'd rather not pursue.

In spite of having Frank and Fearless on her lap and something enjoyable to watch on television, Hattie was very glad to hear Luke's car drive up. He seemed to have been away an age.

'Sorry to be so long,' he said as he came in, holding large white wrapped packets. 'Is the oven on?'

She nodded.

'I'll put these in there to keep warm for a bit. I need a beer. Want one?'

Hattie suddenly felt anxious. Luke was being very casual but she sensed it hadn't been a queue in the chip shop that had kept him.

'It was so exciting, Hattie!' said Xander, coming in, holding an even bigger white packet. 'We saw the car and could see there was a man in it. We parked out of sight so we could spy on it.'

'I'm not sure Hattie needs all the details,' said Luke. 'Do you?'

'I'd rather know the worst,' she said.

Luke nodded. 'You tell her, Xander.'

'Well, we parked quite far away, pulled into a lay-by, next to the wood, but we could see the car. Luke had binoculars in his car. He's a bird watcher, you know.'

Hattie did know this, although not about the binoculars.

'We saw him get out of the car and go up to the house. He banged on the door, really aggressively, and waited. Then he had a good walk round and peered in the windows.'

Hattie shuddered.

'And then…' Xander was very excited. 'Luke rang the police!'

'Not exactly,' said Luke. 'I rang a mate of mine to see if he and his patrol car were in the area. Luckily they were nearby and so were able to find him stalking the house. They had a word, gave him a bit of a warning, and he left.'

Hattie found herself shaking. Luke poured her a glass of whisky. 'Here,' he said. 'It goes really well with fish and chips.'

'OK,' she said, having taken a large sip, choked a bit and swallowed. 'Definitely time to move house.'

Chapter Seventeen

After supper and clearing up, Hattie made up the spare bed with her bedding. She was just wishing Luke and Xander had found her make-up bag and not just her toothbrush when Luke tapped on the door.

'I wondered if you'd like to borrow something to sleep in?' he asked, filling the door frame. 'I haven't got pyjamas but I could give you a T-shirt?'

'That would be very kind,' she said.

'Is there anything else you need?'

She sighed and smiled. 'Not for the moment.'

'Cup of tea?'

She smiled properly this time. 'Always. I'll be down in a tick.'

They sat together on the sofa looking out into the garden. Frank and Fearless were settled at their feet. Frank was trying to sneak his way up on to the sofa. Hattie fully intended to let him. Luke cleared his throat and Frank retreated.

'I'd like you and Xander to move in with me for a while, until we know Lance has left the area,' said Luke.

'I'm ahead of you. I've just emailed my landlord telling him I need to move. I'm fairly sure he'll have somewhere he'll be happy for me to move into.'

'He certainly owns a lot of property,' said Luke. 'I've worked on lots of it.'

Hattie nodded. 'And luckily he's generous about me borrowing it. Although I always pay rent.' Luke knew this, but she felt obliged to remind him she wasn't a freeloader.

'Empty property is hard to insure.' Luke put down his empty tea mug. 'Well, if he's got somewhere, he'll tell you, and if he hasn't, we'll have to make another plan.'

Hattie wasn't quite sure about the 'we'. She was used to looking after herself, and others. Luke considering where she might live as a joint problem was strange to her.

'And for now, how would you feel about staying here for a bit? I've got to go back down West to finish a few jobs and having you here to look after Frank and Fearless would be a real help.' He paused. 'Although it won't be much fun living on a building site.'

'It's hardly a building site, Luke! You've not got much left to do.'

Luke laughed. 'I wish! I'll finish it sometime. We'll get the rest of your stuff tomorrow.'

As she lay in bed, trying to get to sleep, wearing an old shirt of Luke's that was soft with washing and still smelt slightly of him, although it was clean, she realised she felt safe and peaceful. Just before she drifted off she wondered if the perfect home wasn't about location but about who you were with. Could she hope to make the perfect home for herself on her own?

After collecting what Hattie and Xander needed from her house the next morning, Luke set off to Cornwall. Hattie focused on work: she had several tricky negotiations on properties under way, not least Nick's possible new home. After a busy few days she plucked up courage to ring Sheila and ask about Lance. She didn't want to tell her that he'd come to her home the previous weekend, but she did want to find out what was going on.

'He was angry, Hattie,' said Sheila, obviously glad to talk to someone about it. 'Very angry. I am just so grateful that Fiona isn't married to him. I think even Malcolm is beginning to understand what he's really like.'

'Do you expect to hear from him again?' Hattie hoped he'd left town.

'I couldn't say. He's very unpredictable.'

Hattie bit her lip. 'Have you heard from Fiona?' she said.

Sheila's voice brightened. 'She's having a lovely time. That Nick is being so lovely to her. Although, to be honest, I knew she was feeling better after she spent the night with you. The strain seemed to fall away almost immediately.'

'That's so good to hear! And she's happy being with Nick, given they don't really know each other?'

'Very happy! They're seeing the sights, spending time in lovely little cafes, walking hand in hand.' She paused. 'I almost think she's falling in love!'

'I hope it's not too soon after Lance—'

'I don't think she was ever properly in love with Lance,' said Sheila. 'But they're talking about extending their stay — a week isn't very long. Maybe hiring a car and travelling south. Apparently Nick can work from anywhere. It would seem he has fallen in love with Fi already. But he doesn't try and control her, weigh her, or any other of the dreadful things that Lance did, and I didn't know about, until nearly too late.'

A bit more conversation convinced Hattie that her vision hadn't let her down and that Nick and Fiona were destined to be together. And a little later, she had a text from Fiona. *I am so happy! Thank you so much for everything you've done for me. I can't thank you enough. Lots of love, Fiona. PS Nick sends best wishes too.*

It was Friday afternoon before Hattie's landlord called. She really hoped he had something for her. Luke was due back later and she didn't want to impose the two of them on him for longer than she had to. Being able to say she had somewhere to live would be great.

'Hi, Hattie,' Aiden said. 'I got your email. Not quite sure why you want to move on, but it's a seller's market at the moment so I could sell. I'll probably rent it though.'

'And so – have you got anywhere else I could live? Don't worry if you haven't. You're not responsible for providing me with accommodation.'

'As it happens, I have just acquired an old lodge. It's tiny and needs a lot of work.'

'Is that all?' She smiled.

'Well, it's currently quite damp and it being lived in would help.'

Hattie laughed. 'So I'm a just a dehumidifier to you?' she said.

'You're far more than that, my dear,' he said. 'Why don't you go and have a look and see if you fancy it? I'll ping you the location. The key is under the mat. There's nothing in it to steal.'

'It is so kind of you, Aiden,' she said, knowing she'd accept it no matter how damp it was.

'Not at all: you'd be doing me a favour. And could your builder bloke – Luke? – have a look at it and make some running repairs? I won't charge you rent until it's properly habitable.'

Luke was back too late to inspect the lodge that night, so he and Hattie drove over the following morning.

'It's quite near, which is good,' said Luke, pulling up his pick-up in the grassy area next to the house.

'And near Mary,' said Hattie, 'which is better.' She paused, aware of Luke looking at her in a way she couldn't interpret. He seemed to be studying her, but also a bit distracted. 'She needs me to pop in, Luke. You don't.'

'I don't know about that,' he said. 'I might need the occasional casserole or fruit cake.'

Hattie laughed. 'I'll see what the kitchen's like before I start promising you cake.'

They found the key, which was large and old-fashioned, and unlocked the back door that creaked as if it hadn't been opened for centuries. As most of the windows were boarded up, Luke fetched his tools from the truck to remove a couple of panels so they could see.

They went into the kitchen and, now there was some light, she could see a metal sink, a cracked lino floor and a tiled roof, and a four-burner electric cooker of unknown age. There was a good wide windowsill which Hattie always appreciated and a Formica dresser against one wall. Attached to the kitchen was a slightly mouldy bathroom.

Hattie went into the sitting room. It had a good fireplace, working shutters and a quaint built-in cupboard among its original features. While it wasn't large, it was big enough for a sofa, and there was just about room for a folding table and chairs: which was good, as there wasn't space to eat in the kitchen except standing up.

She went upstairs and found two bedrooms, both just large enough for a double bed if you didn't need to walk around it much.

Hattie was aware of Luke's big builder's boots striding around making it seem damper and smaller with every step. She went to look at the outside space. There wasn't currently a garden but there was a small paddock where Hattie could put her myriad pots of herbs and favourite plants.

'It's tiny,' said Luke when they were both back in the sitting room. 'You and Xander would be on top of each other and it has no garden.'

'It has a field,' said Hattie, 'which could become a garden. Perfect for Frank and Fearless to run in.' She was determined to like this little cottage, although it was damp and short on windows.

'Not exactly ideal though,' said Luke. He looked searchingly at her. 'Do you like it?'

Hattie exhaled. 'Well, it doesn't give me the heebie-jeebies, which is good. Properties do that to me relatively often.' She smiled.

Luke returned her smile. 'But if you're looking at properties for other people and are not going to have to live there, it probably doesn't matter?'

Hattie nodded. 'I might steer a client away if I had a very strong feeling.'

'But you'd feel OK about living here?'

'I would, surprisingly.'

'Well, I'll fit a better lock and make sure the windows aren't about to fall out, then.'

'I'll tell Aiden I like it and ask him to get the cooker and boiler properly serviced.'

Luke didn't move. 'It's very small for two, Hattie,' he repeated. 'And where would Xander put all his stuff?'

'We'll squash up. It'll be cosy!'

'Or…' He paused. 'He could stay with me,' he said. 'I'd be happy to have him.'

Hattie took a couple of breaths. This was an amazing offer in many ways. But there was lots to think about, not least the effect it would have on Luke's life. 'That came a bit out of left field,' she said. 'Whatever that means. Are you sure it wouldn't cramp your style, having Xander with you?'

'I don't have a style, you know that, Hattie.' He smiled lazily. 'You know I'm working away a lot at the moment. When I'm not here, you could move back in and enjoy the superior facilities at my house. In fact – you could just stay there full time, until you find a more suitable place for the two of you.'

Hattie blinked. Another amazing offer – but strangely not one she wanted to accept. She remembered how safe she felt at his house: she couldn't let herself come to rely on that. No, she needed to be in her own place, stand on her own two feet. But Xander would undoubtedly prefer the space there. She smiled. 'That's unbelievably kind, but I really think I'd like to live here. Xander probably wouldn't! I'll have to talk to Leonie about it. Shall I ring her now? Or shall we go home first?'

'Do it now. I'll have another good look at what work needs doing here.'

★ ★ ★

Leonie asked a lot of questions but she was satisfied with the answers and on the whole didn't seem too bothered by the thought of Xander staying at Luke's.

'I'll go on being responsible for him getting to college and home again,' Hattie said. 'Though if Luke offers him a lift, I'll probably say yes.'

'That's fine,' said Leonie. 'Get Xander to call me when you've told him about this new plan.'

Hattie hesitated and then said, 'You do seem a bit more relaxed about everything, Lennie.'

'I've realised that Xander has been thriving since he's been with you, Hattie. Your scatterbrain approach to life seems to work for him.'

As so often happened, Hattie ended a phone call with her sister feeling faintly insulted.

'So my sister is on board with it. Now we must ask Xander,' said Hattie, 'and if he's not sure, we can show him this place so he'll know what he'll be missing.'

Luke's deep chuckle gave Hattie a warm feeling.

As predicted, Xander liked the idea of staying with Luke. 'But we'd still have meals together and things?' he asked. 'I like your cooking.'

'Of course!' said Hattie, flattered that the boy who apparently only ate plain pasta enjoyed her more eclectic meals.

He hesitated. 'You won't be offended, will you?'

Hattie flung an arm round him. 'Of course not!' she said. 'I wouldn't have suggested it if I would have been. But I'm hoping it's only temporary. I'm going to be looking for somewhere we can live together.'

Xander sighed. 'It's a shame we had to leave the last place. But I don't blame you for not feeling safe there. Luke will take care of us,' he added.

'We don't need anyone to take care of us. But it will be handy living at Luke's while he's away, while we're getting the lodge sorted.'

'How will we do that without Luke?'

'He's not the only builder on the planet! And I'm not incapable.'

Luke didn't seem to be aware of Hattie's bold words and was at the lodge with his tools the next day.

Luke cleared the gutters and reattached a drain pipe to the wall while Hattie held the ladder. Then he repaired the roof over the kitchen.

'It needs replacing, really,' said Luke. 'But that'll keep the rain out for now.'

Hattie noted this down along with the hours Luke worked, so Aiden could pay him.

'How are you getting on with the painting inside?' asked Luke.

'Come and see.'

Xander was there wearing an old pair of shorts and T-shirt. He was wielding a roller loaded with white paint. 'This is fun!' he said as Luke and Hattie entered the room. 'Mum's never let me near paint before.'

'Maybe try to get a bit more of it on the wall and less on the floor,' suggested Hattie. 'But otherwise you're doing a fine job.'

'You're certainly speedy,' said Luke.

'I know white paint isn't imaginative,' said Hattie, 'but it's brightening the place up a lot and it's only temporary. But let's go back now. You guys must be tired.'

'You mean you're tired, Hattie,' said Luke.

She nodded. 'And hungry! Shall we go home via the fish and chip shop? On me.'

A couple of days later, Rose and Hattie went to the lodge. Rose was donating some curtains and soon the gloomy lodge was a bright, attractive place to live.

'It's still tiny, though,' said Rose, having finished her curtain hanging.

'Fine for one. Or a close couple,' said Hattie. 'I can work from the second bedroom. I wonder if Aiden will bring the bathroom upstairs eventually? It would be too small for living in but a perfect romantic getaway.'

'It's a shame you had to leave your last place,' said Rose.

Hattie hadn't given Rose all the details of why she wanted to move. Now she glossed over it. 'Oh, well, you know me. I never want to stay anywhere too long. And wherever my pots of herbs and things are, that's my home, to massively misquote Bob Dylan.'

Rose didn't comment but Hattie had a feeling that she hadn't got away with that glib reply. 'Are you sure you won't come back and eat with us? Sam is cooking and I know he'd love to see you – and Xander of course.'

'No, thank you. I want to make sure Luke's house is as clean and tidy as possible before he gets back tomorrow. Then I'll move in here.'

'Well, at least it's near Luke's,' said Rose.

Hattie felt annoyed by this but decided not to comment. Why did Rose think she needed to live near Luke? She was perfectly all right on her own.

Hattie was alone at the lodge, watering her pots, when her sister rang.

'Hattie? How's it going? I can't get Xander on his phone. Is he with you?'

'He—'

'But I need to speak to you first.' She didn't even stop for breath. 'He has a parents' evening coming up – an appraisal – whatever they call it – and I need you to go.'

'Lennie! I'm not his parent. It would be quite inappropriate for me to go.'

'You're *in loco parentis,* which means you have to. And how else am I supposed to find out how he's doing? There's no earthly point asking him!'

Hattie had to admit her sister was probably right about that.

'But I'd have no idea what to do at a parents' evening!'

'You make appointments with the different teachers and turn up. They can be a bit shambolic, I do admit. But I don't need you to see every teacher, just his English and maths tutors.'

'Oh? But what about music? He likes that!' Xander had finally told his mother about his passion for electronic music, and how living at Luke's meant he could indulge it.

'He may like it,' said Leonie crossly, 'but it's not exactly going to give him a career, is it?'

'He's very young—'

'I know how old he is. He's my son. And I'm only asking you to see two teachers. How hard can it be? Oh, and record the interviews on your phone.'

Hattie definitely wasn't going to do that. 'I might take notes. People don't often want to be recorded.'

'Oh, OK. Now go and get him, would you? I haven't got long.'

'He's at Luke's. He must have been in Luke's cabin when you called so he didn't hear the phone. I'll get him to give you a call.'

'Please do!' Leonie sounded bossy and demanding. Then she suddenly added, 'I miss him.'

Hattie's heart lurched. She realised that her sister's heart wasn't made of stone however hard she tried to pretend it was. She rang Luke the moment her phone was free.

'Hey, Hattie, what's going on?' he said, when he answered.

'Could you get Xander to ring his mum, ASAP? She's missing him and needs to speak to him.'

'OK. For a moment there I thought you were going to come over and hang out.'

Suddenly extremely tempted, Hattie said, 'I can't. I've got work to do.'

'Ah. I was hoping you were going to say you had a cake just out of the oven.'

Hattie laughed. 'No such luck.'

But before she went back to her laptop, she took butter out of the fridge and checked how many eggs she had. She owed Luke a cake for everything he was doing for Xander, she really did.

The day of the parents' evening, Hattie checked her reflection in the mirror. Xander, whose presence always made the lodge feel small, had been dropped off by Luke. 'Do I look all right?'

'You look fine.'

'OK, come on then. I'm so glad you're coming with me. I'd never find my way round on my own.'

'Actually, Hattie…'

'What? You're not backing out on me, are you?'

'To be honest, it would be far better if I didn't come too. They won't tell you the truth if I'm there. You've only got two people to see. They'll give you a map of the college when you turn up. You don't need me!'

'But what'll you do here all on your own while I'm away?'

'You've got telly, haven't you?'

'I haven't got Netflix!'

'Then I'll listen to music.' He paused. 'I might even read a book! Luke's lent me one.'

'You really won't take pity on your old auntie and come too?'

'Hattie, no one looking at you would ever think of you as anyone's old auntie.'

Not sure if her nephew was paying her some sort of backhanded compliment, Hattie decided to just go. She'd never really believed he would go with her but it would have been so much nicer if he had. Without quite knowing how it had happened, she'd started to really enjoy Xander's company.

Chapter Eighteen

The meeting with the maths tutor had gone well and Hattie was feeling relaxed as she waited in the queue of parents waiting to see the English tutor.

When suddenly she was no longer looking at the back of the person in front of her. Instead, she saw a couple in a pub garden. The man – the English tutor – was facing her and the woman was clearly recognisable, although Hattie only had a back view. The neat blonde chignon, the Chanel-inspired suit, the Loewe handbag on the table in front of her and the large pearl earrings: it was her sister, Leonie. The way the English tutor was twinkling indicated the pair were getting on very well.

It was a glimpse, nothing more, before Hattie found herself back in the noisy sports hall, surrounded by parents. She would have very much liked to sit down and have some water – maybe a paracetamol or some Rescue Remedy, but there wasn't time. It was her turn to see the tutor, and, thank goodness, there was a chair. Hattie sat on it and smiled. Her allotted ten minutes had begun and in this time she now had to get the necessary feedback about Xander's progress and become friends with this man so she could introduce him to Leonie.

While it would serve her sister right if Hattie ignored the vision, Hattie couldn't do it. Leonie may well be bossy and overbearing but she was still her sister.

'Hello, Mr… Saye. As you probably know, I'm Xander's aunt. His mother is away so Xander is living with me temporarily.' She smiled, hoping Mr Saye would take it from here.

'Ah, well, it's good you could come.'

He had a nice voice, no obvious accent – her sister was a terrible snob and required RP English from all her friends – so this was a start. He wasn't dashingly handsome but he looked pleasant and had no visible tattoos or anything. Her sister thought tattoos were beyond the pale.

'So how is Xander getting on?' Hattie smiled a little more enthusiastically than she would have done if it hadn't been for the vision; she had to make this man her friend.

'I don't think English is his favourite subject. Has he been tested for dyslexia, do you know?'

'I don't think so, although I'm sure if there'd been any sign of it my sister would have had that done.'

'It's only a thought. He's very creative when he contributes in class but his written work doesn't really reflect that.'

'Do you think he could do with some coaching? To help him get what's in his head down on paper?' Hattie remembered someone saying something like this during her own school days. Her talents had always been a bit hard to define. Everyone agreed that she had them, but no one could decide exactly what they were.

Mr Saye inclined his head. 'It's hard to say, really.'

'The thing is, my sister, being separated from Xander at the moment, is particularly anxious. I'm sure if I could tell her that he's getting extra support from someone – you, for example – she'd feel a whole lot happier. She'd pay you for your time, of course.' She smiled, she hoped, endearingly.

'I don't know if things really require—'

'Please, Mr Saye. My sister wants what's best for Xander more than anything. I'm sure a few extra lessons from you could really help.'

'But why me?' Mr Saye was looking kind but confused.

'Because Xander really likes you. He mentions you when he's at home. And he's not a talkative boy – at home, anyway.' Hattie hated lying, but all she wanted was Mr Saye's contact details, then she could work something out. Maybe she could persuade Sheila to organise another quiz.

Still Mr Saye hesitated. Hattie produced a business card. 'Do you have a card, Mr Saye?'

'Er – no…'

'Write your contact details on the back of mine. I know you'd be really helping Xander if you'd give him one session, even.' Hattie smiled admiringly, entreatingly, sending out waves of charm towards this innocent man. She didn't want it to look as if she was flirting with him, that would be quite inappropriate, but she did want his telephone number.

'OK.' Mr Saye took Hattie's card. 'Talk to Xander's mother and I'll see what I can do.'

Hattie walked away from the interview feeling sick. She needed to sit down for a few minutes to recover both from the vision and the subsequent manipulation of poor Mr Saye. Then she'd buy pizza to take back to Xander.

She had woken the following morning feeling out of sorts. The previous evening had been lovely, eating takeaway pizza with Xander, but now she felt a bit unsettled. She put it down to tiredness, and the new problem she faced with trying to get her sister and Mr Saye together. Still, she had his phone number, although sadly not his given name.

After a fruitless viewing which caused her to wonder if her new client, Mrs Conway – a charming woman – had any idea at all of the cost of a grand period property. Or if she realised she might have to have her own pond put in and plant a few roses in order to call a place perfect, Hattie found herself near Sheila's house. She decided to call her to see if she was up for a visit.

'Hattie!' said Sheila, delighted. 'I was just about to ring you. I've got some gorgeous pictures of Fiona and Nick.'

'Oh! I had a text from Fiona a little while ago, but no photos. She said she was very happy.'

'I think she is. They've decided they will extend their holiday for a bit so she can really recover from everything Lance put her through.' She paused. 'I could send these pictures, but I'd love to see you.'

'Well, I do happen to be very near your house if you were up for a visit.'

'Lovely! We can have lunch. Malcolm's playing golf.'

Feeling cheery, Hattie drove to Sheila's house.

After showing to Hattie several photos of a very relaxed Fiona, in shorts and T-shirt, looking very happy, with Nick's protective arm around her, Sheila turned her mind to lunch.

'I've only got soup, bread and cheese and a bit of cold meat,' Sheila said. 'And I think I know I can't press you to a glass of wine, but it's sourdough bread from the van, and the cheese is local too.'

'That sounds delicious,' said Hattie, accepting the offered place at Sheila's big kitchen table. 'I've got a client – a really nice woman – but her wish list is a yard long and her budget isn't nearly big enough and tactfully pointing all that out is tiring.'

'How do you cope with that?'

'I try to find out which of her list is really essential, and if her budget could be stretched if we found the perfect house. Every viewing is a learning opportunity. Eventually we'll find a way to compromise but it can feel like doing things the hard way.'

'That does sound exhausting,' said Sheila. 'Let me show you more photos while the soup warms.'

Hattie flicked through the photos on Sheila's phone. There were a fair amount of city views, a couple of Nick holding different wine glasses in different bars and restaurants, but what made her really smile were the ones of Fiona.

'Look at her there,' said Sheila, looking over her shoulder. 'Eating ice cream, not a scrap of make-up, looking as happy as a clam.'

'She is so lovely, she really is. She doesn't need make-up,' said Hattie.

Sheila sighed. 'I can't wait to hear all about it. I told you, didn't I, that they've decided to extend their trip?

Nick is a "digital nomad" apparently, so can work from anywhere.'

Hattie laughed. 'Convenient, in the circs!' She paused and then went on. 'Erm – have you heard anything from Lance?'

'Well, he's not going to be sending me friendly texts, but I have been keeping an eye on him.'

'How have you done that?' Hattie was impressed.

'I'm a middle-class woman of a certain age: I can do anything! No, actually I've got a friend who's been doing a bit of cyber-sleuthing. I think he's planning to move to the States. Which would suit me just fine.'

'And me!' said Hattie. 'I'll feel safer when he's out of the country.' She stopped. She hadn't meant Sheila to know she'd felt unsafe.

'Oh, Hattie! Do you feel threatened? I wouldn't blame you. He's very frightening.'

Hattie put a reassuring hand on Sheila's arm. 'It's fine. I've moved house. He won't know where I am.'

'You moved house? That's a huge thing! We've been here two years and I still haven't got over it!'

'Oh, I move house quite often. It's not that big a deal for me.'

Sheila raised her eyebrows and then smiled. 'So where have you moved to?'

'It's very near where I lived before but smaller. Tiny in fact. It's a lodge. Now we've decorated, it's really nice. Luke did a few running repairs.'

'Is Luke your—'

'No,' said Hattie quickly. 'Just a very good friend.'

Sheila nodded. 'Let's have lunch. I even took a couple of desserts out of the freezer that weren't eaten at the non-wedding reception.'

'Was there much wasted?'

'No,' said Sheila. 'Quite a lot of it was eaten and everything that wasn't, I put in the freezer. I bought a second freezer instantly, so it's all still there. We could have another party!'

'It's a lovely time of year for parties. My birthday is this month and I can quite often celebrate in the garden.'

Sheila's eyes widened in excitement. 'Oh! Let me give you a birthday party! I want to celebrate Fi and Nick coming back but they might think that a bit over the top, but if it was your birthday party, we could invite lots of people. Would you like that? Think it over. Let's eat.'

Hattie accepted a bowl full of salad leaves with a wonderful dressing that Sheila handed her, enjoying the feeling of being mothered. 'This is delicious!' she said a couple of minutes later. 'You're so good in the kitchen.'

'I admit I love entertaining.' Sheila hesitated. 'And we have a lot of wine that no one but me is going to drink unless we have a party.' Sheila shot Hattie a look and then looked more serious. 'I'm so grateful for everything you've done for Fiona. You saved her from a complete disaster.' Sheila put her hand on Hattie's and squeezed it.

'I only did what anyone would have done in the circumstances.' She paused, remembering how angry and threatening Lance could be. 'And you played your part, Sheila. We all did.'

Sheila removed her hand. 'But you initiated it. I can't thank you enough.'

'As I said, we all did it together. But if it wasn't too much trouble, and you let me help, and share the cost, I would quite like a birthday party this year.'

'I'd love that! And we'll argue about costs later. Are you a significant age? Is it your big three-oh?'

Hattie laughed. 'I wish! It's just for fun, really.' It sounded lame but it was the best reason she could think of. She couldn't explain that she wanted a way of getting Mr Saye and her sister together, although inviting him to a party would be awkward. She couldn't guarantee he'd come. 'Or what about another quiz?'

Sheila looked confused. 'I couldn't organise a whole quiz. Why a quiz? It seems a strange way to celebrate your birthday.'

Hattie wished she could explain that you can ask people you don't really know to a quiz in a way you couldn't ask them to a birthday party. But she was prepared to invite a man she didn't know if it meant her sister might fall in love.

She made a dismissive gesture. 'Oh, you know, everyone loves quizzes, but it would be a lot of work.'

'So a party it is. Who do you want to invite?' Sheila got up and found a notebook. 'This is going to be fun!'

'What will Malcolm think of the idea?'

'Malcolm and I have been having words lately. It wasn't until I saw Lance being such a bully that I really realised that Malcolm had those tendencies too. He doesn't want me to leave, and so he's being far more considerate.'

Hattie disguised her surprise behind a drink of water. It was very brave of Sheila to confront Malcolm about his behaviour, and credit to him that he admitted his faults. There was more behind this comfortable middle-class couple than she would have suspected.

'That's amazing, Sheila.'

'It was tough but it needed to be done.' Sheila smiled briefly and moved on. 'Now, the party…'

'How many people do you think the party should be for?'

'How long is a piece of string! We'll put the gazebo up. Rent patio heaters if it's not warm. I think we want a reasonable number, don't we? I don't want Fiona and Nick to feel self-conscious; we'll need enough of a crowd that they can feel anonymous. How many people would you like?' She pushed her notebook across the table. 'I'm always better with a pen in my hand and something to write on.'

Hattie wrote quickly. Rose and Sam, Leonie and Mr Saye. Luke, herself, Xander. She added the names of two more couples. 'It's eleven people. But I could trim the list if you'd prefer fewer.' She sighed. 'I'd invite my old friend Mary, but she might find it all a bit much, she's nearly ninety.'

'I'm sure we can accommodate her if she does want to come. And otherwise, your list is fine – in fact, it could be much longer! I can invite the Jenkinses, they're neighbours, and maybe Rachel Anstruther-Jones and her husband – you remember, the terrifying woman who we went to the quiz for.'

'I remember her! She asked for free advice about her property, although everyone does, so I won't hold that against her.'

'So if they came they wouldn't spoil the party for you?'

'Of course not! I believe in mixing people up at parties. Although I may ask if Xander would like to invite a friend, if that's all right.'

'Please do! And have some more to eat. I've got quite excited about this party. When the wedding was called off, although I was deeply relieved, I felt a bit cheated out of a big do with my daughter…'

It was nearly four o'clock before Hattie got away, glad that Luke was picking up Xander. Sheila had been so enthusiastic it had given her confidence that inviting a man she didn't know at all to a party was actually fine. She would feel better if she discussed it with Rose though. She pulled in next to a hedge and called her.

'Hey, Rose! Do you and Sam fancy coming up for supper?'

'When would you like us?'

'About half six?'

'Oh, I meant which day. Is it urgent?' Rose knew Hattie well enough to spot she had an agenda.

'I do have something I need to talk to you about.'

'Well, Sam's got a council meeting. How would you like just me tonight?'

'Perfect! I'll pick you up and drop you off, then you can drink.'

'I'll get Sam to bring me, it's on his way, but you can take me home afterwards if you like. His meeting might go on forever.' She paused. 'You haven't been drinking much lately. You're not pregnant, are you?'

Hattie giggled. 'Chance would be a fine thing.'

'Then it must be visions you want to talk about,' said Rose. 'I'll be with you by seven – half past at the latest.'

Chapter Nineteen

'Well?' said Rose the moment Hattie had finished putting the plates on the table in her little sitting room.

'The charcuterie is all English,' Hattie said. 'Kinder to the pigs.'

'Jolly good,' said Rose. 'Now tell me what's going on?'

Hattie told Rose all about the party and why she needed to have one.

'Let me get this straight,' said Rose, picking up an olive. 'You're getting Sheila to have a party just so you can introduce your sister to a man you don't know because you had a vision? About your sister? Who you don't get on with?'

'Yes. The thing is, you know I can't ignore a vision. And it could be lovely for Lennie to have a man! I know she annoys the hell out of me but I want her to be happy.'

'Run it by me again – you went to a parents' evening at Xander's college?'

Hattie nodded. 'They called it something else, but yes.'

'Colleges don't always have parents' evenings, as far as I know,' said Rose.

'Well, this one did. Anyway, that's not important. I saw him and I had a vision, which also had Lennie in it. And her Loewe handbag.'

'But you don't have his full name?'

Hattie shook her head.

'Have you googled him?'

'No! You're almost as bad as Sheila. She's got a friend who's internet stalking Lance.'

Rose nodded, reaching for her phone,. 'Never mind about Lance now, let's research your sister's potential new husband.'

It didn't take Rose long to find out Mr Saye's name was Tom and he was roughly the same age as Hattie's sister. He'd only been at the college for a year so was a relative newcomer to the area.

'If he's new,' said Hattie, 'he might be more willing to come, to widen his circle of friends.'

'Possibly. I'm just going to check out his Facebook. He may be Mr Popular already… Ah,' she said, 'you can't get in unless you're an actual friend.'

'How unreasonable,' said Hattie, who had deleted her Facebook account so clients couldn't harass her after hours. 'But hey! We've got a name. All I need to do now is find out when Lennie can come over from Switzerland so we can choose a date for the party.'

'Will she come just for a party?' asked Rose.

Hattie nodded. 'I think so. I'll say Xander really wants to see her. She likes a party and will be impressed my upmarket client's mother wants to give me one. I won't need to give too many details.' She paused. 'She might like to check that Xander really is happy with Luke, although of course he says he is every time she asks him.'

'Surely it would be better if Xander was staying with you, a bona fide family member.'

Hattie nodded. 'You're right. I've got feelers out for something a bit larger, where Xander and I can both live.'

'So, what are you going to wear?' asked Rose. 'Something new, I hope.'

'Or something new to me!' said Hattie. 'Let's have a look on Vinted…'

'I'm sure Leonie would be checking out Vestiaire,' said Rose.

'If you want a vest, go to M&S,' said Hattie. 'It's Vinted for my money.'

By the time Hattie took Rose home, they had found two lovely outfits for the party.

To Hattie's surprise, her sister was able to make the date Hattie first suggested, despite the very short notice. 'That would be delightful! I'm quite impressed that a client's mother wants to give you a party,' she said.

'It's a joint party, for her too. Sheila just thought it would be fun for us to mix up our guests a bit. It's very good for me, of course. I've just added a couple of estate agents I want to get to know better to my invitation list, as well as family – that's you and Xander – and friends.'

Leonie laughed. 'I'm really looking forward to it. It'll give us an opportunity to discuss Mum and Dad's Golden Wedding.'

'Oh, that's not until August!' said Hattie who'd been putting that family occasion out of her mind for months. 'I want to concentrate on my party.' She paused. There was no point in introducing Leonie to Tom Saye if she had found herself a Swiss lover for the summer; she wouldn't be in the right headspace to fall in love. 'So, have you met any nice men while you've been over there?' she asked innocently, painfully aware this was not a subject the sisters usually talked about.

'Hattie! I'm here to work: what are you insinuating? What sort of party is it anyway?'

Hattie was relieved by her sister's chiding. 'Probably in the garden with a gazebo. Sheila's got a lovely garden.'

'And who's in charge of catering?'

'Don't worry! It's not me. Sheila is insisting on doing it all so you're bound to enjoy it.'

'Great!' said Leonie. 'So all we need now is the good weather.'

While good weather was certainly on Hattie's mind, she was more immediately concerned about getting Tom Saye to the party, given that they didn't know each other at all.

Hattie spent a large part of her working days calling people, many of whom she didn't know, on the telephone; she was never anxious about it. But as she tapped in the number Tom Saye had written down for her, she quailed at the thought of the conversation to come.

'Oh, Tom,' she said, quickly stifling the 'Mr Saye'. 'You won't remember me. I'm Hattie Bruckless. I'm Xander Rathbone's aunt. I met you at the college the other day and was asking about—'

'I remember you, Hattie,' he said. Oh, no! He sounded very friendly; he couldn't be allowed to fancy her. He was for her sister!

'Oh, that's good, because I have a rather unusual – um – invitation. I want to ask you to a party.'

'That is usually known as an invitation.'

Hattie could hear that he was amused. This was probably a good thing but she needed to steer clear of any flirtation – from her side at least. 'It's unusual because we don't really know each other but I'm very keen that you should meet my sister. Because she wants to talk to you about Xander, and she'll only be in the country for one night.' Hattie took a breath. 'Would you come?'

'That's very kind of you. When is the party? And where?'

He didn't sound wildly enthusiastic but he wasn't saying no. 'Next Saturday, the thirteenth of July. I'm pretending it's Bastille Day! Only one day out.'

'Any particular reason for celebrating Bastille Day?'

'Well, it's my birthday. It's why I'm having a party but we're not calling it a birthday party because I don't want people bringing me presents.'

'Why don't you want presents?' he asked, sounding a bit surprised.

'You know, clutter.'

'OK. I'll come and I won't bring you a present.'

Hattie was surprised and delighted how easy this had all been so far. Was it because of the vision? Getting Fiona and Nick together had been easy too.

'What sort of time?'

'About seven.'

'And the address?'

Hattie gave him Sheila's address, sounding rather garbled, wanting to get the words out before he could change his mind and say no. 'It's not actually where I live. A friend is holding the party for me. I'm so glad you can come. I don't know how you'd meet Leonie otherwise.'

'Of course I'm delighted to be invited to a party,' said Tom, 'but I'm not at all concerned about Xander's work. There's no need for me to meet your sister.'

'Trust me, there really is. But Sheila's house is delightful. The food will be brilliant, and there will be lots of nice people coming. And of course,' she added, 'do bring a plus one if you'd like to. She – he – would be very welcome.'

She felt she had to say this, but really hoped he'd refuse.

'It's just me,' he said.

'Well, that's a relief.'

'Oh? Why?'

'Oh, you know,' said Hattie with a nervous laugh. 'Numbers! So, bye! See you soon!'

Chapter Twenty

Rose created some very pretty invitations – Sheila was thrilled by them – and these were duly sent out. Almost everybody Hattie asked accepted, despite the very short notice, as she had felt sure they would. A chance to dress up to go to a house they hadn't been to before was always going to be popular, among the women at least.

Sheila had reiterated that she was not impressed by the length of Hattie's guest list, insisting that she wanted her garden – and therefore her party – to be full. So as well as her close friends and the estate agents, Hattie invited a couple of local solicitors – one had been really helpful over the negotiations for Nick's house sale; Hattie was delighted that after some intense haggling his offer had been accepted – and a handyman and his wife. This couple had rescued many a local with a suddenly blocked drain, missing roof tile or mysterious damp patch, several of them Hattie's clients. This was a thank you for their assistance over the years she had been in business. Luke, however, was the only builder she asked, although he said, as he accepted the decorated card, that he was always booked for months ahead and really didn't need to do any more extensions.

'I'd still feel disloyal if I became friends with any other builders,' she said.

'That's only right and proper,' he said with a smile.

A couple of days before the party, Hattie went to see Mary with an invitation. She found her friend sitting in her chair, facing the garden, as usual.

'Hello!' she said brightly, having let herself in. 'I've come to invite you to a party. It's for my birthday,' she added, giving Mary her invitation. 'I know it's a long shot, but if you thought you could manage it, I could bring you, and take you home. You wouldn't need to stay long if you didn't want to.'

Mary took the invitation. 'It's very pretty. Did Rose design it for you?'

'Yes. She's so clever.'

'And remind me who Sheila is?' asked Mary, reading the details.

'The mother of the bride, Fiona. I told you all about it.'

'Oh, yes. The awful man. You were so clever to stop the wedding. So is that why she's giving you a party?'

'Partly. But do you want to come?'

Mary shook her head. 'To be honest, if parties don't start at twelve midday and stop by half past one, I usually give them a miss. I love seeing people individually, but too many at once make me tired.' Mary smiled reassuringly. 'Now, would you like some tea?'

'I'd love some. But I'll make it.'

In the kitchen, possibly Hattie's favourite room in a house she loved, she could see that Mary hadn't done much cooking lately. There was food in the cupboards (Hattie had ordered and put this away herself) but it wasn't eaten. As there was cheese and a couple of tomatoes, she made some sandwiches and cut them into quarters. Mary could have any that were left over later.

'I took the liberty of making us a snack,' she said as she brought in the tray. 'I suddenly had a longing for a cheese and tomato sandwich. I hope you don't mind.'

'They're my favourite!' said Mary, putting one of the small triangles on her plate. 'You make them so neatly. Mine are always so lumpy.'

Hattie stayed until Mary had eaten three sandwiches and drunk two cups of tea. Was she getting enough to eat? Hattie wondered. Her appetite seemed OK, but she obviously couldn't manage very much at a time. Hattie resolved to come over the day after the party with some food and champagne. She couldn't bear the thought of Mary struggling on her own.

Rose called Hattie early on the morning of the party. 'Have you used your Spidey senses to magic this perfect weather?'

'I do not have Spidey senses, so no. But it's good, isn't it? Such a relief!'

'When are you going over to Sheila's?'

'I'm going to pop in at lunchtime to see if anything needs doing, but otherwise, I'm frantically tidying up here so Leonie can stay. The good thing is, with Xander already at Luke's, it's only my own stuff I need file away out of sight.'

Rose laughed. 'Well, call on me, if I can be of use. I've got my favourite mother-and-daughter team in the shop all day. And I'm very happy not to drink, if you and Leonie want to be picked up. It is your birthday, after all, in spite of you pretending it's not.'

'That would be nice,' she said. 'We could always get a taxi back. Leonie might need to stay late if she hits it off with Tom.'

'We'll be fine to stay late. I'll clean out my car.'

'Oh! Surely you don't need to do that?' Hattie was horrified at the thought of putting Rose to so much trouble.

'I collected some lovely ceramics the other day, but they were packed in straw. It's all over the seats now.'

'OK. I will have Ms Picky with me.'

Hattie found herself surprisingly pleased to see her sister. She collected her from the station and they hugged affectionately.

'You will see Xander. Luke's bringing him to the party and you'll have all of tomorrow to be with him. He's such a nice boy.'

'Is he? I've always found him rather difficult.'

'I think college has matured him. And I told you his English teacher is coming to the party, didn't I?'

'Oh? Did you?'

'Yes. Otherwise you won't get a chance to meet him, and you wanted to, didn't you? You couldn't be at the parents' evening.' Hattie felt obliged to remind her sister. 'He's really nice.'

'You always think the best of people, Hattie,' said Leonie, but for once it didn't sound like a criticism.

'I don't always,' said Hattie, thinking about Lance. 'Have you got something nice to wear? It's a garden party, so you don't want to be too formal. It's not Buckingham Palace,' she added quickly, knowing how her sister's mind worked.

'I've brought a couple of options,' she said. 'You can advise me. I don't know our hostess.'

A few minutes later, when they reached the lodge, Leonie said, 'Oh, is this it? It's tiny! No wonder you thought Xander was better off staying with Luke.'

'It's too small for three.'

'It's pretty small for two,' said Leonie.

'It's only temporary,' said Hattie. 'We've done it up a bit for now, but I'm aiming to move on soon.'

Leonie put down her case and eased her shoulders. 'I've agreed to extend my time in Switzerland a little; they're paying me so well. But I won't do it again. I need to come home.'

'But you've enjoyed your time abroad?'

'Oh, yes. And I've saved money, but I'm missing Xander. And you.'

Hattie gave her a little hug. 'And me you,' she said, surprised to discover it was true. 'Now, let me show you your bedroom. There's a shower but no bath, I'm afraid.'

'I do need a shower. Trains are always filthy. Have you a hair dryer? I need to wash my hair.'

Hattie never used a hair dryer herself but she had bought one specially for her sister. 'I'll let you borrow it if you promise to wear your hair down for my party.'

'But I hardly ever wear it down!' Leonie protested. 'It looks so – unprofessional.'

'It looks lovely down—'

'Long hair on an older woman doesn't look good,' said Leonie firmly.

'You're in your early forties, that does not qualify as being older, not these days.' Hattie was being unusually firm, she realised, possibly because her sister wasn't being as bossy as usual.

'OK. I did have it trimmed recently.'
'Don't you want a cup of tea or something first? Rose is taking us so we could have a glass of Prosecco.'
'Oh, go on then,' said Leonie.

As Hattie put her own new-to-her dress on and fluffed up the hair she'd washed that morning, she reflected that she and her sister had never done this 'getting ready to go out together' thing before. It was surprisingly fun. Maybe it was the glass of Prosecco or maybe it was just a change of mood, but Leonie seemed open to Hattie's suggestions about her hair and make-up. The final effect was a dreamier, more relaxed Leonie in a lovely rose-covered vintage-style dress, knee-length and full. It showed off her tiny waist and made her look curvy and slim rather than just thin.

Hattie was pleased with her own appearance too. It was fairly casual in a longer, softer dress, but her hair looked OK and her make-up was nicely smudged under her eyes, making them look extra green. She was just wondering if she needed different earrings when Leonie came into her room. She stood behind Hattie as she looked in the mirror.

'What about this?' said Leonie, and picked up Hattie's hair from the nape of her neck and twisted into a knot which she secured with a clip. Then she pulled out a few extra strands round Hattie's face, letting them fall delicately. 'There,' she said. 'Very Jane Austen. What do you think?'

Hattie was so surprised at her sister doing something so... sisterly that she couldn't speak for a moment. Then she considered her reflection. It was different, but she still looked like herself. 'I think I like it,' she said. 'I may get fed up with the clip halfway through the evening, but it's nice to try new things.'

The sisters were in surprising harmony when they got into the back of Sam and Rose's car. Rose could hardly hide her disbelief.

Sheila's garden looked magical. There was a gazebo with fairy lights and lanterns in the surrounding trees. Beyond the gazebo was a summer house, and soft lights flickered there as well. As Hattie was nominally one of the hostesses, they had arrived early, but there were a couple of people there already. She was longing to see Fiona and Nick although they were nowhere to be seen.

'This is really pretty!' said Leonie as they went through the gate. 'It gives me hope that if – when – I move to this area, I can still have a good social life.'

Hattie knew her sister was thinking about coming to the locality but mostly managed to forget about it. She smiled as their hostess approached.

'Sheila! This looks amazing!' said Hattie, kissing Sheila's cheek. 'Let me introduce you to my sister, Leonie.' She placed her hand on Leonie's shoulder but she needed no encouragement. Leonie was good at this.

'And you know Sam and Rose,' Hattie went on. 'From the quiz.'

'Of course!' said Sheila. 'I'm so glad you could come. Do you know people? Can I introduce you to anyone?'

'Actually,' said Rose, 'if it wouldn't seem too rude, can I have a look round your garden before it gets too busy? It's so beautiful. I can see a sweet pea wigwam from here.'

Sheila was obviously delighted. 'July is a great month for fragrance; we have the lilies as well. Although the dahlias don't smell of much they do like to show off with their huge flower heads like Ascot hats!'

'It's so kind of you to give a party for Hattie,' said Leonie when Rose and Sam had gone off to explore.

'Anything for Hattie!' Sheila began, and then stopped, possibly realising that Leonie didn't know everything that Hattie had done for them. 'I mean, she's been so kind to my daughter and she's become a family friend. Come and have a drink.' She drew Leonie towards the bar area.

Hattie was following when suddenly Fiona appeared and hugged her. 'Hattie! It's so lovely to see you! Isn't it, Nick?'

Nick smiled his agreement. They were both lightly tanned, and looked relaxed, happy in each other's company. Nick had his arm round Fiona's waist as if they'd been together for years. Hattie couldn't help noticing how much he had changed from the slightly taciturn client she had once known.

'I'm delighted to see you too! And you're both looking so... well!'

They exchanged a quick, intimate glance before Fiona went on excitedly. 'I was thrilled when Mum said we were having a party, because although we're not making any sort of announcement as it's so soon after last time but...' She leant in to whisper. 'We're engaged! We haven't told Dad as he'll worry he's got to spend loads of money for a wedding, but this time it'll be very low key. And not until next year. But we wanted you to know.'

Hattie hugged Fiona. 'That is so good to hear! How did it happen?'

Nick looked lovingly at Fiona. 'I may have rushed it a bit. I didn't want to risk losing her, so I blurted it out over the Greek yoghurt and strawberries at a little B and B in France.'

'And I said yes instantly because I didn't want to risk him going down on one knee or anything.' She squeezed Nick's hand. 'But then he asked me again, and I said yes again.'

'So there was no doubt,' said Nick.

'What a great story! I do love a happy ending!'

'Or a happy beginning! And thanks to you we should have a wonderful new home to start that beginning,' said Nick, looking pleased and proud.

A few minutes later, Hattie moved away, leaving Fiona and Nick to wander round the garden hand in hand, hoping her vision concerning her sister would work out just as well. She went to join Leonie, who was chatting away to a nice couple who must have been friends of Sheila's, and took a glass of champagne from a passing tray.

'Hattie!' said Leonie. 'Allow me to introduce you to—'

Hattie responded accordingly and as she did so, she noticed Tom Saye arrive. She took hold of her sister's arm and moved her round a little so she could see him too.

'Oh, he looks rather nice,' said Leonie, sounding surprised.

'He doesn't know anyone here,' said Hattie. 'We should go and say hello. If you'll excuse us,' she said to the couple. 'I hope we'll catch up later.'

'He's happy to talk about Xander,' Hattie said, still holding on to Leonie's arm, in case she suddenly decided to walk off. 'And it would be good to get him while the party is still quite quiet.'

Leonie didn't reply. Unusual, thought Hattie, encouraged.

'Hey, Tom!' she said when they reached him. 'I'm so glad you could come. If you're new to the area, it's a good opportunity to meet some people.' Too late she remembered he hadn't told her he was new; she had found that out through internet stalking. But she couldn't unsay it. 'Let me start with my sister – Xander's mother. She needs to speak to you anyway.' She stopped, aware that she had said too much.

But Tom seemed very willing to meet Leonie, giving her a broad smile, which made his rather ordinary face suddenly attractive.

'It is so kind of you to make the time for this,' said Leonie. 'I do hope my sister didn't bully you into coming.'

'No bullying required, I assure you,' said Tom. 'Shall we find somewhere quiet so we can talk?'

Hattie wasn't given to punching the air, but she did whisper 'Yes!' to herself as she watched them go.

Then Luke was at her side, with Xander. 'Hey!' he said, and kissed her cheek. 'You've done something different with your hair.'

The feel of his cheek against hers and the smell of his cologne confused her for a few seconds. 'Leonie did it,' she said quickly. 'She's got her hair down and I've got mine up. Hey, Xander! You're probably dying to see your mum but she's busy just now, if you can hang on.' She looked at Luke, suddenly a bit shy. 'Shall we find the food? And Sam and Rose are wandering about somewhere.'

The table was laden with every sort of food you could imagine: much more than could have been frozen after the non-wedding party. There were plates of charcuterie, smoked salmon and rare roast beef, interspersed by salads obviously inspired by Ottolenghi. Tabbouleh bright with parsley; chickpea salad with tiny tomatoes, peppers and shallots, sprinkled with fresh herbs. There was a pile of flatbreads and another of baguettes and sourdough rolls. It was the perfect combination of fresh and healthy food and luxurious decadence.

Hattie was just trying to decide where to start when a pretty young woman came up. 'Are you Hattie? Hi! You don't know me but Gavin sent me. He's hoping to come later – it's such a lovely invitation – but he wanted to make sure that at least one of us got here. I'm April, from Rabbet and Such.'

'Oh, hi!' said Hattie. 'So pleased to meet you! I was hoping to catch up with you. Luke? Let me introduce you to April. She works for my favourite estate agent. You might not know of them,' she said to Luke, 'but we work together quite a bit. And this is Luke, the best builder in the county, but sadly, always busy.'

'Hattie's saying that because people do proposition me at parties,' said Luke with his shy smile.

'I promise you I won't,' said April. 'But it's good to have a name to suggest to clients. You can tell them you have no availability!' She laughed.

At this moment Hattie noticed that Tom Saye and her sister had separated and Leonie was heading towards them. Xander broke away and Hattie was pleased he seemed keen to see his mother.

Sheila came up to her. 'I think it's going rather well, don't you?'

'You've made the garden look magical!' said Hattie. 'Did you hire a team of designers to make it look so fantastic?'

Sheila laughed. 'You know I didn't. It's all me and Fiona, helped by Nick. I must say I like a man who can climb a ladder without complaint. I'm no good at heights myself.'

'So you like Nick?'

'I love him! The more I see him with Fiona, the more I realise how wrong Lance was, even before he got controlling. Even Malcolm is coming round to him.' Sheila paused in thought. 'Although in some ways, I have to be grateful to Lance. He made me and Malcolm reassess our marriage. I think Malcolm realised how easily he could lose me.'

Hattie wasn't quite sure how to reply to this so she squeezed Sheila's hand comfortingly. Luckily, Rose didn't hesitate to interrupt their moment. 'Sheila! The garden is so beautiful! You must not only have the greenest of fingers, but work on it every hour God sends! Do you do it all by yourself or do you have help?'

'I had help for tonight,' Sheila said happily. 'But mostly it's just me.'

There was a little dance floor set up on the patio and music came from inside the house. Hattie found herself dancing with various people, including Tom Saye, who also danced with Leonie and then they went off together. She was having a rest when Luke came up.

Her first thought was that he was going to ask her to dance but she quickly realised that he wasn't.

'Xander is flagging and Leonie thinks he should go home. I'm more than happy to take him. Leonie wants to come too.'

'I feel I must stay a bit longer as the party is in my honour. You don't think Leonie would mind?'

Luke shook his head. 'She says she'd like to stay with me and Xander. I can put her in the spare room.'

'Where I slept?' asked Hattie, knowing that her sister liked a pure down pillow with a silk pillow case and a thread count for the sheets that was almost beyond counting. When she'd last been there, Luke's spare room featured a ladder, a saw horse and a load of tools.

Luke nodded. 'Would you like to come for breakfast?'

'That would be very nice, thank you,' she said.

'I think Leonie is taking Xander out for lunch.'

'It'll be good for them to have some proper time together.'

Luke suddenly grinned. 'I thought for a moment you were going to say "quality" time.'

Hattie smiled in return. 'I thought I'd spare you. I know how you hate clichés. I'll see you in the morning.'

Hattie moved away from the dance floor and found a little table and chair next to a bed of night-scented stocks that filled the air with their heady fragrance. She was glad to have a few moments on her own. She had a lot to think about. Had Tom and her sister really hit it off? It seemed as if they had, and with Leonie planning to live in the area, they could become a proper couple. She didn't often question her visions, and so far they hadn't ever been wrong. But for some reason, as this one involved her sister, she felt the need to be extra vigilant.

And then there was Fiona and Nick. She was very happy for them. They seemed very happy.

As if thinking about them had conjured them up they appeared at the little table. 'There you are, Hattie! There are about three people all longing to dance with you! Come on!'

Hattie laughed, allowing herself to be led back to the dance floor. She took the clip out of her hair and began to move to the music; she loved dancing.

Chapter Twenty-One

Hattie opened her eyes cautiously the next morning but realised drinking a lot of water before she went to bed had held off a hangover. A quick shower and she felt good as new before she headed over to Luke's. She brought with her croissants from the freezer and some mixed seeds and berries that she'd bought for her sister. She was a bit anxious; she really hoped Leonie hadn't been critical or disapproving of Luke's house.

'Hi!' she said cheerily as she got out of the car. Frank and Fearless, who reached her first, were followed by Xander, looking sleepy. 'Am I too early?'

'No. Mum and Luke are up. Have you brought food? Mum's not thrilled by the sausages that Luke is offering.'

'I have,' said Hattie. 'Are things… How's your mum?'

'Weird,' said Xander. 'Half her usual quite critical self and half happy.' He smiled somewhat wistfully. 'Living with Luke is so simple.'

Hattie laughed. 'Down, dogs!' she said, and went into the house.

Luke leapt to his feet the moment she appeared. 'Hi, Hattie! Coffee? Tea?' He was looking strained.

'Tea please, and I've brought breakfast.' She put her basket on the table. 'Croissants which will need heating. Berries and seeds which don't. I've got Greek yoghurt too.'

'That's good,' said Leonie. 'Luke and I have very different diet preferences.'

As Hattie unpacked her basket she tried to work out what mood her sister was in but it seemed that Xander had been spot on when he said she was half her usual self and half happy.

'How did you sleep, Lennie?' said Hattie, finding bowls and giving them a quick swipe with a tea towel. Luke's open-shelf kitchen storage looked very attractive but would have worked better for someone who didn't bring dust home on their clothes.

'OK – sort of.' She made a face. 'I had a bit more to drink than I usually allow myself.'

Hattie found her sister a spoon and handed her the berries. 'Me too. Although I seem to have escaped a hangover. I have milk thistle at home if you're not so lucky.'

'Proper food will sort me out,' said Leonie, scattering her yogurt with seeds which made Hattie think of sand. 'I don't need your vile-tasting potions, thank goodness.'

'That's lucky. Milk thistle does taste fairly nasty.'

'Toast, Hattie?' asked Luke.

'Yes, please. Have you got any Marmite?'

Just then, Leonie's phone pinged. As she had very strict rules about phones at the table, this was a surprise. Leonie looked down at her phone and got up. 'Excuse me.'

She came back quickly, but she had a smile on her face she was obviously trying to suppress.

'Sorry about that. Nothing important.' A slight pause. 'Just Tom checking to see he had the right number for me.'

Now it was Hattie suppressing a smile; her sister had a case of mentionitis. That had to be a good sign for her and Tom.

Breakfast had dwindled to final cups of tea or coffee. Xander said, 'Luke? Can I show Mum the cabin? Maybe play her that track we made?'

'We've got time before lunch?' said Leonie.

'Of course,' said Luke.

'Do you want to borrow my car to go to the pub? Or are you just going to the Wagon and Horses?' said Hattie. She didn't think the Wagon and Horses was quite Leonie's sort of place, but she was full of surprises today.

'Your car is a bit big for me,' said Leonie, 'and Luke has kindly offered to take us to the Ragged Cot.'

Luke smiled. 'Leonie didn't fancy driving my truck, either!'

'Come on, Mum!' said Xander. He stopped. 'Oh, by the way, you guys realise that term ends on Friday, don't you?'

Hattie felt her mouth open and quickly shut it. 'I had no idea…'

'Xan!' said Leonie. 'You might have told us!'

'I just have!'

'But, darling, I hadn't realised it was quite so soon. I'll get in touch with your father. I can't take you back to Switzerland with me, I'm so busy trying to wind things up before I leave.'

'Can't I just stay here?' said Xander. 'I'll be fine at home on my own.'

Leonie took a breath but Luke spoke first. 'I'm happy for him to stay here for as long as he wants. I'm still away in Cornwall a fair bit, but of course Hattie comes overnight when I'm not here.'

Leonie didn't speak for a few moments. 'It would only be until Xander goes to visit his father for his usual summer visit,' she said.

'So that's OK then?' said Xander. 'Mum? You coming?'

Leonie got up. 'I do wish I'd had some warning about your term ending,' she said.

'It's been in your diary since before I started at college,' said Xander. 'Now come and hear this track!' With that he practically dragged Leonie from the room.

Luke and Hattie looked at each other in bemusement. 'Are you sure you're happy with this? It won't be long till Xan goes to Scotland.'

'It's fine,' he said.

'But it's so unlike Lennie not to have the date etched on her memory, with a plan in place.' Hattie was amazed. 'And usually she's on my case about everything, all the time. But she's hardly told me off at all during this visit.'

'No,' Luke agreed. 'She was quite relaxed about sharing a bedroom with my tools too. Although I had bought some new bed linen.'

'That would have helped. But anyway, if she's happy, we mustn't stop her. It's lovely that Xander wants to show her your cabin. I just hope she doesn't mind him making music that doesn't involve recognisable instruments.'

Luke laughed. He was, Hattie decided, looking handsome in a rugged way. Maybe it was his casual denim shirt which showed off his builder's physique. Or his recently washed hair which was a bit longer than he usually had it or the fact his teeth looked particularly white against his faint tan. For the first time since she'd met him, Hattie allowed herself to admit it was a shame he was such a good friend.

Xander and his mother came back to the kitchen. 'She quite liked it, didn't you, Mum?'

'I don't really understand that sort of music but it did sound nice,' said Leonie. 'Maybe you'll be able to keep practising when we move here. I'm really hoping to be able to relocate somewhere nearby by September or October.'

Hattie wondered again how she'd feel about her sister living in the same area as she did. It would certainly be nice to see Xander more often. She'd become very fond of him since he'd been under her wing.

Chapter Twenty-Two

'Penny for them?' Luke asked when he came back from delivering Leonie and Xander to their chosen lunch spot.

'I was thinking of calling on Mary, as Leonie doesn't need me. Sheila gave me a whole box of leftovers and I'd like to bring it to her as she couldn't go to the party herself.'

'Good idea. And do you fancy lunch in a pub? We can go somewhere different from Xander and Leonie.'

A flutter of something made Hattie clear her throat. 'Actually, I'd planned to stay with Mary for lunch. I'll share the leftovers. I usually rush in and out when I visit her. I've got time to pay a proper visit today.'

Luke nodded, but didn't comment.

Mary was very pleased to see Hattie, who felt her friend looked frailer than she had when she saw her last, only a couple of days earlier.

'Hi, Mary,' Hattie said, kissing her cheek. 'Shall I set us up outside in the garden for lunch? It's such a beautiful day, and the view is too good to miss.'

'If it wouldn't be too much trouble,' said Mary, who was very pleased to see her. 'I would like to go outside.

But I haven't worked in my garden for far too long. It's a jungle now.'

'Wildlife haven,' said Hattie briskly. 'You're doing nature a good turn.'

Mary laughed. 'I think I was still doing nature a good turn when I kept things a little tidier, but I appreciate your positive attitude.'

'If you like, I could tidy the beds you can see from the house before I go,' she suggested. 'You should ask Clive if he could get someone in.'

Mary shook her head. 'The last time I let Clive have anything to do with the garden it ended in tears. He's a slash-and-burn type and I much prefer a jungle to a wasteland.'

'I do know someone who could come and do it for you. She's a lovely woman and has a team of other lovely women to help.'

'Is there any sort of tradesman you don't know of?' said Mary.

'I hope not! It's part of my job!'

It didn't take Hattie long to set up a wicker table and a couple of chairs. Then she set out the lunch on plates and poured water for them both.

'I've got a bottle of white wine somewhere,' said Mary. 'Would you like some?'

'Ooh! That reminds me! I nearly forgot. I've got half a bottle of champagne wrapped in newspaper in the car. It's got a cork in so it should still be fizzy. Shall I get it?'

Mary paused. 'To be honest, these days I enjoy the idea of wine – even champagne – more than I enjoy drinking it.'

'But you're feeling OK? Mostly?' Hattie handed Mary a plate with some devilled quails' eggs, a tiny quiche, and a savoury profiterole.

'I'm mostly fine. I struggle with the stairs a little bit but as long as I bring everything with me so I only go up once, it's manageable.' She surveyed her plate. 'That looks like a lot of food, but suddenly I find I am quite hungry.'

'What did you have for breakfast?' Hattie asked.

'Oh, I don't bother with breakfast. A cup of tea – or maybe a glass of squash – takes me through until later.'

'Don't you feel hungry these days, Mary?'

Mary finished eating a devilled egg. 'I do, but cooking is so tiring. That's why I like it when you order me crackers and butter from Waitrose. I can always live on those.'

Hattie didn't think this was quite true and was shocked to hear it. 'I could arrange for you to have meals that you keep in the freezer and just microwave,' she said.

'I did try those once,' said Mary. 'I found them a bit bland. Although they might be a good idea. Now, tell me about the party.'

Hattie told Mary as much as she could remember in as much detail as possible.

'So, who's Tom? The man that your sister liked?'

'He teaches Xander at college. Leonie wanted to have a chat with him and she couldn't get to the parents' evening. I'm sure I've told you that she's rather an anxious mother. I can't say I blame her. Bringing up a child on your own in London must have been terrifying.'

'But she's thinking of coming to live down here, you said?'

'Yes.' Hattie paused. 'I rather hope she doesn't ask me to find her a house. I've got enough paid work going on without taking on my sister. She'd be demanding, and I wouldn't feel able to charge her.'

'She could come and live here!' said Mary. 'I won't be here much longer.'

'What do you mean? You may not be a teenager any more but you're not at death's door! And if anyone is going to live here, it's going to be me! I think you'd be a lovely housemate and this house is too beautiful for anyone else, even my sister.'

Mary laughed. 'Well, if ever you do need somewhere – bigger than your lodge perhaps – we could think about it. There's lots of space and even a nice big shed that Xander could mess about in if Luke wants to get rid of him.'

Hattie swallowed. 'Are you serious?'

'Are you?' asked Mary, her eyes lighting up.

'I could be. This house is big enough so we don't need to get in each other's way, and I could keep an eye on you!'

'As long as you didn't stop me having rowdy parties every weekend, I could live with that,' said Mary. 'And while I definitely don't need a minder, I do need someone for silly things, like opening jars, finding my reading glasses. And my phone. Oh, and sorting out my pills and putting them into the boxes.'

Hattie laughed. 'There's certainly an app to help with your phone, although I'm not sure about the other things. But let's have a proper think about it. It's not something either of us should rush into.'

'And I would have to run it past Clive. Although I think he'd be delighted. He wouldn't have to visit me at all then.'

'But before we do any of that, would you like more of what you've had, or would you like to move on to desserts?'

'Pudding, please,' said Mary definitely, obviously delighted at the thought.

After lunch, Mary dozed in the sunshine wearing one of her many old straw hats. Hattie, in another hat, and Mary's wellingtons, got on with the gardening. And as she dug up clumps of grass that had got among the pretty raised beds, and cut back overgrown shrubs and trimmed the lavender, she thought about moving in.

Currently, she and Mary truly loved each other, but would living together change that? She knew that too much proximity could change a relationship and turn friendship into irritation and dislike.

And would Clive agree? He already disliked Hattie and could easily bully Mary into withdrawing her support for the idea. But, as Mary said, with Hattie on the spot, he needn't keep an eye on her.

And she'd make sure she paid rent. That should please him.

Mary woke up, and Hattie agreed to make tea. 'And we'll finish the leftovers. But I'm going to think carefully about this idea for me and Xander to move in. I don't want to upset Clive too much.'

'But you don't mind upsetting him a little bit?'

Hattie smiled. 'Only a little bit. But you must think carefully too, Mary.'

'We don't want to risk our friendship.'

'That's exactly what I was thinking!' said Hattie.

'I thought you might be. It's why you won't make a play for Luke,' said Mary. 'Because you don't want to risk your friendship.'

That stopped Hattie in her tracks. 'But not risking it is the right thing, isn't it? Do you think I'm being silly about that?'

Mary sighed. 'Darling, it's your relationship, but I think he's a very special person and you'd be mad to let him slip through your fingers.'

Hattie pursed her lips. 'I'll go and put the kettle on. Are you happy there? Or would you rather move inside?'

'I'm happy here,' said Mary.

At Mary's suggestion, after tea, Hattie explored the house with her professional head on. She'd obviously done this before but not in the light of their potential new arrangement. She hadn't previously taken an interest in soil pipes and supporting walls.

At one time there had been four rooms downstairs with a passage and staircase in the middle but the dividing wall between the rooms had long since been taken out so there were two sitting rooms that ran from front to back, so she and Mary could be independent. Both rooms were light and of a good size; both rooms had patches of damp. They both had wooden shutters and fireplaces, but in one room, the one Mary didn't use, the paint on the shutters was peeling and the mechanism was stiff.

Upstairs were three generous bedrooms and a family bathroom. There was plenty of room in the largest bedroom, Mary's, to put in an en suite. As getting to the bathroom involved walking along a passage and a small trip could involve falling down the stairs, Hattie felt angry that this job hadn't been done for her friend.

Nobody could deny the potential of the house. If money were spent and a bit of thought put into it, it could be anyone's dream home. But even without the money and the work, it already was Hattie's dream home. She simply longed to live here and now she had the chance. She went back into one of the spare bedrooms, admiring its proportions – large enough to be comfortable; small enough to be cosy – and the view from the window. She could imagine some of her own things installed here: it would be perfect.

She went downstairs and into the garden.

'Well?' said Mary, who appeared to have been waiting for her, possibly a bit anxious. 'What do you think?'

'I'd absolutely love to come and live with you here, if you could put up with me and Xander.'

'Of course I don't know Xander, but any nephew of yours can be a sort of great-nephew of mine.' She smiled, and instantly looked younger. 'I think I'm too old to be living on my own. I worry.'

'And I worry too,' said Hattie. 'But we have to consult with Clive: there are a few things we could do to make you more comfortable here but they'd require a bit of money.'

'I'll ring him,' said Mary. 'But I should think he'd be delighted.'

Hattie wasn't so sure. Clive didn't like her and he didn't like spending money. He wouldn't like her muscling in, as he would see it. But it was still Mary's house and so her decision.

'I'll just have a look in the shed. I'll see if we could make a den for Xander in there,' she said. 'Do you want to ring Clive now?'

'Oh, no. Not on a Sunday. He'd rather I rang during working hours.'

Hattie left shortly after inspecting the shed, which would need clearing out, hoping that Clive would let her move in soon. She hated the thought of Mary feeling anxious about being on her own, especially when there was an easy solution. And she'd enjoy living with Xander again.

She got back to Luke's to find her sister there, preparing to leave. 'I've collected all my things from the lodge,' she said to Hattie the moment she appeared. 'And I've got to go. I really hope to be back soon though.' She glanced at her son. 'Xander and I have had a lovely afternoon. It's been so good to spend some time together.'

These words sounded strange coming from Leonie, who was usually so brisk and despised anything that might be construed as 'touchy-feely'.

'I'm so glad. Let me know when you'd like me to take you the station.' She knew when the train left and felt that Leonie was leaving it rather late to get there. 'If you're sure I can't persuade you to stay another night? The trains will be better tomorrow.'

'Hattie! You know I've had my ticket booked for ages. I want a quick word about the Golden Wedding party though. We completely forgot to talk about it. You know Mum's booked a very smart venue for it? They want to ask everyone.'

Hattie groaned inwardly. 'I didn't know they wanted a big do. How lovely! But it's not until August, is it?'

'No,' said Leonie. 'But to be honest, it's not super convenient. Xan will be with his father for most of August so he won't be able to be there.'

'Shame,' said Xander in a way that made it clear he was delighted.

'Well, we don't need to talk about it yet, Lennie, and if you're going for a train, can we go? You know I always get anxious about missing trains.'

Leonie laughed. 'Yes! It's the one thing that makes you normal. You're so laid back about everything, except that!'

'The thing about the Golden Wedding,' said Leonie when they were nearly at the station, 'is that you will have to wear something respectable. Nothing "pre-loved". I know Mum is worrying about you looking too "hippy dippy". And before you say it, August is in a fortnight.'

'Still plenty of time to worry about it!' said Hattie, furious behind her friendly smile. 'And we're in time for the train too.'

When they were on the platform, Leonie gave Hattie an unexpected hug. 'Thank you so much for looking after my boy. He's loving living with you and Luke. I'm sure he's happier with you than he ever was with me.'

Hattie returned the hug. 'I'm sure that's not true but I've loved having him.'

As she waved off the train she found herself feeling a bit tearful. In spite of all their differences, deep down, she was very fond of her sister.

But Hattie drove away from the station with her mind whirring. Although she had plenty of other things to think about, it had snagged on Leonie saying 'you and Luke' as if they were a couple.

Chapter Twenty-Three

Hattie was on her way to a working breakfast with a group of estate agents when Rose called.

'The visitors' book you ordered for Sheila has come in and it looks gorgeous! The name of the house on the front looks so stylish. The woman who makes them is going to do one for me too.'

'What perfect timing!' said Hattie. 'I could come to the shop and pick it up on my way back from town.'

'Tell you what, if you let me come, I'll gift wrap it for you. I want another look at Sheila's garden. I've got a new member of staff who's working out really well. She only does school hours but can turn her hand to anything.'

'I'll be a couple of hours but I can call Sheila now and see if she'll be home.'

Sheila was delighted to hear from Hattie but insisted that she and Rose came for lunch the following day. 'No need to bring me anything, having a party for you was a joy! But my favourite part of a party is talking about it afterwards and as Malcolm couldn't be less interested in who got off with whom, I'm thrilled to have you. We'll have leftovers. And I might have some news!'

★ ★ ★

Sheila was delighted with her present. Through the maze of 'you shouldn't have' and 'there was no need's Hattie could see genuine pleasure. 'I love entertaining,' she said. 'This is lovely, with the name of the house on it and everything.'

'Rose arranged that for me. She knows a woman with a little company who does it.'

'I'll get one when Fiona and Nick's house goes through,' she said. 'It's such a lovely gift.'

'The perfect gift,' said Rose, 'for the people who have everything.' She stopped. 'Oh, sorry, was that rude?'

'Not at all!' said Sheila. 'It was honest. Now, let's have lunch. It's not quite warm enough to sit outside, I don't think, but that's what we have a conservatory for. Malcolm's playing golf, so we can gossip away. Come through.'

Sheila's conservatory had slatted blinds so that sunlight striped the floor, giving the room an exotic atmosphere, enhanced by the traditional club furniture and large plants. The chairs were large and comfortable and surrounded a glass table that was set with colourful china and attractive glassware.

'This is such a lovely room,' said Hattie. 'Is it original or did you add it?'

'We replaced the one that was here. It was great for keeping the plants watered, but you had to keep moving them round the floor. In other words, it leaked.' Then, refusing offers of help, she left the room.

She came in shortly afterwards with a tray. On it was a large majolica dish bearing an equally colourful dish.

'It's char-grilled prawns, with avocado and salad,' said Sheila. 'When it came to it, I didn't fancy serving leftovers.'

'Well, this looks delicious,' said Hattie. 'So colourful!'

'And did you grow the salad and herbs?' asked Rose.

'I did! Malcolm can only eat a certain amount of salad so it's lovely to have enthusiastic diners. Help yourselves. Have some bread. I don't suppose I can persuade either of you to join me in a glass of fizz? As I said on the phone, I do have something to celebrate.'

Rose gave in to temptation quite quickly. 'It's my morning off and Hattie drove us here. I'd love a glass of fizz.'

'Excellent!' Sheila quickly fetched a bottle. When everyone had a drink, Hattie sticking to sparkling water, Sheila made a toast. 'To parties, to friends, and to people who know their way round the internet.'

Hattie and Rose's glasses landed quickly. 'That sounds intriguing. What do you mean?' asked Hattie.

'This woman I know discovered that Lance – you know Lance?' Sheila addressed Rose. 'The horrible man who nearly married my daughter?'

'I know who Lance is,' said Rose.

'Well, he's definitely making plans to emigrate!'

'How on earth can anyone find that out?' asked Hattie.

Sheila shrugged. 'It's to do with social media. He announced on there somewhere that he's got a new job. I'm celebrating because I didn't think I'd stop worrying about Fiona if he was still in the country. And I'm sure you felt the same, Hattie.'

Hattie nodded. 'I didn't think I was worried in the long run, not really, but now you've told me that, I do feel a weight has been lifted. '

Once in the car with Rose, Hattie gave a little shudder. 'I can't help wishing I didn't have visions. They are such a responsibility.'

'I can imagine but you did a good thing for Fiona as a result.'

Hattie smiled gratefully at her friend.

'Different when it's your sister,' Rose went on. 'Although Tom seems perfect for Leonie, I'd have thought. He's so nice.'

'She seems to think so. Although of course I can't tell her it was a vision. They none of them approve of my wild Irish great-granny, who apparently had them too.'

'You're very different from your sister.'

Hattie nodded. 'And from my parents.' She frowned suddenly. 'That reminds me, they're coming up for their fiftieth wedding anniversary soon – something I keep avoiding thinking about. I wonder what that'll involve?'

'You, to some extent!' said Rose, laughing.

Hattie had dropped off Rose at the shop, refused tea and was on her way home to the lodge when her phone rang. It was Clive.

'Hi,' he said. 'I think we should meet.'

'Good idea,' said Hattie, forcing positivity into her voice, although she felt suddenly anxious. She'd met Clive a few times before and it had never been enjoyable. 'When would be good for you?'

'When would be good for you?' he asked, reminding Hattie that he could be a bit oleaginous.

'Now? I'm in the car. We could find a pub garden or something.'

'Fine. The Fountain? Do you know it?'

One of Hattie's many skills was knowing every pub and café in the area. 'Yup. I'll be there in fifteen.' She wanted to do a drive by on a house to check if there was evening sun later, so this would be convenient.

★ ★ ★

Clive was there before her at a table near the bar, with a pint in front of him. He was wearing chinos and a striped shirt that clung slightly and had one too many buttons undone. He didn't get up when Hattie approached, so she greeted him and ordered herself some sparkling water.

'Shall we sit outside?' she asked, when she had her drink. 'It's a lovely day.' She might feel less uncomfortable being with him if she was in the fresh air.

He shook his head. 'I'm fine here, thanks.'

Hattie sat down opposite him, wondering that he was somehow related to Mary and reminding herself she had to get him on side. 'Cheers!'

'So, you want to move in with Aunt Mary?'

'Yes,' she said, having rejected several longer ways of saying this.

'Why?'

'I need somewhere to live temporarily. Mary and I get on, and the house is big enough for us both. I could keep an eye on her. She's very old to be living on her own.'

'And your nephew will be there too?'

Hattie nodded. 'That's also temporary.'

'Hmm,' said Clive.

He didn't speak for quite a long time and Hattie wondered why Mary couldn't just say she wanted Hattie to live with her. She shouldn't have to ask permission, or run it past her great-nephew.

Hattie wouldn't break the silence. Eventually, Clive said, 'You'd pay rent, of course?'

'Of course,' said Hattie. 'And share expenses. I'd cook and clean, keep an eye. I think Mary would feel safer if I was there.' She took a sip of her water to stop herself reminding him Mary really wanted to go into a care home. He knew that.

'OK,' said Clive. 'It'll be...' He quoted a rent that was about double the going rate.

Hattie shook her head. 'No,' she said calmly. 'I'll pay half that.' She wasn't going to be bullied into paying more than she should. Had she been paying Mary direct, it would have been different, but she knew the money would go to Clive and couldn't see a way whereby it would end up in Mary's account.

He wasn't happy.

'OK,' she said eventually. 'I'll pay what you ask, but I'll deduct all the money I spend on food, repairs, etc., before I pay. Or I could just pay Mary direct.' She knew Mary had a building society account that Clive had no access to.

He sighed and eventually nodded. 'Pay what you suggest. Any money you spend on the house will be refunded but I'll have to agree the expense is valid.'

'I'll keep strict accounts.'

They parted shortly afterwards and Hattie drove to the property to check on the sunset. She had an app on her phone to help her do this but it was never the same as seeing it for herself. 'Evening sun' was right at the top of her newest client's list of requirements.

Afterwards, Hattie drove back to Mary with the news. She was delighted. 'I don't want you to pay rent though, darling! You'll be looking after me to some extent. I should pay you!'

Hattie laughed. 'I'd rather pay rent. I don't want Clive, or anyone, thinking I'm sponging off you. And I won't really be looking after you much. I'll cook the odd meal—'

'And clean, do the garden, heave me back into bed or my chair if I fall out…'

'I'll be happy to do all those things,' said Hattie. 'And pay rent. Now, when would you like me to move in?'

'Have you got plans for tonight?'

Hattie laughed again and kissed Mary's cheek. 'Maybe tomorrow would be better. I ought to at least bring a nightie and a toothbrush with me.'

Chapter Twenty-Four

It was actually a couple of days later that Hattie and Xander moved their things to Mary's house. Hattie's landlord had been understanding as, in the past, Hattie had done him so many favours; he said he thought he'd turn it into an Airbnb for the time being. When they arrived, Hattie brought Xander to meet Mary. She didn't say anything but she was praying that he would speak to her and not be paralysed by shyness.

'Hello, Xander, I'm Mary,' she said the moment Xander and Hattie entered the room. 'I do hope you're going to like living with me. It will take us a while to get used to each other, I'm sure. But I am quite deaf, so you probably don't need to worry about playing your music too loudly.'

Xander laughed. 'I usually wear headphones when I'm playing music,' he said. 'I wouldn't want to disturb you.'

'And we're hoping to turn the shed into a den for you,' said Hattie. 'Although he's not a noisy person generally.'

'I try not to be noisy,' said Mary, 'but I do have the television up rather loud. We'll have to tolerate each other.'

Xander nodded and looked pleasant. Hattie was proud of him. He was so much less shy than he had been when he'd first been thrust upon her.

Hattie had brought her own bedding from the lodge and soon made up beds for her and Xander. Initially, Mary fretted about dampness but once she'd accepted that Hattie could manage, settled back in her chair with a cup of tea.

Xander was surprisingly helpful and volunteered to walk down to the end of the village to get fish and chips. While he was gone, Mary said, 'He's such a nice boy, isn't he?'

'He's usually very shy but he obviously felt at ease with you,' said Hattie, who had made a fresh pot of tea and had brought it into her sitting room. 'I think Luke's been a very good influence on him. And talking of Luke, would you like me to make a list of jobs for him? Nothing major, but maybe he could fix the guttering to stop the damp? And a few other things that would make the house more comfortable for you. Maybe a handrail for that little step into the kitchen?'

'Yes, please, dear.'

Luke came over one evening after work early the following week. 'So what needs to be done?' he asked when he had said hello to Mary.

'Hattie has a list but I think you should tell us what you see needs doing,' said Mary. 'Hattie, you go round with him and take notes. Just in case we need to involve Clive. Financially, I mean. He does have control over most of my money.'

Hattie, who didn't like this arrangement at all, took Luke outside. 'Clive hasn't been maintaining the property properly. It's such a lovely house, it should be looked after.'

'It *is* a lovely house,' said Luke, pressing at a window-sill with his fingers. 'But you work with lovely houses all the time. What's so special about this one? You're different when you talk about it. Almost as if it was a beloved pet.'

Hattie laughed. 'Do you need to ask? It's got such lovely proportions and character. It faces south-west so it gets sun almost all day, and the garden is wonderful. It's hard to find a garden that's remotely level round here. You wouldn't exactly call it flat, but it does have flattish areas. It's also full of very unusual plants. Mary was a great gardener in her day. And I love the shed.'

Luke laughed gently. 'Well, I think that's a good list of reasons as to why you love it.'

'I do love it,' said Hattie. 'It's like home to me, in a way none of the many houses I've seen have. I'm not sure I know why. It's just the way it makes me feel.' It was only now that she realised that she'd missed this feeling of home; she'd thought she was perfectly happy with her peripatetic life.

'Well, I'll keep it standing as long as possible,' said Luke. 'And it's not that bad, I don't think.' He paused. 'Would it be rude to ask for a cup of tea? I'm gasping.'

'I'll put the kettle on!' said Hattie. For some reason she was eager to get away. She felt she'd exposed herself to Luke in some way. A cup of tea would make everything seem more normal.

It was barely a week since Hattie and Xander had moved in with Mary, the night before Xander was due to meet his father in London. They were having his favourite meal, of pasta with peas, bacon and cheese.

'We're going to miss you,' said Mary, spearing a bit of fusilli with skill. 'We've become a family so quickly. And I really enjoy playing Scrabble even if you do often win.'

'I think Luke will miss you too. He said you were really helpful the other day,' said Hattie.

'I'm good at carrying buckets,' said Xander, laughing. 'And will you miss me too, Hattie?'

'Strangely, I will! Who knew having a Gen Z person around could actually be quite fun?' Hattie put a hand on his arm. 'And you're quite happy to go up to London, take the tube to Victoria and then on to your dad's?'

'Of course I am!' Xander was adamant. 'I'll be fine. There's no need to worry.'

These were pretty much the same words as Hattie had said to Leonie when she had tried to persuade Hattie that Xander needed an escort. As it turned out that Xander's father Charles and Tom had both said the same thing, Leonie had to agree.

'I don't suppose I'll ever go to London again,' said Mary, 'but I did used to enjoy it.'

'Would you like to go again?' said Hattie, wondering if she should arrange to take her.

'I don't think so really. I had a job in Knightsbridge and used to go to Harrods in my lunch hour.'

'The food halls?'

'Salon de Parfum as they used to call it. I used to spray myself with as many scents as I could get away with.'

'Didn't they smell weird, all mixed together?' asked Xander.

Mary shrugged. 'I had a scarf which smelt wonderful. Although I dare say others may not have agreed with me.'

'Mary's fun, isn't she?' said Xander as he and Hattie cleared up after the meal. 'I wish my grandparents were more like her.'

'I'm sorry you feel like that, but I agree, they are rather – formal.'

Xander nodded. 'They want a grandchild they can boast about to their friends. I'm not one of those.'

Hattie opened her mouth to argue but she knew he was right. 'I'm really proud to have you as a nephew, Xander. If that helps.'

'I know. But you and Luke are cool.'

Hattie considered reminding Xander that she and Luke weren't a couple, but refrained. 'That's good!'

'But my grandparents? Terrifying. I'm so glad I'm going to be with Dad and won't be able to come to their Golden Wedding or whatever it is.'

'Well, I'll miss you. No one else there is likely to be remotely fun. Now.' She gave the work surface a final wipe. 'I think that's all done. Get the chocolates and we can join Mary. I must say, there's something about a chocolate before bed.'

'As long as you brush your teeth properly before you go to bed, Auntie Hattie,' said Xander with a smirk.

Hattie was sitting in her car in a layby, trying to assess traffic noise for a house that seemed to be perfect in every other way when her sister called.

'It all went very smoothly, apparently,' Leonie said after a brief greeting. 'The Circle Line was behaving itself, and Xan is very clued-up.' She paused. 'Charles is right; I should trust him more. He's old enough.'

'Definitely,' said Hattie.

'Have you time to talk? I just want to make sure you're up to date on the Golden Wedding celebrations.'

'Yes?'

'They've booked a venue, sent out invitations, chosen a menu—'

'I didn't get an invitation,' said Hattie.

'Nor did I! We're family. They wouldn't waste expensive engraved invitations on us.'

'So what do you need me to do? Are they having a cake? I could probably help there if I had to, although transporting it might be tricky.'

'They are having a cake, but they want me – us – to organise a seating plan, ask about special dietary requirements, which they didn't know they had to do until I told them. They need to choose their canapés, decide if they want a cheese course or not—' Hattie heard her sister gulp. 'There's lots that can be done by email but they need help with the menu and I can't do it because I'm in Switzerland.'

'Lennie! I know I work for myself but I am busy, you know!'

'At least you live in the same country. I realise that dealing with our parents is not part of your skill set…'

'I can't be near Mum for more than twenty minutes without her getting upset with me. I'm not your woman for this. Have you thought about hiring a party planner?'

'I've tried! I can't find one that isn't booked. Anyone who does that sort of thing is spoken for. A summer Saturday is peak time for weddings. Who knew?'

It was so unlike Leonie to be ironic, Hattie laughed again.

'I know it's not really your thing, Hattie, it's my thing, and I really wouldn't put this on you if there was an alternative.'

Hattie was so accustomed to being bossed around by her older sister, she was more thrown by Leonie's conciliatory tone. 'I'll do my best, Lennie. But you might need to write me a list.'

'I'll send the list to you now. A spreadsheet will follow. I can't thank you enough for this.'

After Hattie had concluded that the house might just avoid being accused of having too much traffic noise, she drove home. She'd share a cup of tea with Mary before looking through a wodge of legal documents for a house sale. She'd also bought cakes from a stall run by children raising money for the local hospice that she spotted on the journey. She found a little sugar hit prior helped with the paperwork.

'Tea and cakes?' said Mary. 'Is there a reason?'

'My official excuse for cake is the pile of legalese I have to go through later, but you always know when I want to bend your ear about something. It's my sister.'

'Was she pleased with Xander for getting himself to his father without incident?'

'She was! I think she's beginning to let go a bit. She does seem to be less uptight these days. But she's set me rather a large task.'

'You can say no, Hattie darling.'

Hattie shook her head. 'It's our parents' Golden Wedding anniversary party. I can't leave it all to her.'

'I suppose not.'

'And she did at least ask me nicely. She's doing what she can from Switzerland, like checking everyone's dietary requirements, but some of it needs a woman on the ground.'

'In my day you just sent out invitations and people said if they could come or not. One does wonder what happened to the people who were gluten or dairy intolerant.'

'They probably didn't realise that was wrong with them, or they just suffered in silence. Anyway, we have to look after our guests these days. And – and this is the worst part – they need me to work out a seating plan. I don't know who most of the people are!'

'Could you do something like assign a family member to each table, to act as host, and then let people sit where they want?'

'That sounds a brilliant idea but I suspect it's too free-thinking for my parents. They are very dependent on order.'

'Then why don't they work out their own seating plan?'

Hattie nodded. 'When I can work out a tactful way to put it, I will ask that very question!'

Chapter Twenty-Five

Although she missed Xander a lot, having to make do with the odd link to a TikTok or photograph he sent from his dad's, Hattie found herself extremely busy in the run up to the Golden Wedding celebrations. She had agreed to keep a weather eye on the lodge for Aiden as it was turned into an Airbnb, which considering all the rent he had saved her over the years seemed fair enough; there were some niggles with Nick's house to clear up and she had other clients to look after. And now she also spent a fair bit of time looking after Mary and the house. She did it willingly but it was no small undertaking.

With the help of Leonie's spreadsheet, she was working on the seating plan. This meant she had to make a plan for each table, send it to her parents, and then alter it to their ever-changing requirements. While she was on the telephone to her mother, the subject of a dress code came up.

'You don't need to tell people what to wear for a function like this,' said her mother. 'They will know what is appropriate. Except you, of course. I want you to look smart, Harriet. Nothing "pre-loved", please.'

While Hattie was accustomed to her mother telling her what to do, it was a surprise to hear the words 'pre-loved' on her mother's lips. She would have put money on her mother having no idea what the expression meant.

'So it means a shopping trip,' said Hattie to Mary, who was now almost as invested in the preparations as Hattie was. 'Or a borrowing trip perhaps. I just wish I knew more what would be suitable.' She sighed. 'Maybe I should pop into Cirencester or Cheltenham. It can't be that hard to find something nice to wear.' Although as she said this, in her heart Hattie knew it was always far harder than it should be.

'So, long or short?' said Mary.

'I think a lovely summer dress should do it.'

'Come with me,' said Mary, putting her hand on the table and getting to her feet. 'I don't think I've ever shown you my overflow wardrobe, have I? It's in the little room along here.'

Mary, it seemed, had a second wardrobe full of clothes encased in plastic covers. 'I don't keep everything I've ever owned, but I have kept a few really good pieces, that I felt were worth the space.' She pushed the hangers along and then peered at the top of a dress. 'I've written a brief description of what's here – if I can read my handwriting. Yes! This is the one.'

She pulled out a dress and handed it to Hattie. 'Have a look. What do you think?'

Hattie unzipped the plastic covering. 'I never knew you had all these lovely dresses, Mary!'

'I don't mention them because they are my hidden treasure. I can't leave you my house, however much I might want to—'

'That sort of thing only happens in books.'

'But I could leave you my clothes. In fact, I'd like you to have them now. Clive doesn't know about them.'

'Mary, you can't. They're valuable!' But Hattie wasn't concentrating on value, she was just enchanted by the dress that she had pulled from the hanger and held up to her body.

She turned to a mirror in the corner. The dress was navy blue with a cream collar and cuffs round the elbow-length sleeves. Cream satin buttons went down the front. A very full skirt hung from the waist, landing, as far as Hattie could tell, just below her knee.

'I wore it with a petticoat which should be in there,' said Mary. 'It's very Doris Day, but so pretty. Try it on! Look, there's an old-fashioned screen tucked next to the wardrobe. It was my mother's. Open it up.'

'It's probably far too small. Vintage clothes are always tiny.'

'I wasn't tiny and you're by no means large. Go behind the screen and try.'

Hidden behind the black lacquer screen covered in art nouveau birds, Hattie stepped out of her wide linen trousers and pulled off her shirt. Mary handed her the dress and Hattie stepped in. She pulled it up and did up some of the buttons.

'Here,' said Mary. 'Put the belt on. Now, look at yourself in the mirror.'

'It probably doesn't fit—'

'It fits! It looks wonderful. But it needs the petticoat.'

Hattie looked at herself. Her waist looked tiny and she felt wonderful in it. 'I love it! I can't bear wearing normal smart clothes, but this is perfect. Elegant but different. Even my fussy mother will approve. Oh, Mary! I love myself in this! Can I really borrow it?'

Mary was as thrilled as Hattie was. 'It's wonderful seeing this favourite outfit getting another outing. Try the petti – although it is rather discoloured. You may need to have it all cleaned.'

Hattie nodded. 'I know a specialist cleaner. I'll take it tomorrow.'

'Darling, I understand you knowing about builders and mortgage brokers and all those sorts of people, but a specialist cleaner?'

Hattie laughed. 'Nothing to do with work. Rose had her wedding dress cleaned by them. It rained on her wedding day and her dress got covered in mud.'

Mary was now sitting down and Hattie realised she was tired.

'Shall we go back where you can be comfortable?'

'I'm fine here. I want you to try on more clothes. I love seeing them come to life again.'

Hattie tried on a couple more dresses. The sweetheart necklines, tight waists and full skirts suited Hattie's shape, but Mary and she agreed their favourite was a full-length dress made of silk with a halter neck. It clung to every curve and managed to be sexy yet demure at the same time. But it was the colour that made it extra special. It was a dark peacock blue but with just enough green in it to enhance the colour of her eyes.

'You need a long string of pearls and an event, darling,' said Mary, having directed Hattie to the matching clutch bag made of the same fabric. 'Somewhere you can wear that.'

'When's your birthday, Mary? I'll arrange something. I'm somewhat of an expert on party planning now, thanks to my parents.'

Mary laughed but demurred. 'Maybe I am a bit tired.'

'It is past your bedtime. I'll help you upstairs. Or would you like a bath before bed?'

'I think I'll have that in the morning. Now I'd like a mug of Ovaltine to take my pills with.'

'With a tot of something in it, to help you sleep?'

Mary smiled. 'That sounds delightful.'

Hattie spent quite a lot of the night thinking about making changes for Mary, to make living in her house easier. Putting in an en-suite was one idea, though ideally Mary would have a bedroom and bathroom downstairs. Even more ideal would be a move to the care home Mary longed for, though that seemed less likely every day. At least Luke had made a start on a few urgent things around the house.

'So do you really think I should buy this house, Hattie?' asked Hattie's client the next morning. 'It's much smaller than I asked for.'

Nor did it have a stable yard, five acres, an orchard and a wildlife pond with frogs, but Hattie didn't mention that. It had been a daunting list of requirements but Hattie's experience told her that when people started looking at property what they wanted tended to change. And with luck, eventually, they wanted something that was available and affordable.

'It's your decision of course, Mrs Conway,' said Hattie, 'but I do think you could be very happy here. A big house is a lot of work. What this house has is one really gorgeous, spacious room that you can virtually live in, with smaller rooms that won't need much looking after.' She paused. 'Plenty of space for you to put in a wildlife pond too. And if you like, I have someone who could do that for you.'

Mrs Conway didn't reply immediately. 'I've just always dreamed of living in a small stately home. With land. So I could have horses.'

'Are you sure you want horses?' said Hattie quietly.

Mrs Conway sighed. 'Well, I can't ride so maybe I'd better not have them.'

Hattie didn't reply. She could see Mrs Conway was teetering on the verge of making a decision.

'No, you're right, Hattie. This is a very pretty house in a lovely spot.'

'No need to decide immediately, but the owners are keen for a sale and it's not yet on the open market. Why don't you sleep on it, and tell me tomorrow?'

Mrs Conway nodded. 'I will. But I think it's a yes.'

Hattie almost hugged her. Mrs Conway, although a bit of a dreamer, was a lovely woman. Hattie would be delighted if she had finally found somewhere she liked.

'Let me know. And safe journey home!'

As Hattie headed for Mary's house and another pile of paperwork her mother called.

It turned out that Hattie would have to go with her mother to visit the venue, which meant staying with her parents overnight. She told Mary all this when she got back, not happy with the thought of leaving her on her own, even for one night.

It took Mary quite a long time to convince her that she would be fine, for, she pointed out, until very recently she'd spent every night on her own. This didn't stop Hattie alerting Rose and Luke of the situation, and making Mary absolutely promise to ring either one of them should a problem arise.

'It's very kind of you, Harriet, to take the time to come and help us with our little celebration,' said her mother when Hattie arrived at lunchtime the following day. She sounded anything but grateful.

Hattie managed not to tell her mother how many appointments she'd had to rearrange to make the visit possible at the last minute.

'That's OK, Mum!' she said breezily. 'I'm happy to help out.'

This took a small puff of wind out of her mother's sails. Hattie was expected to be apologetic for not dropping everything so she could have arrived in the morning, but Hattie didn't bother to explain. Her parents found the concept of her job tricky. 'So, are we tasting today?'

Her mother nodded. 'Yes. If you can drive us to the restaurant owned by the catering company, they're going to take us through everything.'

Hattie nodded. 'What time are we expected? Do I have time to freshen up?'

Her mother winced at this Americanism, as Hattie knew she would. 'We need to leave in half an hour. I asked Mrs Simpson to make up the bed in your old bedroom. She only comes on Tuesdays now.'

Hattie was expected to commiserate with her mother for only having a cleaner once a week, but she didn't indulge her. 'Great! I'll be down shortly.'

Although it gave Hattie satisfaction to annoy her mother, she knew it wasn't helpful, so she changed into clean jeans, top and jacket. She didn't look as smart as her mother would have liked, but she didn't look scruffy either.

'I'll just go and say hello to Dad,' said Hattie when she came downstairs. 'Is he looking forward to the party?'

Her mother pursed her lips. 'There are some old friends he's invited that he's keen to see. They haven't said if they're coming yet.'

'I'll make sure Leonie contacts everyone who hasn't replied to ask if there's anything they can't eat. It'll inspire them to make a decision. I'll get her to say that Dad is really hoping they'll come.'

Her mother nodded. 'That would be useful, I suppose.'

'I'll go through the invitation list when we get back from the tasting. Everything is going to be fine.'

'How long can you stay, dear?'

'I do have to leave first thing tomorrow, but that's probably long enough for us to sort everything out.' Hattie wasn't entirely sure about this but wanted to be reassuring.

'If you think that's time enough—'

'I can always come again, Mum. It's only a couple of hours' drive.'

'At my age, that seems a lot. Can we travel in my car? I don't find yours very comfortable.'

'Is Dad coming?'

Her mother shook her head. 'Catering is a pink job. He's chosen the wine.'

Hattie sighed. This sounded like par for the course.

The young woman in charge of the tasting was very patient, Hattie thought, and really wanted her client to be happy.

'The thing about family boards, where people share,' she said, 'is that it encourages people who don't know each other to chat.'

'But do people want to be carving and serving when they've been invited out for lunch?' asked Hattie's mother.

The young woman cleared her throat. 'A lot of older people prefer to serve themselves. They don't like to be confronted with a big plate of food. And if the food is still on the table, if they find they do like some particular item, they can have more.'

'That does sound appealing,' said Hattie's mother. 'Many of my husband's friends are older than we are.'

'It would save waste, Mum,' said Hattie. 'You hate waste – not that anyone admits to liking it,' she added, quietly, so her mother wouldn't hear.

'Very well then,' said her mother. 'Now what about pudding? And do we have to have a cheese board as well?'

Eventually, all Hattie's mother's questions and concerns were addressed. There'd be a selection of puddings, arranged on a trolley, so guests could choose but wouldn't have to get up to do so. Several small cheese boards would be made up and left on a serving table and Hattie (and, presumably, Leonie and helpful cousins) would take them to tables if required. Tea and coffee would be provided even though, according to Hattie's mother, it cost a fortune.

Before Hattie left, as early as she could the following morning, she was subjected to the dress-code talk again.

'Promise me you'll be appropriately dressed. I want to feel proud of you in front of my friends.' That her mother did not usually feel like that about her hung in the air, unsaid.

Hattie hugged her mother, trying not to feel hurt by this. 'I'll do my absolute best, Mum, really.'

Chapter Twenty-Six

A busy couple of days later – Mrs Conway had decided to go for the pretty house, so Hattie had opened negotiations with the owners; Nick wanted to press ahead with a survey but all Hattie's usual surveyors were booked up – Hattie got back from going through some conveyancing documents with her favourite solicitor, later than usual, to the news that Luke had visited Mary.

Mary was obviously pleased. 'He wanted to check that the guttering he mended was still holding – he's looked at that patch of damp we were talking about and says it's drying out. He's done a few other repairs. He really is an extremely helpful man.'

Hattie agreed that he was and sipped her tea. Mary had something else to say, she could tell. Since they'd been living together she'd got to know Mary better than she had before and could interpret her body language quite accurately now. 'And?'

Mary laughed. 'How did you know there was an "and"?'

'I just do.'

'I think you have second sight, sometimes,' said Mary, making Hattie jump a little. 'But you're right. He wants to ask you a favour.'

'I'll ring him. Luke has always been such a good friend to me, there's nothing I wouldn't do for him.'

'I know it's nice to have friends,' said Mary, 'but don't you really think Luke could be more than a friend?'

'I don't think so.' Hattie sighed. 'When I was at uni, a friend had a male friend who was very in love with her, and she thought: He's so nice, who would make a better husband? I can't remember why she was so keen to get married so young – family reasons, I think – but she married her friend. It all went horribly wrong, and they both lost their best friend.' She turned her gaze to the floor. 'That was far worse than losing a husband, I thought. I'd never risk that happening with me and Luke, even if he was in love with me.'

Mary started to speak and then stopped. 'Well, give him a ring. Take him out for a drink to find out what he needs. A meal, even.'

'You're not matchmaking, are you?'

Mary shook her head. 'I'm far too old and sensible to do that.'

Hattie doubted this, but didn't argue.

She went into her favourite spot in the garden where there was an old bench, a nearby honeysuckle and a vista that showed glimpses of the river when the sun shone on it. She got out her phone.

'Hey, Luke! How are you doing?'

'Hey, Hattie. I was about to ring you. Fancy a drink sometime soon?'

'I was going to invite you!' said Hattie. 'Maybe even have something to eat? I want to thank you for being so kind to Mary. As well as—'

'What?'

She didn't want to tell him she wanted to know what favour he wanted to ask her, not on the phone. 'Never mind. When's good for you?'

'Tomorrow?'

'I've got nothing else on. Where shall we meet?'

'I'll pick you up,' said Luke. 'In the old-fashioned way. And then you can have a glass of wine with your pie and chips.'

'Pie and chips? You must be talking about the March Hare!'

'Yup. No better place for pie or indeed chips.'

They chatted on for a few moments and Hattie was still smiling when she disconnected. Luke could always make her laugh. And it would be good to have an evening together like old times before he got that job in Cornwall and she became a substitute parent to Xander. She went to tell Mary of the arrangements. Mary nodded approvingly.

'Are you sure you don't want to wear anything from the wardrobe?' Mary asked, obviously disappointed by Hattie's outfit. 'I mean, you look lovely, as usual, but Luke might like to see you in something different.'

Hattie laughed. 'I don't think Luke notices clothes. Now, are you sure you're all right? Shall I bring a pie home with me? Or some chips?'

'Silly girl! Off you go and have a lovely time. Tell me all about it in the morning.'

Hattie was about to say there wouldn't be anything to tell but heard Luke drive up and so waved to Mary and went out to meet him.

'This is very nice!' she said, getting into the front of Luke's big pick-up. 'Being collected!'

'I have a favour to ask you. I need to be nice.'

'Is that how it works? You're always doing me favours. I don't think I'm particularly nice to you.'

Luke laughed. 'This is a big one. And no, you can't ask me what it is now. I need you sitting comfortably, with a big glass of wine.'

'I can't remember when I last went out and had a big glass of wine.'

'Which is why I picked you up. I want your guard to be down a little bit so you'll say yes to my favour.'

'I would anyway, Luke! You know that!'

He was smiling but he didn't comment. He waited until their pies, the vegetables, the chips, had all been served. Hattie had a glass of wine, and Luke had a lime-soda.

'Now you have to tell me what the favour is,' said Hattie. 'I won't enjoy any of this if I'm worrying about what you want me to do.' She picked up a chip. 'I'm only going to eat this one, and let everything else go to waste unless you tell me now!'

'Ask you, rather.'

Hattie exhaled loudly. 'So ask!'

'I want you to be my plus one at an event.'

Hattie was almost disappointed. 'Is that all? Of course I'll do that!'

'It's black tie. An awards ceremony.'

'I can do black tie!' She put her hand on his for a moment. 'Seriously, that's no problem. I scrub up quite well if I put my mind to it.'

He looked down at her hand, turned his over underneath it so they were palm to palm. 'That's not the issue, you always look gorgeous.'

Hattie pulled her hand back.

Luke picked up a chip. 'It's the date,' he said.

Suddenly Hattie was concerned. 'It's not the same day as my parents' Golden Wedding do, is it? That's the tenth of August.'

'Not quite that bad, but nearly. It's the night before. I know because Mary told me.'

Hattie took a sip of wine. 'I was planning to go down the night before.'

'I know. And I completely understand if you say no. It wouldn't be the first time I've been to an event like this on my own.'

'I'm sure I can make it work – go to my parents' early on the Saturday morning – but what's different about this event?'

Luke looked sheepish for a moment. 'I'm up for an award, which I probably won't get, but more to the point is the lads – the guys who work with me down in Cornwall.' He held Hattie's gaze for just a beat before finishing his sentence. 'They – and the architect and various others – have been teasing me for ages about not knowing any women.'

Hattie had heard about this group of people, who had started out as colleagues and now were mostly friends. The thought of meeting them was daunting.

'Really?' Hattie cut into her pie.

Luke nodded. 'You know when you had the dogs for me? They first started teasing me because I would shoot off as soon as possible to come and get them from you. I tried to explain we were just friends but then they decided you didn't exist and that I didn't know any women.'

'Why would anyone think that?'

'There are no photographs of any women on my phone; no one visits me down in Cornwall. They challenged me to produce someone for this do. They don't think I can do it.' He seemed awkward. 'It's all very pathetic. There's money on it.'

Hattie laughed. 'Outrageous! And there's no one else you can ask to be a proxy girlfriend?'

'Loads of people but none I want to actually come with me to an event like this.'

'In that case of course I'll come with you.'

'That's very kind, Hattie.'

'Not at all! It wasn't long ago that you were rescuing me from an angry man with a grudge against me banging on my front door. Frocking up for an evening with you is the least I can do in exchange.'

'I should mention that we're expected to stay over. It's in a fancy hotel.' He cleared his throat. 'But the rooms are big. There'll be a sofa for me to sleep on.'

Would this be awkward? Surely if he was the friend she had assured Mary he was, it would be fine! 'I trust you, Luke. Where is this fancy hotel?'

He mentioned a place about an hour away.

'Oh! That's on the way to where my parents live. So as long as I remember absolutely everything I need to take with me, that'll actually be helpful.'

'Thanks so much, Hattie.'

'Don't think about it.' Hattie knew, if their positions were reversed, he would be there for her.

'I would have liked to drive us both down but even if you weren't going to your parents' do, I've got to go straight off and start some snagging on my previous job that day. It'll take me away for a couple of weeks, possibly longer. But at least I can take the dogs.'

'What will you do with them during the event? Or is the hotel dog friendly?'

'Luckily I have an old friend who'll have them overnight. I'll pick them up in the morning.'

She nodded. 'And it's no trouble for me to drive myself but should we have somewhere to meet up first? Or shall I just rock up and say I'm with the prize winners?'

Luke laughed. 'I'll wait by the door for you. We'll go in together. This is so kind of you, Hattie. Now let's eat!'

Mary was asleep when Hattie got home feeling gently merry, but in the morning extracted every detail from Hattie about the night before over tea and toast. In the end she said, 'You must wear the blue silk dress, darling. You look so lovely in it.'

'I'd love to, but supposing I spill something on it?'

'Then you spill something on it! Not important. You just need to have a lovely evening with a lovely man.'

Hattie shook her head at her old friend. 'Have you finished with your plate?'

'Yes, thank you. I must admit I have got used to being waited on worryingly quickly.'

'But you don't feel smothered? Am I fussing?'

'I love it.' Mary smiled so warmly she almost glowed.

Hattie returned the smile, delighted to see Mary so happy. 'Well, I must go. Give me a call if you fancy anything particular for supper. I'm aware we have a lot of omelettes.'

'I like omelettes. You have a good day, darling, and I'll see you later.'

Chapter Twenty-Seven

Hattie would have preferred not to drive wearing a bias-cut silk gown when she could probably have changed in the hotel room, but she knew Mary was very keen to see her in all her finery. Given that Mary had given her the dress (although Hattie considered it a loan) as well as the one she was wearing the next day, it was the least she could do.

'So, what do you think?' she asked, standing before Mary.

Hattie had been to the hairdresser to have her hair put up – just as Leonie had done it for Hattie's party – and a large silk flower, exactly the colour of the dress, now sat behind her ear. Around her neck was a string of pearls. In her ears were large baroque pearls that made more of a statement than those around her neck.

The dress had a matching stole and evening sandals, but Hattie had declined these, preferring to wear her own, slightly scruffy court shoes which no one would see in the folds of the dress and she knew she could spend all evening in. There was also a matching clutch, but Hattie preferred not to take this either. It would be so easy to leave somewhere. Instead, she had a tiny vintage silver beaded bag on a long strap that she could wear without it interfering with her look.

'You look...' Mary took a breath. '... so beautiful! And even without the matching bag and shoes, you look as if you should be in the pages of *Vogue*.'

'A very old copy,' said Hattie laughing.

'You were so clever to find a flower that matched exactly.'

'I have Rose to thank for that. Her shop has such lovely things. But you don't think it's too much?'

'Don't be silly! I love your earrings too.'

'Also from Rose's shop. I love that they're not regular and really large. I don't usually like dainty jewellery, so the pearls round my neck are a bit of a change for me.'

'It's perfect. Your neck and décolletage are lovely.'

Hattie looked at herself in the mirror again. 'You don't think I'm showing too much cleavage?'

'I don't think Luke will think so.'

'Mary! Of course I want Luke to think I look nice. I want him to be proud of me on his arm, but I don't want to look – you know...'

'Slutty?'

For some reason, Hattie was shocked at hearing this word from Mary. 'Well, yes.'

'Sexy but not inappropriate,' said Mary, possibly guessing that Hattie had found her frankness unnerving. 'Now off you go. You don't want to be late. Have you packed the car?'

Hattie nodded. 'Absolutely. And I've got everything on my exhaustive list. The table plans, the big table plan so people can find their table. The dietary needs, the place names. A list of people who've accepted for my parents – two copies – one each. And some things my sister left behind when she was staying.'

'Then what are you waiting for? And do send pictures if you can. And don't get stopped by the police on the journey. You may be arrested for being a runaway countess.'

Hattie rolled her eyes and then kissed her friend goodbye. 'I'm wearing a jacket for the drive. And flat shoes.'

Hattie pulled into a layby to touch up her make-up and change her shoes. It was a warm day and she was pleased to take off her linen jacket. She pinned the flower in her hair more securely and decided she would have to do.

The hotel had once been the stately home of a local manufacturer. It had extensive grounds and a sweeping drive. The house itself was a fine example of Victorian splendour, with turrets and terrifying carved creatures.

She had parked the car and had just set off with her case on the path towards reception when Luke appeared. He took her case and kissed her cheek.

'Hattie,' he said. 'You look absolutely amazing.'

Hattie looked at Luke. He looked amazing too, she realised. She had never seen him in a suit, let alone a dinner jacket which showed off his broad shoulders and tall frame. His hair was stylishly cut and he smelt of something delicious. She was glad she'd used up the last of her Chanel No. 19 for the evening. She caught her breath but couldn't speak. She was glad when he took her arm.

'Come on,' said Luke. 'We'll get your case sent up to the room and then everyone is very keen to meet you.'

'I hope I pass muster,' she said, suddenly nervous. Although Luke's reaction told her that she did.

'This is Hattie, everyone,' said Luke to a circle of smartly dressed men and women who were drinking champagne in the foyer.

'Hey! Luke!' said one of the men. 'No wonder you've been keeping her hidden away.'

His wife dug him in the ribs. 'Jason! How rude!' Then the woman smiled. 'I'm Carole. Jason is my husband, the architect. I'd better do the introductions as Luke is terrible with names.'

Hattie smiled and nodded and repeated the names as Carole said them. The men all looked a bit uncomfortable in their DJs but their wives had obviously enjoyed dressing up. There were fake tans, fake lashes and a lot of cleavage. Hattie felt her own decolletage was quite tasteful in comparison and she looked forward to reporting this to Mary. And she couldn't help noticing that they all looked at Luke with slight longing. Hardly surprising, she decided. He was definitely the most attractive man in the group.

'Here,' said Luke, taking a glass from a passing tray. 'Have some champagne.'

'You're a bit behind the rest of us,' said one of the women. 'When is it OK for us to get Hattie on her own and really find out about Luke? He's always so mysterious!'

Hattie, who was still holding Luke's arm, gave it a tiny squeeze.

'Give the poor girl a chance to get to know everyone first,' said Luke.

Hattie sipped her champagne. She didn't want to overdo it – she had a very early start in the morning – but a glass of bubbles might make her feel less shy. She was never shy, she reflected. She could talk to anyone. Why did she feel so vulnerable and exposed now?

'So, Hattie,' said one of the women. 'Where have you been hiding all this time? Why hasn't Luke brought you down to Cornwall to meet us all before now?'

'Obviously I can't speak for Luke—'

'I don't know why not,' said one of the woman. 'I often speak for Charlie!'

Hattie smiled. 'I do work rather a lot, and can't easily take time off.' This was a bit of an exaggeration.

'They're calling us in,' said one of the men. 'Has anyone found where we're all sitting?'

'I might pay a quick visit to the Ladies,' said Hattie. 'I don't want to get hemmed in and have to squeeze past everyone.'

'Good idea. I'll come with you,' said Carole.

'So,' she said as soon as they were away from the group. 'How long have you and Luke known each other? We none of us thought he knew any women.'

She was about to say, 'Years and years,' when she realised she didn't know what Luke had said about this. 'I've known him from a distance for ages,' she said. 'But I've got to know him a bit better recently.'

'Oh? Whenever the lads are working on the estate and chatting, Luke gives the impression you and he have been an item for a while.'

'Oh,' said Hattie, not sure what to do with this information. 'So what do you do? If you're on site with the lads? I'd love to hear about it.'

'Actually, I am just going on what Jason said. Here's the Ladies. Then we'd better get seated.'

Hattie took a moment to wonder how she should play the next few hours. She didn't want to make Luke look silly but without knowing what he'd said, it was hard to know how she should behave. She'd have to find an opportunity to ask him.

Luke stood up as she reached the table and pulled her chair out. She smiled her thanks and thought again how very attractive he looked. It wasn't, she realised, because the dinner jacket was so flattering, it was because she just wasn't used to seeing Luke looking so different. Perhaps he was seeing her in a new light too thanks to Mary's dress?

Hattie was good at finding people interesting, but her abilities seemed to fade as everyone around her, apart from Luke, got more and more drunk. They all knew each other well but probably didn't often have the chance to relax and take advantage of free alcohol and food. She was sure they didn't mean to be rude, but she did feel a bit excluded. She couldn't tell if she'd have had more fun if she had been drinking herself. But she didn't dare have very much because she had to leave the hotel by seven at the latest, and had to be on top form to be the dutiful, helpful daughter for her parents' big celebration.

'So, what is it you do again?' asked one of Luke's fellow builders, slurring his words but trying to concentrate.

'I find houses for people,' Hattie had told him before, in more detail, but couldn't be bothered to go through it all again.

'But why can't they go on Rightmove and find their own houses, for nothing?'

'They can! But some people need a bit of help. They may not be local and can't check out properties in real life. I also sometimes get to hear of properties before they go on the market.'

'I wouldn't bother if I was moving. I'd just find the house on Rightmove. Job done.'

Hattie smiled, to avoid saying something that would make her look as rude as she felt like being.

The awards seemed to take forever and, much to Hattie's annoyance, Luke didn't win his. In fact, no one on their table did. It didn't prevent a lot of raucous applause and more drinks being ordered.

Hattie was wondering when Luke might want to leave when he got up. 'Come and have a drink, Hattie,' he said, putting his hand under her elbow.

Hattie stood up immediately. 'That would be great.' She ignored the comments and the 'oohs!' that followed them, and made her way as quickly through the tables as she could.

'I am so sorry about this, Hattie!' said Luke as soon as they'd reached the bar. 'Most of the time they are perfectly nice lads with nice wives and families. But give them free alcohol and they all seem to go crazy.'

Hattie smiled and put her hand on his arm. 'It's OK. I get it. And it's not your fault.'

'Can I persuade you to have a brandy or something? You've hardly drunk a drop all evening.'

'I've got an early start. But a gin and tonic would be nice if we can find somewhere quiet to drink it.' She glanced at her watch. 'I don't want to be late.'

'We could take it upstairs. Sit on the sofa and look at the view?'

The thought of being completely alone with Luke gave her a frisson of something she couldn't identify. 'That would be lovely, but would it look rude to your friends?'

'Tell you what, you go upstairs. I'll make our excuses and come up with the drinks.'

'That sounds a wonderful plan, Luke. Thank you.'

Hattie went up to the room, happy to think she and Luke could have some peace and quiet together. It probably made her a boring person, she told herself, but no one can be a party animal all the time.

She kicked off her shoes and then went to the bathroom to check on her appearance. It wasn't that she wanted to look glamorous for Luke, she told her reflection in the mirror, just that she wanted to make sure her mascara was in more or less the right place. For a moment she considered taking her hair down, but as the flower was still where it was supposed to be, she left it. She did take out her earrings though.

Then she padded across to the window, drew back the curtains and pulled the small sofa in front of the window. The hotel had lovely gardens and they looked enchanting in the summer twilight. Had things been different, she would have liked to explore them but now the prospect of sitting quietly with Luke, having a peaceful drink, seemed exactly what she wanted to be doing. Just for a second, she thought about the outfit she was going to wear tomorrow. She hadn't put it in her case. It was in its plastic cover, hanging up in the back of her car. She could almost hear Mary's voice asking why she and Luke weren't romantically involved, but she pushed the thought away.

Considering he had to say goodbye to his cohort and get drinks, he was quite quick. He had steak sandwiches, chips, chocolate mousse and half a bottle of red wine as well as her gin and tonic.

'I don't think you ate very much, did you? And you may not have time for breakfast in the morning, so I thought a bit of nicer food might be good. And I know you don't want to drink much, but you could have a glass of red with the steak sandwich, if that's what you fancy.'

'Luke! How did you know I'd be hungry? Down there I didn't really feel like eating and I didn't dare drink much, but now, when it's just us, my appetite has come back. I'd love a glass of red.'

She had intended to ask Luke what he'd told his friends about their relationship, but she didn't need to know now. She wasn't going to see them again.

He found a little table for the food and they sat on the sofa. Their arms were touching and it seemed quite cosy, but, as Hattie reminded herself, it was nothing they hadn't done before.

So they ate and drank in companionable silence, looking at the closely mown lawns beyond which was a lake with trees full of fairy lights round it.

'I must get some fairy lights for Mary's garden,' said Hattie. 'It could look really pretty.'

'How is it, living with Mary? I know you're very fond of her but living with her could upset the balance.'

'I don't think it will. We get on very well. And in a way, me being there in the mornings and evenings means we see each other a lot but not for terribly long. So it's casual. She's very self-sufficient really, but we like eating together. It might be different when Xander comes back from his holiday with his dad for the new term. But for now it's working really well for both of us.'

'I'm glad. It is a nice house.'

'I must have told you a dozen times, it's my favourite house.' She gave a deep sigh. 'I'd like to try and buy it when Mary moves. I just can't bear the thought of anyone else owning it.'

'I know Mary would leave it to you if she could.'

'But we know she can't, and besides, if she moves into a care home, which is what she wants to do, she'll need to sell the house to pay for it. Or Clive will.'

'Hmm,' said Luke. 'Unless Clive agrees to spend quite a bit more money on it, it'll affect its value.'

'Which would work well for me!' said Hattie. 'Although, who am I kidding? I have got savings, quite a bit in my eyes, but I won't be able to afford to buy that house.'

'You could look into it.'

She nodded. 'True. I know an excellent mortgage broker. She might be able to work some magic.' A yawn came from nowhere.

'You're tired. You need to go to bed. I'll sleep on the couch.'

'Don't be silly, Luke. The bed is enormous. We'll share it. But I do need to go to bed.'

'Why don't I go and find the crowd in the bar, let you have some privacy? I won't wake you when I come in if you're asleep.'

Shortly after she had drifted off she was aware of Luke coming back and she kept her eyes firmly shut as she listened to him take his suit off and slide into bed next to her. She felt the bed dip as he got in and she allowed herself to move closer to his warmth.

Chapter Twenty-Eight

Hattie woke before her phone alarm went off, as she knew she would. She had been aware of Luke sleeping next to her in the bed, breathing deeply and very occasionally giving a little snore. She wasn't used to sharing a bed with anyone and thought she'd find it difficult, but in fact she found she liked his silent, comforting presence.

Now, she slipped out of bed, gathered her clothes and got ready in the bathroom. She'd showered the previous night to make the process of leaving quicker and quieter. She'd got to her car and put her case in the back before she realised the outfit that she'd pictured so clearly hanging from a hook in the back was missing. Then she remembered it was still on the back of her bedroom door, all ready to go in the car.

She stood in the dawn wondering what she should do. She was due at her parents' for breakfast – they were already annoyed with her for not arriving the previous evening. If she went back now she could get to the venue in time to set out the place cards. But her parents wanted her before that.

She was still thinking about what she should do when Luke appeared. He looked very tall and rumpled. 'I saw you standing here. Is everything all right?'

He shouldn't have been there; he should have been asleep in bed.

'Did I wake you? I tried to be quiet.'

'I woke up and found you gone. You didn't make a sound as you left. But why are you still here?'

'I've left my outfit at home.' She regretted telling him the moment the words were out of her mouth.

'I could get it for you—'

'No! You can't. You have things to do here. I'll just wear what I wore last night. It'll be fine.' She spoke very firmly. She didn't want an argument about this.

Luke didn't argue, instead a slow smile spread over his face. 'I just wish I could be there…'

Hattie found herself smiling. She kissed his cheek, lingering for a moment as his rough skin smudged against hers; then she got into her car and drove away, glancing in the mirror at the man she had left.

As she drove she realised her feelings for Luke had shifted slightly. He was still the always-reliable friend – the friend who offered to drive umpteen miles for her without a second thought – but he was also the very handsome man – a dream date, almost – at her side at a black-tie event. Could he be both those people to her? Would it create a horrible muddle in her life?

To drag her mind away from Luke, she thought of the challenge the day ahead presented. What could she wear with the peacock silk dress to make it more suitable for a lunch do? The linen jacket she was wearing now, with its large pockets she usually used for useful things like a tape measure, notebook, pen and phone, wasn't nearly smart enough. Her sister had told her years ago that jacket pockets were not for putting things in, as that would ruin the line of the garment. But as

Hattie considered the jacket was there to be useful, if the pockets became a little baggy, that was too bad.

She did have with her a bag filled with 'helpful essentials'. Rose, who had once been a wedding planner, had told her she'd need this and what to put in it. Among a selection of hair products, including tongs, there was a garment steamer, a sewing kit, safety pins, parcel tape to remove fluff or dog hairs and double-sided tape for hems, which could double as 'tit tape' in the unlikely event that it was needed. It was galling, she thought, that she had remembered all these little items, but not her actual outfit. And she'd been looking forward to wearing it.

She had brought a cashmere cardigan but it had random daisies embroidered on it, to cover the moth holes. To be fair, it wouldn't have looked nice with the long silk dress even if the moth hadn't got to it. And it definitely looked 'pre-loved' so her mother wouldn't approve.

Maybe she could borrow something from Leonie? Her mother wasn't the sort of person who lent clothes. She might, at a pinch, lend an umbrella or a pair of gloves, but nothing more intimate than that.

Hattie decided she couldn't think about it any more: she might go mad. She would find a solution. It would be fine.

To her surprise and slight annoyance (she wasn't sure why), she found that Tom Saye, the man she had gone to such lengths to introduce to her sister, was with Leonie in the kitchen when she arrived. She stopped being annoyed when she saw how giddy Tom's presence made her sister.

She kissed Hattie (unusual) and ushered her out of the room into the large hallway. Then she whispered, 'I begged Mummy to let me bring him. She finally agreed when I told her it didn't mean she had to let you bring some awful old hippy.'

When she was about seventeen, Hattie had been on two dates with a man with dreadlocks and gnarly toenails. Her parents had never forgotten it. She thought about Luke.

'I haven't had a relationship since my marriage broke up,' Leonie went on. 'It's so lovely to have a man on my arm again!'

'He's not a big fat diamond ring, Lennie!' said Hattie, laughing now.

'No – he's so much better than one of those!' said Leonie, warming Hattie's heart. 'If there's ever a ring it will be very small, he's a teacher, but I won't care. There's more to life than money.'

As Hattie had tried to tell her sister this many times over the years to no avail, now she could only give her sister a hug. 'Well, I think he's super and I hope the parents do too. Where's Mum?'

'Getting ready upstairs.'

'Already? She'll peak too soon at this rate. I'll pop up and see how she's doing.'

Her mother was sitting at her dressing table, looking at herself in the mirror. 'My hair's a disaster!' she said, not bothering to say hello.

'I think it looks lovely. What's wrong with it?'

'It's far too – floppy. Untidy, even.'

'I think it just looks softer, which is very flattering.' She paused. Her mother's anguished expressed hadn't changed. 'But if you like, I could use the curling tongs on it which would define the curls a bit.'

'Could you, darling?' said her mother. 'That would be clever. Have you got any curling tongs?'

'You haven't?'

'Certainly not!'

Hattie quickly fetched her bag with the 'helpful essentials'.

'Why did you bring all that?' asked her mother, watching Hattie find the tongs.

'It's for emergencies, Mum,' she said.

Her mother sighed. 'I do hope there aren't going to be any.'

'There won't be. I've already spoken to the caterers who are really on it.'

'I just wish Leonie could have done all that for me.'

Hattie tested the temperature of the tongs, ever so slightly tempted to let them be too hot. 'It's not easy for her being out of the country.'

'I blame that young man she insisted on inviting. Who is he? We don't know anything about him.'

'I do. He's a teacher at Xander's college. Very nice, very well qualified and destined for great things.' Hattie made up the last part because she knew it would please her mother.

Her mother seemed mollified and was happier with her hair when Hattie had finished. Though she didn't say any of that out loud, of course.

Although Hattie had arrived at her parents' house soon after eight, as instructed, the time seemed to melt away. Her mother wanted Leonie and Tom to travel to the venue with them, so Hattie was going ahead on her own. By the time she was ready to leave (an hour before the others) she had not only tonged her mother's hair, but had zipped her into her dress and jacket, done up the pearl necklace (three strings) that her father had given her on the birth of her first child. She had also taken the clothes brush to her father's suit and removed a small mark from the jacket. She'd had no time to think about her own outfit and was relying on being able to steam the creases out of her dress at the venue.

Her parents, aided by Leonie, had chosen a really beautiful hotel for the Golden Wedding and Hattie had visited it to make sure it was as good in real life as it was on the website. Now, the sun shone on the cream-coloured stone and glinted off the Virginia creeper. It was very traditional, possibly Jacobean, with tall gables and diamond-paned windows. There were arches and small parapets and its history oozed from its walls. The sisters had been delighted with it. Now, Hattie parked and went up to the house with her many bags.

'Hello!' she said at reception. 'I'm Hattie – for the Golden Wedding?'

'Nice to see you. And what a lovely day you've got for it. Follow me,' said the friendly young woman at the desk.

'Is there anywhere I can steam my dress?' asked Hattie.

'We have a ground-floor bedroom set aside for your party. You'll be fine in there. Would like some coffee? Biscuits? Pastries?'

'I'd love some tea! I was up really early this morning but didn't seem to find time for breakfast.'

'I'll send some along to you. And when you're ready, we can organise the table plans and place cards.'

Hattie began to relax, confident that nothing would go wrong. She even managed a quick shower before she put on her freshly steamed gown. The steam had made her hair curl more than ever and her skin glowed, but her dress, although crease-free and clinging to her shape in a very flattering way, was still completely unsuitable.

Hattie walked into the room where the lunch was to take place and gave a sigh of happiness. It looked beautiful. Huge, natural-looking arrangements in front of an ancient fireplace and at other strategic spots consisted of English flowers, 'grown not flown'. Dahlias the size of plates nodded among roses and lacy hydrangeas. There were snapdragons, astrantia, delicate blue larkspur and Japanese anemones. Hattie loved how it looked as if a herbaceous border had been brought into the house. As Leonie had left choosing a florist to her, she had turned to Rose for help. The end result was everything she could have wished for.

'I just hope my parents like it as much as I do,' she said to the young woman helping her with the place names. 'They're a bit conventional.'

'No one could be unhappy with those flowers,' she said reassuringly.

Hattie was in the small hall (dominated by another enormous fireplace) that led into the ballroom (now full of white-clothed tables), ready to greet the guests, when her parents arrived.

'Harriet, dear,' said her mother, having given her a critical look, 'you appear to only be wearing a slip. Could you go and put on the dress that presumably goes over it?'

'There isn't one.' She bit her lips. 'I left my outfit behind,' she admitted. 'I wore this last night to a dinner dance.'

'Well, it's hardly suitable for lunch, is it?' said her mother.

'Otherwise it's my jeans and slightly grubby linen jacket.'

Leonie came forward. 'It's a lovely dress but it is a bit – well…'

'Revealing?' said Hattie.

'I don't suppose you've got a scarf or anything you could drape round yourself?' said Leonie.

'No, or I'd have draped it.'

'OK,' Leonie said briskly. 'You can wear my black leather jacket. Tom?'

'I'll fetch it from the car,' he said obligingly.

'Thank you, darling,' said Leonie.

'Yes, thank you, Tom,' said Hattie.

A few minutes in the Ladies while Leonie fiddled around with her leather jacket, turning back the sleeves a little, experimenting with the collar up and down, and Hattie was ready. 'Thank you so much, Lennie. I remembered everything, all the lists, the table plans, who's allergic to what. I had a whole emergency kit that Rose made up for me, with double-sided tape and everything. I even did Mum's hair. But I forgot the outfit.'

'What was it?' said Leonie, who was now repinning her own hair.

'Knee length, with a petticoat, fifties. It was really pretty.' She sighed.

'Vintage?'

'Borrowed from Mary, actually. You know? Who I live with?'

'Did she lend you that dress too?'

Hattie nodded. Suddenly, for no reason, she wanted to cry. She cleared her throat. 'I was so looking forward to wearing that outfit.'

'Well, this is a lovely dress too. Now.' Leonie burrowed in her handbag and produced a small scarf. 'It needs ironing really,' she said, 'but I think we'll manage.' She folded the scarf and then tied it round Hattie's neck. 'Mum still won't like it, but it actually looks great.'

Hattie looked at herself. 'You've become far less… buttoned-up lately,' she said. 'At one time only a dress and jacket, or maybe a coat and skirt, would have passed muster for this event. But I like this!'

'Oh, I don't think it's suitable,' said Leonie. 'It isn't at all. But as I said, it looks great.'

Hattie kissed her sister's cheek. 'Let's go. The guests will be milling around not able to find their clearly marked tables.'

Having finally got everyone to their places, Hattie took her own. She was on the table designated for people who had to be invited but didn't know anyone and were likely to feel awkward. She had put herself there because she knew she could make sure they enjoyed themselves. They included her mother's cleaning lady, Mrs Simpson, and her husband. She had worked for her parents for at least fifteen years but they were still on Mr and Mrs terms.

'I'm Hattie,' she said to the table as she sat down. 'The younger daughter. Our starters will be here in a minute and there'll be wine, but there's a bar. If anyone would like anything other than wine, I can get it. Gin and tonic? Cocktails?'

It took effort and quite a few drinks but eventually everyone on the table was chatting merrily, finding things in common (*Married at First Sight* proved to be generally popular viewing) and Hattie felt she could relax a bit.

Before the pudding, Hattie got up. 'I'd better check on everyone else. I was having such a good time I'd forgotten I was sort of on duty.'

It was to her parents' table that Hattie went first. 'How are you two? Enjoying yourselves, I hope. It's going well, isn't it?'

'Harriet?' said her mother. 'When is a long silk dress and a leather jacket appropriate for a Golden Wedding Anniversary lunch?'

'Well, it's not what I was planning to wear, as you know, but I think it works better than the dress on its own.'

Her mother nodded. 'Lots of people have said how lovely you look, so it probably does. You did arrange a photographer, didn't you?'

For a moment, Hattie's mind went blank, then she remembered. 'Yes, I did. I'll go and see if he's arrived. Are you saying a few words, Dad?'

As her father either didn't speak at all, or at great length, this was a tall order for him, but he nodded. 'Your mother has checked my speech.'

Hattie shuddered inwardly. 'I'll go and find the photographer.'

Leonie caught up with Hattie while she was in the kitchen, drinking a large glass of water.

'It's going awfully well, Hattie darling,' she said, revealing the fact that Tom was obviously the designated driver and Leonie had been enjoying the wine. 'And your outfit is lovely. I might try wearing something like that myself. You won't forget to give me my jacket back, will you?'

'Of course not,' said Hattie. 'And you would totally rock this look. Biker-girl chic.'

Tom, who had his arm round Leonie, said, 'I totally agree. Although there aren't many looks you couldn't "totally rock", my love,' he said fondly.

Leonie laughed and looked down, embarrassed but clearly thrilled.

The afternoon dragged at the speed of a glacier moving. Hattie, who liked being sociable and was meticulous about thanking staff and giving good tips (there had been firm words spoken to her father about amounts) thought she would never get away. And even then she found herself giving Mrs Simpson – or June, as she had soon come to call her – and her husband a lift home, because Derek, the husband, had drunk a little more than planned and couldn't drive. Hattie didn't blame him. She didn't mind not drinking as a rule, but she had been sorely tempted.

When she got back to her parents' house, she found the full extended family in the kitchen with plastic boxes of leftovers, half-used bottles of wine and a desire to gossip. Hattie slipped upstairs to get into her own clothes before going back down.

She had just put cheese on some crackers (there had been a lot of cheese left over) when she felt her phone buzz in her pocket. It had been out of reach all day. Now, when she looked at it, she saw about five missed calls from Mary. Her heart sank.

There was a message. 'Hattie? No need to worry, but I feel I should tell you, I won't be home when you get back. Clive has got me into a care home. I do hope the lunch went well.'

Hattie went cold, suddenly glad of the cardigan she had on under her linen jacket. She knew there had been a waiting list for the care home Mary wanted.

What sort of a home had he put Mary into with virtually no notice?

'Excuse me, everyone, there's been a bit of an emergency.'

Then she took her phone and went out of the room.

Chapter Twenty-Nine

It was nearly six o'clock before Hattie managed to get through to Mary. 'Are you all right?'

'Yes. A little tired.'

'You sound exhausted! Where are you? Are you in the home you wanted to be in?'

The tiniest of pauses was very revealing. 'Not quite, but I'm sure I can move later if I need to.'

Hattie took a breath. Mary probably didn't want to answer a barrage of questions just now but she felt she needed to know where her friend was. She didn't trust Clive further than Mary could have thrown him.

'I won't interrogate you now. Just give me the name of the care home and its address.'

'The name – well, "Whispering something" is the best I can do, I'm afraid. I don't know the address.'

'Don't worry. I can google it. How far from home are you?'

'It was quite a long drive. I slept through some of it…'

'I'll find it. And if it's in this direction, I'll come and see you tomorrow. And if it's nearer home, I'll call you first and see if there's anything that got left behind.'

'I feel so much better for talking to you. Clive was very – brisk. He didn't give me a lot of time to pack. I'm afraid I forgot my phone charger.'

'Don't worry about it. I'll sort it all out in the morning.'

Hattie noticed a message from Luke when she'd disconnected. For some reason just seeing his name made her breathe faster. She opened the message. It just said, *Thank you for last night. It meant so much. L x.* She didn't reply; she needed time to think of what to say.

Images of Luke in his dinner jacket, and rumpled – was it only this morning? – when he came out to check on her came into her mind. Just for a second she let herself think about him. But then she forced herself to focus on Mary and why Clive had whisked her away so quickly and where had he whisked her to?

She rejoined the family party in the kitchen and found herself next to Tom. 'You look a bit worried if you don't mind me saying so.'

Hattie smiled at him. 'I am a bit. I share a house with a quite elderly woman and her nephew has moved her into a care home with no notice at all. I don't know where she is. Although I'm sure I can track her down!' She laughed to disguise her anxiety. 'I've just spoken to her. She sounded a bit discombobulated. Can't blame her.'

'Do you have any clues as to where she might be?'

'Her home is called Whispering something.'

'But she has a mobile phone?'

'Yes. I've just spoken to her on it.'

'Then you can track her,' said Tom. 'There's an app you can get. I used it when I was on a school trip with a lot of teenagers. Obviously I deleted it afterwards but I can get you on it. Give me the number?'

'I'm not very good at technical things,' said Hattie apologetically. 'Except sites like Vinted and Etsy.'

'Me neither,' said Jacinta, a cousin about the same age as Hattie whom she had always liked. 'But I'm very nifty with eBay.'

'These young people,' said Hattie's mother. 'They seem to speak an entirely different language these days.'

'I suppose it was ever thus,' said Jacinta's mother, who was far more relaxed that her sister. 'I'm sure our parents said the same about us.'

'There you are,' said Tom, handing Hattie her phone. 'She's about an hour from here. And there's the address.'

'Thank you so much, Tom!' said Hattie. 'I am so grateful. I'll go and visit tomorrow and then I can stop worrying. I'm sure it'll be fine,' she added, not believing it.

Hattie left just before lunch the next day. All the clearing-up had been done. Beds stripped, leftovers rearranged into Tupperware and vases found for the very many bouquets of flowers that filled the house.

'Thank you, darling,' said her mother, to Hattie's surprise. 'You were really quite helpful in the end.'

Hattie hugged both her parents and left. Even praise this faint was more than she was used to. Her goodbyes to her sister and Tom were far warmer.

She drove to Whispering Willows (which had turned out to be the name) feeling very gloomy. This was not the elegant mansion in the pictures Mary had shown her of the home she wanted to move to. This was smaller, with random additions to the original building, and a garden that no one appeared to take any interest in. But if the people were kind, and Mary was comfortable, there was no need to make a fuss.

'We do like visitors to make an appointment,' said the woman on the desk, who seemed flustered. 'I don't know where Mrs Stanely is. It's Sunday. The chef's not working this lunchtime and we're very short-staffed.'

Hattie said, 'My friend only arrived yesterday so you may well not have met her. Point me in the right direction, and I'll go and look for her. I'm sure I can find her.'

'I couldn't possibly let you do that! I'd have to accompany you. But I can't leave the desk unattended.'

Panic made Hattie uncharacteristically sharp. 'I know you have a lot on your hands, Mrs – Wilson.' (She thanked goodness for name badges.) 'But I've come a long way to see Mrs Stanely. I'm afraid I must insist on you taking me to her. Or I'll have to write a lot of emails.' Hattie accompanied this with a look she had learnt from her mother.

Mrs Wilson pursed her lips. 'Follow me, then. But you will have to sign in first.'

Apart from a smell of some sort of meal – hard to define and probably eaten several hours ago – and a very faint odour of urine, there was nothing to tell Hattie that Mary wouldn't be happy here. But somehow Hattie knew she wouldn't be.

They found Mary in the television room. She was sitting in a chair and looked suddenly ten years older. Her expression of relief when she saw Hattie caused tears to spring to her eyes.

'I'll leave you to it,' said Mrs Wilson. 'But please don't stay too long. Our residents get very tired.'

'Oh, darling,' Mary said the moment she and Hattie were alone. 'How lovely to see you.'

Hattie swallowed. 'Lovely to see you too! But how on earth did you get here? Did you know you were coming?'

Mary shook her head. 'Clive came round on Friday evening and said he'd arranged a home for me. He expected me to be pleased, and I suppose I had been saying I'd wanted to go to one for a while, but it wasn't the one I had chosen.'

'And he wanted you to go that night?'

Mary nodded. 'He packed me a suitcase, put me in the car and here I am. Of course I haven't got any of the things I really wanted with me. If he'd let me leave it until the following day, I could have packed myself.'

'What about your medication?'

'I've got the little box but I'm not sure about the one I take at night. I didn't take it last night.'

'Well, don't worry. It's probably all right to miss one. We'll make a list of everything you need and I'll go and get it for you.'

'Do I have to stay here?'

Hattie had no idea really. 'It might be best to stay for a few days, to let yourself recover from the drama of being plucked out of your house and deposited somewhere else.' Hattie smiled to imply she was joking, but she wasn't. 'Then, when you've had time to gather your wits, we can make a plan.'

'I'm very tempted to ask you to take me straight home now but I am tired, and I think it would be foolish. The staff are very kind here, even if, aesthetically, it's not where I want to live. There's not much garden. I need a garden around me.'

Hattie nodded. 'Is there anything I can get for you locally? I can find a supermarket and get you underwear, nighties, things like that?'

'Clive tipped my entire underwear drawer into the case, so I don't need knickers. But it's personal things like my little radio. My pillow, my eye mask and my skin cream. I also want my old cardigan. I've had it so long it's falling apart but it's comforting.'

Hattie wanted to cry again. 'Well, don't worry. We'll make a list, and I'll bring everything you need.'

'Maybe I'll make the list tomorrow, when I've had a chance to think what I really do need. I wouldn't want you to have to come twice. It's a long way.' She paused. 'I'd fallen asleep in the car, so I felt very disorientated when I arrived. The nurses called me dear, which I know was kindly meant, but it made me feel old and anonymous.'

'I'm so sorry,' said Hattie. 'Now, have you got anything to read?'

'Apparently there's a library but I haven't found it yet.'

'I'll find it and bring you back some books. Otherwise, as I said, I can pop to a supermarket.'

'I just hope I've got my reading glasses.'

'Let's have a look. They're probably in your handbag, surely?'

Mary shrugged. 'They were probably lying around with everything else. I don't know exactly what Clive scooped up before we left.'

Hattie nodded again. 'OK, you see if your reading glasses are in your bag and I'll find the library and bring you some books. If you haven't got reading glasses I can probably buy some.'

★ ★ ★

It was late afternoon before Hattie headed home. She had left Mary with a pile of books, (Jacqueline Susann, Georgette Heyer and Ethel M. Dell) and a new pair of reading glasses as well as lots of other comforts. Chocolate ginger biscuits, chocolates and a box of Jaffa Cakes. She was planning to go back with Mary's own reading glasses and a lot of other things that Clive had left. She was very tired. So much had happened since she'd set off from home to join Luke for the dinner dance. She decided to have a nap; then she'd deal with everything that needed to be done.

It was a shock to see that the back door had been tampered with and more of a shock to realise her key no longer fitted, which meant the locks had been changed. She took a lot of deep breaths and rushed into the garden for a wild wee. She couldn't do anything about anything while she was so desperate after the long drive.

She rinsed her hands in the water butt and then got out her phone. She pressed on Clive's number, swearing to herself she would be calm and controlled. Being hysterical was what he wanted her to be.

'Clive! Hi!' She sounded as friendly as she could. 'I was just wondering how to get into Mary's house, where I live. Have you left me a key anywhere handy? Under a flower pot? I discovered you've changed the locks.'

'Yes I have and I'm afraid you don't live there any more. I'll be selling the house to pay for Mary's care home.'

'But my things are inside. And I visited Mary: there are a lot of things she needs too.'

'What can she need? I packed everything for her.'

'I have a list.'

'Oh. Well, I'm away at the moment.'

'I can't do without my personal belongings. And nor can Mary. She doesn't even have her reading glasses.'

'I'm sure she can manage without reading for a week or so.'

'How little you know your aunt, Clive.'

'Don't get shirty with me! You've been sponging off my aunt and that doesn't give you the right to tell me what she needs. Anything but!' The line went silent.

Hattie stood outside the house, beginning to shiver. The warmth of the day had dissipated.

At a complete loss, she drove herself to Rose's house. When Rose opened the door, Hattie asked, 'Can I stay the night?' and burst into tears.

Chapter Thirty

Hattie found herself taken into Rose and Sam's comfortable, comforting home. She ended up on the huge squishy sofa, a colourful throw wrapped around her, a glass of red wine in her hand, while Sam made a fire in the big old inglenook fireplace and Rose made cheese on toast.

'I'm sorry I can't offer you supper,' she said. 'We're doing intermittent fasting so ate very early.'

'Although I could easily knock up some quick pasta,' said Sam, now he'd got the fire going.

'Honestly, cheese on toast is perfect. Just the smell is making me start to relax.'

'I've got some fantastic olives,' said Sam. 'If you're in the mood for snacks.' He left the room, heading for the kitchen.

'You know food is his love language,' said Rose. 'Now, tell me everything. I want to know all the details, and not just how Clive changed the locks on Mary's house. Start with Luke on Friday night.'

It seemed to be several lifetimes ago, instead of just a couple of days.

Hattie was being too slow to finish her mouthful for Rose. 'Were you happy with your outfit? The silk dress?'

'Oh, yes, I was! I actually went to the hairdresser and had my hair put up. With the flower from your shop behind my ear. It did feel pretty good.'

'What did Luke think?'

To her surprise, she realised she was blushing. She hoped Rose wouldn't notice, given that she was already blotchy from crying. 'I think he liked it. He looked very good himself. He scrubs up well.'

Rose didn't comment. 'And what are his friends like?'

Hattie crunched a sourdough crust. 'A bit daunting. At least, I think I felt daunted because they'd all known each other for years and looked at me as if I were a mythical creature. One of them told me they didn't think Luke knew any women, let alone that Luke had a girlfriend.'

Rose pursed her lips but didn't comment. 'But you passed muster?'

Hattie thought back. 'Yes, I did.'

'And what was the dinner like?'

'Fairly boring. And Luke didn't win the award he was up for.'

'And you had a room? How was sharing it?'

'Rose! Is this some form of interrogation? It was absolutely fine. The bed was massive. Then I had to get up very early to leave.'

'And so, you and Luke—'

'You know there is no "me and Luke", Rose.'

'You can't give your sentimental friend a little hope that one day you and Luke will be more than best buddies?'

Hattie shook her head and took an olive from the bowl that had just appeared at her side. 'You know me. I can't risk losing him.' But was she still so sure she would lose him? She felt more confused about Luke than ever.

Rose pursed her lips again. 'OK, so tell me about your parents' party.'

Hattie took a big sip of wine, draining the glass. 'Well! The big news there was that I forgot my outfit!'

Sam topped up her wine and put another bowl next to the olives. 'Chocolate-covered almonds with sea salt. I made them myself.'

'You forgot your outfit?' Rose was horrified.

'Sam? You are an actual angel.' Hattie squeezed his arm before he retreated to the other sofa. She turned to Rose. 'I know! I had so many lists. I remembered everything – your bag of emergency supplies really came into its own. I was super-organised and yet, somehow, the outfit is still on its hanger, under its cover, in Mary's house which I may never get into again.'

'Oh, don't worry about that!' said Rose with a flap of her hand. 'We'll break in. So what did you wear instead?'

'My peacock-coloured silk dress! Lennie lent me her black leather jacket and a little neckerchief. To try to make it more daytime.'

'I do hope there are pictures,' said Rose.

'There are loads. Some on my phone. Do you want to look now?'

'Later,' said Rose. 'I want to know about Mary.'

This was the less entertaining bit of the story and by the time Hattie had finished it, Sam and Rose were both looking angry.

Hattie suddenly felt tireder than ever. 'Honestly, I seem to have spent so much time sorting out everyone else and yet somehow I'm homeless, again, and depending on good friends for a roof over my head.'

'Which, considering your line of work, could be seen as bad management,' said Sam.

'But not your fault!' Rose put in hastily. 'You haven't done anything wrong and yet—'

'I still find myself in this ridiculous situation,' said Hattie. 'I am definitely going to make finding myself a home, that's mine to live in, a top priority. Just as soon as Mary is properly settled.'

'I have to leave really early tomorrow. I've got a meeting,' said Sam. 'But if you two want to break into Mary's house in the morning, I'll dig out my tools.'

'It seems the only answer,' said Hattie.

'Haven't you got a locksmith on speed dial?' asked Rose, possibly shocked by Hattie's reaction to the problem.

'Of course, but the call-out fee is terrifying. I'd rather deal with this ourselves if we can.'

'I'll call Anne and ask her to open up the shop for me,' said Rose. 'Now, Hattie? What else do you need?'

After a little more chatting and nibbling Hattie got into a scented bath that Rose had run for her. Then she picked her way round the numerous boxes of stock for the shop that filled Rose and Sam's spare bedroom, got into bed and slept.

Chapter Thirty-One

'How are you feeling this morning?' asked Rose when Hattie appeared in the kitchen the following morning.

'Great, actually,' she said. 'I slept like a log and now I feel I can take on the world! Or Clive, whichever one challenges me first.'

Rose laughed and put a large mug of tea by Hattie. 'So you're not daunted by the prospect of a little breaking and entering? Toast?'

'Yes, please. And no, I've sometimes had to be a bit – er – creative – in how I've got into some houses I've gone to view. Not with clients, of course. But sometimes the doors are completely seized up.'

'Well, Sam's left his tools,' said Rose. She pointed to a worn hessian bag by the back door. 'They were his dad's. I'm not sure what's in there.'

Hattie nodded. 'I'm sure we'll find something that does the job.'

'So, what will you do when you've liberated your things, and Mary's, of course?'

'Once I've got Mary's things to her, I'll see if I can go back to the lodge. But I'll have to make a few calls to rearrange my day first. I need to check if the survey has been done for Nick for one thing.'

Shortly afterwards, Hattie and Rose set off for Mary's house.

'You're quite sure Clive isn't going to come back and catch us at it?' asked Rose, not quite so willing to wield a large screwdriver as Hattie appeared to be.

'I don't care if he does,' said Hattie. 'He kidnapped Mary and put her in a home without her medication.' She had halted her prowl round the outside of the house by the French doors. 'In fact, it's my bounden duty to break in. Although of course I will try not to make our entry visible. And I'll only take what's mine and what Mary needs.'

In spite of trying to be careful, there was a certain amount of splintering timber as she eased open the door. In fact, it turned out that the door was fairly rotten. The lock held, but the wood gave way easily. It was all a lot messier than Hattie had intended.

'It's a shame that Luke can't come and repair that for us,' she said, stepping into the house.

'Can't he?' asked Rose, following her.

Hattie shook her head. 'He's away dealing with snagging on a job, and he's not to know about this.'

'Why not?'

'Because he'd come back and fix it and we can manage without him. I don't want him going to all that trouble. Now, Mary's things. We'd better find a suitcase.'

'And another for your things,' said Rose.

'Fortunately, I brought a suitcase when I moved in. All my other bits and pieces are in a friend's stable.'

'Another reason why you should find a home of your own,' said Rose. 'Stables aren't a safe place really.'

'True! I share mine with chickens and they do not stick to their half.'

'No boundaries, chickens. Now, what's on Mary's list?'

When they thought they had everything that Mary had asked for, Hattie called her. 'I'm in the house, Mary.' She didn't think Mary needed to know how they got in. She then listed everything she and Rose had got together for her. 'Is there anything I've forgotten?'

'Did you find my pills? I don't know what they're for, but I find myself feeling a little odd without them. They can't get a local GP to visit for a while, or I could have asked for another prescription.' She paused. 'I could contact the chemist who sends them to me but—'

'I know,' said Hattie. 'It's not simple. But don't worry, I've found them and I'll pop down with everything later today.'

'I'm putting you to an awful lot of trouble—'

Hattie interrupted her. 'Not at all. I'm quite happy to come and see you again.'

'But it's so far!'

'It'll be fine. Now, is there anything else?'

'There is one big favour…'

'Yes?'

'I want you to take the dresses – you know the ones I mean. I don't know what Clive has planned but he won't know the value of them and I don't want them ending up in a skip.'

'I can't bear to think of anything of yours ending up in a skip,' said Hattie, tears suddenly catching at her throat.

'Nor can I!' said Mary. 'But we must face facts, my dear.'

Hattie didn't reply. 'I could arrange to have all the furniture taken away. It could go in...' She hesitated as she thought of the rustic conditions her own few possessions were kept in. '... my lock-up. There's plenty of space.'

Rose looked horrified. 'What would Clive say? And you don't have a lock-up. You have half a stable!' she said in a stage whisper.

Hattie turned away so she couldn't see her friend. 'Would you like me to do that, Mary? Arrange for everything to be taken out before Clive gets back?'

'He could accuse you of stealing,' said Rose, a bit louder now. 'And he wouldn't be far wrong!'

'What would you like me to do, Mary?' Hattie repeated.

Mary didn't answer. 'I wouldn't want you to do anything that could get you into trouble...'

'But?'

'Yes, I would like that. If I can go to the home I chose I'll be able to have a few of my own things around me. The rooms there are a great deal bigger – I could have a bedroom and a sitting room. It would mean a lot to me to have my familiar things.'

'Right,' said Hattie. 'I'm going to go round the house with my phone, Mary, and you tell me which items of furniture you want to keep. Then we'll come back with a removal van.'

'And I'll stick on a Post-it note as we go,' said Rose, producing a pad of them from her bag.

'Why have you got Post-its in your bag?' asked Hattie.

Rose shrugged. 'It's who I am.'

It seemed to take ages to go through the house, letting Mary look at every piece, including ornaments, and make up her mind if she wanted it or not. But at last they were done. They left the cottage through the French doors and then Hattie tried to close the broken door behind them.

'I think I will ask Luke to sort this out when he's back,' she said to Rose, trying to return a bit of wood to its former home with mixed results.

'How long is he away for?'

'I'm not sure,' said Hattie. 'Clive might be back before he is. We just have to hope he doesn't notice the house has been broken into.'

'But aren't you hoping to get all of Mary's furniture out before then?'

Hattie sighed. 'You're right. A broken door panel won't really matter then, will it? But I want to make it safe from burglars.'

Rose laughed. 'Honey, if we broke in that easily, a professional burglar would have no problem.'

Hattie paused in her gentle hammering. 'So I shouldn't bother with this?'

'You're not making much impression.'

'I don't want to risk breaking the glass.'

In the end they left it so the door stayed shut, aided by a large stone propped against it. It was by no means secure but it was the best they could do.

As they drove away, Rose asked, 'Won't it be difficult to get removers in before Clive's back? Aren't they booked up months ahead?'

'Usually they are,' said Hattie, 'but I'm the house-moving fairy. I can get one when I need one.' She paused. 'Mostly because I've got a friend with a horse box who'll do it very cheaply.'

Rose laughed. 'I must confess to feeling very nervous in there. I thought Clive was going to arrive any minute.'

'I was nervous too. Although I don't know why. He made me homeless in a way that I'm sure is completely illegal.'

'How sure are you?' asked Rose.

'I'm sure he shouldn't have whisked Mary away like that, leaving her medication behind. Or cut me off from my possessions. I pay rent. That must afford me some protection. I'll look it up when I've got a minute. Now, I'd like to get Mary's things down to her immediately. Where would you like to be dropped off? At home or at the shop?'

'Neither! Let's have a road trip. I'll come to Mary's with you.'

'I'd love that!' Hattie said. 'And Mary would be delighted to see you.'

On the way home, after a very enjoyable visit with Mary and a late lunch in a pub garden, Rose said, 'Of course, normally you'd be welcome to stay with us as long as you like but Sam's mother is coming.' Rose frowned. 'Could I use you as an excuse so she can't come?'

'No. And it's OK, I'm going to move back to the lodge. It's perfect for one, though not for the long term when Xander comes back.'

'Isn't it an Airbnb now?'

'Which means I can rent it. I'm sure it'll be fine!' She wasn't quite as sure as she sounded but she didn't want Rose to worry.

'And you won't have to pay?'

'No, I will have to pay. But when Xander comes back, I can ask Leonie to go halves till I find a long-term rental.' She paused. 'She's so much nicer and more approachable since she met Tom.'

'Your visions do come in handy, don't they?' Rose laughed.

Hattie sighed. 'Yes, but don't tell anyone about it.'

'Hattie! I never would. You know that! I haven't even told Sam and he benefited from your visions directly.'

'I know. I just wish I wasn't so weird, sometimes!'

'We love you weird.'

'Well, you do.'

'And Luke does—'

'Luke and I are just good friends!'

'You may see him as a friend, but he adores you. You must know he does.'

'He's a very good friend indeed.'

'And he loves you.'

Did he love her? she wondered. Could he? And could she love him? Hattie sighed deeply. 'I haven't got head-space to think about any of that now. I'm practically homeless.'

'Don't say that! I feel guilty enough already.'

'Don't be silly!'

'I'd much rather have you there than my mother-in-law. She's quite sweet really, but I sense her disapproval. She talks about clutter a lot, and you know I hate it when people do that. My house isn't cluttered; it's just I'm a maximalist.'

'I love your home, Rose. I won't hear a word against it.'

'And as your reward for your support of my style, I'm going to create some proper labels to put on the furniture. The Post-its might drop off.'

'That would be very kind.' Hattie sighed. 'I'm going to text Clive again,' she said. 'See when he's due back. We need to get the furniture moved before then.'

'Is he not due to inherit the furniture?'

'I don't think so. Mary would have said. She's very meticulous.'

'But I'm not entirely sure that taking the contents would be legal, even if they're not due to be his,' said Rose.

'I agree it feels very much like stealing,' said Hattie.

'Do you know anyone in the legal profession?'

Hattie laughed. 'Of course I do! But actually, I'd rather not ask them about this. I wouldn't want them to think I had a side hustle as a burglar.'

Rose laughed. A few seconds later, she said, 'Ask them anyway.' She paused. 'What about Mary's vintage clothes? They can't go in a lock-up or a stable,' she said. 'They could be ruined.'

'What else can I do with them?' said Hattie. 'I don't want to leave them for Clive. He'll sell them but for not nearly enough money.'

'Besides, Mary wants you to have them. Don't worry. I'll find somewhere for them. Sam's mother can't need an entire wardrobe for her things, can she? She's only staying for a few nights.'

'But she'll moan!' said Hattie.

'I don't care. She'll moan anyway. She might as well have a reason.'

Hattie stayed one more night with Rose and Sam, earning her keep by helping Rose put several boxes of shop supplies in the loft the following morning. 'I will need to get this room a lot clearer before she comes.

Sam is lovely, most of the time, but he treats his mother as if she's the queen and has to have everything perfect.'

'Oh dear! That can't be easy to live with.'

'It's not great, but as we only have his mother about once a year, it's not really worth the trouble of divorcing him for.'

Hattie laughed. 'I'm glad of that! My visions are supposed to pair people for life, or what's the point of having them?'

'You don't like having them, do you?'

Hattie shook her head. 'Life would be so much easier if I didn't. But on the other hand, finding a man for Leonie would be a real result.'

'When is Xander due back?'

'I'm not entirely sure. He's spending August with his father, which means at least another couple of weeks or so. I suppose he might go and stay with Lennie afterwards. I'm sure someone will tell me. I gather their summers are always a bit fluid.'

'Have you got time for another cup of coffee before work?' asked Rose. 'I should go myself but I'd love an excuse to linger a bit.'

'No, I must get on. I have a lot to do today.'

Since she had not heard back from her landlord about the lodge, Hattie decided to sleep at Mary's house for a few days, trusting Clive wouldn't find her out, even though it made her a bit anxious. She fleetingly considered phoning Luke and seeing if she could stay there, but decided she'd rather manage on her own. She couldn't let herself get dependent on Luke.

It was two nights later, as she went round the house replacing Post-its with some very pretty labels that

Rose had designed especially ('Only the best for Mary,' she'd said), that Hattie realised the stable just wouldn't be big enough. She would have to rent a lock-up to fit everything into. Moving from room to room she found herself redecorating in her head. The rooms were so full of light she could have dark colours or wallpaper – things that could have made another house seem smaller. She sighed. She'd never get the opportunity to do anything to the house now.

Knowing she was wasting time, Hattie still couldn't help looking on her phone for wallpaper. She found the perfect thing for the bedroom. It was Zoffany, with small flowers. It managed to look vintage but not dated. But seeing the price per roll made Hattie almost relieved she wasn't going to have it in real life. She would be tempted to have a washstand to go with it, and a large jug and basin. Rose would help her source a cheaper version of the wallpaper if she ever found herself actually living here.

She shook her head sharply and ran her fingers through her hair; it was all just a dream anyway. This house could never be hers.

When she'd done the labels, she settled herself with a cup of tea before getting out her phone again to look for storage solutions. She did hope Mary could go to the home of her choice very soon and not just for Mary's sake – the units were expensive!

Hattie got lucky and by the evening of the following day everything Mary had wanted to save from the house was stored; she had added a frighteningly large amount to her credit card and still didn't have anywhere to live herself but it felt as if she'd done the hard bit.

She was just in a supermarket, getting some things for supper, milk, bread, things like that, when there was a ping on her phone. It was a text from Fiona.

Hattie! Just checking in to say hi! I'd love to get together so we can thank you for everything and have a proper catch up. I love Nick's new house, by the way! You could almost have had me in mind when you found it for him! I also want to hear all your news.

She was tapping out a reply as her old landlord finally called to say the lodge was – unfortunately for her – booked up.

She added some wine and chocolate to her trolley: she'd have to slink back to Mary's. At least there was a bed to sleep on, heating, light, a kettle. And Clive hadn't come near the place. She'd be fine.

Chapter Thirty-Two

Hattie came home from the supermarket to find Clive sitting on her bed.

'Well, well, well,' he said. 'If it isn't the glamorous house hunter I've caught squatting in my aunt's house!'

Hattie put her bag on the floor, glad most of her possessions were safely in her car. 'If it isn't the man who made me homeless.' She wanted to add 'totally illegally' but she hadn't had time to check if that was actually true. 'You know perfectly well that Mary wouldn't mind me staying here.' She held his gaze trying to convey confidence.

'Have you asked her?'

Hattie felt herself blush and hoped Clive wouldn't notice. 'She's got a lot to get used to, being put in a home which was not of her choosing and far away from everyone who visits her.'

If she was trying to make Clive feel guilty she immediately knew she'd failed.

'She wanted to be in a home and she's in one. Now it's up to me to sell this place to make enough money to pay for it!'

'Well, you'd better get on with it, then.' Hattie was boiling with rage.

'How did you get in? I had the locks changed.'

'I noticed. But this house isn't very secure, as you must have realised.'

'I can make it secure.' He glared at her as if this was a threat. 'Anyway,' he went on. 'I thought you wanted to buy this house.'

This gave Hattie pause. Surely Clive wasn't going to be helpful? 'In an ideal world, I would, yes.'

'I'll sell it to you. But it needs to be fast. I can give you till the day after the bank holiday, otherwise it'll go on the market.'

Hattie studied him. Surely there'd be a catch. 'What price are you hoping to achieve?'

He told her. It was at least twenty thousand less than its market value, even in its current condition. Her heart rate increased. Was her dream home suddenly within reach?

'OK,' she said calmly. 'I'll undertake to have my mortgage in place by then.'

'You seem very certain.'

Hattie shrugged. 'I am in the business. I have contacts.'

The following morning she started early. She had a lot to do. She needed to chase up some paperwork for Mrs Conway, her lovely client with champagne tastes on beer money, she needed to show another client round another house that she knew wasn't going to be the one and she needed to see her friend who arranged mortgages. The last one was for her.

By the time she landed at her friend's place she felt exhausted. It wasn't the running around after people and searching for rural properties down country lanes, it was the anxiety rumbling in the back of her mind. Could she really buy Mary's house?

'Coffee or tea?' asked Susie, seeing Hattie collapse in the chair opposite her. 'Or just water?'

'Water and then tea, please.'

Susie also produced biscuits. 'Now,' she said. 'What's going on?'

Hattie explained. 'He's given me ten days to get it all together, which will not be easy.' She handed Susie a sheet which had all her calculations on it.

Susie put on her reading glasses and studied the paper. 'That house is a bit under underpriced, actually, but you know that.'

Hattie nodded. 'I can just about manage at that price, if you can get me a mortgage – at a decent rate.'

Susie bit on her bottom lip, her eyes still on the paper. 'I can probably get you a mortgage if you've got at least three years' accounts – which you have, don't you?'

'Yes, of course.'

'And deposit. I see here you have some savings, and you've got some Premium Bonds.'

Hattie nodded. 'I bought them with money my grandmother left me. I don't have quite enough but I'm hoping I can get there. I could sell my car but I would have to buy another one.'

'The Bank of Mum and Dad?' suggested Susie.

Hattie shook her head. 'They are never open!'

'Really?'

Hattie shook her head. 'They never had a hand up when they were starting out; "neither a borrower nor a lender be"; and I have to make my own way in the world, I am not a child.'

Susie laughed. 'It sounds as if you've asked them for money before.'

Hattie shook her head. 'Not since I wanted to buy a second-hand bicycle when I was ten. And to be fair they didn't say I wasn't a child back then, but I'm in no doubt what the answer would be should I ask for help. It's for my own good,' she finished.

'How annoying!' said Suzie. 'Have you any other savings?'

'I could try and get a loan—'

Susie frowned. 'Mortgage lenders don't like loans as part of a deposit. They think you'd be over-reaching yourself.'

'Once I've got the house I can get a lodger, maybe take on an extra job.'

Susie obviously didn't approve of this idea. 'I'll have a good look and see what I can put together, but every penny you can add to that deposit figure is going to help your chances.'

'But you might be able to help?'

Suzie made a face. 'They don't call me the Mortgage Queen for nothing.'

Hattie couldn't help laughing. 'I didn't know they called you that.'

'It's a title I aspire to.' Susie said primly and then smiled. 'Don't look so gloomy. I'm sure there's something I can do.'

Rose had invited her to dinner, to 'dilute the mother-in-law'. Hattie accepted gladly.

Rose's mother-in-law seemed pleasant enough, but she sat in Rose's gorgeous house, full of pattern and colour, wearing a beige skirt and cardigan as if she was in a strange land, one not of her choosing.

Hattie could see the lengths Rose was going to to make her comfortable and how her mother-in-law was refusing to enjoy the attention.

It wasn't long before Rose whisked Hattie away on the pretence of showing her something in her garden, so Rose could unburden herself.

'I try so hard to make her happy but nothing seems to work! And Sam just tuts at me all the time. He turns into a needy child when she's around. Nothing I do is good enough!'

'Oh, Rose! That's awful! I'm so sorry. When does she go?'

'Tomorrow. I'd have to kill her if she stayed any longer.'

'Maybe you're making her too welcome?'

Rose laughed. 'Perhaps I am! Now, what's going on with you?'

'I'm not sure I've got time to tell you. Won't your mother-in-law wonder where we are?'

'Sam can look after her. I need to know about you!'

'Clive has given me ten days to sort out my finances. If I do, he'll sell the house to me. It won't go on the open market.'

'Imagine if you could actually buy Mary's house – the dream!' Rose squeezed her friend's hand. 'And the deposit? Can you get one together?'

'That's the problem. Probably not. I have some savings but not enough – and I gather getting a loan from the bank is not usually acceptable.'

Rose hesitated. 'Have you told Luke about this?'

'He doesn't need to know. Besides, he's miles away on a job. Why should I tell him? We're just friends!'

'Honey, I'm your friend. But you're telling me,' said Rose quietly.

Hattie took a few breaths. She was worried that if Luke knew she was short of money, he'd offer to lend it to her. 'Cheaper than a bank loan!' She could almost hear him say it. He might offer her his house to live in. But she didn't want him to sort out her problems for her. She wanted to do it herself.

She smiled at Rose. 'You're different.'

Rose appeared to accept this and changed the subject. 'So what do you think about my mother-in-law? Sweet old lady? Or a witch?'

Hattie laughed, relieved Rose wasn't pressing her about her feelings for Luke. 'She is quite hard work.'

'Ain't that the truth! We'd better go back.'

'I'll try and engage her in conversation. What does she like?'

'She doesn't watch TV or read modern novels. How are you on classical music?'

Hattie came home from a long day to discover that the gas and electricity had been turned off. She stood in the kitchen, breathing deeply before testing the tap. She could manage without power but not without water. Luckily the tap still ran.

She went out to her car to find the box she thought of as 'for emergency use only'. It included a camping kettle. She brought it in, hoping there was some gas in the cylinder.

She sat at the kitchen table with a couple of candles for light. This was mad behaviour from Clive, and could she trust him to do what he said? But if she got him the money, it would be worth it. She'd have her dream cottage and never have to speak to him again.

She moved one of the candles nearer, and found the calculator option on her phone. She was redoing her sums, hoping to get a different answer this time. She had a few days left until Clive's deadline. Susie had found her a likely mortgage lender, but the problem was still the deposit. What with her savings, Premium Bonds, now cashed in, and a small pension from when she'd had a job as an estate agent, she was nearly there. But nearly wasn't good enough, she knew.

When her phone rang, she nearly dropped it.

'Oh, hi! Lennie!' she said.

'Hello. You sound a bit startled,' said her sister.

'I'm fine. I was just doing some calculations.'

'Sorry to disturb you. I was just confirming that Xander can come back to you – just for the beginning of the term? It's been so good to have him here, I think he likes Switzerland. He seems to get on with Tom really well…'

With everything else that had been going on, Hattie had totally lost track of Xander's movements, and had never really grasped when the new term began. When had he gone to Switzerland? She'd thought he was fixed in Scotland for August. 'So Tom's been there?' she said to cover her startlement.

'The advantage of working in education,' said Leonie. 'Very long holidays.' Her sister was obviously smiling when she said this, something that Hattie was very glad to hear.

Now Hattie laughed. 'I'd love to have Xander back but I'm just not sure where I'll be living.' And whether it will have heat, light and cooking facilities, she added silently.

'Oh? I thought you were in Mary's house?'

'I am, but Clive wants to sell it. I'm trying to buy it.'

'What's stopping you?'

'The fact I'm short on the deposit and his ridiculous deadline is looming. Oh, Lennie! I want this house so badly!'

Her sister didn't reply immediately. 'How much are you short? Granny left us both money and I haven't spent all mine.'

Hattie gave her the figures, and found herself telling Leonie all the things she'd thought of doing to get herself out of this mess. Leonie interrupted. 'I'm not absolutely sure how long it will take for me to get the money into your account, but I assume if the money is in the ether, on its way to you, that will be enough? I can send you confirmation of the transfer request.'

Hattie was overcome. 'Lennie! You can't do that! I—'

Her sister interrupted her. 'Think of all you've done for Xander! And anyway, you don't need to be too grateful, it's a loan—'

'Which I'll pay back as soon as possible.'

'I'm sure you will.'

Hattie felt tears gather in her throat making it impossible to speak for a moment. She coughed. 'Lennie, I can't tell you what this means to me. It isn't only that this is the house of my dreams, but having it will mean I'm not always camping in other people's houses, wondering when I'll have to move again.' She sniffed, found a tissue in her sleeve and blew her nose. She looked around her; the building was old and in need of a lot of care, but it would be hers. She could make a life here.

'Are you crying? No need for that! Go and make yourself a cup of tea.'

When the sisters had disconnected, Hattie's tears had turned to laughter at her sister's ever-practical reaction and then did as she was told. Luckily there was enough camping gas.

Clive arrived on the Tuesday morning, at least an hour earlier than they had arranged. Hattie found it very difficult to be civil to him, but grateful that she was dressed, at least.

'You turned off the gas and electricity,' she said, as he entered.

He smiled. 'All part of prepping for the house sale.'

'How kind,' she said. 'But it means I can't offer you anything to drink now.'

'That's fine. I've already had a very nice cappuccino and a pastry from the bread van. I don't need anything.'

Hattie could tell he was hoping that she would be desperate for coffee and a shower, and while both would have been welcome, she'd been having showers at Rose's house; Rose and Sam had been delighted at the good news about her sister helping her find the money just in time. She had also bought a new gas canister; he had obviously wanted make her very uncomfortable but hadn't succeeded: she wasn't going to feel bullied.

'Well, as my duties as a hostess are not required we can get down to business. I've got the finances sorted.'

She had the satisfaction of seeing him look surprised for a moment.

'I have a lender—'

'Prove it.'

Hattie showed him the offer she had in principle.

'That's not a firm offer—'

'You said I had to have everything sorted by today. You didn't specify I had to have it done' – she glanced at her phone – 'by seven twenty in the morning.'

Clive raised an eyebrow, as if acknowledging this.

'The deposit will be in my account later today.' Hattie mentally crossed her fingers. 'And I've arranged for the lender's valuation survey to be done this afternoon. I am going to visit Mary now,' she went on. 'Would you like to give me a message for her? You haven't been to see her since you put her in that home, have you?'

'It's a perfectly good establishment,' he snapped. 'Nothing wrong with it.'

Hattie inclined her head. 'Apart from the fact it's many miles away from her family and friends. And it smells.' She drew a breath. 'Now, if you don't mind, I've got a long day ahead of me. I need to get on.'

Chapter Thirty-Three

Hattie hadn't intended to tell Mary quite how awful Clive had been but she found herself doing it anyway. Mary was appalled.

'I can't believe he turned off the gas and electricity,' she said.

Hattie shrugged. 'It was only for a short while. I mean, he probably won't put it on again, but once I know the house is mine, I won't care! Although I do hope I'll be able to sort it all before Xander comes back.'

'Darling, I am so sorry you're having to buy it! I wanted to give it to you.'

'But, Mary, if you'd left it to me in your will, like you've always said you wanted to, I wouldn't have you!' She took hold of Mary's hand. 'I'd much rather keep you forever. And my buying it means we'll be able to get you moved to the home you really wanted. Clive – or rather you – will have the money so you can go where you want. Or you could come back and live with me! There'd be plenty of money for alterations if they were needed.'

Mary smiled and patted Hattie's hand. 'That is a lovely offer, and I'd certainly like to come and stay, but although my current home isn't quite what I'd have chosen, the staff are very kind. They are around all day and I... well, I feel safe here. My room may be small, but it's nicely cosy. And I have lots of company.' She pursed her lips. 'Clive handled it all very badly, but it hasn't ended up too bad. Apart from being so far away from you.'

'If you're sure. The offer is always there.'

Neither of them spoke for a few moments. Hattie felt very emotional and could see that Mary was too.

Then Hattie cleared her throat. 'Well, once I'm settled in you can come and look round it and tut at the changes I've made.'

Mary laughed. 'I shall look forward to it! Although I will be having words with Clive. He's my nephew, not my jailor. In fact, I'm going to do that right now. You go and explore the gardens – such as they are!'

Hattie could see Mary had made up her mind, so she dutifully took herself outside. Her first impressions were borne out – the gardens were definitely unloved. After a few minutes she came back to find Mary looking rather cross, so made haste to distract her. 'Now, have you thought where you'd like to go for lunch? And maybe we can go round the supermarket afterwards. You can go in one of those wheelchairs with a basket attached to the front.'

'Which would beat having to sit in the baby seat on the top,' said Mary. 'And as for lunch, there's quite a nice hotel we can go to; one of the residents took her son the other day and had good things to say. And lunch is on me. I am very aware of how much I've cost you recently. Now come on! Before the smell of fish pie reaches us from the dining room.'

Hattie and Mary ate lunch looking on to a very well-kept garden which made Mary ask about Hattie's plans.

'Have you had any ideas about what you might do in my old garden?' she asked.

'Well, not very much. It's so well planted and I really love it as it is. But I would like to make the paths wider, and take out the steps where I can. I want to be able to wheel an old lady I know round it.'

'Darling! I'd love that! Latterly, for a few years really, I hadn't been able to get to the level at the top of the hill, where my bench is. I'd love to see that bit again.'

'And so you shall.' Hattie smiled.

'And while I've got you softened up, I'm giving you this cheque. I gather people do still use them. It's for the storage unit. I've been chatting to an old chap who's in here – probably ten years younger than I am – and he was telling me how expensive they are.'

'I didn't think I'd told you that I'd rented one.' Hattie thought hard but couldn't remember doing it.

'You didn't tell me. I worked it out. Now,' she went on briskly, obviously changing the subject, 'let's look at the puddings. It'll make me uncomfortably full, but then I won't need supper.'

'That's a very good point,' said Hattie. 'A raspberry tart with clotted cream seems positively sensible!'

After a delightfully long lunch and a shopping trip, Hattie delivered Mary back. Having put all the little treats they had bought at the supermarket to hand, and had a cup of tea, she took her leave of her. Before she set off for home, she checked her bank account. Leonie's money was there! She had her deposit. The repairs Luke had made meant she was not worried about the lender's valuation survey, especially as Clive was asking less than he could for the property. Before the year was out she'd be living in the house of her dreams and she'd never have to speak to the odious Clive again.

Chapter Thirty-Four

The moment she opened the back door Hattie was aware that something was wrong. Maybe she'd been burgled. She found her phone and put on the torch, there was no point in trying the lights. In the kitchen, she found that the cooker had been removed.

She moved quickly through the house. In the bathroom there was even more mess, there was no bath and no wash basin and, most importantly, no lavatory. She knew immediately what Clive had done. He had had the kitchen and bathroom removed so the house would be unmortgageable. And he had somehow managed to do it in a single afternoon. The valuation survey would be a disaster.

Back in the kitchen, Hattie found a note. 'So Aunt Mary wants you to have the house without buying it! Well, good luck with that now!'

Hattie pursed her lips. It was hard to imagine the conversation Mary and Clive must have had to prompt this reaction but he must have lost his temper and then jealousy made him do all this.

It was an utterly crazy thing to do. Was he unstable as well as horrid? It would be far harder to find a cash buyer — why didn't he just sell it to her? Because he didn't want her to have it – simply because Mary did. It was a nasty little trick from a nasty little man. Why did he need to ruin the house as well as dashing her dreams? He could have simply refused to sell to her. Now only a cash buyer could buy the house and it would stand empty, deteriorating, until one could be found. And what was worse, somehow, was she wouldn't be able to bring Mary here again, to show her the garden, let her know her beloved old home was in good hands.

Hattie didn't want to cry. She put her lips together and bit down on them, gulping back tears. She couldn't give in now. She'd fought too hard.

Instinctively she found her keys and looked for Luke's. It wasn't there. Had she given it to Leonie? Whatever: she couldn't escape to his house. She clutched her phone and perched on her bed, pulling her duvet around her. When her phone rang she dropped it, she was so shocked. She saw Luke's name on it and connected. But she couldn't say hello.

'Hattie?' he said. 'Are you OK?'

Hattie opened her mouth to speak. Out came the most enormous sob.

'Right,' said Luke. 'I'm coming up. I'll be with you in about four hours – maybe less. Will you be OK until then?'

Hattie nodded, and then managed to clear her throat enough to say yes.

Just knowing Luke was on his way made her feel a hundred times better. She lit candles and considered lighting a fire but it seemed too much like work. She just sat, watching the evening light drain from the room. She was very tired. She'd worked so hard but it had all been for nothing.

Soon, she needed the loo. She got up and went out into the garden and up the path to the little outhouse. It might be horribly spidery but here was a lavatory Clive knew nothing about. Using it gave Hattie a little moment of satisfaction.

She walked back through the scented garden. It had so nearly been hers but now, who knew what would happen to all Mary's beloved plants? Would a new owner destroy the little wilderness areas Mary had left there for the birds?

The house seemed darker than ever and she must have dozed off because all of a sudden she was being made a fuss of by Frank and Fearless, waking her fully and climbing on the bed. Luke followed moments later. He appeared less pleased to see her.

'Why didn't you call me?' he said.

Hattie pushed the dogs off and got up. This was not the Luke she'd been hoping for – expecting even. 'You were miles away.'

'That's no reason not to tell me what's going on.' He produced a large flashlight and put it on. 'What's wrong with the lights? And why has half the kitchen been ripped out?'

'Clive took them out, and switched off the facilities.'

'For fuck's sake! Why?'

Luke hardly ever swore so this was a shock. 'I don't really know,' said Hattie, wanting to cry again.

Luke sighed. 'Come on. I'll take you back to mine.'

While Luke didn't shout any more, Hattie was aware that he was angry, although she wasn't 100 per cent sure who with. The dogs sensed it too as they went to their beds straight away, without being asked.

Although to be fair, thought Hattie, as she perched on the edge of Luke's sofa, not daring to let herself sink back into its feather-filled embrace, he was being the perfect host.

'I think we need hot chocolate,' he announced. 'With a shot of brandy in it.' He looked at Hattie. 'Unless you'd prefer tea?'

'Hot chocolate sounds lovely.'

'I'll just get the fire going first,' he said, setting light to the paper and kindling that was already in the wood burner.

By the time he came back into the room with mugs and a bottle, the dogs had migrated from their beds to the sofa next to Hattie. Luke rolled his eyes but didn't comment.

He handed Hattie a mug. 'So, tell me what's going on?'

Hattie told him as briefly as she could.

'Why didn't you come here instead of camping out like a squatter?' he asked when she had finished. 'You've got a key.'

'I couldn't find it.' This was true, but she had other reasons for not calling on Luke for help.

'You could have rung me.'

'Luke! I'm a grown woman – perfectly capable of sorting out her own problems.'

Luke snorted in disbelief. 'Yeah, right.'

Hattie knew she was on shaky ground. She had patently not sorted anything out. 'You weren't here. You were… snagging or something! Or back in Cornwall. I didn't know! I couldn't expect you to come back and sort out my mess for me. The idea is ridiculous!'

'I'd have come up. Like I just have. You should have known I'd do that.'

'I couldn't assume that.'

'You could assume that.'

'But why?'

'Because you know I'd do anything for you.' He looked at her in a way that made her stomach flip.

'Now, finish your hot chocolate,' he went on briskly. 'I've got an early start in the morning. But I want you to stay here until things are properly sorted out.'

Hattie nodded meekly, aware she was in the wrong, but not absolutely sure why.

'The bed is made up,' said Luke, taking her to the spare room. The room, which previously had been full of Luke's tools and other things, was now a comfortable space with nothing extraneous in it.

'This looks very inviting – when did you have the time to do this?' said Hattie.

But Luke didn't answer her question. 'Please stay as long as you need to, Hattie. I want you to.'

Hattie felt the tension leave her. She didn't need him to fix her problems, but he had scooped her up and looked after her and she had perhaps needed a little of that. Climbing between the soft sheets, she felt safe for the first time for a little while.

Chapter Thirty-Five

Hattie slept deeply, appreciating the good mattress and the lovely bed linen. Did Luke always have bed linen like this? she wondered. Or was it a new thing? Then she remembered he'd bought it recently.

Although she would never have admitted it, even to herself, Hattie was disappointed to have missed Luke that morning. There was a note and a key on the kitchen table. 'Sorry I had to go before you were up. Please help yourself to anything you can find and stay here as long as you like. Luke'.

There was no kiss, but she shouldn't have been surprised. Luke wasn't the sort of person to put kisses on notes. Hattie had been known to add an X to notes to delivery men telling them where to leave a parcel.

She'd missed Luke, she realised, ever since she'd gone to the dinner dance with him, when she'd felt so close to him, so in danger of stepping over the line of friendship. She would enjoy staying in his house, she decided. It would be nice to feel close to him again.

She made herself breakfast, enjoying the fact that Luke had nice mugs and crockery. He appreciated quality and she liked that.

Safely installed at the kitchen table with tea and toast, she used her quiet morning to unpick everything she'd put in place to satisfy Clive's ridiculous requirements. Now that her dream home was only ever going to be a dream, she resolved to see what was on the market within her budget. Paying back Leonie was her first priority. She called her.

She explained what Clive had done and her sister was suitably furious. 'But it means I can pay you back straight away.'

'I'm sorry it didn't work out for you. You must be desperately disappointed.'

Hattie sighed. 'It can't be helped. But I'm at Luke's now – while he's away – so I can have Xander any time. It must nearly be the start of the new term?'

'Yes, next week. If you could have him from Friday, it would be amazing. As you know, I'm hoping to come back as soon as I can arrange it.'

'I know Luke would be happy for him to be here.'

'That's really kind, Hattie! Thank you!'

'I love having him and he'll stop me getting lonely.'

'It's not like you to be lonely.'

'I know. I'll get over it. So what are your plans for when you come back from Switzerland?' Hattie asked to take the attention off her. She really hoped her sister's plans included Tom.

'The moment this contract is over, I'm going to come and live near you,' Leonie said.

'So Xander can carry on at his college?'

'Of course.' There was a moment's pause. 'But actually, you live in a really lovely area…'

'And?' Hattie prompted.

For a moment her sister didn't answer; then she said, 'Well, Tom and I are thinking of getting somewhere together.'

'That's great news!' said Hattie. 'I really like Tom! You must let me know what sort of thing you want, and I'll keep an eye out for you.'

Hattie was aware she had dreaded her sister asking for help but now, she didn't mind. She felt her relationship with Leonie had shifted, and in the right direction.

'So we'll be getting the services of a house hunter for nothing?' asked Leonie, laughing now.

'It looks as if you are! Don't tell everyone.'

Feeling a lot happier about life – it was such good news about her sister – she reflected that the thought of living near Leonie would once have been her worst nightmare. Now it felt like something to look forward to.

Next, she rang Rose, who was suitably excited about Leonie and Tom getting a house together and equally outraged and sympathetic about everything that had happened with Mary's house. After she'd called Clive every insulting name she could think of she said, 'Can I come house hunting with you? My mother-in-law has gone and I managed not to be rude. I need treats!'

'Of course you can. I'll ring Susie, my mortgage advisor, and tell her what's happened and that my budget is now lower, but at least I won't owe anyone anything for the deposit and getting a mortgage agreed might be less stressful next time.'

'Don't rush into buying something you're not really happy with just because you can afford it,' Rose said.

'I'm not going to rush into anything.' Although after she'd disconnected the call, she realised that she wasn't going to waste a moment. She knew she couldn't go on living in the haphazard way she had been for years. She had come so close. If she couldn't have Mary's house, then the new dream had to be a country cottage of her own, and soon.

She drove over to Rose's house and they sat together at her kitchen table with Rightmove open. Because of her job, Hattie was able to add the kind of detail often left off house listings – how near the properties were to busy roads, what the area was like and how far she would need to go for milk.

'I don't know how you know all this about these very modest little terraces,' said Rose. 'It's not as if your clients want houses like these… and is this what you really want?' Understandably perhaps, her friend was still indignant about Hattie having to give up her dream of living in Mary's house. 'And what about a garden? And you probably need room for a shed.'

Hattie laughed. 'Don't worry, I'll run all my choices past you, Rose. Did I tell you I'm looking out for suitable houses for Lennie and Tom too? Unfortunately I haven't got her wish list. Or maybe it's fortunate. It won't be short!'

'Well, let's just concentrate on finding you somewhere to live first. How many bedrooms?'

'I only really need two. I won't have Xander by the time I've bought anything, I don't suppose.' She sighed. 'I'm going to miss him. I used to love living alone, but now it just seems a bit pointless.'

Rose pursed her lips but didn't speak. She didn't need to. Hattie knew exactly what she wanted to say but she couldn't talk about whatever was or wasn't going on with Luke at the moment. She had much more urgent things to worry about.

The next day, the day before Xander was due to join her, Hattie and Rose set off on a couple of viewings, set up at short notice. She had fitted in as many emails as she could, one of which involved Nick's house that was now also going to be Fiona's house. All was going well with it, and the slight glitch regarding a right of way was easy to sort. Now she was spending a bit of time on her own house hunt. Rose insisted on coming with her because, she said, she didn't trust Hattie not to buy just anything in order to gain the independence she now desperately craved.

'There's nothing wrong with this house,' said Hattie after she and Rose had gone over the little two-up two-down. It was modern, with practical plastic window frames, laminate floors and pale mauve paint. From a practical point of view it was fine, but it wasn't making Hattie feel excited.

'There's nothing right with it, either,' said Rose. 'It has no character, faces the wrong way, it has a concrete yard instead of a garden and it's miles away from your friends. By which I mean me.'

Hattie laughed. 'OK, you've got me there. Let's go to the next one. It's quite a bit more expensive and it's very near you.'

'That's why it's more expensive,' said Rose seriously. 'Living near me puts houses at a premium.'

Hattie laughed, feeling a little cheered.

As she drove nearer to where Rose and Sam lived, she was aware that her gloom about losing Mary's house did indeed risk luring her into buying the first thing she could afford. She'd be appalled if any of her clients did that. Her new house might have to be small and affordable but it still had to be somewhere that made her happy. That meant plenty of light, morning and evening, a big enough garden for her pots of herbs and a deckchair, and room for a table in the kitchen. And before Mary's house was sold, she was determined to liberate cuttings of all her herbs and maybe some of the plants as well. Then at least she'd have a bit of her dream home, even if it was only some rosemary and mint.

'Well, it's not really "you", is it?' said Rose as they pulled up for the second viewing.

Hattie didn't speak. Even from the outside it was obvious it was no better than the first house. 'No. If I bought this it would be like buying a dress because it fits and you can afford it. I can't see the joy in living here. But we'd better go inside.'

'To be brutally honest,' said Rose, 'I think even my home-making skills would struggle here, and even if we made it pretty, the second bedroom is too small for a home office.'

Hattie sighed deeply. 'I think you're right. Let's go.'

'Well, that's a relief! I thought I was going to have to convince you. Come back to mine for a cup of tea?'

Hattie glanced down at her phone. 'I'd better get back to Luke's. I'm expecting Xander tomorrow and I need to make sure Luke's cabin is ready for him.'

As she drove back to Luke's she was aware that it felt a bit like she was going home. Once back, with a mug of tea to hand, she called her sister.

'Oh! I was just about to call you!' Leonie said, sounding a little startled. 'Perhaps you *have* got some weird second sight or something.'

Hattie laughed gaily. 'What were you going to call me about?'

'To give you Xander's train times for tomorrow. Can you meet him at the station? Why were you calling me?'

'To ask about Xander. I'm still at Luke's.'

'But Luke won't mind having him, will he?' Leonie asked.

Hattie knew he wouldn't but for some reason she had been putting off asking him. 'No…'

'I'll ask him. Not fair to get you to ask Luke to do me favours.'

Before Hattie had a chance to respond, her sister had disconnected.

Hattie had just gone back on Rightmove, having widened both her search area and her budget, when Luke called her.

'I've just had Leonie on asking about Xander staying for a bit. Of course it's OK, but you know that.'

'That's very kind, Luke. I'm intending to get out of your hair as soon as possible—'

'Please don't! I've got a favour to ask you.' He paused.

'Anything, Luke. You've been so kind to me.'

'Do you remember Jason and Carole from the dinner dance?'

'Vaguely, yes.'

'Well, they want to come and stay for the weekend. Coming tomorrow night. I know we'll have Xander but they're on their way to somewhere else and they want to break their journey here, and as I've often stayed with them, I couldn't say no.'

'Of course not.'

'But I want you to host with me. At the award ceremony they assumed we're a couple. I've let them think that because they were always matchmaking for me and the women were absolutely terrifying!'

'I promise never to try and matchmake for you,' said Hattie, suddenly acutely aware that she'd never had a vision for Luke. What would she do if she did? Shouldn't she be pleased if he was happy? For now she felt relief.

He laughed, although there was something a bit odd about it. 'But it's a big ask, Hattie, they're foodies.'

'I can cook, Luke,' said Hattie, a little offended. 'What's the schedule?'

'Before we get to that, there's one more thing. They'll have to have the spare room.'

'Yes. I've noticed that it's all very comfortable now. Lovely bed linen.'

'I thought I should finally finish doing it up. Although it was mostly just clearing it out. Anyway, we'll have to share the main bedroom, but don't worry, I'll go and sleep on the sofa when Jason and Carole have gone to sleep. Xander will be OK in the cabin. We don't have to disturb him.'

Hattie took the phone and went to Luke's bedroom and opened the door. She hadn't gone near it since she'd been there. She didn't want to intrude on Luke's privacy. 'You've got quite a big bed, Luke.'

A sound like Luke clearing his throat came down the line but he said nothing.

'Please don't worry about where we're going to sleep,' said Hattie. 'Tell me how many meals we'll need.'

'Honestly, you don't need to cook. I can't say exactly when we'll arrive.'

'Then I'll do something like a lasagne that can stay in the oven. So that would be Friday night? Lunch on Saturday?'

'No!' Luke was adamant. 'We'll all go out.'

'So, Saturday night dinner, then. What about Sunday lunch?'

'We could go out for that too.' Luke sounded less convinced this time.

'I can do a roast lunch,' said Hattie.

'You can buy the Yorkshire puddings, and the roast potatoes…'

'Actually, since Rose told me that you just have to jack the oven up to record heights my Yorkshires have been quite reliable. Will they need dinner after all that?'

'No,' said Luke. 'They'll definitely be leaving after Sunday lunch. I'll be staying, of course.'

Hattie nodded. 'I'll make some lists and get shopping.'

'OK. But if you're doing a whole Sunday-lunch production then we'll get a takeaway Saturday night. There's just one more thing – although it's quite big…'

'What?' asked Hattie after Luke had remained silent for what seemed like years.

'Would you mind – er – would you mind making the house look as if we live there together? It's what I've told them.'

Hattie also needed time to answer. He was going to some lengths to avoid a few blind dates. 'The house does have quite a masculine vibe.'

'I'm aware. Would it be difficult to – er – soften it up a bit?'

'I might have to do a fair bit of moving things around. Maybe putting things into boxes and hiding the boxes in the cabin. I do know how to dress a house.'

'Do whatever you like. Spend whatever you like, on food, on scatter cushions, on things from Rose's shop that no man would ever buy – just go for it!'

'There are women who'd almost literally kill for this opportunity, Luke.'

'I know you're not one of them, Hattie, but I'd be so grateful…'

Hattie laughed. 'You're more than welcome, and I owe you so much already, putting a few pink unicorns on the wall—'

He interrupted her with a wry laugh. 'Thank you!' he said jauntily and then disconnected.

Chapter Thirty-Six

Hattie took a few breaths and then checked the train time that Leonie had given her. After she'd picked up Xander tomorrow morning, she'd want to give him some attention as well as explain the situation, so she'd have to get as much as she could done now.

Although he had asked her to do it, Hattie still felt as if she was intruding on Luke's privacy as she faced his desk in the corner of the sitting room. Of course she didn't have to feminise it, but she did think it had to be tidier. As dealing with it seemed like too big a task, she went into the garage and found some boxes. No woman she knew would be prepared to share the dining table with a power drill and Luke had two of them on his. As Hattie knew he travelled with an entire tool kit she wondered why he felt the need for so many. She put them both in the box.

She got into her work. She put music on and cleared and cleaned until she'd removed almost all traces of building equipment. It was amazing how much of it was scattered through the house. She made sure she left lots of traces of Luke himself, but when she was done there wasn't a table drill or router in sight.

She found a large jug which did well as a vase when she'd found enough greenery, plus a few flowers, to fill it. But the house still looked bare. She needed props. She rang Rose.

'You're not going to tell me you've put an offer in on that house!' said Rose, not giving Hattie time to say hello.

'No! Something far nicer!' Hattie explained what was going on.

'OMG!' said Rose. 'I'd be over in a shot if we weren't going to friends for dinner. But I'll bring over all the throws and cushions and bits and pieces you could possibly want tomorrow, early. I'm driving tonight so I won't drink and will be up with the actual lark!'

The two friends disconnected shortly afterwards and Hattie realised how joyful it was to have a happy conversation with her friend. Recently their discussions had been so serious.

Having collapsed on to the sofa to call her friend, Hattie realised that she was hungry. She'd done enough for the evening, she decided, and, heaving herself out of the sofa (which definitely needed more cushions – and not just for the aesthetic), she made her way to the kitchen. She found bread in the freezer, some cheese which looked quite new and made toast. A quick hunt through the cupboards and she found a bottle of Lea and Perrins; Luke had inadvertently provided her favourite meal.

Rose was on the doorstep at eight o'clock. 'I know it's early, but I didn't know what time you had to pick up Xander and I've got a lot on. Friday is always super busy at the shop. The car is full of props. Come and help me in with them.'

'You are the best friend anyone could ever have, Rose!'

But when Hattie saw everything piled into the back of Rose's car, she said, 'You haven't gone too over the top, have you? I'm not sure Luke is ready for a chandelier in the kitchen, although I love the idea myself.'

Rose laughed. 'That's not for you! It's almost all soft furnishings and of course I kept Luke firmly in mind when I made my selection. Some of the cushions I want back first thing on Monday morning; they belong on my sofa.' She made a face. 'And I brought you loads of chunky candles. They always look nice.'

Hattie took hold of the oversized shopping bags Rose extracted from the boot of her car and handed to her. 'You didn't need to sacrifice your own things for this, Rose!'

'I thought it best if we had lots of choice.' Rose hung another couple of bags over her arm and closed the boot of her car. 'Come on, get the kettle on. We haven't got all day! Where are you planning to cook for them?'

Hattie did have to keep Rose a bit in check. While Hattie really liked Rose's ample, exuberant attitude to interior decoration, she had to remind her it was Luke's house and although for the duration of the weekend it was her house too, it couldn't be too over the top.

'Luke's a minimalist,' she explained, handing Rose a cup of coffee.

'But we all know it's the woman who sets the style really, isn't it?'

Hattie nodded. 'But it's not my house in real life. I don't want him to think I've actually moved in.'

'You know he'd be fine with it.'

As there wasn't time to start an argument, Hattie didn't comment. She just tucked in the throw that Rose had flung over the sofa.

By the time they finished, the house looked homely but stylish, comfortable but not so feminine that Hattie couldn't imagine Luke living there. Throws and cushions covered the two sofas. A glass vase, full of the flowers that Hattie had put in a jug plus a few more, now graced the coffee table. There were extra utensils in an old pottery storage jar in the kitchen. (Hattie liked this so much she resolved to buy it when she had a house of her own to put it in.) Some wicker baskets hung from the beams in the boot room and a mirror hung over the washbasin in the downstairs cloakroom. A blue enamel jug had been filled with dried lavender. Rose had even gone to the trouble of digging out a couple of her own jackets to hang there too. The house looked as if a couple lived in it. Hattie was pleased and she hoped Luke would be too.

In the end, she left Luke's desk almost exactly as it was. She just put all the papers in piles and squared them off. He should be able to find everything but it looked fairly neat. But as she finished the job, her eye was caught by a business card that had escaped the neatening process. She went to tuck it out of sight when she saw the name. It was April, the local estate agent she had introduced to Luke at her birthday party. On the back of the card was a handwritten note. 'I called by but missed you! I'll try again.' Then the initial A followed by an X.

Hattie rammed it into the papers and went to find her car keys. Although she tried to focus on Xander and how much she was looking forward to seeing him, that little X niggled at her all the way to the station.

'Why do we have to pretend you and Luke are an item? Why aren't you an item?' said Xander.

She had received a surprisingly strong hug from the boy when he had emerged from the station with his luggage, one she had gladly returned. But once they'd put his things in the car, he was all business.

'We have to pretend because his friends are coming for the weekend and they think we're a couple because we went to a dinner dance together. These people keep trying to find dates for him. If they think he's already in a relationship, they'll stop.'

'And?'

'And what?'

'Why aren't you and Luke an item?'

'We're friends, Xander. That works fine.'

'I'd be OK with it if you did get together.'

This took Hattie aback rather. 'Glad to hear it, Xan, but don't worry, it won't be an issue.'

'Mum was really awkward asking me about Tom. But honestly, she's so much less stressy now she's got him. And he doesn't try and be my dad, so it's cool.' He turned to look at her. 'Luke's cool, you know.'

'That's very good hear to hear,' said Hattie. 'Now, I want to swing by Mary's house. There's a garden full of herbs and I need some. They'll bring my salad to life this evening.'

'Would that be scrumping, Hattie?' said Xander.

'I'm surprised you know that concept, and I suppose it would be. Although "scrumping for mint" doesn't sound quite like "scrumping for apples", does it?'

'I think you'll find it's the principle of the thing,' said her nephew.

It was a bit disconcerting to see an estate agent's sign in the front garden of Mary's house. It wasn't a local agent, or Hattie could have called to find out what was going on with it without Clive knowing.

'I'll park a little way away from the house,' she said, pulling off the road. 'I'll show you what to pick. I'll get the rosemary and thyme as it's harder to pick without scissors.'

'Have you got scissors?' asked Xander.

'I have my trusty Swiss Army knife,' said Hattie.

When Hattie and Xander had liberated enough herbs to keep her going for a few days they went back to the car.

'So, you'd like me to drop you off at Luke's and I'll go shopping on my own? I do have a very long list.'

'That would be good, if you don't mind. I'm a bit tired.'

'Fair enough but don't untidy anything, will you? I've tidied and gussied up the house for these people. I don't want to do it again.'

'I'll just lie on the sofa and watch YouTube.'

Only briefly did Hattie wonder what her sister would think about this plan.

Hattie had made her list carefully and it included a few labour-saving items on it. Ready-chopped *sofrito*, pre-made cheese sauce and fresh pasta slices were among them. For pudding she planned to make Mary's classic trifle recipe which didn't faff about with jelly and took about ten minutes to assemble. She was prepared to provide a very nice meal for Luke's friends but she wasn't prepared to spend a lifetime doing it.

She was soon home and cooking. She had added a nice heavy frying pan to her purchases that she intended to keep for herself; she deducted it from Luke's grocery bill.

The lasagne was all ready to go into the oven and Hattie had started on the trifle when Xander came in, obviously hungry. He looked at the trifle ingredients. 'I'm not sure I'll like that,' he said.

Hattie sighed. 'OK. I suppose it's nice to offer a choice of pudding. I'll try to think of something else. Only it can't be difficult and we have to remember Luke's cupboards aren't terribly well stocked.'

Hattie had bought flour in case she hadn't been able to get ready-made cheese sauce and had lots of butter.

'I really don't want to have to go shopping again,' she said to Xander, who was making inroads into the olives and salami intended to go with the pre-dinner drinks. 'I'll have a look in the freezer. Ah!' At least a year ago – it could possibly have been two – Hattie had given Luke some stewed apples from Mary's garden. And here they were. 'Apple crumble will be delicious. And I bought extra cream.'

The house looked delightful, thought Hattie, trying very hard not to think about the little card stuffed between the papers on Luke's desk. As it was a little chilly for the end of August, she'd get Luke to light the wood burner when he got here. The flowers all smelt lovely, and even the fake ones (very high-end from Rose's shop) had a delightful, subtle fragrance. The throws and cushions were bright and uplifting and Hattie was very happy with her temporary home. Xander had already taken refuge in Luke's cabin, promising to come out when there was food.

She was less happy when the guests, Jason and Carole, arrived before Luke did. And she was a bit taken aback when she realised they weren't the couple she'd thought they were, which made her worry she'd been calling people the wrong names for the entire dinner dance. But her professional skills didn't desert her and she welcomed them warmly.

'How lovely to see you! Luke's not here yet but do come in. It's not as warm as it should be, is it? I'll get Luke to light the wood burner when he gets here. I'll show you up to your room. When you're settled, come and get a drink!'

While Jason and Carole were sorting themselves out, Hattie lit the candles, got out the good glasses and found the wine. The dinner table was already set and the lasagne was bubbling away in the oven. But where was Luke?

It was hard work entertaining people you didn't know in a house that wasn't yours, Hattie realised quite quickly. Carole in particular seemed very curious about her and she did feel she was being interviewed, as if for a job. When Frank and Fearless bounded into the house, she was so pleased to see them she didn't even mind when the vase of flowers went flying.

Luke greeted his guests warmly and then there was a moment of awkwardness before he took Hattie into his arms. 'Hello, darling, the house looks amazing!' Then he kissed her cheek. He hadn't shaved recently and his face was rough against hers. He kept his hand in the small of her back for a few moments in a way that would have looked entirely natural if they had been a couple.

Hattie hadn't rehearsed this moment in her mind although, belatedly, she realised she should have. She felt a bit taken aback.

'Well.' She searched her mind for a suitable reply, feeling slightly hysterical. 'Don't make it sound as if the house usually looks dreadful! I'll get you a drink at the same time as I put more water in the vase for the flowers. Frank? Fearless? Go to your beds.'

Frank and Fearless weren't used to being ordered about by Hattie. With her, they usually called the shots; but, sportingly, they went to their beds and regarded the company eagerly, seeking praise. 'You're very good dogs,' said Hattie.

Luckily, Luke's presence encouraged them to stay in their beds. If Hattie had praised them like that on her own, they'd have taken it as an invitation.

'I think you're very tolerant about the dogs,' said Carole to Hattie. 'One small dog would be fine, but this house isn't really big enough for two of them, is it?'

'It's fine,' said Hattie. 'Anyway, they've been with Luke longer than I have.'

'So how long have you and Luke been together?' Carole went on.

'Quite long,' said Hattie vaguely. 'Now I must have a look in the oven. Are you all hungry?

Luke could answer the awkward questions, she decided, finding a bottle of beer in the fridge.

Hattie was very pleased with how the meal went. Xander came in and joined them, enthusiastically shovelling down lasagne, garlic bread and salad. When he'd finished he said to Hattie, 'That was great. I don't want anything else to eat, thanks. Can I go back to the cabin?'

Hattie nodded. She knew he wanted to get away from the slightly strained conversation and get back to his game. When Xander had nodded goodbye and left, Hattie got up.

'I'll go and get the puddings.'

'Plural?' said Jason. 'That's amazing. We don't have puddings at home, do we?' He looked at his wife.

'Because we don't want to end up the size of houses,' said Carole.

'We only have them if we have guests,' said Hattie, feeling judged. 'Luke? Can you give me a hand?'

It seemed to take a while before the table was cleared and the trifle, cool, covered with cream and toasted flaked almonds, and the crumble, hot with a biscuit-coloured crusty topping, were waiting for Hattie's spoon to go in.

'Wow, can we have both?' asked Jason. 'I can't decide.'

'Of course, but not at the same time,' said Hattie. 'Oh. We need cream. And ice cream.' She got up.

'I can get it,' said Luke.

Hattie shook her head. The cream was in a carton in the fridge but she wanted it in a jug. Rose had brought jugs with her but Luke wouldn't know where they were. 'You carry on here.'

When she had come back into the room, everyone had pudding in front of them; Hattie sat down and smiled at Luke before taking a fortifying sip of wine. Luke patted her knee under the table in return. Then

Carole said, 'Well, now we're all here, can we finally find out how you and Luke met?'

Hattie mentally kicked herself and Luke for not getting their story completely straight before they started on this charade.

To her surprise, he chuckled. Everyone looked at him. 'I can remember the exact moment I first saw Hattie.'

As Hattie couldn't remember this she wondered what he was going to say.

He slipped his arm round her shoulder before speaking. 'I was doing some repairs on a house Hattie was trying to convince some people would be perfect for them if only they were prepared to do a bit of work. She was so passionate. Her hair was curling round her head and her skin was glowing. As I came further into the room, I saw that her eyes were as green as gooseberries.'

Hattie felt herself blush, deeply uncertain if it was because of his hand which was now on her arm, or his description of their meeting. She did remember it now. She had been going out with David at the time – a relationship that had fizzled out soon after. Luke had been with someone too, but she couldn't now remember her name.

'And was it love at first sight?' asked Carole, to Hattie's extreme discomfort.

Luke laughed again. 'We did become friends quite quickly but let's not get into too much detail.'

'We were both with other people,' said Hattie, 'so we stayed friends for a while.'

'So hard to get out of the friends' zone, isn't it?' said Carole.

'It is,' said Luke. 'Now, does anyone want a glass of Armagnac with their second helping of pudding?'

There were nods of agreement and then Hattie said, 'I hope you remember where we put the glasses, darling, because I've completely forgotten.

'We had a bit of a sort-out,' she explained, desperately wishing she could have left the room to look for glasses. 'But Luke will remember.'

'You do make a lovely couple,' said Carole, who, Hattie suspected, had had just a little too much to drink.

'Now... Jason?' said Hattie smoothly. 'Would you like more trifle?'

'That would be his third helping,' said Carole.

'Three's my lucky number,' said Jason and Hattie took his bowl from him and filled it.

Hattie felt she was on her knees by the time they finally got into bed. She wasn't sure if it was because she wasn't used to entertaining people she didn't know or if it was pretending that she and Luke were a couple that was so exhausting.

They tiptoed around each other in Luke's bedroom, getting ready for bed. Hattie abandoned most of her nightly rituals, just brushing her teeth and getting into bed. She was wearing substantial pyjamas because she'd be sleeping next to Luke and she didn't want it to be awkward.

'Are you sure you're OK with me sleeping in the bed?' Luke said in a low voice, although it was unlikely Jason and Carole would hear him.

'Fine! I just want to sleep. I feel as if I've run a marathon – although obviously, not ever having done it, I don't know how it feels, really.'

'I'm so grateful for this, Hattie. It's gone brilliantly. And the food was outstanding.'

'Thank me tomorrow; now just let me sleep!'

Hattie did sleep for a bit, but she woke in the pitch dark, aware of Luke sleeping by her side. To his credit, he didn't snore and the sound of his steady breathing was soothing. But she couldn't help thinking of the way he had described their first meeting. That didn't sound like the meeting of friends for the first time, it sounded more like the meeting of lovers – or potential lovers. She was just turning this thought over in her mind when she remembered the business card she had found.

She turned on to her back, careful not to touch Luke as she did so. She thought she'd never get back to sleep. Her mind was full of conflicting thoughts and feelings. Did she want Luke to see her as a potential lover, as April obviously was? Was she prepared to risk losing his friendship if things went wrong? Maybe it *wouldn't* go wrong?

Chapter Thirty-Seven

Hattie woke again when Luke got up to let the dogs out. He came back with a cup of tea. 'No rush to get up,' he said, handing it to her. 'Jason and Carole are still asleep. At least Jason is. He's snoring like a train. I'll leave you to have your tea in peace.'

'You're very welcome to have yours in here with me,' she said. 'Otherwise you've got to wander around in your PJs.' They were jogging bottoms and a T-shirt, she realised. Which told her he didn't usually wear anything in bed and had also put on extra layers to share a bed with her.

'No. I'm going to clear up a bit. I don't want you to have to lift a finger this morning.'

Not only did Luke clear up the kitchen, he set the table for breakfast, and when Jason and Carole appeared – quite late – he cooked them a Full English, together with pastries and good bread from the van, and made an exquisite pot of coffee.

Luke was showing Jason something in his cabin (Hattie hoping that Xander wasn't too caught out by the visit), so Carole and Hattie were alone.

'You're so lucky having Luke,' said Carole, adding butter to a croissant. 'He knows his way round a kitchen.'

'I knew he could cook before I got together with him.'

'Very wise. And you don't mind the dogs? Always begging.'

'Frank and Fearless don't really beg,' said Hattie, offended on their behalf. 'They just like to be around when there's food in case they can be helpful hoovering up the crumbs.'

Carole laughed. 'As long as you don't mind them, I suppose they're all right. And are wedding bells in the offing?'

Hattie winced inwardly. 'Moving in has been enough of a commitment for the time being.' She couldn't let Carole continue this line of questioning in case she contradicted something Luke had said to her. 'Can I make you some tea? I'm gasping for some myself.'

'I'm on coffee,' said Carole, raising one of Rose's very pretty mugs as if in a toast. 'But you carry on.'

Hattie wondered how long she could spin out making a cup of tea when to her relief she heard the men come in. They were talking and then Luke's phone rang. 'Excuse me,' he said, staying in the hallway to take his call.

Jason came into the sitting room, which doubled as a dining room. 'Still some pastries left, I see.'

'Do have something,' said Hattie, returning to the table. 'They are so delicious. We're very lucky to have a van that brings them practically to our door.'

Luke came in. 'More hot drinks?'

'I'm absolutely stuffed!' said Carole. 'What are we going to do this morning?'

'I really hate to be boring,' said Hattie. 'But I have to do a bit of work. The downside to being self-employed.

I hope to be able to join you for lunch but I can't promise.' She had actually promised herself that she wouldn't join them, but didn't feel she could make it a definite no. She just needed some time away from the pressure of entertaining.

'Oh!' said Carole. 'That's a shame! Surely when you work for yourself you can choose your own hours?'

'In Hattie's case, working for herself means she often has to work at weekends,' said Luke. 'We've been lucky that she's been able to take off as much time as she has.'

Hattie gave him a very warm smile. His support made her feel properly appreciated.

'And I don't expect Xan wants to come on a healthy walk,' he said. 'If you like the idea I thought we might walk along the canal for a bit and look at the round houses. They used to be lengthmen's cottages, in the old days. There's one that needs a bit of work. I might tender for it. I'd like to be more home-based for a bit. Driving up and down to Cornwall is exhausting.'

'Are you sure you won't come with us?' asked Carole a little while later, when they'd pulled on their Barbours and Le Chameau wellingtons which looked suspiciously new, as if bought for their stay with Luke. 'I've a feeling the boys are going to bore me silly talking about architecture and traditional building methods.'

'Get Luke to take you to my friend Rose's shop,' Hattie suggested, determined not to sacrifice her time alone and, indeed, time to work, which had been piling up frighteningly. 'She has some lovely things. There are quite a few samples round here.' She gestured. 'I can't resist her stuff.'

★ ★ ★

After Hattie had got through quite a lot of paperwork, she made some tea and thought about her options. Rose was right, she didn't want to buy just anywhere out of panic, but she couldn't stay with Luke for ever and renting was expensive. It would eat into her deposit terrifyingly quickly. She sat at the table with her notebook and pen, doodling, hoping it would create a solution to her problems. Then Xander joined her.

'What's going on?' he asked.

Hattie sighed. 'Trying to work out where we're going to live. I'm sure if your mum realised that I'm not very good at making a home for you, she wouldn't let you stay.'

'Why can't we stay here? Luke seems quite happy.'

'Erm…' Hattie thought how best to explain to Xander the subtle and not entirely logical reasons she wasn't keen to rely on Luke indefinitely.

'I won't be here for too much longer anyway. When Mum moves back to England I'll be back with her.'

'Are you looking forward to that?' Hattie asked, feeling that Xander wanted to talk about it.

'I am, and I like Tom. He makes her laugh.'

Hattie smiled, feeling like a fairy godmother – which, in a way, she was. 'It's because she's found her person.'

'But you haven't found your person?'

Hattie shook her head.

'Shame. I think Luke's found his.'

Hattie frowned, not quite sure what Xander meant. Had Luke confided in him? About April? It was possible. She pushed the thought out of her mind. 'Really? Well, that's great. But I'm supposed to be working so I'd better get on. I could drop you off at the pub for lunch, otherwise it's leftovers.'

'Happy with leftovers. My mum says you're an over-caterer.'

'Guilty as charged,' said Hattie, 'now let me get on!'

Rose called in at about three with a batch of cheese scones.

'This is a thank you for sending Carole to the shop today,' she said. 'She spent a fortune! It was partly because Luke and her husband had gone off somewhere and left her there for ages. But she was very happy with her haul.'

Hattie laughed. 'That's good! But you didn't need to bake for me.'

'Well, I only really made these so I could hear how things were going,' Rose admitted.

'I knew that,' said Hattie, buttering a scone 'just to make sure they're OK for the guests'. 'But I don't mind telling you: Luke is a really good actor, it turns out, and makes it look as if we're a proper couple.'

'What do you mean?' asked Rose.

'Well, you know, he makes the little gestures, that hand on my back when he's squeezing behind me, the occasional hand on my knee – but only very briefly… I think even Xander thinks there's something going on although he knows we're not together.'

'Hmm,' said Rose. 'Well, keep up the good work!'

'We're in tonight, but we've decided to get a takeaway, so I've just got to do a roast tomorrow for lunch and then they'll go. It's been exhausting!'

'I bet it is.'

'It's not the physical thing of looking after them. If they were my real friends, I wouldn't notice that. It's the fielding the awkward questions, and…' She paused. 'You know.'

'It's like when my mother-in-law comes to stay.'

This made Hattie smile. 'At least Luke has been brilliant.'

Rose put an arm round Hattie and hugged her. 'I'd better go. I don't want to be caught here.'

'Thank you so much for the scones. They're just the thing to fill that hungry half-hour between lunch ending and dinner beginning.'

Rose was laughing now. 'It's not that bad!'

Luke and Hattie stood at the door watching Carole and Jason reverse down the drive. Luke had his arm round Hattie's shoulders and they were both smiling and waving. When at last they were out of sight, Luke removed his arm. 'Come on in. You need tea!'

'We've only lived together for a few hours and already you know me so well.'

'I knew you needed frequent tea before we lived together.' He steered her back into the house and she collapsed on to the sofa.

When he had brought her tea and a fancy chocolate biscuit from a little hamper that Jason and Carole had brought, he sat down in the armchair.

Hattie couldn't help remembering how the previous evening they had been sharing the sofa with Carole while they all watched a film. To save space, Luke had put his arm round her and Hattie found herself resting her head against his chest. A little while later she awoke with a start. But because it would have looked odd if she'd moved away, she'd stayed where she was for the rest of the movie.

She had been gently teased for nodding off and blamed the brandy.

'I've known Jason for years, as a colleague, and although he's a good bloke, he wasn't the easiest house guest. He seemed to be quite demanding.'

'He was fine!'

'And Carole was quite nosy.'

'Honestly, her questions only put me on the spot a bit because I didn't know what you'd said, but they were quite normal questions.' Even as she said the words, Hattie felt herself relax, knowing she wouldn't be asked anything more about potential weddings or whether she wanted children.

'Well, you did me proud,' he said. 'I couldn't have asked for a better girlfriend.'

But she wasn't his girlfriend, Hattie thought in response. And based on what Xander had said, it seemed April was. Hattie felt a sudden rush of jealousy. She coughed and shook her head, trying to banish the feeling. It was a huge relief when Xander came in.

'Have they gone?' he asked.

Hattie nodded. 'The coast is clear.'

'They were OK people, but I just never know what to say to strangers,' said Xander. He smiled. 'Still, the food was great, Hattie!'

'I can cook,' she said with dignity. 'But I don't do it often. Or at least, not to that extent.'

'Now, what can I do for you in return,' Luke said. 'All that cooking should have a proper reward.'

'A cold beef sandwich a bit later would be pretty good,' said Hattie.

'I was thinking something a bit more than that.' Luke's expression was serious suddenly. 'Please stay here while you're house hunting.'

At that moment Hattie was very tempted but if he and April were developing a relationship, having her in his home would be very awkward. 'I'm very grateful, but it's not necessary. I'll work something out. And don't forget, tomorrow this house has to be turned back into a bachelor pad. All the pretty props will have to go back.'

'I think I might negotiate with Rose and keep some of them,' said Luke. 'Those big squashy cushions are comfortable.'

'Rose will be delighted.' She yawned theatrically to change the subject. 'I think I need a film.'

'Just so you can go to sleep? You could just go to bed and have a proper nap,' said Luke, but Hattie shook her head.

'I'd sleep for too long if I did that. I just want something to doze in front of.'

While she adjusted cushions and made herself comfortable, she allowed herself to consider Luke's offer of a home, just until she found her own house. She found she very much wanted to accept.

Hattie was supremely content, with a dog's head on each leg. They had just settled down in front of something Xander recommended and drowsiness was overtaking her when Luke's phone went. He looked at it and got up. As he left the room, he said, 'Sorry, April, now is not a good time. Can I call you back?'

The words sent a jolt through Hattie and she closed her eyes tightly to stop the sudden tears escaping.

Chapter Thirty-Eight

There was a certain amount of morning chaos involved in getting Xander back to college. The traffic seemed bad but they got there on time and as Hattie watched him go through the door, chatting to people, she gave a sigh of satisfaction. He had so much more confidence now than when he first started.

She glanced at her phone. She had a house to show a client who wanted a stately home but could only afford a semi – albeit a very nice one. (She reminded Hattie rather of Mrs Conway.) In fact, they'd seen it together before and the client had rejected it for not being grand enough. But Hattie had shown her a couple of other properties since and felt that the client was ready to be a bit more realistic. The house could be made to look a lot grander, after all. Hattie would need to be firm.

Either Hattie was firm, or the client had come to terms with what she could afford, but this time, as they walked round the house, admiring the geometric Victorian tiles in the hallway, the dado rail and the cornicing, the client said, 'You're quite right, Hattie. It's a charming house and I'd be mad not to snap it up. Can you try and buy it for me please?'

Hattie hugged her. Not only was she delighted that her client was going to end up in a house which was just right for her, but Hattie would have space to take on a new client, and so acquire a fee which would make her own house hunt a little easier.

Afterwards, she drove up on to the local common, where the views went across the Severn plain to the Welsh mountains. She was hoping it would give her comfort. She'd spent a lot of time recently appearing to be cheerful and positive, but inside, she felt she was crumbling. She had lost the house of her dreams and now, thanks to Clive, had no prospect of ever buying it.

Then there was Luke. She'd made such a mistake with him with her stubborn insistence he was just a friend. Now, as she looked at the familiar vista of distant hills, clumps of trees and the river beyond, she realised that she should have got out of the friends' zone, as Carole had put it, long since. But it was too late. Now he was involved with April – who was a lovely woman; she couldn't even hope that April would let him down and that they would break up. She'd managed to find love for her sister, for Fiona and Nick, and even for Rose, many years ago. But she'd let the very thing standing in front of her slip through her fingers. Tired, she felt tears very near the surface.

Later that afternoon, she had an appointment to view a house for herself which ticked all the boxes: all the dull boxes which were about as inspiring as a page full of sums. But she couldn't go on staying with Luke; she had to make a plan and it was time to put sentiment and dreams aside and buy something sensible. And for now, she wanted to breathe calmly, until she felt more positive about it all. It might take some time.

She was interrupted from her self-hypnosis by the telephone. It was Fiona.

'Hi, Fiona, this is a lovely surprise!'

Fiona laughed. 'I'm so glad you've said that because what I'm going to tell you is a bit of a surprise. I'm pregnant!'

For half a second, Hattie felt a pang of envy for Fiona and her happy relationship. 'Oh, that's lovely news. How exciting.'

'Dad isn't absolutely delighted, and to be honest, it wasn't planned, but me and Nick are thrilled and Mum is over the moon!'

Fiona's joy was audible. 'I bet. She will be the perfect grandmother, generous, spoiling and utterly supportive.' Hattie couldn't help but smile at this image, although felt a pang of regret that her own mother would never be like that.

'I know! I'm so lucky to have her. So, to make everyone completely happy, we're going to get married before the baby arrives.'

'Nice,' said Hattie, briefly wondering where all her party dresses had got to in her various recent moves.

'And we'd really love it if you'd be our celebrant.'

This took Hattie aback. 'Oh my goodness! I've never done it before, you know.'

'That doesn't matter. Me and Nick thought – and Mum – that you somehow brought us together and so you should be the one to… well, bring us together! We'll get married in a register office beforehand, so we won't need to worry about the legal stuff. We just want a lovely party with you officiating at the beginning.'

Hattie suddenly wanted to cry. She cleared her throat. 'That's so – romantic,' she said. 'I'm very honoured.'

'We've chosen the venue. We did think of having it in the garden at home, but you can't guarantee the weather, not in September.'

'Where have you chosen?'

'It's a new place. I'll send you the details. Mum insisted on having proper invitations printed; she wouldn't let me just send emails, and you'll need one of them. What is your address at the moment?' There was a long pause while Fiona waited for a reply. Eventually she said, 'Sorry? Hattie? Are you still there?'

Hattie coughed and cleared her throat again, but even then she was certain her tears were evident. 'Erm – I don't really have an address.'

'What do you mean?'

'I – me and my nephew – are... between addresses.' She could have given Luke's address. He wouldn't have minded. But she couldn't bring herself to. Although she had definitely made his house a home for the weekend, she knew she couldn't stay, not the way she was feeling.

Fiona didn't reply immediately. 'Tell you what, let me have a word with Mum. Dad's due to go away on a golfing holiday and she hates being on her own for any length of time. Nick and I are living in his house, waiting for the sale on the new one to go through, so she's feeling it rather. She'd love to have you. There's a guest suite – it's got two bedrooms. I'll call you back.'

In spite of her sudden feeling of desolation, Hattie couldn't help smiling. Fiona was so happy, she wanted to make everyone else happy too. And as Hattie looked at the view and sipped water from her flask, she felt a bit more in control of her emotions – until her phone ringing again interrupted her thoughts.

'Oh my days!' Fiona was obviously thrilled. 'I can't tell you how excited Mum got when I told her you needed somewhere to live for a little while.'

'It's not just me, it's my teenage nephew as well—'

'She knows that. She is thrilled at the thought of having you both to stay! She'll be distracted from the wedding prep by trying to overfeed your nephew. I think she's scarred by what happened last time so it would be perfect.'

'Are you sure? Having two people – people you either don't know at all or hardly know – to stay can be very stressful.' She knew this only too well.

'Not for Mum. Really. She knew you'd say something like that but wants you to know she really would love to have you both.' She took a breath. 'I'm getting off the phone now. Mum wants to ring immediately!'

'Hattie? Is Fiona right? Are you and your nephew really up for coming to stay for a few weeks? I would be SO thrilled!'

'Well, if you're sure that would be OK,' said Hattie, touched by Sheila's enthusiasm.

'I'd love it!'

After more excited conversation, it was agreed that Hattie and Xander would arrive at five, for pre-dinner drinks. This would give Hattie time to finish off her work, collect her things and explain to Luke – and later Xander – where she was going. The 'why' would be more complicated.

She drove to Luke's at lunchtime, hoping not to see his truck or his car so she could let herself in, take her belongings, leave a note and disappear. But no, the truck and the car were both there.

She rang the bell, which sent Frank and Fearless to the window so they could see who it was. Their keenness to see her was evident through the window. Would that make leaving even harder?

'Hello,' said Luke, surprised to see her. 'Why didn't you use your key?'

Hattie wondered the same thing for a minute. But she couldn't have sneaked in and out without him knowing about it. 'I've come to get our things. Xander and I are moving out.'

Luke frowned. 'Why? I didn't think the service was that bad.'

Hattie put her bag down on the table. 'The service was amazing. Couldn't have been better. But I don't want to impose.' She paused. 'Can I make a cup of tea?'

He gestured to indicate that of course she could and followed her into the kitchen.

'Sheila – remember her? Fiona's mother?'

'Of course.'

'She's got a two-room annexe and she's on her own for a while. She's very keen for us to go and stay. Fiona and Nick are getting married.'

'I think I knew that.'

'Imminently. They're going to have a baby and so are rushing things along rather. They've asked me to be celebrant.'

Luke, who had been looking a bit forbidding, relaxed a little. 'Nice! You'll do that very well. The right mixture of warmth and formality.'

Hattie found herself blushing at the compliment 'Tea?' she said quickly to cover her embarrassment.

Luke nodded. 'Will you come back here afterwards?'

'I really hope to have bought something before long – and although I know I won't be in it for a couple of months—' She stopped, not knowing how to carry on. 'The lodge won't be so booked up in September; we might go back there. Can you get the milk out?' she finished.

'When will you move out?' asked Luke while they sipped their tea.

'Now.'

'Why the sudden rush? I thought you, me and Xander rubbed along well together.'

'Sheila wants us. She's lonely.'

Luke put down his mug. Then his phone beeped and April's name came up.

Hattie clamped her lips tightly together so she wouldn't comment on how often April seemed to get in touch with Luke. If you assumed that Luke got in touch with her as often, they were obviously very close. It was weird, she decided, she and Luke were best friends, but somehow, with April's name popping up every five minutes, he suddenly felt like an acquaintance. She needed this space from him to get her feelings in order, otherwise she worried she might lose him as a friend as she'd always feared. And without the reward of anything more.

Chapter Thirty-Nine

'Hi, Hattie!' said Xander, sounding surprised when he saw her parked outside the college where he couldn't fail to see her. 'I didn't know you were picking me up. Or did I?'

Hattie laughed. 'No, it is a surprise. Get in. I've got quite a lot to explain to you. But don't worry, it's all good.'

Xander was not convinced that going to stay with some random woman he'd never met instead of living with Luke was going to be anything but uncomfortable. He didn't express his disapproval in quite that way but Hattie understood his misgivings.

'Honestly, it won't be for long. I'm looking into renting somewhere as well as seriously finding somewhere to buy.'

'But why can't we stay at Luke's?' Xander said for the nineteenth time.

'Because I don't think he can have a proper love life if we're there!' said Hattie finally, hoping her frankness would make her nephew stop asking that question. It did.

★ ★ ★

Sheila could not have been more welcoming. She ushered Hattie and Xander into her kitchen. 'Let's have a glass and some nibbles, then I'll show you to your rooms. Xander, I've got a good selection of soft drinks for you. Would you like to go and look in the fridge and see what you might like? I'm so utterly delighted to have you here!'

'There's enough for a small shop here,' said Xander, coming back with his favourite. 'Thank you!'

'I didn't know what you liked, so I just got everything I could see on the shelf. I'll go and get the food.'

It took several trips to and from the kitchen, even with Xander helping, to get it all to the table. Sheila had gone to epic lengths to find things likely to appeal to Xander as well as Hattie. There was charcuterie of all kinds, plain cold meats, several sorts of cheese, French bread, crackers, Scotch eggs and miniature quiches as well as olives and fancy crisps.

'I was going to do supper as well,' said Sheila when everything had been fitted on to the table. 'But this is probably enough.'

'For us and about twenty other people,' said Hattie. 'This is so generous of you!'

'Yes,' said Xander. 'It's amazing.'

'You know me,' said Sheila, half embarrassed and half pleased. 'I like to feed people.'

To Hattie's huge relief, Xander tucked in enthusiastically, any issues with food he may have had at one time long forgotten. She made a point of loading her own plate and, unusually, she allowed her glass to be filled a couple of times.

'I'm so delighted Fi and Nick asked you to be celebrant,' said Sheila, topping up her own glass. 'I've always felt you brought them together in some way.'

Hattie nodded. Fiona had said the same thing. If only they knew she had done exactly that, she thought. 'It's lovely that they're obviously so happy.'

'I know! They both exude joy! It's bliss.'

'This food is bliss,' said Xander, awkward but making an effort.

'You are so welcome, darling!' said Sheila.

'But we must work out how we're going to arrange things. We must pay you rent and contribute to housekeeping, cook meals sometimes.'

'But I love cooking for people,' said Sheila, in case Hattie and Xander had missed this about her. 'Appreciative people. Malcolm doesn't really like my cooking. He only likes school food, not spice and nothing fancy in the vegetable line. Which means he eats peas and carrots and sometimes green beans.'

'Oh.'

'And as we have lots of veg in the garden it seems a shame. I'll have some bread. It's just possible I may have had too much to drink already.'

'We could have some water. Xan? Could you get us some?'

Xander got up good-naturedly. 'There are about three different kinds of sparkling water in the fridge.'

'Anything will be fine,' said Sheila. 'I've got overexcited having cheery company.'

'And we're very happy too. But you must let me contribute financially.'

Sheila remained very resistant to the thought that Hattie might pay rent and so, after much haggling, it was agreed Hattie would help Sheila in the garden and Xander would take over the lawn mowing. It wasn't proper remuneration, Hattie knew, but it was the best deal she could get and privately she was grateful not to be spending any of her precious deposit money.

The days leading up to the wedding went quickly. Hattie had a lot of work on and she tried to fit in as much gardening for Sheila as she could.

Sheila seemed to be very busy with her daughter's upcoming ceremony although actually Fiona and Nick had it all worked out. Sheila was insistent that the village hall, which had only just become a wedding venue and where they were having the reception (or 'bun fight', as Sheila called it), should be decorated with flowers from her garden. Although her garden was full of flowers, she felt there wouldn't be enough sweet peas. Hattie was happy to dig holes and put up wigwams for support although she and Sheila accepted they were pushing it a bit to expect many of them to be out in time. Hattie found getting her hands in the soil soothing when her own house hunting was going badly. There was simply nothing in her budget that made her heart sing. She was as bad as her clients.

Hattie went past Mary's house once. The 'For Sale' sign now had 'Sold Subject to Contract' on it. She could probably have used her contacts to find out who was buying it but she didn't want to. It was all too painful. Somehow her not being able to buy the house had become linked with things going wrong with Luke and the thought that she had let so much slip through her fingers was too painful to dwell on.

The next day she went down to see Mary, who was very pleased to see her.

'I'm really quite content being here,' she said when Hattie asked. 'I didn't realise the chef who was cooking was a substitute and the food has improved a lot. And my first impressions of the staff were right: they are all very kind. I've also found a wonderful woman who is a botanist. We have very interesting conversations. But it is far away from you and all my friends. The more elderly among them find it hard to visit me.'

'Is Clive looking into moving you somewhere nearer?' Hattie asked.

'Like the care home I had picked out for myself, you mean? He says he is. But apparently my house has to be sold before that can happen.'

'He should have sold it to me, then,' said Hattie.

Mary nodded. 'He's a bit too clever for his clogs sometimes, that young man. Apparently he's negotiating to sell it to a developer.'

Hattie sighed. 'Well, it'll get a good price if they can get planning permission. I doubt that they could, frankly.'

'Couldn't you find out? A woman in your position?'

Hattie smiled ruefully. 'I could possibly find out how likely they are to get planning, but will it change anything?'

Mary put her hand on Hattie's.

'And we want the very best price for the house, don't we?' Hattie went on. 'If I can't have it, you should get millions!'

Mary laughed. 'And there's no good crying over spilt milk, not at this stage. Now tell me, are you enjoying living with Sheila?'

'I am. We all rub along together pretty well. Even though Malcolm came back from his golf trip unexpectedly early, he has learnt to tolerate me. He and Xander have quite long conversations about motor racing – of at least three sentences.'

Mary laughed obligingly.

'And one night when Sheila was out, I made him scrambled eggs, and he loved the way I did them.'

'I liked your scrambled eggs too,' said Mary. 'I loved our short time of living together. We had such fun.'

'The best fun!' Hattie's throat closed with tears and she had to cough a lot, trying not to start sobbing.

Mary patted her hand again. It helped.

Chapter Forty

As the wedding grew nearer, things got busier. Leonie came over to spend the weekend with Tom and Xander. They met at a pub for an early supper on the Thursday, when Leonie first arrived.

'Remind me why you left Luke's?' asked Leonie. 'I thought it all went well when you were staying?'

'It was fine,' said Xander.

'I just thought we were cramping Luke's style a bit, living there,' said Hattie.

Leonie raised an eyebrow but didn't comment.

Hattie thought she'd avoided further questioning when Xander said, 'There's a woman called April who calls him quite often. Hattie thinks she's his girlfriend.'

Hattie felt herself turn scarlet.

'Is that right, Hattie?' said Leonie.

'I don't want to make things awkward for him. Now I think we should order, and what about another round of drinks? My turn!'

Her sister gave her a curious look but, again, didn't comment further. Hattie felt she'd dodged a bullet.

★ ★ ★

Two days later, on the morning of the wedding, Hattie awoke to hear rain drumming on the roof of her guest apartment. No point in worrying about that, she realised, she had other things on her mind. She got dressed quickly into loose linen trousers and a top and then went along to the main house. She had a secret and was worried that she might have the fact written on her forehead in large red letters. Sheila shared the secret and they exchanged furtive glances but couldn't speak. They'd have to be very careful.

Fiona was at the table looking a bit glum. 'It's raining,' she said, in case Hattie hadn't noticed.

'But it doesn't matter,' said Hattie, 'because it can all happen inside. And the hall is looking wonderful!'

Sheila, who was pulling a croissant apart but not eating it, nodded. 'I must say, the WI all came up absolute trumps. They gave up their very best blooms and their time and talent.'

'They did,' said Hattie, reaching for toast. 'Decorating it last night was one of the most enjoyable experiences I've had in a long time.'

'It was fun, wasn't it?' said Fiona, distracted from the rain. 'It turns out that ladder holding and fetching water is quite fun if you're with pals.'

'We couldn't let you climb ladders in your condition,' said Hattie. 'And I had fun climbing them. And fixing flowers to the proscenium arch.'

'I didn't know that bit of the stage was called that,' said Fiona. 'Until last night.'

'It's not the sort of thing that comes up in conversation,' said Hattie, saying almost anything to avoid mentioning what was on her mind.

'It would be a good question for a quiz,' said Sheila randomly. They exchanged quick glances; Sheila was obviously feeling the same.

Sheila poured more coffee. 'Should I get your dad up, do you think?'

'No, no,' said Fiona. 'We're fine. Let him take his time.'

'It would have been easier if the village hall had been picturesque to start with,' said Sheila, temporarily thwarted in her desire to fry bacon for her husband, and possibly slightly resentful that she hadn't got to choose the venue. 'Some have lovely beams and things to hang things from.'

'We did try for one of those,' said Fiona, 'but we wanted to be near here. And it looks brilliant now.'

'It does, darling,' said Sheila, holding her daughter's hand. 'I'm just a bit tired.'

'And emotional!' said Fiona. 'I don't know how much you had to drink last night, but it was a lot.'

Sheila laughed. 'Just because you're not drinking, any more than one glass and you think people have gone on a bender!'

'Dad went on a bit of one,' Fiona said. 'But luckily it didn't make him grumpy this time.'

Hattie's mind went back to Fiona's first wedding day. Malcolm had definitely had too much to drink then. Although that time it had worked to Fiona's advantage.

'I think I need more tea,' Hattie said. 'Can I make some for anyone else?'

'Oh, I'd love a peppermint!' said Fiona.

'I'll pop out and pick some leaves so you can have it fresh.' Hattie left the kitchen followed by Fiona's protests that a bag would do.

'One of the things I like best about this house,' said Sheila when Hattie had returned, 'is having herbs so handy for the kitchen.'

'I want that in my new house too,' said Hattie, pouring boiling water on mint leaves. 'But so many houses around here have steep gardens you can't easily get at.'

'I don't understand why you can't find yourself a lovely house, Hattie,' said Fiona. 'You were so brilliant with us.'

'I don't expect she applies so much energy to finding her own house,' said Sheila. 'A cobbler's children and all that.' Sheila realised that Fiona and Hattie were looking confused. 'You know, the cobbler spends all his time making shoes for other people, he doesn't have time for his own children? I had a friend whose father was a dentist. She said it was a nightmare trying to get an appointment.'

'I wish it was time to get dressed,' said Fiona. 'I want to get this party started!'

'You could get out of your dressing gown, darling,' said Sheila. 'Unless you want a cooked breakfast. I'm going to do one for Dad, just in case there's a delay before the food appears.'

'Nick's booked some very expensive caterers,' said Fiona, possibly a little offended. 'There won't be a problem.'

'Why don't we go and visit Rose's shop?' suggested Hattie. Fiona could probably recite a list of the items for sale by heart but Hattie was desperate to get her out of the house.

Fiona did not look terribly excited by this thought.

'She's got some new things in. Come on! We'll get out from under Sheila's feet.'

'Are we under your feet, Mum?' said Fiona, suddenly petulant.

'No – yes – not really. But do go out with Hattie, then I can focus on Dad. You know he gets tetchy if he's surrounded by women.'

'Nick's not like that,' said Fiona, looking happier. 'He made me have a hen do, and hired a minivan to get us all to the venue.'

'He's a keeper,' said Hattie.

'So, so different from Lance!' said Fiona, saying what they were all thinking.

'Come on,' said Sheila. 'Have a quick shower and get going. You'll feel less nervous if you're doing something.'

'It's only shopping, Mum!' said Fiona, but she got up and gave her mum a quick hug as she passed her.

Sheila and Hattie exchanged glances. 'I wish I'd thought of something better to offer her than Rose's shop. We were there the day before yesterday.'

'It's fine,' said Sheila. 'I'm so excited!'

'Me too!' said Hattie.

'I know I'm pregnant and a bit distracted because we're getting married today, but this isn't the way to Rose's,' said Fiona after a little while.

'No. We're not going to Rose's. We're going somewhere much more exciting.'

'Oh my God! Where?'

'Sapperton.'

'I know Sapperton, but why?'

'Not telling. Oh, I say! There's a house for sale. I wonder if I'd like to live there.' Hattie indicated a middle terrace high on the hill. 'The views would be amazing.'

'Hattie! I know you're not really thinking about buying it, because you will have seen it already if it's remotely suitable. You may be a cobbler's child, or whatever cobblers Mum was going on about, but I know how you work.'

'I was just distracting you. Now look at the scenery. We're nearly there.'

Hattie hoped that Fiona wouldn't notice the picture of the Labrador above the name of the house on the open gate. She drove in, as instructed, parked, and then got out. 'I'm just going to close the gate.'

Fiona was waiting for her by the front door. 'It's not a surprise party, is it? I mean, they're fun and all but it's a bit early and I've only just had breakfast.'

'Well, it's a surprise, and sort of a party, but you won't be required to eat anything.' Hattie rang the doorbell.

It was opened quickly by an attractive woman wearing an apron. 'Hello! You're right on time! I'm Natalie.'

'I'm Hattie and this is Fiona,' said Hattie. 'She doesn't know why she's here.'

Natalie chuckled. 'Well, I don't think you'll be disappointed. Come on through. We're all in the kitchen.'

Natalie's kitchen was large, beamed and full of the sort of things that Rose sold in her shop. But neither Hattie nor Fiona noticed the decor, attractive as it was, because in the corner of the kitchen, next to a huge old Rayburn, was a large pen. And in the pen was a litter of sleeping puppies and their mother, who was obviously dying to say hello.

'This is Amanda,' said Natalie, letting out a very friendly black Labrador. 'Proud mum. And there are her babies. They're a bit too young for too much excitement but now Mandy's abandoned them, they'll wake up and you can see them bumble around.'

'Oh, they are gorgeous!' said Fiona. 'I love that they all have different colour collars. What a lovely treat to distract me from my wedding! I'm getting married this afternoon,' she told Natalie.

'I know!' said Natalie.

'And we're not just here so you'd be distracted,' said Hattie.

'You're here to choose a pup,' said Natalie. 'Although they are quite small so you could come back. They're only two weeks old.'

Fiona made a noise between a gasp and a cough. 'A puppy? For me?'

'Nick has arranged it all,' said Hattie. 'It's a wedding present.'

'I've always wanted one!'

Hattie felt a mixture of envy and delight at the thoughtfulness of Fiona's husband-to-be. The little creatures, like miniature seals, moved slowly about, occasionally opening their mouths and revealing pink insides. They were adorable.

'And if you find it too difficult when you have a baby,' Natalie was saying, 'your mum is going to have him – or her – until you're ready.'

'Sheila is a bit worried about you managing a puppy and a baby at the same time,' said Hattie.

'I had a puppy and a baby at the same time,' said Natalie. 'I did get confused. You obviously wash your hands after playing with the pup before you pick up the baby and I found I washed my hands after playing with the baby before dealing with the pup. I washed my hands a lot!'

'But you managed OK?' asked Fiona. 'I have always wanted a dog but obviously, the baby must come first.'

'If you have a secure garden,' said Natalie, 'and you have, it should be fine. I know that because Nick showed me round both your present house and your new one. I've already checked everything out.'

Fiona sat on the kitchen floor, surrounded by puppies. One attempted to climb her shoe and Fiona picked it up and put it in her arms. The puppy snuggled into her elbow. 'This one is lovely.'

'He's a little chap,' said Natalie. 'Cuddle a few more. None of this litter is spoken for yet so you can have your choice.'

'I can't decide if I want a girl or a boy,' said Fiona. 'I know you're not supposed to describe it as that.'

'It's fine!' said Natalie. 'We all know what you mean. And if you can't make up your mind today, don't worry. There's no rush.'

Just then a puppy toddled towards Fiona and gave a tiny yap. Fiona instantly took it into her arms. 'I think I want you!' she said.

'That's a bitch – little girl,' said Natalie. 'But both sexes make lovely pets. They're bred almost entirely for temperament.'

By now, Fiona's ear was getting a thorough clean by a little pink tongue. 'I'm going to call her Petronella,' Fiona said. 'I've always liked the name but it's a bit much for a person.'

'That's a lovely name,' said Natalie. 'I expect it'll get shortened but it'll look great on the pedigree.'

'Well done you for deciding,' said Hattie. 'They are all so lovely.'

'It feels more like Petronella chose me,' said Fiona.

★ ★ ★

By the time Hattie said they really had to go now, it wasn't only Fiona who was in love with the thought of having a dog. Although in some ways she thought of herself as already having two dogs: Frank and Fearless. But if Luke and April moved in together it was unlikely that she'd be needed to look after them much. Just for a second, it felt to Hattie as if this was something else April had taken from her. Hattie was not given to self-pity – perhaps it was the emotions of Fiona's wedding day – but just for a moment she let herself feel that as well as the house of her dreams and the man she hadn't even realised she wanted, she'd lost the animals she thought of as partly hers. If she hadn't been driving, she'd have been overtaken with tears.

Chapter Forty-One

Hattie hadn't thought she'd be nervous about being a celebrant. She didn't have to learn her words by heart, she could read them if she wanted. And although Fiona and Nick were exchanging vows, they were very short and simple. Once she'd said her bit, the party would start. She was wearing Mary's gorgeous navy and cream dress which had never reached her parents' Golden Wedding celebrations, and knowing she looked good should have given her confidence.

And yet, when she was standing at the front of the village hall – it was still pouring with rain – she felt almost overcome with twitchiness. It wasn't even proper nerves, she realised. It was as if electricity had somehow got under her skin.

Outwardly she was calm but her blood was fizzing inside her veins. She clapped her hands to get everyone's attention when the time had come for Fiona and Nick to walk down the makeshift aisle together, and Sheila changed the music from Fiona's classical playlist to Pachelbel's Canon in D.

It was a delight to watch them walk up between their friends and family. Everyone was smiling; the couple were holding hands, looking at each other, their expressions full of joy.

Hattie had practised her lines often enough so she did know them by heart. Nick standing with his bride whom he so obviously adored and Fiona looking up at her groom, full of trust and love, was inspiring. And although her skin still felt electrified and her heart was racing, she enjoyed saying the few lines that would unite this couple in the presence of everyone who loved them. She took a moment to look at her audience. She noticed Malcolm squeezing Fiona's hand and then getting out his handkerchief and giving it to her. She just had time to appreciate the change in him before she had to speak.

She finished with a triumphant 'You may exchange kisses' and the whole party erupted in cheers of congratulation as Nick and Fiona leant in for a deeply felt kiss.

Afterwards, someone put a glass of champagne into her hand but she didn't dare drink it. She felt strange enough without adding alcohol even if she wasn't driving. Hattie wished she'd fought to take her own car. She felt a bit trapped now.

Rose came up to her. 'It's a shame Luke couldn't come.'

It was typical of Rose to get straight to the point. Sheila had invited him although Hattie had tried to imply she didn't want him to come, and Hattie realised that part of her was disappointed he couldn't make it.

'Some business meeting, I gather.'

'But it's a Saturday!' said Rose indignantly.

'I know! But business goes on at weekends for some.' Now Hattie wished she hadn't put her champagne glass down. Her mouth had gone completely dry. 'I must get some water—'

'Sam? Would you be a dear?' Rose asked her long-suffering husband.

'For Hats, I'll be an antelope!'

'You think he'd wait to actually be a dad before making dad jokes,' said Rose. 'And no, I'm not pregnant, though I am thinking about it.'

'Rose! That's so exciting! I thought you were wedded to your shop.'

'I am, but now I want a baby too.'

'I will insist on being godmother. I'm so thrilled!'

She gave Rose a quick kiss on the cheek at the same time as Sam arrived with a glass of sparkling water.

'Thank you so much for this,' said Hattie. 'I'm feeling dreadfully on edge for some reason.'

'But you've done your bit – very well. You can relax now,' said Rose.

'I know. I think the water will sort me out.' Hattie sipped and while it stopped her feeling thirsty, it didn't calm her much.

She managed to chat to a few people – Fiona and Nick, some friends of Sheila's who were also staying with her for the wedding, but then she felt she had to get some fresh air.

The rain didn't help. She opened the back door in the kitchen of the hall and stood on the step, risking upsetting the catering staff who were all around her.

Then it happened. It was a vision. This time it was Luke she could see so clearly. He was wearing a suit and was looking at someone in a blue dress – Hattie couldn't see who – with love in his eyes. There was a tiny glimpse of what looked like the lining of the jacket the woman was wearing, fabric she'd never seen before. It was white with a small filigree pattern in blue on it, beautiful. Frank and Fearless were standing next to what was probably the woman's knee. Hattie stepped out of the kitchen and held on to a garden bench until the vision and its accompanying nausea left her. She breathed deeply for a few seconds, her brain whirling. Then she made a decision which probably broke every rule but she found she didn't care. She had to act. After all, if the vision hadn't yet happened in real life, she could stop Luke meeting the woman in the blue dress. She went back into the building and found Rose.

'Did you drive?' she said.

'Of course – what's the matter?'

'Can I borrow your car?'

'Where do you want to go in such a hurry? Would you like me to drive you anywhere? It's not Mary, is it?'

'No. I just need to get somewhere. Immediately.'

'You've had a vision, haven't you?' said Rose.

Hattie nodded. 'I need to go now.'

Rose delved in her handbag and found the keys. 'It's Luke, isn't it?'

Hattie nodded. 'I have to stop him falling in love with the wrong woman!'

'Alleluia!' said Rose, but Hattie had gone.

Hattie was at Luke's house almost without realising how she'd got there. There was a strange car on the drive she knew by instinct was April's, but she didn't allow that to slow her. She had her key in her hand this time, so she opened the door. The dogs rushed up to her, jumping and yipping their welcome. She pushed past them into the sitting room.

Luke and April were at the table with some papers – architectural drawings, perhaps – she couldn't really make them out. They both got up when she appeared, looking guilty. 'Hattie!' said Luke.

Hattie didn't reply. April looked at him, obviously acutely embarrassed. 'I'm not going to say it's not what it looks like,' she said to Hattie. 'Luke, you're going to have to tell her everything!' Then she picked up her handbag and left.

Hattie thought her knees were going to give way. She got herself to the sofa and sat down. She felt hot and cold at the same time. She knew it was only partly the aftermath of the vision. The rest was shock at what April had said. Frank and Fearless sat at her feet, looking anxiously up at her.

Luke came over. 'You don't look well. I'll get you some water.'

He seemed concerned but no longer guilty. She took the glass when he handed it to her. 'It's all right,' she said when she'd taken a sip and her mouth became less dry. 'I know you and April are together – and – well – you're perfectly entitled.'

When she'd been flying through the country lanes, she had been set on telling Luke how she really felt. But now it was too embarrassing to declare herself without really knowing how he felt; all she knew was that she wanted to try. The certainty her vision had given her had faded somewhat.

'Don't be ridiculous,' Luke said. 'Stay there and drink your water.'

He left the room and a moment later she saw him crossing the garden to his cabin. She sipped and closed her eyes. Fearless crept up on to the sofa beside her. Frank had his head on her knee. They kept her from fleeing the house but they couldn't prevent the tears seeping out from between her lids.

Luke was back in a few minutes. He had something in his hands which he put into her lap. She looked down to see a Bag for Life stuck up with parcel tape. It was wrapped round something quite large and she wondered what it could be. But what on earth was going on? She'd come here to declare herself, had her worst fears confirmed and now she was apparently about to open a present.

'It's for you,' said Luke. 'I intended to wait until Christmas to give it to you.'

There was a lot of tape, and she didn't know where to start.

'Here,' he said, handing her a knife.

She took the knife but was in too much of a state to be able to think how to use it.

Luke picked up the parcel. 'I'll start it off for you.'

Hattie started to pull away the tape where Luke had made a cut.

'I'm no good at wrapping presents,' said Luke.

'You never have been,' she said, looking up at him. Hattie took out a white cardboard box, too big to be held in one hand.

'Open it!' Luke demanded.

She reached inside, thoroughly confused by a cool, smooth surface. Then she realised what it was. 'It's a snow globe!' she said, pulling it free from its box.

Luke nodded. 'Can you recognise it?'

In it was a house and as she turned it round, snowflakes danced through the sky above it. She realised she knew it. 'It's Mary's house!' she whispered. Luke didn't speak as she turned the globe in her hand. There was the water butt, the seat, the stone sinks filled with herbs. 'It's perfect, like in a model village or something.'

Luke laughed gently. 'When I realised you couldn't buy it in the normal way, I wanted you to have it in some form or other.'

'And so you made it for me.' Hattie inspected it, noting the detail: the roof tiles, the double doors that opened on to the veranda; it was perfect. She couldn't speak or see for a few moments as tears overcame her. She cleared her throat and blinked. 'I don't know what to say. It's wonderful. I didn't know you could make things like this.'

Luke relaxed. It was if he hadn't known earlier if she'd like it or not. 'I started building things with balsa wood when I was a boy.'

'But it must have been so difficult to create anything so small, so detailed. And painting it.'

'That took a steady hand, I tell you. And a very fine brush. But I enjoyed doing it. For you.'

Hattie's mouth went dry again. She shivered. She was so unbelievably touched by Luke's thoughtfulness and, at the same time, unbelievably sad. She had lost this wonderful, handsome, thoughtful man through her own inability to see what was under her nose. 'It's so beautiful. I love snow globes.'

'I knew that,' said Luke. 'I remember, a couple of Christmases ago, you and Rose saying how much you liked them.'

'Oh, Luke!'

'What?'

Hattie could never have expressed her feelings in words, her thoughts were like fog and her heart was too full to make sense of anything. She suddenly felt hemmed in on the sofa. She got to her feet. 'I don't know how to thank you.'

She opened her arms. She'd have to hug him; it would be weird and unnatural not to.

'Hattie – I feel—' He stopped, gazing down at her. She looked up at him, willing him to finish his sentence, but instead, his mouth came down on hers and the need for explanations vanished. They were holding each other so tightly neither of them could breathe, kissing as if they would never stop.

The dogs, confused, jumped up and down next to them. Luke brushed them away but didn't take his mouth from hers. At last, they had to part. Luke swallowed. 'I hope I haven't made a mistake. I've loved you for so long, I really hope I haven't stuffed it up.'

Hattie was still short of breath. 'By making me a snow globe?'

'No! By kissing you!'

Hattie shook her head in exasperation, so happy she couldn't stop smiling. 'But what about April?'

'April? What are you talking about?' He seemed genuinely bewildered.

'Aren't you together? You're in touch with her so often! She's always messaging you and I assume you message her back.'

'Yes, but – you don't really think that she and I are an item, do you?'

He seemed to think the idea was so ridiculous Hattie began to wonder herself. 'Why not? She's a very attractive woman!'

He seemed confused. 'But I'm in love with you.'

The way he said this made Hattie suddenly feel weak and lose concentration. She almost missed what he said next. 'Why would I think about her? The messaging? She helped me with the snow globe. I needed some drone shots to get the 3D effect for the house. She knew the right people to arrange that.' He laughed. 'I couldn't ask you, although I'm sure you know the right people too!'

'I see.'

'You introduced us!'

'I know – sorry – I'm feeling a bit odd,' she said. 'Put your arms round me again.'

He obliged and they sank on to the sofa. Luke kept his arm round her shoulders, but he was diffident.

Hattie decided to be brave. 'What did April mean when she said you had to tell me everything? She couldn't have just meant the snow globe. How could anyone be anything other than utterly delighted about that?'

'I'm so glad you're delighted. If you hadn't had feelings for me too, it could have just been the most over-the-top, embarrassing present ever.'

'We've established I adore the snow globe. There couldn't be a nicer present in the whole world.' She took a breath. 'And I love you too.' She moistened her lips. She and Luke had spent so much time pretending to themselves to be just friends, it wasn't easy to say the words. 'But we can't have secrets. Not if we love each other.'

His arm tightened. He pulled her into his chest and kissed her hair. 'I can't believe what I'm hearing. I never thought I'd hear those words from you.'

'We've been "just friends" for so long.'

'You were never "just friends" for me.'

A sigh of happiness that was almost a sob made her need to clear her throat. 'So? What else?'

'It's complicated.'

'Then explain,' she said gently. The longer he held back, the more she feared what he was going to confess.

'I'm buying Mary's house.'

This was a shock.

Luke rushed to fill Hattie's silence. 'Once Clive took out the kitchen and the bathroom I knew you couldn't buy it without a mortgage, so I put in a cash offer. Mary's nephew didn't know I had anything to do with you. I offered for it in my company's name. I said I was a builder and he took that to mean developer.'

'And did he charge you more?' asked Hattie.

Luke nodded. 'He thought I was going to apply for planning permission to build houses. Of course he charged me more.'

Hattie was horrified but not surprised. 'And you could pay cash for it?'

'With a bit of fiddling about, yes I could, just about. And once it's all gone through…' He paused. 'I'd like to sell it again, to you.'

'To me?'

'I'd give you the house, gladly, but I know you wouldn't accept it. You don't want a gift—'

'Not when I've got a snow globe, which I love, with all my heart.'

He laughed. 'If you've got a snow globe, who needs a house?'

'You're right. I wouldn't want to be just bought a house. That would be weird.' She paused. 'I'm in shock,

Luke. This is everything I could have wanted, everything I thought I'd lost coming back to me.' She paused to take a breath, unsure what to say. 'The first thing I'll do after I've moved in is to make the garden secure for the dogs, so they can stay whenever they want to.'

Frank and Fearless knew when they were being referred to, and wagged their tails. Luke looked down at them, colour creeping up his neck. 'I was hoping—'

Just then Hattie's phone beeped in the pocket of her dress. 'Oh! It's Rose. She needs her car. I borrowed it,' she explained.

'OK,' said Luke, 'do you want me to follow you back to the wedding?' He looked at her then, caught between a smile and something more serious. 'I'd follow you anywhere, Hattie.'

Hattie felt tears of happiness spring to her eyes. She smiled back at him, hoping her loss for words would say it all. 'Come on,' she said.

As she drove to the village hall and Fiona and Nick's wedding, Luke in his truck in her rear-view mirror, Hattie thought about the vision. She never thought she'd have a vision of Luke and it had been a shock, enough to jolt her into action. But who was the woman? Perhaps not April, but someone else? And what if that woman, not Hattie, was the one for Luke after all? She remembered how tricky it had been working out whom she'd seen in her vision of Nick. But the fact that she couldn't recognise whom Luke was with in the vision was troubling.

She tried to brush away her anxiety. Her visions had never been wrong before, but then there was everything that Luke had said and done. The efforts he had gone to in order to make the snow globe – that alone was enough to send her into a cloud of pure joy. And he had saved Mary's house from developers for her. Her entire life had changed, going from chaos to happiness in a few minutes. She glanced back at Luke and he blew her a kiss. Her wave of longing for him almost made her drive into the ditch.

Rose was waiting for her in the car park of the hall. 'Oh my goodness!' she said, the moment she saw Hattie. 'No need at all to ask if it went well with Luke. It's written all over your face. You are happiness personified.' She took Hattie into her arms and hugged her. 'And here's the man himself!' Rose hugged him too. 'Congratulations.'

Sam arrived at this moment and looked at Luke and Hattie. 'Oh, I see! Are you two engaged?'

'Not yet,' said Luke with a laugh and a very fond look at Hattie. 'Give us a moment.'

Chapter Forty-Two

Hattie was desperate to make her excuses, grab an overnight bag from Sheila's house and go back with Luke. She set off to find Sheila.

'Hi—' she began.

'Oh, Hattie!' Sheila exclaimed. 'I thought I'd missed you. I wanted to say thank you again for taking Fiona to see the puppies and doing such a splendid job as celebrant.'

'That was all an absolute pleasure,' said Hattie, 'but now—'

'It couldn't have gone better, could it?'

'No, but, Sheila—'

Something about the way she said it finally got Sheila's attention. 'It's me and Luke,' said Hattie. 'We've got together—'

She didn't have time to finish her sentence before Sheila embraced her. 'Oh, my darling! I couldn't be more delighted! But how? He couldn't make the wedding. Did he show up at the last minute?'

'I went to see him, on impulse,' said Hattie. 'Inspired by the wedding,' she added, feeling the need to provide some sort of explanation. One day she'd tell Luke about the visions, of course she would, but not now. 'And now I want to get some things from your house as well as my car—'

'Go! And I want all the details very soon!'

At last she was back with Luke in the car park.

'Rose and Sam had to go,' Luke said.

'I know. That's why I got the panicky text.' She smiled. 'If you drop me back at Sheila's, then I can pick up my car and drive to yours?'

He smiled. 'Don't hang around.'

Luke hadn't waited for her at Sheila's, and when Hattie arrived back at Luke's house, she understood why. He had done a rapid but effective tidy-up. There were flowers, picked from the garden, in a jug on the table. There was a bottle of champagne in a bucket – a black polythene builder's bucket.

He kissed her briefly. 'Stay here for a moment or two. I haven't finished in the bedroom.'

Hattie found her place on the sofa and the dogs instantly got up and sat next to her, leaning into her embrace. She sat there, anticipation and even slight anxiety mingling with her desire for Luke. How could she get through the next few moments, waiting for him to come and fetch her? Could you actually die from longing? Luckily, she didn't have to wait long.

Luke put out a hand and pulled her to her feet. Then he swept her up into his arms and carried her, right past the unopened champagne and up to the bedroom. She could smell line-dried sheets and his cologne. He dropped her on to the bed and had a stern word with the dogs before shutting the door.

Hattie was happy. Just now, she didn't want to share Luke with anyone.

The following morning, Hattie and Luke were in bed drinking tea. The bottle in the builder's bucket was now empty and upside down. Frank and Fearless had joined them on the bed. Hattie had never felt so happy before in her life.

Then suddenly the dogs were on full alert. Luke sat up. 'Who on earth could that be?' He looked at his watch. 'It's nearly eleven.'

'Oh,' said Hattie, feeling very caught out.

The doorbell rang and Luke got out of bed and started pulling on his clothes.

'We could pretend we're not here,' suggested Hattie, getting up too now. She realised her overnight bag had never made it to the bedroom and she didn't fancy fighting her way back into her wedding finery. 'Can I borrow something to wear, Luke? A shirt?'

He pulled one from a hanger and threw it towards her.

'It might be a delivery or something.' Luke was now dressed. 'I'll go and see who it is.'

'And can you get my case for me?'

'Sure,' he said, and left the room.

Soon she could hear voices and Luke being welcoming; it was obviously not a delivery.

Hattie had an extremely quick shower and pulled on the shirt which was long enough to make her almost decent. Then she peeked out of the window and saw her sister's car parked behind hers.

Although she was alone, she blushed from head to toe. Quite why she felt so embarrassed at the thought of her sister knowing she had sex, she wasn't sure. She couldn't possibly go downstairs in Luke's shirt now. She was just starting to panic when Luke opened the bedroom door and pushed her case through, giving her a knowing smile as he did.

She was delighted to see it but found it very carelessly packed. Her underwear and toiletries were there, and a pair of jeans, but somehow no top. What had she been thinking last night? Luke's shirt would have to do.

In the hallway, she spotted a metal tape measure on a shelf. Almost weeping with relief, she picked it up and went into the sitting room.

'Oh, hi, Lennie! Tom! And Xander! I didn't know you were coming! Luke? I think standard curtains would be fine in there. Or you could have a blind.'

Her sister, Tom, Luke and Xander all looked at her. Hattie realised she had no idea of what had been said. Had Luke announced the fact that they'd got together as he'd opened the door?

Even the dogs paused in their making a fuss of Xander to look at her quizzically.

'It's no good pretending you were measuring up for curtains,' said Leonie, appearing amused. 'It's perfectly obvious that something's going on between you. Quite apart from the fact that that shirt is way too big for you, there's this.' She indicated the builder's bucket, the champagne bottle and the glasses.

'We were celebrating,' said Hattie, unwilling to admit defeat. 'Luke is buying a house!'

'Another one?' said Leonie.

'You can never have too many,' said Luke, seriously.

'Mary's house! He's buying it for me,' said Hattie. 'Not for me, but on my behalf.'

'Oh, that's amazing!' said Leonie. 'Your own home that you won't have to keep moving out of. That's brilliant! Well done, both of you.' She gave her sister a tight hug; Hattie was rather taken aback.

'We're celebrating too!' said Tom, brandishing a full bottle of champagne.

Hattie relaxed. With news of her own to share, Leonie wasn't going to be interested in the details of what Hattie and Luke had been up to.

'I'll get some glasses,' said Hattie.

'Do you know where they are?' asked Leonie, suddenly very innocent.

'Of course. We lived here, remember!'

Leonie gave her a sisterly smile which made Hattie want to kick her.

Hattie found glasses and some unopened snacks.

'Can I go to the cabin and make a bit of a track, do you think?' asked Xander. 'I realise no one is going to give me champagne.'

'Of course!' said Hattie, grateful for one less embarrassed person in the room before realising that it was Leonie's job to give permission really.

'So, what's your excuse for champagne?' asked Hattie when Tom had filled the glasses and Luke had passed them round. 'Although I hope I can guess!'

Tom nodded. 'We're engaged!'

Hattie swooped on her sister and hugged her. 'That's such lovely news!'

'Yes,' said Leonie. 'And we're going to have an engagement party – where Mum and Dad had their do.'

'As well as a wedding?' asked Luke.

Leonie nodded. 'The wedding will take a while to organise and Mum and Dad want everyone to have met

Tom beforehand. And, Hattie, I'm taking you shopping for a proper outfit. You may have looked amazing in that slip dress but Mum was not impressed.' She shot Luke a look before continuing, 'I'm assuming you'll have a plus one.'

'She will,' said Luke. 'And I liked the slip dress.' He gave Hattie a lingering look.

'So, when did this happen, then?' asked Leonie, nodding at Hattie and Luke. 'I want all the details.'

'You can't have *all the details*,' said Luke firmly, 'but maybe – Hattie? Do you want to show Leonie and Tom?'

'Oh, yes!' Hattie went to the sideboard where she'd put the snow globe. 'Luke made me this.'

'Hattie! What an amazing present. You've always loved snow globes.'

'It's Mary's house,' said Hattie.

'It was when I thought she couldn't have the real house,' Luke explained. 'It was painstaking work but satisfying.'

'It's amazing,' said Tom, turning it round and round in his hands. 'All I gave Leonie—'

'Is this!' Leonie held out her hand. On her finger was a very attractive ring: amethysts and pearls set in gold. 'It's Victorian. We bought it in a lovely little antique shop.'

'It's so pretty! I love it,' said Hattie.

'I must say it was the first one we saw and although we looked at others, we kept coming back to this one.' Leonie got to her feet. 'Hattie, I'm not going back to Switzerland until the middle of next week. Any chance we could go outfit shopping before then?'

'Er, I'm sure we could.'

'Maybe also buy a skirt or a pair of trousers?' Leonie put her arm round Hattie's waist and led her away from the men. 'I'm so pleased that you and Luke have finally got together,' she said quietly. 'What took you so long?'

Hattie shrugged. 'I don't know really. But we worked it out eventually.' She didn't mention the vision, though the question of the other woman flashed into her mind once more.

'Well, thank goodness! Now, do you know where you'll be living until you're installed at Mary's? I'm leaving Xander with you again next week. Will you be here or with Sheila?'

Luke, who apparently had the hearing of a bat, joined them. 'I really hope Hattie will be here. And Xander, of course.'

Hattie found herself blushing again.

Leonie gave her a squeeze. 'Jolly good! I'll fetch Xander and we'll get out of your hair for now. I'm sure you have… things to do.'

If Hattie had thought she could take her and Xander's things and run, Sheila had other ideas. She sat Hattie down at the kitchen table and produced tea and biscuits.

'So, you and Luke!' said Sheila. 'Tell me the details. I know you're old friends but when did you start to feel differently about him?'

'It sort of crept up on me, Sheila.' Hattie found herself determined to change the subject. 'Now, what I want to know from you is, are you and Fiona both going to have puppies? I don't think you should miss out on the fun. You can look after each other's dogs when you go away. It would be ideal.'

'I can see you don't really want to talk about it, Hattie, so I won't insist. But I am very happy for you, and yes' – Sheila looked flushed with excitement – 'I think I do want a puppy.'

On the way back to Luke's, Hattie pondered as to why she didn't want to talk about getting together with Luke. Much as she didn't want to admit it, she knew it was because there was that niggling doubt about the vision which wouldn't leave her. Who was the other woman, and was she a threat to Hattie's newfound happiness? And, more importantly, how would Hattie ever know the answer to that question?

'Are you sure you're happy for me and Xander to live with you until the house sale goes through?' asked Hattie over a late lunch at Luke's. 'I don't want to take advantage of your good nature.' She'd tortured herself with thoughts of the vision for the whole drive over and decided to simply try and enjoy herself with Luke for the time being. It wasn't as easy as she'd hoped it would be.

'Sweetheart! You don't have to ask. I feel I can speak for Frank and Fearless here too: we're all delighted for you and Xander to stay forever if you want to. Well, maybe not Xander forever, but quite a long time.'

Hattie used a piece of bread to wipe up the last of the salad dressing on her plate. 'That's so kind.'

Luke put down his fork and picked up her hand. 'I want to spend every minute I can with you. Why would you doubt that?'

Hattie smiled as broadly as she could manage. 'I just don't want to take advantage of your good nature.'

He kissed the hand he was holding. 'Don't be silly. Now let's go to bed. An afternoon nap is always a good idea.' He gave her a look to suggest that he had no intentions of sleeping.

Hattie smiled and then her phone pinged. She saw Luke look irritated. 'It's all right,' said Hattie. 'It's Fiona. Aw – she's just saying thank you for yesterday. It was such a pleasure. And she wants to meet up later this week as they're not going away.' She tapped out a quick reply and then said to Luke. 'Where were we?'

Much later, Hattie and Luke were on the sofa flanked by Frank and Fearless. Hattie was playing with her snow globe, turning it over and over.

'You should show it to Mary,' said Luke.

Hattie turned to him. 'What a brilliant idea,' she said. 'I can do some rearranging and see her tomorrow. I'm pretty busy but can fit Mary in after my house viewing if I press on.' She felt happier when she'd made this decision. Mary was full of wisdom and knew her well. She would help her dispel the small niggle that was spoiling her joy.

'Darling!' said Mary, turning the snow globe over and over just as Hattie had been doing. She watched the snow settle on the model of her old home. 'Luke must love you very much to take so much trouble and spend so much time to make this for you.'

Hattie nodded. 'And I love him. It took me a while to realise I did, or rather to feel brave enough to take the leap.'

Mary looked at her carefully. 'So why aren't you jumping up and down with happiness? Especially as he's making it possible for you to have the full-size version of my house as well as this one.'

'It sounds so silly – it is so silly – but I can't shake off the doubt…'

'What doubt? And don't worry about sounding silly.'

Hattie took a breath. It was almost impossible to explain this to Mary with any certainty without mentioning her visions.

'I just… I can't shake the feeling that there is someone else out there who Luke might be destined to meet. A feeling came over me at the wedding that he might meet someone and I'd miss my chance with him so I rushed to him to stop him meeting her, but that was probably wrong.' She shrugged and looked down at her hands. 'Call it female intuition?'

Mary didn't speak for some moments. Hattie could almost see her holding back the words telling her she was an idiot to place so much trust in something that couldn't really be real. Except she didn't.

'I wish I could think of something to say to you that would make you stop worrying. But I do think that Luke loves you so much – it's always been very clear to me how he feels about you.'

Hattie sighed. 'I suppose.'

'I hate to be predictable but I can't help telling you to just let yourself be happy about all your recent good fortune. I think you might have simply got cold feet. It's perfectly normal. You've been on your own for so long. You have a lovely man, you will have a lovely house—'

'And a lovely snow globe—'

'The best snow globe,' Mary went on.

'So you think I should just be grateful and go on my way rejoicing?'

'You're welcome to stay as long as you can,' said Mary.

Hattie laughed. 'Fair enough! Sadly, I can't stay any longer. I've just about got time to get back for my sister to take me shopping. She wants to find me something for her engagement party that our mother will approve of.'

She drove away feeling more cheerful, if not entirely reassured.

Chapter Forty-Three

She just had time to put on a clean top before her sister arrived, full of beans and on a mission.

'Tom's put me on the insurance of his car,' she said excitedly, having kissed Hattie and refused use of the facilities. 'Isn't that just lovely?'

Hattie and Luke had put each other on their car insurance quite a long time ago; it seemed practical and it somehow lowered their premiums. It hadn't felt romantic at the time.

'It's a lovely car,' said Hattie, smiling. Her efficient, businesslike sister getting soppy over car insurance. It was adorable!

'It is! Now, remind me which way Cheltenham is again?'

Leonie may have been hazy about where Cheltenham was but once there she knew exactly where she wanted to go.

The sisters paused on the threshold of a lovely shop and Hattie looked in the window with wonder and joy. Instead of the elegant taupe, biscuit and ecru colours that her sister usually favoured, here was turquoise, Schiaparelli pink, orange, scarlet and yellow the colour of the dawn. And the styles were flowing, generous, not the sharp well-cut suits that Leonie usually loved.

'This is a surprise, Lennie!' said Hattie as they went in.

'I'm not always the sensible sister, you know,' said Leonie. 'Sometimes I'm positively giddy!'

The woman in charge of the shop – who turned out to be the owner – was friendly and helpful but didn't interfere until Hattie, exhausted by trying find something her mother would find acceptable that she also liked, flopped into a chair. She refused to buy something she would never wear again.

'Can I lead you over here?' she said. 'These are on this sale rail because so far no one has bought them. But I think they're lovely and definitely worth a look. They're well reduced too.'

'Now, Hattie! No buying anything weird just because it's cheap!' said Leonie, looking at jumpsuits, unaware she may have been sounding rude.

'I love a bargain,' Hattie breathed to the woman as they moved through the shop.

'Me too! Now look at this. It's unusual, but I think it might just be you.'

Superficially it was a long sleeveless dress with a fairly deep round neck and Nehru jacket, very elegant, stylish, much more Leonie than Hattie. But then the owner took it off the hanger and revealed the jacket lining. It was exquisite: a blue filigree pattern on a white background. 'Try it on,' said the owner of the shop. 'There's a matching scarf—'

Suddenly feeling light-headed, Hattie allowed herself to be guided to the ample changing room.

'Let me know if you need any help,' said the owner. 'But I think it will be perfect for you.'

As if in a waking dream, Hattie slipped on the dress, which was the perfect length, and then the jacket. She slung the scarf round her neck and emerged into the shop. With a deep breath and a big smile she admired the outfit, particularly the lining. She felt as though a cloud had been lifted. It was the fabric she had seen in her vision about Luke: she no longer had to worry; she was the woman in the vision.

The owner instantly came forward and adjusted the scarf. 'There,' she said, in the satisfied tone of an artist who was happy with their picture.

'Lennie?' said Hattie. 'What do you think?'

Leonie didn't speak for a few seconds. 'It's absolutely fabulous! It could have been made for you, designed for you, it looks so amazing. But it's far too perfect to waste on my engagement party. Keep it for the wedding!'

In her mind's eye, Hattie saw Luke in his suit, smiling at her in the vision. She beamed at the owner, whom she wanted to hug. 'I'll take it. But now can you find me something less amazing?'

'You're looking surprisingly happy for someone who's just spent so much money on new clothes when usually you stick to charity shops and Vinted,' said Leonie as they drove back to Luke's house.

'Well, you do have to splash out for special occasions, don't you?' said Hattie breezily.

'You've never thought that before! Is your business doing extra well or something? Or is living with Luke giving you financial security?'

Hattie considered everything that was good about living with Luke: financial security didn't seem an important factor.

'I don't think it's that,' she said, aware she couldn't possibly tell her sister why she was suddenly full of joy. She couldn't wait to see Luke.

Hattie didn't invite her sister in, she just got out of the car and retrieved her shiny carrier bags from the back and ran into the house. She found Luke in the kitchen. She threw her bags on to a chair and ran up and put her arms round his waist; she hugged him, her head on his chest.

'Hey!' he said, returning her embrace. 'What's all this about?'

'I've bought a wonderful outfit for the wedding and it's making me so happy!'

'Whose wedding? Ours? Is there going to be one? That's wonderful!' He took her into his arms properly now and kissed her so thoroughly she had to push him away so she could finish what she was saying.

'Actually, I was talking about Leonie's wedding.'

'Damn it!' said Luke. He looked down at Hattie, who was looking up at him adoringly. 'We could have a wedding too, couldn't we?'

Hattie nodded. 'One of us would have to propose though.'

Luke grinned. 'Hattie, will you marry me?'

Hattie stared at him, almost unable to breathe with the joy of loving him so much and knowing he loved her back. Before, she'd tried to keep her feelings in check and hadn't allowed herself to be completely happy in case it was all going to be taken away from her. She had no doubts now. 'I absolutely will!'

Epilogue

Late June the following year

'So, Xander, would you mind giving me away?' Hattie asked her nephew. They were sitting on the veranda at Mary's house, looking at the view over the valley. It was Hattie's favourite place on earth. 'It's not really that you're giving me to anyone, I'm giving myself. It's more for me to have someone to prop me up as I walk down the aisle.'

Xander had been invited for lunch without his mother and stepfather and although Leonie, who knew why, had been encouraging, Hattie was worried in case Xander thought the whole idea was ridiculous. Luke was keeping out of the way.

'In case you fall over?'

'I'm not going to do that, I just might feel a bit wobbly. Nerves or something. I would ask my dad except he's only just done it for your mum and, to be honest, she gets on much better with him than I do. I'd rather have you.'

'That's cool,' said Xander, obviously extremely flattered.

Hattie put her arm round him and gave him a squeeze, a 'PDA' he wouldn't have accepted when he first came to live with her. 'Thank you so much. I'm sure you know my parents do not approve of us not getting married in church.'

'I love my grandparents,' said Xander, 'but they are quite – you know – old-fashioned.'

'Which is a grandparent's role, to be fair,' said Hattie.

Xander nodded. 'Deffo. But we don't all have to be like them.'

Hattie nodded. 'And Luke needs to have Frank and Fearless with him. Like bridesmaids – except, obviously, he's not a bride and the dogs are – well, dogs.'

Xander nodded. 'I understand. Nerves or something,' he said.

'And you'll help us get the garden all ready – with your college friends?'

He nodded. 'Mary's house is going to be a great place to have a wedding.'

Hattie nodded. Although it was her and Luke's house now, they were all still in the habit of referring to it as Mary's. 'She's going to love seeing it all gussied up for our wedding.'

'And it was so cool that Luke managed to make her a snow globe too.'

Hattie nodded, remembering when she and Luke had watched her unwrap it. Her face had genuinely lit up, making her look like a girl again. 'And she's really happy in her new care home. Thank goodness Clive finally got that sorted out, although I'm not sure if he did it to make her happy or because he was worried that Mary might disinherit him if he didn't.' Hattie laughed. 'Although perhaps I'm being unfair.'

'Will he come to the wedding, do you think?' asked Xander.

Hattie shrugged. 'I shouldn't think so. I'm not quite sure why Luke invited him.' She glanced at her phone on the table in front of them. 'I'm going to have to go. Rose wants to see me to check on things. Is Luke dropping you back?'

Xander nodded. 'Did I tell you he's taking me on the track driving day that Mum bought me for working so hard for my exams? She asked him as I think she knew he'd enjoy it too.'

Hattie laughed. 'He did mention it. And he'll love it! I hope not more than you do.'

'No fear of that,' said Xander.

Hattie gave him a friendly squeeze.

The wedding day couldn't have been more beautiful. Hattie woke early to see the sort of mist that meant it was going to be lovely. Luke was staying with a friend, for superstition's sake. Rose and Leonie were sleeping, soon to awaken to help her get ready. Now, Hattie went quickly down the stairs in her bare feet and into the garden.

There was dew on the lawn, every rose seemed to be flowering and the fragrance reminded Hattie of an upmarket flower shop. Mary had always had a lot of roses and Hattie and Luke had planted more. And there were peonies, irises, stately white crambe covered in tiny white flowers. Perennial geraniums, and aquilegia, like old-fashioned granny's bonnets, their country name. There was ammi, like cow parsley, in abundance; and cosmos, like coloured stars.

In the marquee were buckets of sweet peas grown by Sheila especially for the occasion. Swags of flowers on ropes hung under the eaves and every chair had a bouquet tied to it. Sheila had convinced half the WI to help decorate for Hattie and Luke and the result was like a fairyland.

She gave a shiver of happiness. As much as she had dreamed of living in this house, her imagination wouldn't have let her add Luke, now the man of her dreams, sharing it with her. Or a pregnant Rose and Leonie as matrons of honour. She realised her slight nerves were perfectly normal; in fact they sharpened her feelings of joy.

Hattie's bare feet began to get cold and she went inside. Rose and Leonie were up now. 'Nervous?' asked her sister, handing her a mug of tea.

'Just a bit.'

'I would be too if we had to follow you down the aisle,' said Leonie. 'But of course, if you want us to, we can. Even without matching outfits.'

'I just want you both here now,' said Hattie, feeling a sudden rush of love for her sister and friend.

'It's going to be amazing,' said Rose. 'I can't wait!' She went to Hattie and hugged her.

Leonie came up and joined in from behind. 'This is my first group hug,' she said. 'I rather like it.'

'So do I,' said Hattie, suddenly fighting tears.

'I'm going to cry now!' said Rose. 'Has anyone got a tissue?'

Xander and Hattie stood behind a potted olive tree, waiting out of sight for the music to give them their cue. Xander, taller than Hattie now by quite a lot, squeezed her hand. 'OK, Auntie Hattie! We're on!'

Hattie dug him in the ribs with her elbow and they set off.

She couldn't help smiling. Everyone she loved was there and now they were all on their feet, turned towards them.

She saw Mary, looking elegant and ageless. Her parents, overdressed and uncomfortable with the informality. Sheila and Malcolm, Sheila in a very stylish hat, sitting next to Fiona, ready to hold the baby should Fiona need her to. Next to them was Nick, proud of his family, whispering something to Fiona that made her giggle. Leonie and Tom beamed their own happiness back at her. Then Rose and Sam and several other friends and relations. On the other side were Carole and Jason, all the friends who'd been at the dinner dance. Smiling broadly was April with her partner.

Then she looked at Luke, who, it seemed, only had eyes for her. Frank and Fearless, who had been waiting silently at his feet, broke free of his spell and came bounding up before remembering they were there to support Luke and bounded back as Hattie and Xander approached.

Luke couldn't wait for Hattie to reach the end of the aisle; he stepped forwards to close the gap. He took hold of her hands and stared down at her. Hattie met his gaze, wrapped in the love that shone from him, utterly certain of their future happiness.

Acknowledgements

To Tania Thompson, Cotswold House Hunter, who I met when planning to move house and knew I had to write a book about.

My children, Guy, Frank and Briony. You are being amazing, thank you.

To Bill Hamilton and Rebecca Ritchie and the entire team at A M Heath. You are the best agents ever, and I am so grateful.

To Darcy Nicholson, Caroline Hogg, Maisie Mc-Cormick, Amy Donegan, Fran Owen, Mari Yamazaki, Joe Roche, Fabrice Wilmann, Charlotte Phillips, Thea Hirsi and everyone at Bloomsbury. You have been so welcoming and kind to me and very supportive during this tricky time.

And as always, Richenda Todd who's saved me from making hideous bloopers for more years than I can remember.

I'm not exaggerating when I say I couldn't do any of what I do without you.

A Note on the Author

KATIE FFORDE lives in the beautiful Cotswold countryside with her family. Each of her books explores a different profession or background and her research has helped her bring these to life. She believes falling in love is the best thing in the world, and she wants all her characters to experience it, and her readers to share their stories.

A Note on the Type

The text of this book is set in Bembo, which was first used in 1495 by the Venetian printer Aldus Manutius for Cardinal Bembo's *De Aetna*. The original types were cut for Manutius by Francesco Griffo. Bembo was one of the types used by Claude Garamond (1480–1561) as a model for his Romain de l'Université, and so it was a forerunner of what became the standard European type for the following two centuries. Its modern form follows the original types and was designed for Monotype in 1929.